Random Road

Books by Thomas Kies

Random Road

Random Road

Introducing Geneva Chase

Thomas Kies

Poisoned Pen Press

First Edition 2017

10 9 8 7 6 5 4 3 2 1

Library of Congress Catalog Card Number: 2016952646

ISBN: 9781464208003   Hardcover
      9781464208027   Trade Paperback

Poisoned Pen Press
4014 N. Goldwater Blvd., #201
Scottsdale, AZ 85251
www.poisonedpenpress.com
info@poisonedpenpress.com

Printed in the United States of America

For Jessica and Joshua, Alexander and Jessie,
Thomas and Gillian, Henry and Jake

Acknowledgments

I'd like to thank my fabulous agent, Kimberley Cameron, for pulling me out of the slush pile and matching me with a wonderful publisher. Through your incredible patience, grace and friendship, you've changed my life. I'll always be grateful!

I want to thank Poisoned Pen Press, including Barbara Peters, for taking a chance on me, Annette Rogers, my incredible editor who helped guide me through the editing process, and Diane DiBiase who put up with all my dumb questions.

I'd like to thank Dawn Brock from Coastal Press who, when I needed yet another hard copy of the book to work from, would drop everything and print a copy.

Thank you, Allie Miller for the photos and making me look good.

And finally, I'd like to thank my incredible wife, Cindy Schersching, who believed in me from day one and kept telling me that I was a good writer. I might have quit a long time ago if it wasn't for your love and encouragement. Hugs.

"Creativity is the ability to introduce order into the randomness of nature."

—*Eric Hoffer*

Chapter One

"Last night Hieronymus Bosch met the rich and famous."

That was the lead sentence of the story I filed later that night with *The Sheffield Post.* My editor spiked it, saying, "Nobody who reads this newspaper knows who Hieronymus Bosch is."

Instead, the story began, "Six people were found brutally murdered, their nude bodies mutilated, in the exclusive gated Sheffield community of Connor's Landing."

My name's been on the byline of hundreds of stories over the last twenty years, in four newspapers, three magazines, a half dozen websites, and, for a very short, shame-filled stint, Fox News. I've honestly lost count how many crime scenes and murders I've covered—drug deals gone bad, jealous lovers, random shootings, bar fights, gang hits.

This one was different. It felt surreal.

These murders happened in the wrong place. These weren't supposed to happen here.

The three-story turret of the 1898 Queen Anne home stood like a guard tower looming over a two-acre carpet of manicured landscaping perched on the shoreline of Long Island Sound. Wicker chairs and glass tables rested on a massive wraparound porch, waiting for crystal glasses of Pinot Grigio and plates of warm Brie. Antique panes of leaded glass overlooked the harbor where schooners once docked. A gentle sea breeze rustled the leaves of hundred-year-old oak trees.

Connor's Landing was a small island community named for a nineteenth-century whaling captain, and is separated from the mainland by salt water tidal pools and connected by an old wooden bridge.

Even in the dark of night, I could see how beautiful it was. A haven of sprawling grounds overlooking the water, houses the size of small hotels, yachts worth more than some small corporations, lifestyles of the rich and the super-rich. All owned by people who, even in this economy, continued to manufacture money.

This particular estate was fabulous. The crime, however, was horrifying.

The cops wouldn't let me beyond the yellow tape and into the crime scene itself, so I waited in the suffocating, hot July darkness until I could get enough information and at least one official quote. Then I'd rush back to my desk and put together a story before press-time.

Leaning against my ten-year-old Sebring, I felt the heat and humidity frizzing up my hair. Whining mosquitoes kept trying to zip into my ears. Sweat trailed slowly out from under my bra and down my ribcage. Every so often I'd glance up at the sky where stars poked glimmering holes in the darkness and the moon hung like a pale sliver in the night.

While I absently fingered my smartphone and squinted through the darkness at scribbles I kept in a tiny notebook, police were coming and going throughout the house with uncertain regularity. Lights were on inside. Windows showed me cops moving slowly around, the flashes of cameras recording the scene.

So far, I was the only member of the Fourth Estate who had shown up. My competition was the local TV cable station, WTOC, and another local newspaper, *The Bridgeport Times*. I chalked up my good fortune to someone else's tough luck. The police scanner app on my phone had said that there was a jackknifed tractor trailer on I-95 and traffic in both directions was stopped dead.

Any other reporters in the vicinity were frustrated behind their steering wheels, covering a traffic accident instead of a multiple homicide.

I'd been waiting in the driveway behind the yellow tape for nearly an hour when Mike Dillon, the deputy chief, finally came out of the house. He's about forty, tall and lean, with brown eyes and an angular face that looked cunning to me, wolf-like. He was wearing a summer uniform with short sleeves but no hat. The sheen of sweat below his receding hairline glistened in the staccato red and blue lights of the police cruisers. Mike walked deliberately toward me, acknowledging my presence with a grim expression and a nod.

"Hey, Mike."

"Hey, Genie." His voice sounded a little more somber than usual, for good reason.

"I've been listening to the chatter. Sounds pretty bad in there." I nodded toward a small cluster of paramedics who'd been called earlier that evening, but weren't needed. Like me, they'd been standing outside in the oppressive heat and wishing they were in an air-conditioned bar back in town. They were waiting, not to take the injured to the hospital, but to take the dead to the morgue.

"I hear you've got six bodies." It was more a statement than a question.

Mike came up beside me and crossed his arms. He took a deep breath, using the moment to compose his thoughts. Mike Dillon was accustomed to talking to the media. He hated to be misquoted; he hated it when anyone took cheap shots at him or the police department; and he hated pushy reporters.

But it was pretty evident that he liked me. And it isn't because I'm not pushy, because I am, or that I don't take the occasional cheap shot, because I do.

Mike liked me because, even though I'm a few months shy of forty, time has been kind to me. Men in bars still tell me I'm pretty and I haven't had to resort to Botox yet, although I've thought about it. The treadmill has kept my weight in check and I've still got great legs.

I know that it isn't PC to admit this, but Mike thinks I'm hot, simple as that. With men, it always amazes and amuses me how much concession that'll buy.

Taking a long breath, he answered, "Yeah, six bodies, all homicides."

"How'd they die?" I had my notebook ready.

"Hacked to death. Blood and body parts everywhere."

I glanced up. He was looking away from me, staring into the darkness toward Long Island Sound. He wasn't seeing the water, though; his mind was still visualizing what he saw in that house, something unspeakable.

"Hacked to death?" I repeated, stunned.

He answered in little more than a whisper. "They were cut to pieces."

It took me a second to process what he'd just told me. I've covered a lot of murders and this was surprisingly gruesome.

"Jesus Christ."

"I've never seen so much blood."

"What was the murder weapon? Machete?"

"Don't know yet."

"Got a motive?"

"Don't know yet."

"Robbery gone bad?"

"Not ruling it out."

"Does it look like it could be some kind of ritual?" I was fishing.

Mike glanced back at me to see if I was pulling his leg. He frowned. "No pentagram on the wall, if that's what you're asking."

I thought a moment. "Who found the bodies?"

"We did. We got an anonymous call."

I nodded. "Time of death?"

Mike took a moment to frame his reply. "Coroner thinks sometime around one o'clock this morning."

They'd been lying dead in that house for over eighteen hours.

"Ready to release the victims' names?"

He shook his head. "Can't."

"Can't or won't?" The police liked to contact the next of kin before releasing names to the press. "I already know that this house belongs to George and Lynette Chadwick." I held up my smartphone to show him how I'd uncovered that fact. "Are they two of the victims?"

He didn't answer.

"Who are the rest?"

"We don't have positive ID's yet."

"No?"

Mike cocked his head. "The victims are all naked. Bodies are all stacked up in a pile. The killer or killers took all the wallets and purses with them. None of the victims have any identification."

"Did you say the victims are naked? Were they naked when they were killed?"

He nodded slowly in the affirmative.

I glanced back up toward the house. In the circular driveway, past the police cruisers and the ambulances, there were three SUVs and a Mercedes E350. "I'll bet the victims belong to some of those, and I'll bet you've already run the plates, Mike."

While the cop shrugged, his eyes stared into my own. "Look, Genie, I've got to notify families before I can give you names, you know that. And I also know that you'll be running those plates yourself once you get back to your office. Unless you've already done it." He pointed to my phone.

I had, of course, but before I could print the names, I'd need confirmation from the cops. Two of the SUVs belonged to the Chadwicks. The third, an Escalade, belonged to John and Martha Singewald. The Mercedes was the property of Kit and Kathy Webster.

None of the names meant anything to me. Not yet.

"Any idea on who might have done it?"

Mike gave the stock answer. "Yeah, we've got some solid leads and we expect to make progress on this case over the next few days."

That was the deputy chief's way of saying they didn't having any suspects. If he did, he would have said that he expected to make an arrest.

Instead, he'd said that he expected to make progress.

Big difference.

That meant that the cops didn't have a whole lot to work with yet. But I couldn't write that because that wasn't what Mike said.

"Well, there's not a lot of story here, Mike."

"What? Are you kidding me? You got naked, and you got hacked up bodies stacked up like cordwood. Makes a hell of a front page." Even though Mike likes me, he sounded disgusted.

I held up my hands. "Sarcasm, Mike. It was sarcasm."

He was right, of course. This was a big story. Six naked people cut up into pieces in one of the most exclusive neighborhoods on the Gold Coast of Connecticut. And right at that moment, the story was entirely mine. On the one hand, I was repulsed to my very soul that six people died like this. The final moments they endured must have been absolute hell. Nobody deserves that kind of ending.

But on the other hand, I was at a low point in my life, bottomed out. If I didn't screw it up, this could be the catalyst to put my career back on track. I desperately needed to get it right.

I tucked my phone and notebook into my oversized handbag. "So, how's Phil doing?"

I was referring to Officer Phil Gilmartin, twelve-year veteran of the Sheffield Police Department.

"He's okay. Still a little sore."

"I didn't hit him that hard."

"You gave him a black eye."

"Tell him again that I'm sorry, okay?"

"Genie, I like you. But don't hit any more cops. It really pisses them off."

I shrugged and raised my hands. "I'm payin' for it, Mike. You know that. I'm on probation and attending AA meetings for the next six months."

"You humiliated him."

"So next time he'll remember to keep his guard up."

"Not funny."

I pointed to the house with the six naked bodies still inside. "Call me if there's a break in the case?"

"You know I will." Mike spoke the words but I was almost sure he didn't mean it. Knowing Mike, he'd call me when it was good for Mike.

• • ● • •

Twenty minutes later, I was at my desk watching my editor chew on the stale corner of an old tuna fish sandwich. He stared intently at his computer screen, silently editing my story on the Connor's Landing murders.

Earlier in the day, the ancient air-conditioning system in the building had gone belly-up and, even that late in the evening, the internal office temperature hung in the low nineties. As he looked over my story, Casper Wells took out his handkerchief and absently wiped away the beads of sweat trickling down from his graying scalp and pooling in his bushy, overgrown eyebrows.

Finally, blessedly, Casper hit the Send button, looked up, nodded, and gave me a sour grin.

Time for this girl to go.

I took a look around the building. This was when I enjoyed the office best. It was quiet. Most everyone in the editorial office had gone home for the night. The ubiquitous chatter of the police scanner was silent as were the computer keyboards. The screensavers' ghostly, silver glow threw odd shadows over the chaos of the newsroom. Random piles of newspapers and manila folders were strewn around the floor next to ancient metal desks, littered with more folders and dirty coffee cups.

The office, like the business itself, was showing her age.

With a sigh, I picked up a couple of file folders from my desk, shoved them into my bag, waved at Casper, said good night to the pre-press guys, and walked out.

Glancing at my watch, I had to make choice. I could head over to the Paradise Lounge for a vodka tonic or go to AA.

Chapter Two

You never know what freaky cards the universe is going to deal you. On the same night the cops discovered six bodies—giving me a once-in-a-lifetime chance to claw out of my career abyss—I crossed paths with an old friend. I had no idea then how profoundly it would change my life.

I hadn't seen Kevin Bell since college. But here he was at an AA meeting with the same resolute expression on his face that he wore when we were both eleven and he'd just gotten his ass kicked by the schoolyard bully.

A lifetime ago, my family moved from Cincinnati to Sheffield, Connecticut, and it was the first day of school. I was already way too tall for my age. As I stepped off the bus, I felt like a stumbling giraffe walking alongside my brand new classmates. I clutched my lunch nervously to my skinny chest, feeling and hearing the wax-paper wrapped PB&J sandwich that my mom had tucked inside a brown paper bag crushing up against my windbreaker.

I was certain that all the other kids were staring at me like I was a sideshow freak.

At least that's how I felt, right up until the fight started…and then I was sure that all eyes were on Kevin Bell.

Kevin, much shorter than me at the time, barely five feet tall and hardly a hundred pounds, had been sitting on a stone wall, which was more decorative than functional, alongside a dozen other kids outside the doorway of John F. Kennedy Elementary. We were all waiting for the front doors to be unlocked when

Danny Allan, a brutish kid with limited intelligence and few social skills, decided that he'd be better served if he had his butt planted where Kevin's was.

At first Danny's request was cordial. "Hey, dickhead, I wanna sit down. Get outta my spot."

Kevin answered with equal grace. "Screw you. I was here first."

Danny reacted like any kid who was older, bigger, and stronger than the rest of his classmates. He got up close to where Kevin was sitting and, without warning, shoved him hard with both fists, slamming them like hammers into Kevin's chest. The smaller boy pitched backwards off his perch and dropped with a solid thud to the ground.

Danny laughed and sat down on the wall. He gloated, "Nice of Kevin to save my spot...he kept it nice and warm."

Kevin struggled to his feet, embarrassment and pain in his eyes. I was amazed at how it quickly faded, replaced with blind rage. He brushed the dirt off the seat of his jeans and walked angrily around the end of the short stone wall, planting his feet directly in front of the bully. Before either of them had a chance to say another word, Kevin balled up his fist, reared back, and punched Danny under his left eye.

I'd fully expected the bully to fall over backwards, very much like Kevin had only seconds before. But instead, Danny Allan remained in place, looking surprised. Then he rubbed the reddening area under his eye and stood up, easily demonstrating that he was a full head taller than Kevin.

The bully's thin lips split into a grin that sent a cold shiver down the back of my neck.

Without another word, the carnage began.

Kevin did his best to cover up and block the damage that Danny's huge fists inflicted. He even attempted to land a wild punch or two of his own. But, in seconds, Danny had battered and bashed Kevin's face badly enough that one eye was purple and almost swollen shut and his nose looked to be at an odd angle, most likely broken. Blood flowed freely from Kevin's nostrils and down onto his shirt.

I kept hoping that Kevin would just fall down. Maybe then, mercifully, Danny would quit beating on him.

But in front of a growing mob of kids screaming with gleeful bloodlust, Kevin stood there and took it, vainly trying to ward off the blows. Over and over, he kept getting hit while I watched like it was a bad dream you can't wake up from.

Little more than a target, Kevin stood his ground. Weeks later Kevin told me that, for him, beating Danny didn't mean kicking the crap out of him, not that there was a snowball's chance of that happening. It meant not losing to him.

No matter what Danny Allan did, he couldn't knock Kevin down.

Mr. Wordin, the vice principal, appeared from thin air and grabbed Danny's collar, pulling him away from the mauling. "What's going on here? Who started this?"

Pointing at Kevin, the bully honestly answered, "He hit me first."

"That true?" Mr. Wordin snapped, so angry that his bloodshot eyes bugged out like a Saturday morning cartoon character's.

An exhausted Kevin swayed side-to-side, his eyes nearly closed, a steady stream of blood from his nose splattering to the ground around his sneakers. When he sighed and nodded yes, it broke my heart.

Without thinking, still holding my paper bag lunch, I stepped up and stated emphatically, "But that's not the way it happened. It was *this* boy who started the fight." I pointed defiantly at Danny Allan.

I recall hearing everyone in the crowd take a collective gasp of air, shocked at my courage. *Who is this girl who dares to challenge Danny Allan, the bully with the vicious temper and the vengeful fists?*

At least that's how I want to remember it.

The reality was that the school door had already been unlocked, the bell was ringing, and the other kids were already drifting into their classrooms. Mr. Wordin ignored me completely and hauled both boys off to the principal's office for further interrogation and eventual detention.

But Danny Allan had heard me.

That boy would become my sworn enemy until we reached the tenth grade, right about the same time he discovered the joy of drinking beer, smoking dope, and nailing cheerleaders. Then he just forgot who I was.

But, unfortunately before that happened, Danny Allan would hurt me horribly, a pain that's never gone away to this very day.

Kevin, however, would become one of my best all-time friends, right up until we graduated from high school.

And then, attending colleges hundreds of miles apart, we lost touch.

But here he was, in the basement of the Sheffield Unitarian Church. It took me a minute to recognize him. Of course he was taller than I remembered. I'd forgotten that by the end of high school Kevin had grown to the point that he was even taller than me. His hair was shorter now. Most of it was still brown, some of it was starting to go silver, and it was cut close enough to his scalp that you could easily see the widow's peaks of his receding hairline. His eyes were still as blue, but they seemed tired, like he'd seen a lot of things he'd just as soon forget.

I smiled when I saw that he'd never gotten his nose fixed. At the time of the fight, his Dad was out of work and they didn't have insurance so Kevin never saw a doctor. When it healed, his nose had a slight, angular crook to it. It was nothing ugly… it made him unique and ever so slightly asymmetrical. As a matter of fact, I always thought it made him look kind of cute in a rugged sort of way.

He was wearing a blue cotton work shirt, rolled up at the sleeves, and a pair of well-worn jeans. His face had enough lines and creases to give him character, and he was wearing the look that I'd seen a lot when we were kids. It was Kevin's *"I wish I were anywhere but here"* expression.

Because this was an Alcoholics Anonymous meeting, we were supposed to *be* anonymous, so I resisted the urge to run across the church basement and give him a hug. Seeing him again after so many years made my heart skip a couple of surprising beats.

He stood along the far wall, his arms folded, face intent as he listened to the speaker. I'd come in late and he hadn't seen me sneak in, which allowed me to study him with impunity.

I'd obviously missed the coffee, doughnuts, serenity prayer, and opening words from our host. We were already into the portion of the evening in which people got up and shared how well they were doing in their struggle with booze. I was still pretty new to AA and had yet to be one of those folks who would proclaim their first name, admit to being an alcoholic, and then tick off the number of weeks, days, hours, and minutes since they'd last ordered a vodka rocks.

This was the very first time I'd been to this particular chapter. I'd been attending the Westport AA meetings. Westport's a pretty affluent town and I was hoping that maybe it had a better class of drunks. In the end, I decided to try this group because it was closer to where I live.

About forty people sat in metal folding chairs or, like Kevin, stood along the cinderblock walls. They formed a kaleidoscope of diversity; alcohol doesn't care about gender, age, or race. Some wore ties, their sport coats slung over the back of their chairs. Some, like Kevin, wore denim work clothes. Everyone was concentrating on the speaker—a man at the front of the room in his mid-thirties, with a thick head of dark hair and pale blue eyes. He was handsome in a boyish way, but he was a big man, a little over six feet tall with the solid, chiseled musculature of a weight lifter

He said his name was Jim and stated that he was an alcoholic. The entire room, including me, answered in unison, "Hello, Jim."

"I been sober for over a year…" he started, then sighed. After a lengthy pause, he continued, "…until yesterday."

Jim stared down at his shoes, clearly ashamed. The room was tomb-silent.

"Yesterday would have been my tenth wedding anniversary, except about a year ago my wife left me for another man." He fell silent again, then continued, "No, that's not honest. She left me because I'm an alcoholic. When I drink I get stupid and when I get stupid I hurt people."

Now I could quite clearly see tears welling in his eyes. "So yesterday I got out our wedding album and I watched our wedding video. When my wife left, she didn't care enough to take them with her. Thinking about our wedding day made me realize just how lonely I am, how much I miss her. I wanted a drink so damned bad."

When he next spoke, his voice had dropped to almost a whisper. "So I bought a bottle of Jack and didn't stop drinking until it was gone."

While he talked I watched his hands clench into fists and unclench, over and over. His hands were massive. Unfortunately, I've been on the receiving end of angry fists and I was certain that man's hands could do some real damage.

"And then I wasn't sad anymore." His voice still low. "I was angry. I wanted to hurt somebody. I wanted to hurt my wife and I wanted to hurt the man she married. I wasn't in my right mind. I wanted to hurt 'em bad."

I was startled by how threatening his voice had become.

A second man suddenly stood up, about three rows back. He was tall and wore a closely cropped beard, his head shaved to the scalp and his eyes as blue as the speaker's. He wore a gray tee shirt that said *Jesus, take the wheel.*

The man said, "But he didn't. He didn't hurt anyone because Christ took him by the hand and guided him back to the road of righteousness."

Everyone turned to look at the new speaker.

The big man at the front of the room nodded in agreement and took a deep breath of contrition. "I've got my brother here with me now, and he's a minister, and he and I prayed over it, and we know it's all gonna' work out. I'm sober now. Today. And with the help of the Lord, I'll be sober every day for the rest of my life."

As he walked back to his seat, he paused to shake hands and listen to words of encouragement. When he got to his seat, his brother hugged him.

I'd only been doing AA for about a month, but the stories were running together in a dark blur of regret, tragedy, and endless pain. Nobody was here because they were tired of having a good time. They were here because they'd caused someone else unforgivable suffering.

I looked over at Kevin, wondering what his story was.

How did you get here, Kevin?

If I'd thought I'd find out that night, my hopes were dashed by the intrusive, high-pitched twitter of my cell phone. Glancing guiltily around me, I faced a room full of annoyed stares. A slight jolt of electricity snapped in my chest as I noticed Kevin looking directly at me, his mouth slightly open with a grin of recognition and amused surprise.

Stepping into the hallway, I recognized the number on caller ID. "What do you want?" I snarled.

"The wife is out of town, you want dinner?"

"I haven't heard from you in a month."

"It's been complicated."

I heard the anger in my own voice as I hissed, "Don't call me again." I hit the End Call button, stalked out of the church, and promptly forgot about Kevin Bell. Then I stopped at the liquor store, drove home, and killed the better part of a bottle of Absolut.

Chapter Three

The incessant chirping of my cell phone felt like an ice pick digging around behind my retinas. I kept my eyes closed and tried hard to ignore it.

When it finally, mercifully stopped, I slowly opened my eyes to see Tucker, my Yorkshire terrier, sitting on the pillow inches away from my face. Little more than two bright, shiny eyes tucked into a ball of brown and gray fur, Tucker wagged his tail furiously and licked at my cheek.

The vodka from the night before had left its usual cruddy taste in my sand-dry mouth. A humming nest of angry bees buzzed furiously around in my throbbing head. I reached up and lifted the cell phone off my headboard.

The caller ID said it was someone from my office. Reluctantly, I listened to the voice message. It was brief. "It's Laura, give me a call." Laura Ostrowski is the daytime copy editor at the newspaper.

The digital clock on the cell phone told me it was a little after nine. Since my shift doesn't start until three, it was way too early to be awake.

I hit the return call button and put a hand over my eyes to mitigate the daylight punching its way past the curtains into my bedroom. "Hey, Laura, what's up?" The smoky, low timbre of my own raspy voice surprised me.

"Nice job on the Connor's Landing story."

"Thanks. How did Casper play it?"

"Six columns, top of the page. It's a hell of a piece. The Associated Press picked it up, CNN too. Charlie told me that all the morning news programs were quoting your story."

Even hungover, I felt that strange thrill in my stomach, the one you get when you're the lead dog on a story everyone wants a piece of. I hadn't felt it in a long, long time.

"Hear anything more from the cops?"

"Not yet. I'll give 'em a call after I've had a cup of coffee."

I was waiting to hear what she wanted. Laura simply didn't have it in her DNA to call for a little chitchat.

Finally she got to it. "I heard from the prosecutor's office that Jimmy Fitzgerald's going to cop a plea this morning."

Jimmy Fitzgerald is the son of Henry Morris Fitzgerald, the owner of Regius Opus, a hedge-fund firm in Greenwich. At nineteen, Jimmy is a child of extreme privilege. Reared in the spacious, velvet halls of Gold Coast mansions, educated at the most expensive private schools in New England, promised a monster trust fund that kicks in at twenty-one, the boy quite literally had it all.

And then he killed someone.

He and a friend had raided the old man's wine cellar and cannon-balled about four thousand dollars' worth of rare Pinot Noir. While they were chugging the finest wine that Napa Valley has to offer, they were also smoking high-end Jamaican cannabis.

Having exhausted their supply of ganga, they decided to slum it, hopping into Jimmy's Porsche to fly on down to Sheffield and purchase another couple of ounces.

At the same time, Elena Bermudez had just finished her shift as a checkout clerk at Shop-Rite and was crossing the street to reach the bus stop. She was late and didn't want to miss her ride. She needed to start dinner for her three children.

When Jimmy hit her, he was going nearly sixty miles an hour in a thirty-five-mile-an-hour zone.

He was charged with leaving the scene of an accident, driving under the influence, and manslaughter. The young man hadn't spent an entire night in jail before a hyper-priced attorney sprung him on a quarter-million dollars bail.

"Cop a plea, huh? What's that got to do with me? Audrey's on that story."

"Audrey slipped getting out of the shower this morning and threw out her back," Laura explained.

I glanced over at Tucker looking back at me expectantly, tongue lolling out of the side of his mouth. He was waiting patiently for me to walk him. "I didn't get to bed until late," I whined. "There isn't someone else on the day shift that can cover this?"

Laura ticked off her list of disasters. "Eric's getting a root canal, Don's on vacation, Anthony's in Westport covering the regatta, and Ann is on the mayor's speech. I'm out of available bodies and you owe me a favor."

I sighed. "I need to take my dog for a walk and grab a shower. What time is the Jimmy Fitzgerald Show taking place at the courthouse?"

"Ten-thirty. If you hustle, you can do all of that and still grab a cup at Starbucks."

"All right, I'll do it. Hey," I interjected, clearing my throat, "have you heard anything more on the Home Alone Gang?"

"Not since they did the 'twofer' a couple weeks ago." Her answer was terse. "Everyone thinks they've already blown town."

The Home Alone Gang was a sophisticated group of cat burglars who'd broken into more than a dozen mansions in the most expensive burbs of Fairfield and Westchester counties with startling regularity. A week and a half ago, they hit two houses on the same night at almost the same time. One was in Wilton and one was twenty miles away in Ridgefield. The last time I talked with Mike Dillon about them, he theorized that they were showboating for a grand finale before leaving the state for fresh pickings someplace else.

Ah well, it was good ink while it lasted.

"Hey, Genie."

"Yeah?"

"Staying straight?"

I massaged the side of my throbbing temple while I assured her. "Like an arrow."

"You said you were up late."

"I was at AA."

"And that went late?"

"Last night it did," I lied.

The pause on the other end of the line seemed to last forever. Finally, Laura said, "Okay. See you when you get here."

Tucker got his walk and I took my shower. I spent longer than I should have trying to cover my hangover with Visine and high-end makeup and, yes, still had time to buy a latte that I carried into the courthouse. My ice-pick headache had subsided into a dull throb as I sat toward the front of the room and pulled my tiny recorder out of my purse. Then I waited.

I don't like covering courtrooms because they're arenas of greed, complaints, whining, tragedy, and despair. Besides, they never stay on any kind of reasonable schedule.

If you've ever been called for jury duty, you know exactly what I'm talking about. Something that should take anyone else about thirty minutes to accomplish, attorneys and judges can stretch out into a hellish eternity.

Plus the wooden seats are hard. They don't just punish the guilty, they punish everybody.

At about eleven o'clock, Jimmy Fitzgerald showed up in court with his lawyer. The kid was easily six feet tall, looked like he knew his way around a gym, had spiky, stylish hair that appeared deceptively disheveled, and wore a dark gray suit that probably cost several thousand dollars special-ordered from London.

Walking in with him was Jimmy's attorney. Stephen Provost was shorter than his client, around sixty years old, had a full mane of silver hair, and wore a pair of tiny, steel-gray glasses perched on his patrician nose. His suit looked almost as expensive as Jimmy's.

Glancing behind me, I saw the husband of Elena Bermudez sitting on a bench two rows back. Three weeks ago, at Jimmy's indictment, I'd read in our newspaper that Julio Bermudez had brought all three kids with him to the courtroom.

Today he was alone. He wore a wrinkled, blue short-sleeved shirt and a tie, no coat. His face was dark from long days in the sun and there were creases around his brown eyes and the corners of his mouth that were his rewards for a hard life. He was a day laborer who worked construction jobs, when they were available. I'd bet that Julio Bermudez didn't own a suit.

His face was grim. He rocked ever so slightly as the judge swept onto the bench.

It was over almost before it started.

Presiding over the courtroom was Judge William Cain who'd been on the bench for over a decade. He was known as a tough, no-nonsense judge but had a reputation as a political power broker. He recited the state's charges against James M. Fitzgerald.

The prosecutor, Andy Sutton, and the attorney, Stephen Provost, both acknowledged the judge's accurate description of the charges. Then the judge rhetorically inquired, "Am I to understand that a plea agreement has been reached?"

Once again they both replied yes. The judge instructed them to approach the bench.

After a few moments of conference and nodding, Provost and Sutton stepped back. The judge peered across the room at Jimmy and said, "Stand up, Mr. Fitzgerald."

The young man did as he was told. With his head slightly bowed, he appeared properly contrite.

"The prosecution has informed me that the state is ready to drop the charge of manslaughter if you're willing to plead guilty to the charges of leaving the scene of an accident and driving under the influence. You'll serve community service and pay a fine, as yet to be determined, and provide compensation to the family of Mrs. Bermudez," the judge stated in a flat voice. "Is that correct?"

Jimmy replied, "It is, Your Honor."

"Is the husband of Mrs. Bermudez in the courtroom?" The judge's eyes scanned the courtroom.

I glanced over at Julio Bermudez. He was still rocking, almost imperceptibly, in his seat. The muscles in his jaw were working as he ground his teeth. The man slowly stood up. In a voice that was barely audible, he answered, "Yes, Your Honor."

"Are you aware of this agreement, sir? Has it been explained fully to you?"

He nodded, staring down at the floor. "Yes, sir."

"Are you satisfied with the proceedings of this court?"

Mr. Bermudez nodded once again. "Yes, sir." His voice was little more than a whisper.

"Please be seated," the judge said. He turned his attention to Jimmy Fitzgerald. "Young man, your plea is accepted. Your sentencing will take place two weeks from today."

I took a look at Julio Bermudez one last time as he sat back down. Tears ran down his face, leaving trails that glimmered on the sunburned skin of his cheeks.

• • ● • •

I collared the assistant district attorney outside the courtroom. "Hey, Andy, how did that kid get away with murder?"

His face was deadly serious. "Turn off your recorder, Genie. This is all off the record."

I made a show of putting the tiny silver machine back into my purse. "So?"

Andy surreptitiously glanced around to see if anyone was listening. "C'mon, Genie, you know the deal. Money talks and the rich kid walks."

"How much?"

He shrugged. "Does it matter?"

My head was throbbing again. "It does to me."

He leaned in and put his lips close to my ear. He whispered, "This has gotta be off the record."

"Yeah, yeah, off the record." I held out my hands to show him I wasn't holding a notebook or a recorder.

"I only know for sure what his old man is paying the family—three hundred thousand dollars."

"And?" I knew there had to be another quid pro quo hidden in this woodpile.

He bit at his lip and then quietly said, "I'm getting this from someone who works in the judge's office, so take it with a grain of salt, okay? She told me that a check was sent from Henry Morris Fitzgerald in the amount of a million dollars to a PAC attached to a United States congressman, a congressman who's tight with the judge."

I held up my hands like I was weighing cantaloupes. "Let's see, a million dollars over here," I let my hand drop, then continued. "Over here we have three hundred thousand dollars. Is that what the life of a mother of three children is worth these days?"

Andy Sutton shrugged. "Look, I'm not happy about this. But for a guy like Julio Bermudez, who has *nothing*... that kind of money and a green card is like hitting the lottery. Oh, yeah, the congressman is getting this guy a green card. Maybe you don't know, but Julio Bermudez is an illegal. At first, Jimmy's old man thought he could get the charges thrown out if Mr. Bermudez was sent back to Columbia. But then he decided it was easier to buy him off."

Andy glanced down at the floor for moment and then met my eyes. "Genie, Elena Bermudez was in the wrong place at the wrong time. I know that. It was an act of God, bad luck, whatever you want to call it. But now these three kids have a chance to live in a nice apartment and maybe get themselves a college education. I know it sounds harsh but in reality, it's the best thing that could ever happen to them."

Losing their mother because some rich kid was taking a drunken joyride, the best thing that could ever happen to them?

I looked at my watch. "Hey..." I felt really tired. "All part of the grand design. Maybe Jimmy Fitzgerald should get a friggin' medal for making mom a hood ornament."

Okay, sometimes I have a really hard time restraining my anger and sarcasm. But I'm pretty sure that nobody had seen Mr. Bermudez crying that morning except for me.

When I left the courthouse, I was certain I'd be writing about Jimmy Fitzgerald again. The kid had no moral compass. Over the last three years, he'd been charged with identity theft, aggravated assault, and rape. In every instance, any witnesses or accusers had recanted and the charges were subsequently dropped.

Jimmy Fitzgerald was a sociopath. I was convinced that either he'd end up in prison or running for public office. I guess it depended on how much money his old man could afford to burn through.

Chapter Four

"I know who killed those people."

The moment I heard those chilling words on my office voice-mail, a jolt of adrenalin hit hard.

I touched the button and listened again.

"I know who killed those people out on Connor's Landing. I read the story this morning and I got your name and number out of the newspaper. I can't talk to the police and I can't tell you who I am. But I know why they were killed and I know who did it."

There was a short silence while the caller considered what he should say next.

All he came up with was, "I'll call back."

Caller ID said the number was "unavailable." I listened to the message three more times to see if I could capture a single clue that might tell me who the caller was. It was a male, a baritone. He sounded nervous. There was nothing else, no stutter, no accent, no ambient background noise.

Could this guy be for real?

Or was he a nut? A high-profile story like the Connor's Landing murders, you're bound to hear from a few. In the years that I've been a journalist, the crackpots outnumbered the genuine tips by a gazillion to none.

But every once in a while, I'd get a real one. It's like getting hit by lightning.

Why the hell hadn't he told me *when* he was going to call back? What was I supposed to do, sit by the phone?

Typical freakin' man.

I momentarily struggled with the notion of calling Mike Dillon and telling him about the phone message. After all, this was *his* homicide investigation. But then I thought it through. The guy said he couldn't go to the cops. If the caller was legitimate, then he was a source and a reporter doesn't give up her sources.

And there was no guarantee the caller was even for real.

The tiny red light on my phone continued to blink, reminding me that there were still other messages waiting in my voice-mailbox. Maybe the mystery man had called a second time?

The next message was nearly as interesting as the first.

"Geneva Chase…this is Kevin Bell. What a surprise seeing you last night. I get The Sheffield Post delivered at home and I see your byline all the time. I was going to call you weeks ago, but I thought that maybe working for the newspaper, well… I'm sure they keep you pretty busy. You're a good writer. Um, look, I'd love to catch up with you sometime. Could you and I grab a cup of coffee when you have a few minutes? Call me if you think you can find some time and if you don't, hey, I know you're busy. But I'd love to see you again."

He left me his phone number.

My heart gave an extra thump and wondered why.

Kevin had been my best friend through high school. But we'd never been romantic.

Not really.

I chalked it up to the adrenaline high I'd gotten from the mystery caller a few minutes earlier. That and too much caffeine. I'd skipped breakfast to get to the courthouse on time and my blood sugar was getting pretty low.

The rest of the calls were follow-ups from other stories I was working on. Nothing more from the tipster who wanted to talk about the Connor's Landing homicides.

I'd settled in and started working on the Jimmy Fitzgerald piece when Laura Ostrowski stopped by my desk. She's been a newspaper editor for over twenty years and has the tired, bag-laden eyes and pasty, prison-like pallor to prove it. "Just wanted to thank you for covering the courthouse today."

I smiled. "No problem, but we're square now on the favor thing, right?"

She didn't smile back. "Not quite. Almost."

Laura had covered for me one evening about three months ago after I'd stopped off at the Paradise Lounge, knocked back three vodka tonics, and then came into the office. She knew I'd been drinking the minute she saw my lush flush and sent me home with a whispered lecture. She told Casper that I had the flu. If he'd known the truth, he would have fired me.

She was right, of course. I owed her more than just the one favor.

Laura continued, "I need you to cover a black-tie fundraiser tonight."

I squinted up into her face. "What?" My voice was clearly incredulous.

"The Fairfield County Bar Association has a dinner dance tonight at the Shorefront Club. They're raising money for the American Cancer Association. I'm still shorthanded. I've already talked to Casper. He says it's okay if I assign you to the story."

I argued. "I don't want to sound ungrateful. God knows I could use the evening out, but take a look at my business card. It says I'm the crime reporter. I do the police beat."

Laura shrugged. "A lot of cops and judges will be there. Good place for you to network. Here's the information." She dropped an invitation and two tickets on my desk. "You're not drinking, right?"

That was the second time she'd grilled me about that.

Do I look that hungover?

I blinked and tried to sound sincere. "I'm even attending AA. I've become absolutely boring." Holding up the tickets I asked, "Two?"

She shrugged again. "Take a date."

As Laura walked away, my phone rang. Thinking it might be the mystery caller with more information about the homicides, I sprang to pick up the receiver. "Geneva Chase," I stated quickly.

"Got time for lunch?"

"I told you not to call me anymore."

"C'mon, it's only lunch."

"I'm in the middle of a story," I snarled. I started tapping away at my keyboard as much for effect as for honesty.

"Portofino's?" Frank Mancini has a wonderfully deep voice and even the most mundane words can sound seductive when they come out of his mouth. Plus, he wasn't playing fair. He knows that Portofino's is my favorite restaurant.

"I don't hear from you for a month and now you expect me to drop everything and go with you to lunch?" My voice had a clear edge but I was working hard to keep it low enough that I wouldn't disturb anyone else in the office.

"Portofino's," he said again. "Think of it as an apology lunch."

"Maybe I wasn't clear. I'm in the middle of a story." I hoped that he couldn't hear my stomach rumbling.

"Yeah," he said, "those murders out on the island. That was some nasty business, huh? I know some people who live out there. You got names on the victims yet?"

Feeling testy, I snapped, "Not that story. Another story."

"What's the story? It can't wait?" Frank was speaking from his cell phone. From the ambient noises, it was obvious he was calling from his car.

"Jimmy Fitzgerald, the rich kid from Greenwich, beat a manslaughter charge this morning. Another victory for the American system of justice. It's the best that money can buy."

Frank was silent for a moment. I like being critical of our country's judicial train wreck. Frank's an attorney and it really gets under his skin.

After an appropriate second or two, he took a deep breath. "Portofino's?"

Casper had just come into the office. He's the nighttime copy editor. Laura runs the day shift. They were talking with each other and glancing toward me.

Suddenly I feel the need to get out of the office.

"Okay. Give me half an hour."

• • ● • •

I like Portofino's because it's really comfortable. The colors on the walls, the curtains, and the tablecloths are all muted earth tones. The lighting's obscured without being dim. The menu is familiar yet adventurous. The wait staff is friendly and attentive.

It's comfortable and expensive.

"Miss Chase, so nice to see you again." Massimo, the owner, greeted me with a hearty kiss on the cheek and a hug as I walked through the door with Frank.

I responded, "Massimo, you know, sometimes I think that having lunch here is better than sex."

He stepped back, blushing and making a small hand gesture of apology, smiling sheepishly at Frank. "Only if it's the osso bucco, Miss Chase." He was good at thinking quickly.

I glanced over at Frank, hoping that I'd embarrassed him as much as I had the restaurant owner. He was giving me his bemused "you're such a bad girl" stare.

I hate to admit it but I had missed Frank Mancini.

For one, I like the way he looks. He's tall, over six feet, is graced with a dark Mediterranean complexion, chocolate brown eyes, full head of black hair, and a closely cropped George Clooney beard that's showing the slightest hint of gray. He smiles easily, has a charming, old-world sense of humor, and speaks intelligently on almost any subject. Frank wears expensive suits and fills them well. He's fifty and determined to keep his body as hard as a young man in his twenties.

Frank spends enough money to prove that he's a very successful attorney. He's usually even-tempered, but on occasion, I've seen flashes of anger and pettiness that lead me to suspect that Frank Mancini possesses a secret dark side. It makes him all the more attractive to me.

He's everything I've ever wanted in a man.

Except for the wedding band that he wears.

It's not mine.

"A table overlooking the harbor?" Massimo asked, as we walked through the dining room.

"Please," Frank answered.

Once we were seated, my eyes immediately checked the view. It was a clear, perfect summer day and the restaurant overlooks a marina on the edge of Long Island Sound. Dozens of boats were tied to docks that were less than forty feet from where we sat. I figured there wasn't a craft out there that was worth less than a quarter million dollars. Even though I went to high school in this part of Connecticut, I'm still amazed at the ostentatious displays of wealth. The rest of the world can be crumbling and broke, but Fairfield County raked it in.

When I turned my attention back to Frank, I was a little startled to see that he was watching me. "What?"

"I just like looking at you. I haven't seen you in a while."

"A month," I stated flatly, taking a drink from my water glass. "It's been over a month."

Before he had a chance to respond, a young man swooped by our table with menus and asked us if we'd like something to drink.

Frank quickly ordered a martini and then glanced over at me.

I clenched my jaws angrily. "Thanks for the support."

"What do you mean?"

"You know I'm not supposed to drink. And you order a martini? The least you could do is order an iced tea."

Frank made a small production of scanning the busy dining room. Then he quietly announced, "I don't see any police here. I don't see any judges here. I just see you and me. If you want to order a cocktail, then order a cocktail. I promise, I won't tell a soul."

I looked up at the young waiter, who was clearly befuddled, and scrunched up my nose. "I'll have a diet Coke, please."

Frank waved his hand in the air and ordered, "Bring the lady a vodka tonic."

The waiter nodded and quickly left.

I shook my head and muttered, "Asshole." I tried to sound angry, but secretly I was glad that Frank had ordered me a grown-up drink.

"So, look, I'm sorry I haven't called you sooner." He kept his voice low. "The way it all shook out, I thought it might be best if things between us stayed quiet for a little while."

"Stayed quiet," I repeated. "You mean on the down low?"

The hint of a smile played on his lips. "Yeah, on the DL."

I growled, "Down low, my ass."

Frank rubbed his forehead and glanced around, wishing the waiter would come back with his drink.

"So how is Evelyn?" I asked icily.

Frank scowled. "The morning after all that unpleasantness happened at the Z Bar, Evelyn told me she wanted a divorce."

I don't mind telling you that for a brief moment, I felt a hot flash of euphoria. "I hope I don't sound too unsympathetic, but isn't that what you and I've been talking about for the past two years?"

"Predicated upon my first acquiring custody of the children. Evelyn threatened to take them away from me. The children, both of the houses, the cars, and all of our investments. She said that if I ever saw you again she'd take it all."

"And yet here you are."

Before Frank could respond, the waiter placed our drinks on the table and asked if we were ready to order. We'd been there enough times that neither of us needed to consult the menu. Frank ordered the seared tuna and I ordered a Caesar salad.

When we were alone again, Frank held his glass in the air. "Cheers."

I picked up my glass and held it to his. "Cheers," I repeated, taking a sip. "So are you saying that Evelyn doesn't want a divorce now? Everything's good at home?"

Frank took a deep drink from his martini. "You know that it's never good at home. But, no, she doesn't want a divorce."

"What changed her mind?"

"An apology and a new BMW."

I shrugged. "So what are you going to do?"

His eyes looked misty and he seemed genuinely sad. He was very good at that. "Well, I know that I can't walk away from you."

"And you can't leave your wife."

"Are things really so bad?"

"The way they are? You mean right now?" My voice rose angrily.

He took a breath. "Except for the last month, we manage to see each other a couple of times a week. We have nice dinners together, we have nice lunches. We go to shows together, see movies. I think the sex is, well, pretty damned fantastic. We have a warm, fun, open, wonderful relationship. Our interests are alike; our politics are the same and I love being with you. How many married couples can say that?"

In reality, the fact that Frank Mancini was married wasn't necessarily a liability. Would I like the freedom to see him when I wanted? Sure. But I also liked the "alone" time that I had. I wasn't ready to share my life with someone right now, so I tacitly agreed to share him with his wife.

And honestly, the fact that he was married? That we were committing adultery? Always worried that we might be "found out"? In a twisted way, that made him all the more appealing to me.

He reached over and softly touched my hand. "So after lunch, are you busy?"

"I have to finish the Jimmy Fitzgerald story."

He squeezed my hand. "Do you have time for dessert?"

Sexual tension suddenly raised my body temperature by about ten degrees. He wasn't talking about splitting a chocolate mousse. Frank was asking me if I was in the mood to go back to my apartment and slip inside my queen-sized bed.

Now, I'm not some teenager whose hormones are constantly boiling over. No matter how hard I lean against it, I can feel my age trying to squeeze its way through the biological door. Let's face it, my interest in sex isn't what it used to be when I was in college or even in my early thirties.

It had been over a month since I'd last been with Frank.

Or anybody else for that matter.

And he wasn't lying when he said the sex was fantastic. His desserts were fun.

And calorie-free.

But I answered, "I really have to get this story done." And having forgotten that I had agreed to cover the fundraiser, I asked, "How about we get together later tonight?"

His face took on a pained expression. "I wish I could. I have a black-tie thing I'm attending tonight. The Fairfield County Bar Association is raising money for some charity."

My spirits rose. "Hey, what a coincidence! As it turns out, I have to cover that very same event tonight. Want to be my date?"

Frank's hand was on mine and I could feel his palm start to sweat. He didn't say anything for a moment. Then he explained, apologetically, "Um, I have to take Evelyn."

"Have to take Evelyn?" I snarled. "Someone got a gun to your head?"

"Everybody at our table's bringing their wives."

Lunch came just in time for the waiter to hear me growl, "I wouldn't expect dessert from me now or anytime in the near future. How about if you want dessert, you give your wife a big slice of apple pie and a freakin' can of Reddi-wip on top of her new BMW?"

Later that afternoon, I called Kevin Bell.

I asked him to be my date.

And to my delight, he said yes. He may have hesitated and stammered a little, but he finally said yes.

Chapter Five

Kevin's address was an oxymoron.

He lived on the corner of Providence Avenue and Random Road. As I drove up his driveway, I wondered if this might be the universal nexus where fate meets chance. Where God's grand plan is really only a roll of the dice? A place where design rises from chaos?

Once I got a look at Kevin's house, I decided it was all the above.

Kevin's modest two-story home was in a blue-collar neighborhood about five blocks from the harbor. Most of the houses were Cape Cods built forty years ago, when houses and land were still within the price range of the average Joe. Situated on tiny, well-tended yards, the homes were neat. Many owners had obviously added rooms over garages or constructed decks jutting out onto their back lawns. Because property was at a premium, the best way to add value to a home was by building up or out.

Almost every driveway hosted at least two cars as well as a small powerboat parked on a trailer. Slip rentals in this part of Connecticut are incredibly expensive. For the people who lived in Kevin's neighborhood, boats are affordable. Places in the water to keep them are not.

Finding his house, I pulled up behind a faded red Ford pickup truck with the words *Kevin Bell Construction* stenciled onto the side doors. There were sawhorses in the truck bed. Scarred by a dozen dings, dents, and multi-colored scrapes, the vehicle may not have been plagued by age but certainly had been cursed by misused mileage.

I noticed that Kevin did not have a boat in his driveway.

Getting out of my car, I could easily see that Kevin's property was out of sync with the neighborhood. His scruffy-looking lawn, losing its fight with thick patches of weeds, was about two weeks overdue for a trim. Behind his house, I saw a six-foot wooden fence encircling a yard filled with tall stacks of lumber and multiple piles of gravel. My guess was that Kevin wasn't going to get the "good neighbor" award.

When have I ever picked up a guy at his house to take him out on a date?

Earlier that afternoon, Kevin had balked when I'd asked if he wanted to accompany me to the Lawyer's Ball. "I appreciate the offer. I really do. I'd love to see you again. But how about we just go out for pizza?"

"I have to cover this black-tie thing tonight," I explained. "I've got two tickets…free tickets. C'mon. Be my date."

He sighed. "I don't own a tux."

"It's black tie optional," I replied. "A suit and tie will be just fine."

"I don't know, Genie. I'm thinking I might feel a little out of place."

"Aw c'mon, Kevin. It'll give us a chance to catch up," I gently argued. "And I don't want to go alone."

I could almost hear the gears in his head grinding away and then, finally, he slowly replied, "Okay, um, just one thing. Would you mind driving?"

That had taken me completely by surprise. "Car trouble?"

"Something like that. What time you want to come by?"

I shrugged as I talked into the phone. "I don't know. Cocktails at six, pick you up about a quarter to?"

Just as soon as I'd said the word *cocktails,* a picture of him at an AA meeting flashed in front of my eyes. "Not that we have to drink anything," I mumbled.

Sometimes I can be such a dope.

As I walked up the front steps and rang the bell, I shook my head at my stupidity.

A young girl, about thirteen, answered the door. Wearing jeans and a short-sleeved shirt emblazoned with the UConn Huskies logo, she was thin, had long blond hair, deep blue eyes, and a pretty smile. "Hi, you must be Miss Chase."

As I came in I told her, "You can call me Genie," and I shook her hand.

"I'm Caroline. Dad's almost ready. He'll be down in a minute. Can I get you a cup of coffee, soda, maybe a glass of water?"

"Glass of water would be great." While the young girl disappeared into the kitchen, I wondered where her mother might be. I had assumed that Kevin was single when he'd called and asked me out for a cup of coffee. And now, a little late in the game, I silently hoped that I was right. Dating one married man was okay. Two would be overkill.

I followed Caroline into the kitchen and stopped cold in my tracks.

The room looked like a bomb had gone off.

All the cabinet doors were missing. Plates, bowls, glasses, cans of food, cereal boxes, and spice containers were all on display. Then my eyes fell to the countertops. Half of them were gone as well. Upon further inspection, I saw that most of the ceiling tiles had been removed and the beams were showing, along with copper pipes and electrical wiring.

Caroline handed me my glass of water. Still looking around, I quietly asked, "So, what's your dad do for a living, honey?"

She blushed. "He's a contractor."

I'm no expert, but it looked to me that the kitchen had been like this for a while. "Doing a little remodeling?"

She looked around her and shrugged. "Dad started this before Mom died. He was remodeling the whole house. I've seen the drawings he made of what it all should look like. When he gets it finished, it's gonna be beautiful. But after Mom passed away, I think maybe he lost interest a little."

Her mom was dead…Kevin's wife.

I took a sip of my water. I didn't know what to say.

Then I heard Kevin coming down the stairs. "Did I hear the doorbell?" he shouted.

When he came through the doorway and saw me standing in the kitchen, he glanced around the room as if he was seeing it for the first time and said, clearly embarrassed, "Um, sorry about the mess."

I quickly put my glass down on the kitchen table and hugged him. I held him close. I hadn't seen him since high school where, up until graduation, we'd been best buds. I suddenly realized how much I'd missed him He put his arms around me and I could feel his strength through his suit coat, his muscles solid from hard work. He smelled nice, like soap and aftershave, Old Spice maybe.

I pulled back a little. "How long has it been?"

He grinned and thought a moment. His face had a world-weary look to it, but he had a warm smile. "I don't know. Twenty years?"

"Yeah," I put the flat of my hand against his chest. "You look great."

"You too." His smile got brighter.

I glanced over at Caroline leaning against the refrigerator, hands in her pockets, watching us with a bemused look on her face. "And you have a beautiful daughter."

"I had help." His smile faltered for a brief moment. "Look, I'm sorry that I had to ask you to drive. That's a little embarrassing."

"Is your car in the shop?" I recalled the truck in the driveway.

Caroline balled up her fist and coughed into it, saying at the same time, "Restrictions."

When I looked over at her, she had an odd smile on her face.

Kevin nodded. "Restrictions. When did you get back into town?"

"About four months ago."

"Ah, well, about a month before you got here, there was a major power outage that affected over a quarter of the city."

"Yeah? I remember that, Valentine's Day, wasn't it? I was in town visiting a friend." What I didn't tell him was that I was in a hotel having dessert—okay, sex in a king-size bed with Frank Mancini that afternoon. "I heard some guy ran his car into a pole knocking out a power transformer. Shut down a whole power grid."

"That's my Dad," Caroline announced, patting him on the shoulder. She kissed him on the cheek and walked out of the kitchen.

He raised his hands. "My fifteen minutes of fame. Over ten thousand people didn't get their power back on until sometime after midnight. I was the most hated man in Sheffield. And, yeah, it was on Valentine's Day."

The memory of that day was quite vivid. I'd been working at a magazine in New York and taking the train into Sheffield once or twice a week to see Frank. We were snuggled up at the Doubletree when the lights went out. It didn't bother us, of course, because what we were doing required no illumination.

I remember being annoyed, however, not because of the power outage, but because Frank was taking Evelyn out to a Valentine's dinner later that night.

On that particular evening, while he and his wife were having lobster and champagne in New Canaan, I was on my way back to New York via Metro-North, eating a cold slice of pizza and drinking vodka from a thermos.

"So, after five months your car is still in the shop?"

"Ah, well," he explained, "the car is completely gone. It was totaled."

"Didn't want to replace it?"

"No point. The accident was clearly my fault. I was impaired. The judge gave me a fine and put me on probation and driving restrictions. I can only drive to get back and forth from work and during daylight hours. I was lucky he didn't take away my license completely or throw me in jail. There are a lot of people in town who think I got off way too easy. Somebody told me that my neighbors had considered getting together for a barbeque and a lynching."

"Yikes. How long before you can drive like a grown-up?"

"Seven more months. I can petition the court for my driving privileges again next February."

"So it was Valentine's Day. Were you on a date?"

He shook his head and chewed at his lower lip. "It was the first anniversary of Joanna's death."

I reached out and delicately touched his arm. "Your wife?"

He nodded, eyes lowered. "It was breast cancer. I'd spent the whole afternoon in a dark bar, alone, trying to drown her memory in a bottle of scotch. It was stupid."

"And that's why you're in AA."

He pointed at me.

My heart ached for my old friend and I took his hand. "So you want to be my date tonight or what?"

He looked into my eyes and smiled. "Yes, that would be nice."

"So, have you had a good life?"

When Kevin posed that question, he was staring idly out the passenger's side window of my car. He was trying to fill an embarrassing lull in the conversation.

"Good…yeah." My simple answer to a simple question. But then I went on, because I was nervous and when I'm nervous, I never know when to shut up. "Well, for the most part it's been pretty good. The journalism thing's interesting. You're never going to make a ton of money."

"Did you ever get married?"

I hesitated but then decided to be honest. "Yeah, three times."

He turned to give me an odd, inquisitive look. "I'm sorry, how many times did you say you've been married?" He couldn't believe what he'd heard.

I winced and held up three fingers. "It's one less than Hemingway."

"Married now?"

I shook my head. "No, but the guy I'm kind of seeing is."

God, don't you know when to shut up?

It was Kevin's turn to wince. He turned back toward the window and gazed out at the landscape as it whizzed by.

"Disappointed?" I started fiddling with the air conditioning.

He shrugged. "I always thought that if you weren't going to marry me, you'd end up with a novelist or a real estate tycoon."

I frowned and smiled at the same time. "You thought we were going to get married?"

It was his turn to smile. "I had a crush on you when we were in high school."

"You never showed it." I clearly felt myself blushing.

"So you were really married three times?" He changed the subject. "What do you have, like ADD?"

"I got married straight out of college but it only lasted about a year. I caught him in our bed with another woman."

Kevin cleared his throat and muttered, "Sorry."

"Husband number two was the city manager for Couders-port, a town just outside of Boston. He was arrested for taking kickbacks and bribes from city contractors. I was working for *The Boston Globe* at the time. I'm the one who broke the story. Blew the whistle on my own husband. He filed for divorce during the trial."

Kevin was quiet for a moment. "Yeah, I can see how that might sour a relationship."

"Husband number three was a homicide cop in New York. He died about five years ago, killed in the line of duty."

"Oh, my God! I'm so sorry."

"Sal was a good cop but he liked to drink. He could put me under the table and that's saying a lot. His partner told me that Sal had been drinking before he'd gone on duty. He put himself at the wrong place at the wrong time."

We both went silent. I pulled onto Gregory Boulevard and headed toward the harbor. We were only a couple of blocks from the Shorefront Club.

"Kids?" he asked.

"What?"

"Did you ever have any children?"

I shook my head.

I can barely take care of myself. How the hell could I take care of kids?

"So," Kevin asked, "how did you end up back in Sheffield, working for your hometown newspaper?"

I took a deep breath. I'd already told him way too much but I never did know when to quit. "No one else would give me a job, Kevin. I pretty much drank myself out of a career and that's the truth. I'm kind of at the end of the line."

"Sheffield's the end of the line?"

I could hear the hurt in his voice. This was his home, but for me, yes, coming back to Sheffield was the end of the line.

As I drove, I reached over and put my hand on his. "I meant working for the local paper is kind of the end of the line. Really, I like being back here."

No I don't. And, by God, if I can get my name back out there with a story as big as the Connor's Landing murders, and get it right, I might be able buy a ticket out of Sheffield and back onto a real newspaper again.

Chapter Six

The southern wall of the Shorefront Club is glass, nearly three stories of it. It offers an unparalleled view of Long Island Sound, the islands of Sheffield Harbor and, on a clear evening, tight to the horizon, the skyline of Manhattan. When we arrived, the sun was easing behind a bank of deep blue and pink cumulous clouds.

Kevin and I stood in front of the glass and watched the sunset. While we talked, our hands touched, accidentally?

Tiny lights on the distant shore of Long Island formed a fine line of flickering stars. Closer, red and green boat lamps bobbed and floated like fireflies just above the surface of the water.

It was a quarter to seven, nearly the end of the cocktail hour. The crowd was growing in number and as the alcohol flowed, the laughter and conversations were getting louder.

Neither Kevin nor I were drinking.

It was odd but illuminating to be completely sober while the rest of the room caught a collective buzz. Certainly a new experience for me. I felt slightly superior to everyone else.

Kevin did not. He whispered in my ear, "I feel a little awkward. I don't see anyone else here who isn't wearing a tux."

I leaned in. "You look terrific."

"I feel like I'm wearing an old shirt and a beat-up pair of jeans."

"You're the best looking guy here. Now, just keep in mind that I'm working tonight and, at some point, I'll have to leave you for a few minutes to do a quick interview."

"No problem. Did you see how much it cost per plate to come to this party?"

Honestly, I hadn't. I was a little embarrassed to say so. The ticket price to any charity event can sometimes be part of the story. The pricier the better.

He relieved me by answering his own question. "Three hundred-fifty dollars each. I couldn't afford to come to this thing if you hadn't invited me, so if you have to get some work done, you go do it. Okay?"

I smiled at him and touched his arm. He was dressed in a dark blue suit that was a lot like his truck; it had seen better days. His cuffs were a little scuffed and his lapels slightly askew from too many visits to the dry cleaners. But tucked into his white shirt and burgundy tie, he exuded rugged good looks.

Kevin was clearly uncomfortable in this place of chandeliers, champagne, and canapés. This was a man who didn't sit behind a desk looking at spreadsheets or legal briefs all day. This was a man who worked hard, spent his days in the sun and the wind. His hands were calloused and hardened from physical labor and his skin was tanned from his time outside in the elements.

Looking at our reflections in the window, I thought we made a nice couple. Kevin was the handsome contractor. And me? Well, my hair was brushed back and curling coquettishly just right. My blue eyes sparkled. I was dressed in heels, gold necklace, earrings, and bracelet that accented my favorite black dress, cut low in the front and high enough in the leg to garner attention but still be classy.

"Okay," I said as I patted his arm. "I'm going to talk to a few people and get work out of the way so that we can relax and just enjoy dinner. Fair warning, though, we may have to skip the chocolate mousse. I'll have to run back to my office and write this up for tomorrow's paper."

He took my hand and squeezed it, making my heart take an extra thump again. "It's nice to spend some time with you."

Why had I lost track of this guy after high school?

I went looking for Amanda Cain, organizer of the dinner dance. Coincidentally, she was the wife of Judge William Cain, who'd presided earlier in the day at Jimmy Fitzgerald's sentencing. I wanted to ask her how it felt to be married to a man who equated jurisprudence with the size of one's checkbook.

But instead, I asked her the requisite society page questions.

"How many people do you expect will attend tonight?"

"Over four hundred."

"How much money do you hope to raise for the American Cancer Association?"

"What with the silent auction, we think it's going to be nearly three hundred thousand dollars."

The first thing that came to my mind was that was the exact amount that Jimmy Fitzgerald's dad had paid to Elena Bermudez's family. But it was far less than the million dollars paid out to a PAC belonging to an unnamed congressman.

I had to wonder how much of *that* million dollars might end up in Judge Cain's pocket.

I asked Mrs. Cain for the names of some of the celebrities and dignitaries that would be attending and who would be honored with the cheesy plaques that were always given out at these things. After she listed some well-known Broadway and movie stars, a few politicians, and a writer or two, I asked a few more banal questions, then the interview was over. Other than going back to the office and writing the story, my job was pretty much officially finished for the evening.

As I headed back where I'd left Kevin, I ran into the deputy chief of the Sheffield police department. "Hey, Mike." My voice rose to be heard above the other conversations swirling about the large room.

"Genie!" For a cop, he looked darn good in a tux.

"You clean up well," I purred. "Nice party, huh?"

His smile got bigger. "It's a room full of lawyers. Being here is a little like swimming in a tank full of boozed-up sharks."

I liked Mike Dillon's sense of humor. "What's new with the homicides?"

"You're getting some competition," he answered. "Not only am I getting media calls from all over the state, but I'm catching some from newspapers in New York."

Great, I need more journalists on this like I need a skin rash. I'm going to have to run faster to stay ahead of them.

"Six naked rich people sliced and diced. It's good ink. I don't like having other reporters on my turf. What did you tell them?"

"No more than you already know."

"So tell me something I don't know."

"Bodies are with the medical examiner and the evidence is with forensics. We're still looking for the murder weapons. We think there are at least two."

"Does that mean more than one killer?"

He knew he was on the record and he considered his words. "We don't know for sure, yet, but there were two sets of bloody footprints exiting the room. We're interviewing the neighbors and the security guard on Connor's Landing and we're talking with friends and the families of the victims."

"Was I right on the victims' names?"

He nodded and pulled a small notebook out of the inside breast pocket of his jacket. Opening it, he read out loud, "George and Lynette Chadwick, 39 and 35, they were the owners of the house. John and Martha Singewald, 41 and 40, and Kit and Kathy Webster, both of whom are 42. Interestingly, these three couples didn't seem to have any prior relationship before that evening. At least none that we've discovered."

"Really?"

"George Chadwick is a VP for Connecticut Sun Bank. His wife was recently named to the board of directors at the hospital. John Singewald is the CEO of Fairfield Mutual Insurance and his wife is a real estate agent. Both Kit and Kathy Webster are schoolteachers at a private school in Greenwich. Their families and friends aren't aware of any time that they've ever been together or even talked with each other before the night they were killed."

Unconsciously, I pulled the cell phone out of my purse and took a peek at the screen, wondering if I'd missed any calls since

I'd gotten to the Shorefront Club. I'd had all of my office calls forwarded to my cell phone. The screen was blank.

"Expecting a call?" Mike inquired.

I nodded but didn't tell Mike from whom. I was hoping that I'd hear from the man who'd left a message on my voicemail that morning. The one who claimed he knew "who killed those people."

I put the phone back into my purse. "Just checking."

Mike looked at me doubtfully. "Anyway, we've got warrants to search the victims' homes, their phone records, take their computers and shake 'em down. We'll take a look at e-mail and websites they frequented. See if there's a common denominator."

I nodded.

He gazed at me suspiciously and inquired, "You know something you're not telling me, Genie? If you do, I'd appreciate it if you'd let me know. This was really bad and I mean crazy-ass bad. Three of the vics were decapitated. All of them had limbs sliced off. It was a slaughterhouse in there. I don't want whoever did that to those people walking around on the streets, you know what I mean?"

At this point, I *really* didn't know any more than he did. So I deadpanned, "All I know is what I read in the newspapers."

Mike Dillon looked at me with an odd, appreciative expression on his face, sipping his martini. He said, "You look very nice tonight, Genie."

I blinked at him provocatively. "I've got to get back to my date."

He glanced over at Kevin who'd struck up an animated conversation with a man and woman who didn't look familiar to me. "I see you came with Kevin Bell."

"Yeah, you know each other?"

"No offense, but you can do better."

"Oh?"

He was staring at Kevin across the room when he said, "Used to be a damned good contractor. He did our kitchen. Then he crashed and burned. About four years ago, he tanked his construction company and put his family and friends through hell. I like you Genie, just be aware, the man's an alcoholic."

The moment he said that, my estimation of Mike dropped precipitously.

"Kevin and I are old high school friends," I replied. "I ran into Kevin at AA. If he crashed and burned, I think he's turning his life around."

Suddenly realizing that he'd just been incredibly stupid, Mike backpedaled. "Oh God, look, no offense intended. I'm sure he's back on track." It was a weak defense. "Kevin's had some tough breaks. I think the worst one was when his wife died."

I put my notebook back on my purse. "Cancer, right?"

"Yeah. If I remember right, it was a pretty rough time. Look, I'm sorry I was such a shit about Kevin. That was really out of line."

His eyes seemed genuinely apologetic.

I attempted a polite smile. "Got to go, Mike. Look, something comes up on this Connor's Landing thing, call me, okay?"

"I will." He added, "You too. This works both ways."

Walking away from Mike, I was torn between being pissed off at him and wondering what he had meant when he said that Kevin had put his family and friends through hell. *What was that all about?*

As I made my way across the crowded ballroom, Kevin was handing a business card to an attorney I'd seen a few times around the courthouse. When I came up beside him, I heard him say "Call me" before Kevin reached over and touched my hand.

"That guy wants me to talk to his wife about remodeling their kitchen." Kevin pointed.

"Great," I responded. "Get the job and then you can take me out to dinner at a really expensive restaurant."

He blushed. "I'd like that very much."

I took his arm and started leading him past the bar and toward the dining room. "I've finished my interview. I'll have dinner with you and then probably leave just before the speaker goes on. I'll head over to my office, write this up while you're having dessert and then come back here, pick you up and take you for a cup of coffee at Dimitri's."

"Sounds like a plan."

Of course, then I saw him. Frank Mancini was coming through the front door. He had on his tuxedo and a million-watt smile as he swept into the ballroom.

His wife, Evelyn, was close by his side. A redhead, she's tall and svelte, wearing a long black gown that clung to her body like a coat of expensive paint.

Even though I knew in advance that the two of them were attending the event, seeing the both of them startled me enough that I squeezed hard on Kevin's arm.

"Yikes," he exclaimed in surprise. Then he followed my line of sight until he spotted the Mancinis walking into the party. "That him?"

"Who?" I tried to feign indifference.

"The married guy that you're seeing?"

I glanced at Kevin and then turned my full attention back to the Mancinis. Holy crap, they were walking straight at us. Oh wait, they weren't walking toward us. Frank was bringing Evelyn to the bar and we were standing between it and them.

I tried to drag Kevin through the crowd so that they might not see us. "Yeah, he's the married guy. But we're not seeing each other anymore. C'mon, let's go find our table."

"Wow," Kevin remarked, "Good-lookin' guy."

I looked up. They were closing in on us and the crowd had jammed up at the dining room doorway. We couldn't move, we were stuck there. Kevin was right, though. Frank Mancini looked great in a tuxedo. "Yeah, yeah. He looks like James Bond and his wife looks like a supermodel. Nice couple."

Kevin leaned in close, sensing my unease. "You're much prettier than she is."

I squeezed his arm again and pulled him a little closer. "You're full of shit, but thank you for saying that."

Suddenly they were there, standing right in front of us.

It was one of those embarrassing moments that you hear about but hope never really happens to you. For a long, pregnant moment, no one said a word.

Finally, Evelyn broke the ice. "Oh look, Frank. It's your whore."

Frank was aghast. "Evelyn!" He held out his hand clumsily to Kevin. "I'm Frank Mancini and this is my wife, Evelyn."

Kevin shook his hand. "Kevin Bell. It's nice to meet you."

Frank nodded toward me and mumbled, "Genie."

The four of us settled into an uncomfortable silence until Kevin spoke up, "We were on our way into the dining room."

Frank said, "We'll be headed that way ourselves. Just want to get us a glass of wine first."

"I should have known that she'd be near the bar," Evelyn sneered. Glancing at her diamond-encrusted watch, she added, "Cocktail hour is almost over. I'm amazed she's still on her feet."

I could feel the anger coloring my face. I was about to say something really crass, but Kevin cut in. "We're going to take our club sodas into the dining room. It was very interesting to meet the two of you."

Kevin started to pull me along, but not before I winked at Frank and growled at Evelyn, "Kiss my ass, sweetie. Your husband has."

Kevin's grip on my hand tightened as we moved through the dining area and found our seats. "Well, that didn't go so well, did it?" he remarked.

I glanced around behind me. Through the crowd, I could see that Frank kept his hand on his wife's arm and the two were heatedly talking to each other.

Kevin pulled out my chair for me and I sat down. "No, not so well."

"She knows that you're having an affair with her husband?"

"Had. It's over." I surprised myself.

"It shouldn't come as any shock that she's not fond of you, then."

"Makes her downright hostile." I took a drink of my club soda, wishing to God that it was vodka, straight up.

Other people settled around us. I was extraordinarily grateful that fate hadn't played a cosmic practical joke and put the

Mancinis at our table. We all introduced ourselves to each other and then started working on our salads.

"How long have you known that guy? What's his name? Frank?" Kevin speared a cherry tomato from his plate.

"Two years. After Sal died, I was still living in Manhattan and freelancing for a couple of magazines. When Mom passed away, she left me the house here in Sheffield. I wanted to sell it and I needed an attorney to help settle some probate problems. Frank was the guy."

Kevin watched the Mancinis glide slowly through the room, carrying glasses of Cabernet, stopping to talk to people at tables as they passed by. "Not to take anything away from you," Kevin observed, "but his wife *is* pretty attractive."

I knew what his unasked question was. "So why was Frank having an affair with me?"

Kevin shrugged.

I got on my soapbox. "Why do CEOs who make more money than god feel the need to steal even more from employee pension funds? Why do some politicians take bribes or cheat on their wives?" I frowned. "They can't help themselves. What they have isn't enough. They have to have more. They feel entitled."

Kevin pretended to understand. I knew that he didn't.

"Frank does it because he can. Plus, there are two things that I'm very good at, writing," and at this point, I leaned in and whispered into his ear, "and sex."

Kevin burst out laughing, his face a bright crimson.

I laughed as well and the rest of the table awkwardly stared at us.

It was Kevin's turn to lean in close and whisper. "How long has Evelyn known about you and Frank?"

I chewed on a mouthful of arugula and thought for a moment. "I'm not sure. She might have suspected for quite a while, but she found out for sure about a month ago when she caught us at the Z Bar near closing time."

Kevin listened intently while he tore a piece from a dinner roll and popped it into his mouth.

"Frank and I had spent most of the evening together." I didn't tell Kevin that it was at a local Hilton Garden Inn. "We decided to have a couple of late cocktails and dance a little bit. Unfortunately for us, Evelyn had attended a musical at the Westport Country Playhouse that night with a group of her rich friends and they thought they'd go clubbing."

"Let me guess," Kevin said. "They ended up at the Z Bar."

"In all the world, in all the towns and all the bars, she ends up in mine." I paraphrased Humphrey Bogart. "Anyway, she sees me snuggling up to her husband on the dance floor and decides that she wants a piece of me. So she takes both hands and grabs up as much hair on my head as possible and pulls…hard."

The waiters were taking the salad plates away but Kevin kept his eyes locked on my face.

"I'd had a few cocktails at that point, so it didn't take much to yank me off-balance and I fell flat on my ass. I tried to get back to my feet, not easy because I had four-inch stilettos on and all I could see were her fingers and nails going for my eyes. She actually gouged me under the left one here. Can you see the mark?" I pointed to it.

He leaned in close again and slowly shook his head. "It's barely noticeable."

"I came up swinging. It was self-defense. The problem was, I was pretty blasted so I was swinging wild. It just so happened there was an off-duty cop there, sitting at the bar, guy we went to high school with. You remember Phil Gilmartin?"

Kevin scrunched up his face, trying to recall. "Yeah he was a year behind us, used to run cross-country."

"Same guy. Anyway, Phil's a cop now and even though he was off-duty, he felt the need to get between me and Evelyn before we killed each other."

"And?"

"And he pushed his way in just as I was swinging my fists and I clocked him right in the eye. Gave him a hell of a shiner."

"Oops."

"Yup. Bought me a night in jail. I'll give Frank credit. He posted bail and put me in touch with a good criminal attorney."

"What did you get?" he asked. "You didn't have to do any time, did you?"

I shook my head. "Nah. Small fine plus court costs. I had to publicly apologize to Phil for punching him. That embarrassed *him* more than it did me. And I have to stay off the sauce for six months."

The light bulb went on above Kevin's head. "Which is why you're attending AA."

I held up my glass of club soda in a mock salute. Then I nodded to a woman sitting two tables over from us. "That's the presiding judge over there. Judge Beverly Rath."

Kevin peeked around me to see. "The lady with the bad dye job?"

I snickered. "It's hard to miss, isn't it?"

"She's sitting at the same table with the guy and his wife who want me to remodel their kitchen."

I turned and looked.

Kevin continued. "They live on Connor's Landing, just a couple of houses down from where those murders happened."

I looked at them with renewed interest. "Small world."

I finished the last of my chicken Florentine, then I leaned over and told Kevin that it was time for me to run back to the newspaper office for about an hour. "Will you be here when I get back?"

He shrugged. "Most likely. You're my ride. You sure I can't come with you?"

"It'll go a whole lot faster if I concentrate and bang it out. I'll be quick, I promise." I gave him a peck on the cheek and I was off. I should have felt guilty leaving him there but the conversation at our table had turned to baseball and Kevin seemed to be enjoying himself.

• • ● • •

It didn't take me long to hammer out a puff piece about the Fairfield County Bar Association assuaging its collective guilt by raising an obscene amount of money for the Cancer Association. I didn't write it like that, of course, but I wanted to.

No sooner had I sent the story to Casper's queue on the server than I started working on a follow up to the homicides. I'd made some phone calls earlier in the day to some of the neighbors out on the island and discovered that nobody knew much about the Chadwicks. I was a little luckier in getting background information on the Singewalds and the Websters. The consensus was that they were nice people and didn't deserve to die like they did. Since Mike had confirmed their names, I could use it all in the story.

Throughout the day, I'd kept in touch with my police contacts but there wasn't much new to report. They were trying to reconstruct where the victims might have been earlier in the evening and what they'd been doing, but hadn't made much progress. So while there wasn't much more about the official investigation I could put into the paper, I was able to incorporate what Mike had told me at the party into the first paragraph of the story.

Casper loved it. The story was the lead on page one again. His headline read *Cops Call Murder Scene 'Slaughterhouse.'* It wasn't going to win me a Pulitzer, but it made me grin.

Chapter Seven

"So, other than when I left you all by yourself, did you have fun?" I nosed my car out of the parking lot of the Shorefront Club.

I'd gotten back as they were clearing away the tiramisu and the band was winding down with the last few songs of the night. Before the end of the evening, Kevin and I managed to mangle two fast dances and one slow grope. I *do* recall dancing with him at our prom when we were in high school, even though we weren't each other's date, and frankly after twenty years, he hasn't gotten any better at it. Kevin is one of the nicest guys I've ever met, but he's got the rhythm and grace of a spastic giraffe.

However, I'd spotted Frank Mancini out on the dance floor with Evelyn, and damn it, I wanted him to see me with Kevin. Okay, so at one point when we were slow dancing, I might have let my hand drift down from his lower back and gently, quickly run my palm down Kevin's butt, just so Frank could watch. The way I did it, it could have been an accident. Or it could have been on purpose.

It's disconcerting to me that, even when I'm sober, I can be childish and bitchy.

"Yeah," Kevin answered. "I actually I did have fun. It was fun *and* profitable."

"Really?"

He pulled a couple of business cards out of his shirt pocket. The only illumination in the front seat of the Sebring came from the dashboard so showing me the cards was purely for effect. "I met your judge, Beverly Rath. I'm driving out to her place in Darien tomorrow morning to give her a quote on putting in a guest room. And in the afternoon, I'm going out to Connor's Landing to take a look at remodeling a kitchen for that lawyer's wife, Becky Elroy. She was there tonight, with her husband, Pete. You know them?"

I searched my memory and then slowly shook my head. They hadn't looked familiar when Kevin pointed them out earlier in the evening.

"She's a little bit of a nut," Kevin said. "You know what she wants to put in her kitchen?"

"A personal chef?"

He waved his hand. "Don't be silly, she already has one. No, she wants to put in a backsplash that's mined from a quarry in Wyoming. They sell slabs of stone imprinted with fossils from a subtropical rainforest that's over fifty-million years old."

"Let me guess, it's expensive."

"I love working with people who have more money than brains," Kevin laughed.

"So what do you want to do now?"

"How about we go get a cup of coffee?"

I glanced at the digital clock on the dash. "How about we have a cup of coffee at my place? I've got a dog that's ready for a walk right about now."

He didn't answer right away. Had I made him a little nervous by asking him back to my apartment? He was most likely remembering that I'd brushed my hand along his tush during "Unchained Melody." I tried to put him at ease, 'We're two old friends having coffee, Kevin. No strings, know what I mean?"

"Sure," he mumbled. "Yeah, of course, okay."

• • ● • •

My Yorkie spent about two seconds growling at Kevin when he first came through the door and then the dog must have decided that, if he's with me, the big guy must be okay. My pup started dancing around, tail wagging, and yipping that he was long overdue for a stroll through the neighborhood.

Kevin leaned down to give him a scratch behind the ear. "What's his name?"

"Tucker."

"Tucker," he repeated, low and friendly. "What a good boy."

"This good boy needs to do some serious business," I told him. "If you'd like, you can turn on the TV while I'm out."

He looked around the apartment and for a moment I wished that I'd picked up a little before I asked him in. I have two bedrooms, a kitchen, tiny dinette and a single bath in an old Victorian home that's been chopped up into apartments. I'm on the ground floor and I have a private doorway and access to the front porch, which I use often, drinking wine, relaxing in my chaise, and reading mysteries. The ceilings in the apartment are high, the windows offer a view of the wetlands behind the house and I sometimes pretend that I'm staying in a bed and breakfast.

I'm happy with where I live. I'm just not a great housekeeper.

It's not like I have piles of dirty clothes and old pizza cartons lying around. But I *don't* run the vacuum or dust the furniture every week and there are a few scattered magazines and news-papers on the floor next to my place on the couch.

Showing Kevin that I was serious about the TV, I picked the remote off the coffee table and handed it to him. *It's as domestic as I get.* "The TV section of the newspaper is on the floor next to my chair over there," I pointed out. He'd have to get that himself.

He shrugged. "Would it be okay if I tagged along with you and Tucker?"

He made me happy. "Sure."

My neighborhood is in the process of being gentrified. At one point, about fifteen years ago, it looked like South Sheffield was going into the terminal phase of urban blight. There were empty storefronts, old houses boarded up with plywood, and drug dealers who bought and sold with impunity.

And then an amazing thing happened. Property values in the area soared.

Because Sheffield is so close to New York City, there are no parcels of real estate in town anymore that aren't worth a fortune. Businesses on the harbor-front, their doors closed and windows dark for so many years, became trendy restaurants, nightclubs, and boutique shops. Old manufacturing buildings, some burnt out, mostly empty and gutted, were transformed into million-dollar homes or torn down and reborn into chic condominiums. The drug dealers? They either left the city for other rat-holes or else they got into something more lucrative: They started buying and selling real estate.

My house was right around the block from the line of night-clubs. I liked it because, when I was drinking, I could hit as many of the bars as I could afford and then walk safely home. If I get caught in a DUI again, I'll lose my license for a very long time.

Tucker likes it because we're a short walk to the docks. We can be on the waterfront in about seven minutes. Pleasure boats are tied alongside oyster trawlers and the ferry. There's the sound of the waves gently slapping against their bows and there's the smell of the sea air and saltwater. When I let him off his leash during the day, Tucker likes running back and forth on the wooden docks, terrorizing the gulls, who rise up reluctantly into the air and scream shrill epithets at the little dog while wheeling in slow circles a few yards above his head.

Kevin had left his suit coat back in my living room. His collar was unbuttoned, his tie loosened, and his sleeves rolled up.

I was still in my black dress, but I'd traded my high heels for a pair of flats.

As we walked along the waterfront, streetlights glittered on the black, rippling surface of the water. I glanced over at Kevin. "Thanks for being my date tonight."

He looked down at his shoes, adorably shy. "Thanks for asking me."

"I'm sorry we didn't get to spend as much time together as I would have liked."

"It was nice being with you again," he said. "I've missed you."

It was dark, so I'm not sure if he could see me smile. "I never even had a chance to ask how things have been for you."

"Okay," he said, uncertain. "It's been good, most of it."

"Life?"

"Yeah."

"Well, that's the abridged version. How about you fill me in on your life...let's see, say after we graduated?"

"Well," he brightened, "after high school, you know I was a psych major at UConn. I lasted about three years, ran out of money and figured that I'd had enough higher learning. I'm not sure what I would have done with a degree in psychology anyway. I certainly wasn't going to go on and get my PhD. So I moved back home and I can't tell you how much that thrilled my dad. But only for a few months and then I went to work for my Uncle Jack."

I interrupted, "Your Uncle Jack. Jack Bell? I remember him. Wasn't he...?"

"Killed by lightning." Kevin filled in the blank.

I'd finished college and was just starting to write for a newspaper in upstate New York when my mom sent me a clipping about Kevin's uncle. She'd sent it with a note saying that this was the kind of story that sells newspapers.

Honestly, Mom was right, and it was a lesson I took to heart.

Kevin told the tale. "Uncle Jack was patching over some weathered spots up on the steeple of the Silver Hill Methodist Church. He'd been a loyal member of the church for over twenty-five years. In all of that time, it was rare that he missed a service. Plus, he was always doing odd jobs for them. On that particular day, he'd supplied the lumber for free and was donating his time, and he was just about finished when the storm hit. Uncle Jack owned and operated his own construction company for over thirty years. He taught me everything I know about contracting, which includes not handling metal tools and getting to a safe location during an electrical storm.

"But for some odd reason," Kevin continued, "Uncle Jack kept on working. Maybe it was because he was almost done with the job or maybe it was just because he wasn't paying attention. Anyway, the storm clouds moved in fast, riding a stiff wind off the sound. I heard that when the sky opened up, the rain fell so hard you could barely see your hand in front of your face. I wasn't there, but one of the deacons said that he thought he'd seen Uncle Jack start down the ladder and that was when he was hit."

All I could say was, "Oh, my God."

"It literally hurled him off the ladder and into the air. He dropped almost a hundred feet to the ground. The doctor said that the lightning had probably stopped his heart and that Uncle Jack was dead before he hit the parking lot."

I reached over and took his hand.

"For a while after that," Kevin said, "a lot of people wondered how God could do something like that to someone who was so devout. Jack practically lived in that church. He was always helping them raise money or he was doing repair work in his spare time either for the church or for some parishioner who was down on his luck. People wondered how something like that could happen to a man who was fixing the steeple of a church, God's own house. At the funeral, Reverend Cleese said it had to be the Lord's way of rewarding my uncle for his good works, and now and forever Uncle Jack would sit at the right hand of God in the Kingdom of Heaven."

I watched as Tucker trotted up to Kevin and put one paw on his shoe, looking for attention. He knelt down and scratched the pup behind his ears. "Then the rumors started. About how Uncle Jack and Reverend Cleese's wife had been having an affair, maybe going on for years. That was why Uncle Jack was spending so much time at the church. And then everyone started talking about how the bolt of lightning had been just punishment for committing adultery."

Yikes, "just punishment" for committing adultery. I don't like the sound of that.

"No matter who you talked to," he mused, "it amounted to the same thing. Whether he was being rewarded or he was being punished, it wasn't an accident. There was a purpose for Uncle Jack being struck by lightning."

Kevin stopped petting Tucker and we started walking again. I tapped his arm. "Is that what you think? That everything happens for a reason?"

He nodded. "In this case, yeah. The reason Uncle Jack died was because he didn't put his tools away and get down off that scaffolding when he saw the storm coming."

• • ● • •

As we walked back to my apartment, he finished telling me about his life. He'd started his own company soon after his uncle died. He'd met Joanna, married her, bought the house on Random Road, and Caroline was born. They never were rich but they were never poor. They took vacations to places like the Grand Canyon and Disneyworld. When he was single, Kevin had owned a motorcycle, but after he'd gotten married, all he drove were minivans and SUVs. Their lives were full and happy even if, at least to me, it all seemed a little non-eventful.

But maybe in the grand scheme of things if you're sharing it with the right person, that's a pretty good way to live.

Suddenly Mike's words came back to me, "Kevin put his family and friends through hell."

By the time we got back to my place he hadn't said anything about the death of his wife and I didn't ask.

Once we were inside, we went straight into my tiny kitchen and I started bustling around, getting a filter for the coffeemaker, pulling a bag of coffee out of the freezer, getting cups out of the cabinet. Once I had everything on the counter, I turned and sighed.

"Now," I said, "I promised you a cup of coffee."

Kevin leaned against the refrigerator with his hands in his pockets, much like his daughter had done earlier that afternoon at his house. He waited for what I was about to say next.

"But I have a confession to make, and I hope you don't think less of me because of it." I put my hands flat on the counter.

"According to my court sentence, I'm not supposed to drink for six months." I reached up and opened a cabinet door. Inside, clearly in sight, were bottles of wine, scotch, bourbon, and vodka. "I'm not supposed to drink," I repeated, "but sometimes I cheat."

He pushed himself away from the refrigerator and stepped up close to me, staring at the alcove of alcohol. Kevin pursed his lips and softly whistled. Then he said, "You know, sometimes I cheat, too. Scotch? Neat?"

Hot diggity damn!

I poured a healthy serving of Glenlivet for him and a tumbler of Absolut over ice for me. Then I suggested, "How about we go out and sit on the porch?"

We sat in chairs next to each other and breathed in the night air, thick with the sweet scent of roses that my landlady, Mrs. Soldaro, has planted all around the base of the front porch. A history of the universe twinkled down at us in the form of a sky full of stars. Crickets and cicadas hummed and chirped giving auditory proof that the earth was a living, breathing entity.

I took a long hard sip of vodka, the ice tinkling against my teeth, the liquid lighting a fire in my throat and igniting a familiar heat in my stomach. Almost immediately, the warmth and a sense of well-being stole into my consciousness. I took a deep breath. The world was okay.

"So," Kevin sipped his scotch, "are you going to see that Frank guy again?"

I felt a cool breeze coming up from the harbor and pondered the question he'd just posed. Finally, I answered, "I don't think I'm going to be seeing him at all. I think that book's closed."

Kevin looked out into the darkness. "I'm not sure I have a lot of respect for a man who cheats on his wife."

"You were always faithful?"

"Yes."

"Never thought about it?"

"Cheating on Joanna?"

"Yeah."

He shook his head. "Nope."

"She must have been quite a woman."

"Once in a lifetime."

"You were a little sketchy on how you met her."

He laughed. "I'm sorry. Joanna was never too proud of how we met. It was in a bar. Figures, huh? It was my birthday and a bunch of us were hanging out at Whaler's Café. This really pretty brunette down on the end of the bar sends our group a whole platter of Jell-O shots."

"Joanna?"

"Yup."

"Nothing says love like Jell-O shots."

"Maybe you knew her," Kevin suggested. "Her maiden name was Lewis, Joanna Lewis? She graduated at our high school a year after us?"

I shook my head. I couldn't place the name, but high school was a long time ago and I've killed a lot of brain cells since then.

"Anyway, while the rest of my group worked on the shots, I went down to the end of the bar and thanked her. I asked her why she'd done that. She said that I looked kind of cute *and* it was my birthday."

I took another sip of my vodka, listening.

"Strange thing, she wasn't even supposed to be there that night. She was supposed to be meeting a friend of hers for drinks, a guy she worked with. But Joanna had written down the wrong date. It was a weird quirk of fate that the two of us even ran into each other. I fell in love with her that night, right then and there. We got married six months later."

"Nice story." I raised my tumbler in a toast.

"We'd been married for twelve years when one morning, after taking a shower, she came out of the bathroom and told me that she'd found a lump on her breast. I remember the sound of her voice. She was scared. I've never heard her scared before."

Kevin stopped talking for a moment and I didn't feel it was appropriate for me to say anything. The only noise was the distant rush of cars and the quiet symphony of crickets.

Then he started again. "The doctors diagnosed it as breast cancer. It was pretty far along. A few days later, they performed a mastectomy. But by that time, the cancer had already metastasized into her liver and lymph nodes. They began treating her with aggressive chemo treatments."

Kevin was silent again. Then shaking his head slowly from side to side, he said, "It made her sick. She lost all her hair, of course. She couldn't eat, couldn't sleep. Joanna kept her sense of humor and her dignity for as long as she could. Finally, she didn't know what was worse, the chemo or dying."

I reached over and held his hand.

"When it was obvious that she was only getting worse, they offered her experimental drugs. They gave her hope, gave all of us hope. But in the end it didn't help.

"She died on Valentine's Day. While she was lying in the hospital bed with all those tubes running into her arms and her nose, as weak as she was, more morphine pumping through her veins than blood, barely able to move, she touched her heart with the tips of her fingers and then, with what little strength she had left, she reached over and touched my hand. It was her Valentine's present to me."

I heard his voice crack. And then, in the dark, I heard him silently sobbing, trying hard to keep it from me. But in the shadows, he held a hand up to his mouth and his body shook.

Then I felt my own eyes water and my throat tighten, feeling his grief and wishing that I could take away the pain, feeling as helpless at that moment as Kevin was when he watched his wife die.

I looked up at the stars and wanted to say something profound. Like she was in a better place now or at least she wasn't in pain anymore.

But I knew that wouldn't help.

So I just held his hand.

● ● ● ● ●

We didn't talk much after that. We finished our drinks and went back inside. Without asking, I poured us two more.

He looked at me with eyes that were red. "I shouldn't." He pointed to his glass. "I should go home."

"Is your daughter waiting for you?"

He shook his head. "She's staying overnight with her aunt."

I stepped closer to him, close enough I could hear his breath quicken. "Look Kevin, I don't want to be alone tonight." I reached out and took his hand. "And I don't think you should be alone tonight either. I want to hold you and I want you to hold me. Please?"

When we got to bed, we held each other a very long time, two old friends who had found each other after a life time apart.

And as long as we held on to each other it was okay. We were safe and the rest of the world was a faraway place.

And then he kissed me.

Before that night, Kevin had only kissed me once. Oh sure, he'd bussed me on the cheek a million times. But there was one time when we were seniors in high school, after we'd drank a few Budweisers and found ourselves in his parents' basement playing pool. At some point, we were standing a little too close to each other and he looked at me and I looked at him and we kissed, right square on the lips.

And then we both did the damnest thing. We burst out laughing.

We'd been such good friends for so long, the kiss seemed silly. It was like I was kissing my brother.

But that night in my bed, after not seeing him for so long, we kissed and we didn't laugh. We kissed some more and held each other.

And then we made love.

Chapter Eight

For the second day in a row, Laura Ostrowski reached me at home with an assignment. This time it was before ten in the morning. Mike Dillon had called to say that at noon the cops were going to make an arrest in a string of high-profile burglaries, specifically the Home Alone Gang.

The police wanted to have a reporter and a photographer there to capture the moment. Because I'm as adept with a digital camera as I am with a computer keyboard, the deputy chief had specifically asked for me.

It's possible he was still feeling guilty for dissing Kevin last night.

It didn't matter. This would be a good story.

I'd already been up since eight anyway. Tucker, true to form, had started to lick away at somebody's face. Only this morning, it wasn't mine. Kevin Bell got the Tucker treatment.

Waking up with Kevin naked in my bed was both exhilarating and embarrassing. Seeing him as he tried to protect his face from puppy slobber was absolutely adorable. After gently persuading Tucker to stop, Kevin gazed at me with sleepy eyes and smiled.

I couldn't decide whether to kiss him or to pull the covers over my head. I know what I look like when I wake up in the morning and Medusa's got nothing on me. I was amazed that Kevin didn't take a look, throw himself screaming out of the bedroom window, and run like the wind.

Instead, he leaned over and kissed me. "Thank you for last night."

"My pleasure," I answered honestly. "I still owe you coffee."

"I'd like that."

"Mind if I take a shower first?"

"Only if I get the shower next."

Then, of course, a natural progression of logic took over and I suggested, "It might be more expedient if we showered together."

Sometimes I simply surprise myself at how slutty I can be. Although, now that I'm more mature, I prefer to think of myself as being lusty and provocative.

He ran his hand down the small of my back and let it rest on my derriere. He whispered, "I'm nothing if not expedient."

• • ● • •

Being together for the first time was an affair of the heart. We'd known each other our entire lives. We'd literally grown up together, been to each other's birthday parties, known each other's parents, taken high school classes together, done homework together, gotten drunk together, shared joys and victories, shared sadness and failures, shared our acceptance letters into college. We'd even shared the flu.

Up until then, we'd done and shared everything together except for sex.

We certainly changed that.

What we did that night was hold each other, comfort each other, and share our bodies and our love. It was warm and special and I'll always remember it as such.

What we did in the shower was just raw animal sex.

And I'll always remember *that* as such.

There's something about hot water, steam, and slick, slippery skin that just really drives me nuts. We took turns under the showerhead; rubbing soap all over each other, making sure every inch of exposed skin was squeaky clean, some of it twice and three times. We even shampooed each other's hair, which I found to be *very* erotic, especially when Kevin slowly and gently massaged my scalp.

I could have spent the rest of the year standing in the tub with that man.

But the problem with taking a long, leisurely shower in an old Victorian home with a lot of other people who share the hot water tank is you're apt to run out of hot water.

And when my shower turns cold, it does it fast.

We both cried out in surprise and dismay when the first splash of icy spray replaced the warm lusciousness and it took only the blink of an eye for us to rinse off the soapsuds and get the hell out.

But we really weren't finished.

Kevin spent a great deal of quality time drying off my body with a fluffy towel. Of course, he concentrated on certain parts, like my boobs and tush, and when he got down on his knees to get my feet, legs and inner thighs, well, between the gentle toweling and the delicious little kisses and licks he gave me, I about lost what little composure I had left.

Then I did the same with him. He has a really great body. Time always takes its toll, but hard work has kept him trim and muscular. True, fried foods and the booze put a few pounds around his middle, but his arms are buff, his legs are toned and his ass is hard as a rock. I took my time with the towel. When it was my turn to kneel in front of him, it was obvious what the height of his interest level was.

We adjourned back to my bed.

By the time we were done, we were so sweaty that we needed another shower. So much for expedience. And hot water.

After we got dressed, Kevin barely stuck around long enough have coffee and a couple of slices of whole wheat toast. He wanted to get home, change out of the blue suit that he'd worn the night before and get into his work clothes before Caroline got home. He didn't think staying out all night with an old high school friend set a very good example for his daughter. Plus, Kevin had those two potential jobs from last night that he wanted to go out and take a look at.

He promised to call me later and, since it was Kevin Bell, I believed him.

• • ● • •

Fifteen burglaries had been committed over the course of six months in seven different towns in both Fairfield and West-chester counties. The last two had been staged only a little over a week ago in the towns of Wilton and Ridgefield, both north of Sheffield on the same night.

They would choose their victims carefully. Targeting the very wealthy, they'd raid homes that were repositories for easy cash, jewelry, high-end electronics, furs, and antiques. They knew when the owners were out of the house, attending the theater, a party or out to dinner. They knew which alarm company had wired the home and how to bypass it. Even the cops admired their professionalism.

After the seventh burglary, the press started calling them the Home Alone Gang. Full disclosure: I'm actually the one who gave them that name.

Their average take per house was estimated to be well over half a million dollars. They could crack wall safes, ransack jewelry drawers, empty closets, and take priceless pieces of art and furniture in under eleven minutes.

They left nothing behind that could identify them. Not a single shred of usable evidence.

The cops were stymied until the night of the Connor's Landing murders. At about the same time I got the phone call from Casper telling me about the homicides, a beer truck on I-95 swerved to miss a Honda Accord that had cut in front of it. The driver of the tractor-trailer lost control and his vehicle overturned, sliding sideways along the highway for nearly a hundred feet. By the time it came to a stop, cases of Coors were strewn all over the road.

As fate would have it, an Escalade was following a little too closely behind the beer truck and a case of Coors Light twelve-packs crashed through the windshield. The driver of the SUV ended up in the hospital with minor facial lacerations from the broken glass.

An unexpected outcome of the accident was what police discovered in the back of the crippled Escalade. The SUV had been transporting over three hundred thousand in furs—furs that were quickly identified as having been heisted during one of the last two Home Alone robberies.

After the driver of the SUV, David Lobel, age thirty-five of Queens, was stitched up, the police charged him with possession of stolen property. While he was still in the emergency room, he was read his rights and asked if he wanted an attorney. He was also informed that if he cooperated, he might get an agreeable plea bargain instead of facing the myriad charges implicating him in fifteen burglaries.

He skipped the attorney and went for the deal. According to Mr. Lobel, he'd never taken part in any of the burglaries. He was only fencing the furs, buying them from the Home Alone thieves and taking them to New York to ship to Asia where they could safely be resold.

The police then pushed Mr. Lobel a little harder. Being a fence still made him an accessory. If he wanted to avoid serious jail time, he was going to have to help them find the Home Alone burglars.

Having been incarcerated once before, Mr. Lobel was justifiably reluctant about going back to prison. He told the police that while he had no way to contact the thieves directly, they'd already set up a meeting for him to appraise the last of the loot, a meeting that would take place in two days in the parking lot of a local grocery store.

That was all the cops had to hear. This was the break in the case they'd been waiting for.

• • ● • •

Shortly before twelve, I was sitting in Mike Dillon's black Jeep Cherokee in the middle of the Stop-n-Shop parking lot. Not far from the front entrance of the grocery store, Mike had backed into a parking space, facing out, just in case he needed to move fast.

There was a storm rolling in from Long Island Sound but it was still unbearably hot and humid. Mike had left the engine running so we could sit in air conditioned comfort.

All around us, people pushed shopping carts. Cars pulled into the parking lot and cars pulled out. It was a blacktopped ant-hill of constant movement. "Why in hell are they meeting here, Mike? There're people all over the place."

"Ever hear of hiding in plain sight?"

I looked over at him. Mike Dillon had on a polo shirt, jeans, and a Yankees cap. I had on almost the same outfit, except for the hat. Mine had a Boston logo.

Go Sox.

Oh. One more thing that was different. Mike had a gun in a holster on his belt.

Nodding at the pistol, I asked, "Think you'll need that?"

He smiled. "Genie, if I thought this was really dangerous, you wouldn't be here. Cat burglars never carry guns. They know that if they ever get caught carrying a weapon, they're looking at seriously hard time."

"Okay, so what's the plan?"

"We have four unmarked vehicles parked in locations that can easily block all the exits," Mike said. "Because Lobel's SUV is still being repaired, he's going to drive up in an Escalade that we borrowed from the Cadillac dealer over in Darien. The chief warned me that this knucklehead better not put so much as a scratch on it."

I chuckled and watched the Hampshire Avenue entrance to the parking lot. "What's to keep him from driving off into the sunset and not showing up at all?"

"We've got him fitted with a GPS and an ankle bracelet, plus I have an officer trailing him," Mike explained. "Lobel will circle the lot until he hears from the bad guy. He'll let Lobel know where he is and what kind of vehicle he's in. Then Lobel gets into the bad guy's car and he appraises the loot. After money changes hands and Lobel leaves the vehicle, we'll move in and make the arrest. Here, Lobel's wired for sound." Mike handed me a small receiver the size of a cell phone rigged with an ear bud. "I've got mine, here's one for you. Listen to everything that's going down."

"Roger that." I placed the bud in my ear canal, feeling voyeuristic.

Mike continued, "The wild card is we won't know which car the bad guy will be in. We don't know if he's already here waiting or if he'll drive in some time behind Lobel."

I gazed around the parking lot. All I saw were regular-looking people, some of them obviously moms with their kids, going into the store and coming back out again pushing carts piled high with groceries. I spotted men carrying out plastic bags of frozen pizza and six-packs of beer. Almost everyone walking into the market held a slip of paper, a list of what they needed to buy. Nobody walked back out empty-handed.

"Thanks for letting me be part of this, Mike," I said. "What's the catch?"

"Just write a good story, Genie," he winked.

What he didn't say, and what I knew, was that the chief of police was going to retire next year. There's a review board that recommends who the mayor appoints for that position. Mike Dillon wasn't stupid. The more good press he got, the better his chances at getting that job.

I spotted a black Cadillac SUV as it drove into the entrance. It was five after twelve. "That our boy?"

Mike nodded, adjusting his earpiece.

Both of us heard the words as they crackled through the airwaves. "I just pulled into the parking lot. I'm waiting to hear from my contact." It was Lobel talking, his words picked up by the tiny microphone hidden in the pair of sunglasses given to him by the police.

I glanced over at Mike. Even I could hear the nerves in Lobel's voice.

Then, through the earbud, I heard a cell phone, the theme from *The Godfather*. The bad guy was calling. We could only hear the conversation from Lobel's point of view, "Yes, okay, a black and silver HumVee."

Mike and I both automatically started scanning the parking lot, looking for a black and silver Hummer. The acid in the pit of my stomach started churning hard when I spotted one, parked only one space away from us on our right, closest to my side of the car. The only thing separating us from the bad guy was a Chevy Suburban.

I couldn't get a clear view of what he looked like but it was obvious he was talking on a cell phone. Plus he'd pulled into the space nose-first so that he was sitting on the other side of his vehicle. I had to peek through the windows of the SUV between us to see anything. The man was in his mid-thirties, his hair was cut short, military-style, and he was wearing wire-framed glasses. He could have been the branch manager of my local bank.

"I see it," Lobel said. "Let me park and I'll be right there."

Then, incredibly, Lobel pulled into the space across the aisle directly in front of us. If we were any closer to all of this, we'd be sitting in the front seat of the Hummer.

Mike handed me a grocery store supplement that he'd brought with him. "Genie," he said, calmly. "Pretend like you're reading this. Rip out a couple of coupons so that we look like we're about to go shopping."

"Really? Think that'll fool anybody?"

Through the windshield, I surreptitiously watched David Lobel get out of the Escalade. When he saw us he stopped dead in his tracks, blinking his eyes, not quite believing that we were that close.

I was silently shouting at him. *Keep moving, you dumbass!*

As if Mike heard me, he whispered, "Keep walking. Keep walking."

Lobel snapped out of it and continued over to the HumVee. He was wearing a pair of black slacks and a long-sleeved, button-down white dress shirt, open at the throat and rolled up at the wrists. There were bandages on his forehead, left cheek and chin, and puffy purple patches under both of his eyes.

"Jesus Christ, Lobel," a disembodied voice in our ears said as the fence crawled into the Hummer. "What happened to you? You get hit by a truck?"

Pretty good guess.

I could imagine Lobel shrugging. "I got mugged. I was in the city two nights ago, heading down to see some friends in the Village. I got jumped on the subway by a couple of guys who punched me in the face and stole my wallet."

"Oh, man, looks like they hit ya' pretty hard," the bad guy responded. "How much did they get?"

"About a hundred bucks and my credit cards, a Visa and my American Express Platinum card. And my driver's license. That's gonna' be a bitch to get replaced."

I looked at Mike again. Lobel's voice was really pitched high, talking way too fast. He was a wired mass of frazzled nerves.

I could see the bad guy shake his head. "What's this world coming to, David? World's full of barbarians. I'm sorry, man. Anyway, I hope you still got some of your money left. Take a look at this, it's the last little bit of the last job. We're thinking it's worth about thirty G's."

"Let me see," Lobel said.

Over the next couple of minutes, all Mike and I heard was silence. I glanced over at the Hummer. The guy sitting in the driver's seat was tapping impatiently on the steering wheel.

Lobel, sitting next to him, had the police sunglasses tipped up on the top of his head and was studying something in his lap through a jeweler's loupe. A case filled with jewelry?

Finally Lobel said, "I read in the papers that you guys have done fifteen jobs."

Another silence.

"Is that true?" Lobel asked.

"What?" The bad guy sounded annoyed.

"Did you guys do fifteen jobs?"

"What's it matter?

Lobel explained, "You only brought me in on thirteen. If there's another fence in the area, I need to know. Nobody likes competition."

Mike was shaking his head. "What's Lobel doing?"

The bad guy responded. "Don't be a pussy. You're the only one we've been working with."

"The papers said fifteen jobs," Lobel insisted.

"What...the hell...is...he...doing?" Mike whispered again.

I heard the impatience in the bad guys' voice. "Thirteen. We did thirteen jobs."

Lobel argued. "The newspapers can't count? Why would they say you did fifteen? If I got a competitor, I need to know."

The driver leaned forward. "Because, you dumb shit, it happens everywhere we go. Somebody reads about our action in the papers or sees it on TV, and they think they can do it as good as we do. Somebody else did those other two jobs. When we start seeing copycats, we move to another location. As a matter of fact, if you can focus and we can get this done, we're headed out this afternoon."

Copycats? Which two jobs did they do? I've got a great hook for another story. There's a second gang of crooks out there.

"So let's get down to business, Lobel," the bad guy snarled. "We're saying thirty thousand."

Lobel looked back down at his lap. "Twenty-seven."

Mike shook his head again and whispered, "He's sounding way too nervous."

"How much?" the bad guy asked.

We heard Lobel clear his throat and say, "Twenty-eight?"

There was a long silence. Then the bad guy said in a low, careful voice, "Lobel, you're one of the tightest weasels I've ever worked with. You've lowballed me at every turn, usually insulting my intelligence with an offer that's about a third of the real price. You're a professional worm and I've respected that out of professional courtesy. So how come now, on our final transaction, you're offering me a price that's obviously more than what this shit's all really worth?"

There was another silence.

Mike surprised me. "Buckle up."

And then I saw the bad guy lean toward Lobel and snatch the sunglasses off his head. Mike and I both heard him snapping the frames. "You're wearing a wire? You son of a bitch! You're dead!"

I could feel my heart stop.

The Jeep jerked forward and Mike tore out of our parking space. He immediately slammed on the brakes, stopping behind the HumVee. "Stay down," he snapped. He was out his door and barking commands into his radio, ordering his men to move in. His gun was in his hand.

Portable red and blue lights placed atop four unmarked police cars started to flash and whirl almost simultaneously. Mike cautiously moved around his side of the vehicle until he was behind the hood of his Jeep, his gun aimed at the SUV. He shouted, "Police! Put your hands on the steering wheel."

The HumVee's engine roared to life and David Lobel leaped out of the passenger's door, bouncing hard against the parked Suburban, crumpling to the ground.

The Hummer backed up fast, squealing into my side of the Jeep. The Cherokee rocked sideways, the door buckled and the window glass shattered, shards flying through the air. I was thrown hard against the door, stunned.

The Hummer pulled forward and then, engine shrieking, it flew backwards again into my side of the Jeep. The impact slammed me sideways, the seat belt and harness digging hard into my shoulder and chest.

My airbag exploded, blasting against my face and chest like a giant fist, pinning me against the seat.

The Hummer's motor screamed and tires screeched and I smelled rubber cooking. The HumVee was pushing against my door, trying to power the Cherokee out of the way. The Jeep shook under the pressure and I felt the world sliding underneath me.

A single gunshot split the air and multiple voices shouted simultaneously, "Get out of the car, put your hands up, get down on the ground."

The howling engine went silent and the Jeep stopped moving.

I'm not sure how much time passed before I felt hands reach in through my open window and unbuckle my seat belt. Someone else pulled me across the center console and out the driver's side. Once I was outside in the fresh air, Mike held me, keeping me upright on unstable legs. I could feel drops of rain falling on my face

People were running and screaming in all directions, mothers with children, old men with shopping carts. People were down on the hard surface of the parking lot, having thrown themselves to the ground when Mike fired a warning shot.

The bad guy lay on his stomach on the oily asphalt, hands cuffed behind his back, surrounded by cops.

I spotted David Lobel leaning against a Toyota, both hands clasped against his face, trying to staunch the bleeding from his nose where he'd bounced off the Suburban. He wasn't having much luck keeping his face in one piece.

I heard an ambulance siren in the distance.

"Genie," Mike asked, "you okay, honey?"

Taking my camera out of my bag, I said, "I'm fine. Let me get some shots, okay?"

"Jesus, you're bleeding."

I felt a tiny shard of glass sticking out from my forehead. I gingerly plucked it out, then pulled a tissue from my handbag to put on the cut. Dabbing at it, I checked out the amount of blood on the tissue.

It was more than I anticipated. I felt woozy.

"We're taking you to the hospital," Mike stated.

I frowned and shook my head. "All I need is a Band-Aid." Then I touched him on the arm and brushed a few raindrops away from my eyes. "I'm all right. You want to get out of the way so I can get a couple of pictures?"

David Lobel walked up to us on legs that wobbled. "So, what happens to me?" He held both of his hands on the sides of his nose, trying in vain to stop the bleeding.

Mike crossed his arms. "Looks like we're taking you back to the hospital. Then we'll find a judge to get you arraigned and arrange bail."

"I could drive the Escalade."

"What are you, crazy?"

"I get my deal, right? I mean I did good here."

Mike squinted at him. "Other than you almost blew it."

"I was a little nervous," Lobel argued. "Is that a crime? And I thought the rotten bastard had cut me out of two jobs."

As I snapped photos and took some more notes, I ruminated on what Lobel had just said. There was still another gang of crooks out there somewhere.

I kept taking photos while they loaded the bad guy into a squad car and drove away. Mike came up to me. "I'm sorry, Genie. There's about ten acres of parking lot here. What are the odds the bad guy is going to be parked right next us? I put you in danger. That's unforgivable."

Mike wasn't really worried about putting me in danger. He was worried what the chief would say if he knew there was a reporter in his car during an arrest that got rough. "Look, Mike, I love this stuff. How about I leave out the part about my being in your SUV? It's really not part of the story."

I watched as a broad smile broke out on his face. "I owe ya, Genie."

"Nah, I got some great photos and it's a cool story. Hey, you think there's another gang doing burglaries?"

"Sure looks like it, darlin'. Let me get one of the EMS guys to look at your forehead."

• • ● • •

Some days are crummy and stay that way. But once in a while, and not very often, you get a day that starts out great and *stays* that way.

It all started with Kevin in my shower. And then I got an exclusive on the arrest. True, I had a nasty headache, but it was nothing a tumbler of vodka and an aspirin wouldn't take care of.

I didn't think there could be anything left that could top that.

Until I got into my Sebring and noticed that I'd gotten a cell phone message. It must have come through at the same time I was getting rammed by the Hummer.

It was a call forwarded from my office phone.

"Geneva Chase...I'm the one who called you yesterday. I know who killed those people on Connor's Landing. I'll try to call you later tonight. I hope you can be by your phone at nine. That's when I'll call again."

Just try to keep me away.

Chapter Nine

I decided that since I was on a roll, I'd press my luck. Once I was back in my office and I'd finished pounding out the story about the arrest, I punched up Kevin's number.

"Hello?"

"Caroline?" I recognized her voice from yesterday.

"Yes?"

"Hi, honey. It's Genie Chase. Is your dad around?"

"No. He's out bidding on a couple of jobs. You want his cell phone?"

Her voice sounded a little odd. Like maybe she'd just gotten out of bed.

"Were you taking a nap? Did I wake you?"

"No. Let me give you his cell phone."

She did and I wrote it down. I asked, "Everything's okay?"

"Yeah." Her voice perked up a little. "Just a little tired is all."

It's the middle of summer. School's out. The kid's on vacation. How tired can she be?

"Well, I'll give your dad a call. Get some rest, sweetheart."

"'Kay...thanks."

Weird. Not the same confident, poised young lady that I'd met yesterday.

I punched up Kevin's cell phone.

"Hello?"

"Kevin, it's Genie." My voice had unconsciously taken on a softer, sexier tone.

"Hi!" He suddenly sounded warmer as well.

"Hey, I hate to bother you"

"No bother. It's nice to hear from you."

"My shift started early today so I'm off around six. Want to go grab something to eat?"

"Actually, I'll make you a counteroffer."

"Yeah?"

"I'm a pretty good cook. How about you have dinner at my place tonight? I'll grill some salmon."

"Sounds great. Can I bring anything?" Then, without thinking, I added, "Bottle of wine?"

He didn't say anything and when I heard the embarrassing silence, I winced.

Then he quietly said, "Hey, we're adults. Sure, how about a nice Chardonnay? See you around six-thirty?"

After we hung up, I put my hands on my eyes and shook my head, amazed at my own stupidity.

• • ● • •

After my arrest and sentence of sobriety, I started buying my booze surreptitiously. When I'd first moved back to Sheffield, I was a regular customer at Yankee Wine and Spirits over on Walnut Street. It's one of those liquor super-stores that stocks pretty much anything in the world that has alcohol in it. I liked the broad selection and shopped there often. They quickly came to know me as a regular, greeting me by name when I walked in the doorway.

But after my trial, that sort of familiarity became a liability. I started shopping at Pete's Liquors off West Avenue. It was barely bigger than my closet and the representative client demographic purchased malt beverages, inexpensive whiskies, and wines that came in jugs with screw tops.

Even so, on that evening, I found a nice Chardonnay in the cooler behind a six-pack of hard lemonade. I'm not a hundred percent sure, but I think it was Pete's only bottle of wine that cost more than eight dollars.

Feeling self conscious, when I got to Kevin's house I had the bottle hidden in my oversized bag that also held my notebooks, camera, and cosmetics. After all, we were both supposed to be on the wagon.

"Genie!" Kevin exclaimed as he opened the door. He had a big smile on his face.

"Hi." Even though we had seen each other naked only nine hours before, I reached up and gave him a huge hug. "I've got the wine in my bag," I whispered into his ear, sounding like a spy trying to hand over some microfilm.

"Well, let's open it," he said cheerfully, completely without artifice.

I reached into my bag, grabbed the bottle, and handed it to Kevin. He gave me a quick kiss on the lips. "C'mon in." And then he noticed. "What did you do to your head?"

I touched the bandage the emergency medical crew had placed on my forehead. "I'll tell you over dinner."

Caroline was sitting on a couch in the living room, looking much more animated than she had sounded earlier that day. "Hi, Genie." She was wearing a pair of denim shorts, a Sheffield High School shirt, and a pair of beat-up sneakers.

"Hi, honey."

Caroline's smile faltered when she saw her father walk through the living room with a bottle of wine.

I was a little surprised when I spotted another woman sitting on the sofa on the other side of the room. She stood up. "Hi, I'm Ruth Spence, Caroline's aunt."

"Geneva Chase." I introduced myself.

"I have a standing invitation." Ruth's eyes were studying my face.

"Aunt Ruth comes over for dinner a lot," Caroline announced. *Aunt Ruth?*

Growing up with Kevin, I knew that he was an only child. That had to mean Ruth was Joanna's sister.

Her brown hair, accented professionally by expensive high-lights, was cut stylishly short, framing her face. The lack of worry lines around her eyes and forehead indicated Botox injections and her dentist had obviously whitened her teeth. She was attractive in a stern, dominatrix sort of way. Her posture and attitude made her seem taller than me, even though she and I were about the same height.

"Was that a bottle of wine I saw Kevin carrying?" She clenched her teeth.

I nodded, "Yup."

"How nice. We haven't had alcohol in this house for quite some time." She barely concealed her disapproval.

I glanced at her left hand. No wedding band.

Was Ruth trying to make time with Kevin?

I turned to Caroline. "So your dad tells me he's quite a chef."

She nodded. "Mom used to do most of the cooking."

Ruth interjected, "After Joanna passed away, poor Kevin couldn't boil water. I was over here all the time helping him find his way around the kitchen."

I'll bet you were.

"It's nice that Kevin has a sister-in-law who's so helpful." I sounded less than convinced.

Before anyone could say anything else, Kevin came through the door with a wineglass in each hand. "Here you go," he announced, handing one to me and the other to Aunt Ruth. "Hang on, I'll be right back."

Seconds later, he was back with two more glasses, one of them less full than the other. He handed that one to Caroline. Then he held his own glass in the air and toasted, "To my favorite women."

Caroline immediately touched her glass against her dad's. Ruth and I did so more slowly.

"I've got to run out to the grill and check the salmon," Kevin said. "Lucky it's just about done. Looks like it's going to start raining again. The salad's on the counter in the kitchen. Why don't you guys go start your plates? I'll bring the fish into the dining room."

After he left, Ruth turned to Caroline and said in a low voice, "I don't think your father should be giving you wine, dear."

Caroline answered by defiantly draining the glass.

• • ● • •

Like the kitchen, the dining room was a project in disarray. The light fixture over the table was a hole in the ceiling with a knot of exposed wires tucked inside. Around the room the wallpaper had been stripped, leaving the naked sheetrock to glare blankly at us as we ate our grilled salmon.

Caroline had compensated with candles on the table.

"Kevin tells me you're a reporter for the *Post*." Ruth popped a tiny forkful of romaine lettuce into her mouth.

I nodded and sipped at my wine. "Recording the first draft of local history." I hoped that I sounded witty.

"What?" she asked.

"I'm paraphrasing a famous quote."

She stared at me without saying anything.

Sometimes when I get nervous, I start talking, often with nasty consequences. I felt one of those moments coming on. "For example, today I witnessed the arrest of somebody suspected in a string of big-time burglaries."

Caroline piped up, "You saw somebody get busted today?"

"This guy even tried to make a run for it."

"No kidding?" Caroline nodded her head in approval.

"What happened?" Kevin asked.

I slowly sipped at my wine, wondering if this was the only booze Kevin had in the house. "I was sitting in the car belonging to the deputy chief of police and he was outside pointing his gun at the bad guy. And the bad guy tried to make a run for it in one of those massive HumVees."

"And?" Kevin cut into his salmon.

"I discovered what happens when an irresistible force meets an immovable object." I touched the bandage on my forehead again.

Caroline asked, "What happens?"

I laughed. "The airbags go off. The bad guy kept ramming the car I was in so he could get away."

Kevin leaned forward and put his hand on mine. "Oh, my God! Are you okay?" He was studying the bandage on my forehead.

I loved the concerned look on his face. I wanted to lean over and kiss him. Instead, I said, "Never better. I got some great photos. Wait 'til you read the story. Front page, tomorrow's paper."

Caroline slowly shook her head in admiration. "Cool."

"So how do the two of you know each other?" Ruth was apparently bored with my story about the arrest.

"Genie and I went to high school together," Kevin explained.

"Really? Were you high school sweethearts?"

I shook my head and grinned at Caroline. "Hardly. More like high school buddies. We used to hang out together."

"Never dated?"

Kevin smiled. "Never dated. But because we'd spent so much time together, a lot of our friends just assumed we'd eventually get married."

"*Were* you ever married?" Ruth looked straight at me with a bemused smile.

"Well, not to Kevin."

"But you were married."

"Yes," I decided not to elaborate.

"Are you married now?"

"No, ma'am." I felt my annoyance grow. "I'm a big believer that, if it doesn't work out, you either leave 'em or kill 'em."

Caroline snorted out a laugh and Kevin quickly stifled a grin by sipping some wine.

"In our family," Ruth purred, "we take marriage a little more seriously."

"Have *you* ever been married?" I responded.

Aunt Ruth slowly, but clearly, turned a bright shade of crimson. Her superior smile was quickly replaced by a tight-lipped expression that I can only compare to the look of someone who has just bitten into a fresh lemon. I'd apparently poked at a raw nerve.

A film of tears glistened in her eyes. Haltingly, she whispered, "It's a subject of a deeply personal nature that I'm going to decline to discuss."

• • ● • •

After dinner, I helped Kevin carry the dirty dishes into the kitchen. "I hope I wasn't out of line asking Ruth if she'd ever been married. She brought it up first."

"Yeah, she started it." Kevin rinsed the plates off and handed them to me to put into the dishwasher. "Ruth married well," he said in a stage whisper. "And while it was a painful process, she divorced even better."

I looked at him quizzically.

"She was married to Harry Spence, an investment banker working out of Manhattan," he explained in a low murmur. "He was obscenely successful even after the economy soured. They seemed happy. He made money, Ruth spent it and it looked like a relationship that worked pretty well. Then Harry started spending more and more time away from home, working late in his office in New York, traveling a lot on business. When Ruth discovered a number on his cell phone that Harry was calling repeatedly at all hours, she hired a private investigator."

No surprise there.

"*His* cell phone?" I asked.

"He always recharged it at night from an outlet in the kitchen. Ruth took a look while he was asleep."

I tried hard not to pass judgment. I've done much worse.

"As it turns out, Harry was living the cliché. He'd been having an affair with his administrative assistant for about two years. I've seen some of the photos that the private investigator took: Harry and her leaving the office together, Harry and her in a restaurant together, Harry and her going to her apartment, Harry and her having sex."

"Having sex? They have photos of them having sex?"

"That private investigator was very expensive and wasn't above breaking, entering, and hiding a camera."

"Ah, did you see any of those pictures?"

He raised his eyebrows and whispered, "Not the X-rated ones."

"Ruth filed for divorce?"

He shook his head. "Actually, no. She confronted Harry and hammered him with an ultimatum. Either he stops seeing the 'whore,' as Ruth refers to her, or Ruth takes Harry for half of everything he owns." Kevin paused for a moment and then explained, "She really didn't want the marriage to end. In her family, divorce equals failure and, in her way, I think she still loved him."

I was confused. "So Ruth didn't file for divorce?"

"You want another drink?" Kevin changed the subject.

I snuggled up close and whispered, "You got some more wine?"

He kissed my forehead and answered in a low voice, "I've got some Absolut. Want some?"

"Yes, please."

Kevin squatted down and rummaged around in an open cupboard. Like everything else in his kitchen, the door had been removed. After rearranging a few boxes of Special K and Cheerios, he brought out two hidden bottles, vodka and scotch. He stood back up, glanced around to make certain that no one was watching, and poured a glass for each of us, neat.

"Cheers," he whispered.

"Cheers." I tapped my glass against his. Then I kissed him, long and hard. Sighing with pleasure and touching his chest with the flat of my hand, I sipped my vodka and then asked, "Ruth and Harry?"

"Ah, yes. It was Harry who filed for the divorce. He'd had quite enough of Ruth, and even if it cost him half of everything, he was going to leave her."

"And?"

"He did," Kevin said. He took a swallow of his own drink and contentedly closed his eyes. Without looking at me he continued. "The proceedings took almost two years. Harry wasn't stupid. He tried his best to hide his assets from her. But she was patient and vindictive. She ended up with a settlement that left her with more than six million dollars, not counting the house, which is worth another million or so."

I puffed out my cheeks and exhaled. "Wow. Ever thought about hooking up with Ruth? It sounds like you'd be set for life."

He smiled enigmatically. "I'm inclined to believe that Ruth has thought about it more than I have."

I got up close to Kevin and wrapped my arms around his waist. "I watched her tonight. She's attracted to you."

He slowly shook his head. "I don't think she and I would be a good match."

I agree.

"Why not?" I didn't care what his answer might be. I was just happy we were thinking the same way.

He sighed. "Joanna and Ruth might have been sisters, but they're very different. Ruth is efficient, organized..." He hesitated, looking for the right adjective.

"Cold-blooded?" I offered. "Tight-assed?"

"Exacting. I think Ruth is exacting. She knows precisely what she wants."

"And Joanna?"

His face warmed to the task and he beamed. "Joanna was gentle, forgiving, understanding. She had an incredible sense of humor. She had to have a sense of humor to put up with me." Kevin rolled his eyes. "I put her through an awful lot."

"Ruth doesn't have a sense of humor?" I already knew the answer.

Kevin looked down at his loafers and took a drink of his scotch. He shook his head. "No." A small smile played across his mouth. "I don't think I've ever seen her laugh. As a matter of fact, I think she only smiles when somebody else is in pain."

She is so like a dominatrix.

We finished putting the dishes away and sipped at our drinks, like an old married couple. It was nice. I almost laughed at myself when I asked, "So, honey, how was your day?"

He grinned and held his glass up in the air. "I got both jobs."

I put my glass down and clapped.

"Judge Rath doesn't want me to start the guest room addition until the end of the month, but tomorrow I'm ordering the materials for the kitchen job out on Connor's Landing."

As soon as he mentioned Connor's Landing, I remembered the mystery caller and looked at my watch. I wanted to be back at my office at nine. It was a little after eight. "Nice house?"

"Beautiful place. Right on the water, five bedrooms, four baths, three fireplaces, a swimming pool. They want me to knock out a wall for a breakfast nook."

"And they want the fossil backsplash from Montana."

"Wyoming."

"Same thing." I was feeling a little buzz coming on. "Are they nice people?"

He nodded. His eyes were getting glassy from the scotch. "Yeah, Pete Elroy wasn't there so I was working mostly with his wife, Becky. She's nice enough. Wants a kitchen she can show off to her friends, even though she has a cook and can barely find the refrigerator on her own. I thought her sons were a little odd, though."

"Oh?"

"Can't remember their names. Becky introduced them to me as they paraded out the door to get to the pool. One's a freshman at Yale, the other one's a junior at some expensive prep school in Greenwich."

"The pool? It was raining most of the day."

"Yeah, that's what I thought was so odd. At one point, I looked out the window and saw them both huddled under the cabana drinking beer and playing video games."

I checked my watch again. "The idle rich. Hey, I have to go into the office for a little bit."

He looked disappointed.

I put both my hands on his chest. "I won't be long. Want to meet me for a drink when I'm done?"

He brightened again. "Sure, where?"

"My place."

He was flustered until I added, "I'll come back here and pick you up, Mr. Restrictions."

Chapter Ten

At nine o'clock that night, the newsroom of *The Sheffield Post* was busier than usual. A half-dozen reporters were in the office knocking out their stories, the pre-press guys were burning plates and hustling them out to the pressroom, and the editors, including Casper Wells, were staring at their computer screens as they frantically read and edited tomorrow's newspaper.

The one thing everyone has in common is the clock. It's your king, your master, your archnemesis. With every sweep of the second hand, you have sixty seconds less to complete your assignment. The press starts promptly at midnight and God help you if it's late. Every minute the press isn't running means union overtime, advertising inserts waiting to be stuffed, drivers parked idle in the lot, newspapers late on readers' doorsteps, and worse— a possible loss in an ever-dwindling pool of circulation numbers.

Circulation is an apt term for a newspaper. If you don't have it, it's like losing blood. Lose too much and you die.

And like every other newspaper in America, the *Post* was slowly dying. The paper was over a hundred years old and had won dozens of awards. But the terminal combination of the economy and the Internet was slowly squeezing the *Post* of both advertisers and readers. *The Sheffield Post* had a website, but couldn't sell enough advertising to make up for the steady losses in the print version of the paper.

The clock on the wall wasn't just the nemesis of the reporters and editors; it was counting down time for the paper itself.

• • ● • •

"Good job on the arrest this afternoon."

I turned and looked up into my editor's face. Heavy eyebrows peeked over black horn-rimmed glasses; a smile revealed yellowing teeth that probably hadn't seen a dentist in years. "Thanks, Casper."

"So what are you doing back here in the office? I'm not paying overtime."

"Tying up a few loose ends."

"What did you do to your head?" He touched his forehead in reference to the bandage on my own.

I couldn't tell him about being in Mike's Jeep. "Oh, I dropped something under my kitchen table and when I stood back up I just nicked the corner."

"You okay?"

"Hell yeah, no problem."

"Nothing a martini couldn't fix?"

I could have sworn his nose was twitching, trying to catch a whiff of booze. Had Ostrowski told him about the night she had to cover for me? It didn't matter. He knew about the incident at the Z Bar. Everyone at the newspaper knew.

I turned back around to face my computer screen. "Wouldn't know, boss," I said, angrily. Privately, I was happy that I'd popped a couple of Altoids before coming into the office. Even though I was off the clock, I didn't need to enhance my reputation as a boozer.

Without a word, Casper turned around and walked back to his desk.

I glanced up at the wall clock. It read six minutes after nine. The phone rang.

"Geneva Chase," I snapped.

I was greeted with silence, as if the individual on the other end of the line was shocked that he'd gotten a real person instead of an answering machine. "Um…" said the voice, "I called earlier. I have information about the Connor's Landing murders?"

It was my turn to be quiet. Finally, I answered, "Can you tell me your name?"

"You're not recording this are you?"

"No."

There was another awkward silence while I waited for him to say something.

"Shouldn't you be asking me questions or something?"

"What's your name?" I asked again.

"I'm not telling you that."

"Then we're off to a bad start. What *can* you tell me?"

"I know why those people were killed."

"How do you know that?"

There was yet another moment of silence and then he spoke. "Because my wife and I were supposed to be there that night, out at George and Lynette's house."

My mind was working furiously. "Um, look. I think it would be better if we met."

"Oh God, no!"

"I don't need to know your name."

"I can't let anyone know who I am."

"Yeah, I get that." I cradled the phone to my ear. "Look, you have to believe that I protect my sources, but I really need to actually see you."

"Why?"

"To make certain you're telling the truth. To make sure you're not some kind of nut."

The caller was quiet again, thinking. Finally he said, "Can't I just tell you what I know over the phone?"

"No, but you can name the place where we meet, someplace where you feel safe."

I heard him sigh. "Fine, do you know where Bricks is?"

Yeah, it's right around the corner from where I live. "Yup."

"Meet you there in twenty minutes."

"How will I know you?"

"You won't. I'll find you. Carry a copy of your newspaper tucked under your arm so I can see it."

• • ● • •

There are plenty of fancy restaurants and trendy dance clubs in South Sheffield, but Bricks isn't one of them. It's your basic, neighborhood pizza joint with a tiny bar tucked away along the back wall. It's dark, it's quiet, and it's a good place to talk.

Walking from my place, I wore flats, black slacks, and an off-white blouse under a windbreaker that did little to keep out the rain. Holding a copy of the paper over my head hadn't done much either.

When I came in out of the weather, I brushed wet hair away from my eyes and looked around. At nine-thirty on a Saturday night, the place was pretty deserted, except for a few tables occupied by young couples out on a cheap date.

One lonely guy sitting at the bar, who, hunched protectively over his cocktail, was furtively stealing glances at me.

Either he was entranced with my soggy appearance or he was my source.

As I got up close, he spotted the rolled up newspaper I had in my grip. It was pretty wet, having served as a makeshift umbrella. The man stood up, briefly eyed the bandage on my forehead, and reached out his hand, "Geneva Chase?"

He was about six feet tall, balding, with a graying mustache, weighed about two-hundred-thirty pounds, and was somewhere in his early fifties. He wore a cheap watch, a simple gold wedding ring, dark green golf shirt, and a pair of black jeans. He hadn't been there long; the jacket on the back of his bar stool was still wet. If I had to guess, I'd place him as a middle manager in an insurance company or something equally nondescript.

I shook his hand. "And you are?"

He smiled, bit his lip, and shook his head.

"I have to call you something. How about you just tell me your first name?"

He blinked as he thought. Then he said, "Ted."

I sat down at the bar. "Good start. How ya' doin', Ted?"

He sat down as well and took a deep swallow of his drink, which smelled like bourbon.

The bartender came by and I ordered an Absolut and tonic.

Ted leaned over, his lips close to my ear, and said in a low voice, "Nobody can know who I am."

"So you've said." I started to take out my recorder.

He put his hand on mine. "You can't tape this."

I shook my head and put the recorder back in my bag. "Jesus Christ, Ted. You want to tell me what you know?"

"I know why those people were killed."

I looked him in the eye. "Why?"

"They were in an alternative lifestyle."

"Alternative lifestyle?"

The bartender slid by and dropped off my drink. I took a fast gulp. Then I took out my notebook and pen.

"You're writing this down?"

"I'm a writer." I raised my eyebrows and tried to appear genuine. "It's what I do. What kind of lifestyle?"

I was envisioning S&M maybe, BDSM, pagan rituals, witchcraft, devil worship.

He took another drink for courage. "Open marriage."

"What?"

He hesitated, then said, "Swinging."

"You mean like exchanging sexual partners?"

He nodded.

"How do you know?"

Ted didn't say anything.

"Ted, are you and your wife part of this lifestyle? Is that how you know?

He slowly nodded again.

"Is that what those three couples were doing out on Connor's Landing?"

He nodded a third time.

"You and your wife were supposed to be out there that night?"

He sighed. "There's a club here in Sheffield. It's open on Wednesday and Saturday nights."

"A club."

"Yeah, it looks like a regular, big old house from the outside. The inside has been completely retrofitted. It has a dance floor, a sound system for a DJ, a bar area, private rooms, hot tubs, Jacuzzi's. It has an orgy room."

I felt myself blushing. "Orgy room?"

He sipped his bourbon. "Yeah, it's a large room with wall-to-wall mattresses where a couple dozen couples can all play at the same time."

"Where's this club?"

He shook his head. "I can't tell you that, but it doesn't take a genius to find it. Google 'swingers' and 'Sheffield'. They have a website. It's a nice place. Hell, they get couples who come in from Hartford and Manhattan."

"How many couples belong to this club?"

"No idea, but they always have a crowd, especially on Saturday nights. Fifty or sixty people isn't unusual."

"Really? I kind of thought this went out with disco in the Seventies."

Ted eyed me, and smiled. "Everyone needs a little 'naughty' in their lives."

"So what typically happens?"

"It all starts around nine, we eat a little, we talk a little, we drink a little, we flirt, and we dance."

"And then?"

"And then around eleven, we go off and do our thing," He stared into his bourbon. "We might join another couple or two and hop in a hot tub or go up to a room. Or head off to somebody's home for a private party."

I raised my eyebrows. *Another couple or two?*

Ted was boring, the kind of guy who does your taxes. But every now and then, he and his wife, who was probably equally as dull, could pretend to be sexy and party like there was no tomorrow, doing things that are usually only sweaty late-night fantasies, things that you only see in porn movies.

And then they weren't so boring.

I didn't quite know how to feel about the whole thing.

Was it any worse than what I was doing with Frank Mancini? He was having a sexual relationship with someone other than his wife. He was having sex with me.

"So is that what happened this past Wednesday night?" I looked down at my notebook. "You were at this club with George and Lynette Chadwick, Kit and Kathy Webster, and John and Martha Singewald?"

He shook his head sadly. "You know, until I read the story in your paper, I never knew their last names. We're not big on talking about who we are in the real world."

"So I noticed."

"We rarely know what someone else's job is or how much money they make. You go to these things and it's a party, people gravitate to each other for whatever reason. Could be looks, personality, maybe they're just acting really hot. But after you've been there a few times, there are certain couples who are comfortable being with each other, you know what I mean?"

In the way he was talking about, no. But I didn't tell him that. I nodded in agreement.

"But those folks and my wife and I, we'd all spent time together over the last few months, you know, partying. Sometimes in a private room at the club, sometimes we'd go to somebody's house."

"Is that what happened last Wednesday night?"

"George and Lynette were inviting everyone over to their place out on Connor's Landing."

"Had you been there before?"

He picked up a couple of peanuts out of a snack basket on the bar and popped them into his mouth, chewing. "It's a beautiful house."

"I've seen it from the outside."

"They've got a sunken living room with lots of these big couches and plush rugs and pillows and a fireplace. Know what I'm talking about?"

I could only imagine. "Sure."

"My wife and I have been there a couple of times. George and Lynette are terrific hosts. Good food, expensive booze, soft lighting, they have a huge collection of porn and a big screen TV with surround sound. We always had a good time there."

"So, just to be clear, you and your wife have had sex with other couples there, at George and Lynette Chadwick's house?"

Frowning, he slowly turned to face me. "Yes, we had sex with other couples there. See why I can't give you my name?"

"Sure."

"My wife and I can't have that all over the news."

"I understand."

"And you see why I don't want the cops to know who I am?"

"What you do isn't against the law." At least I didn't think it was.

He took a drink. "Then maybe I should have gone to the police." He had an edge to his voice.

"George and Lynette invited you back to their place out on Connor's Landing but you didn't go. Why not?"

He drained the last of the bourbon from his drink. Holding up his glass, he pointed to it and the young man behind the bar immediately went to get him a refill. "There was bad mojo that night. Lynette's ex-husband showed up at the club."

We'd printed the names of the victims along with their photos in that day's newspaper. I recalled Lynette Chadwick. She was in her mid-thirties, high cheekbones, brunette with an expensive cut, pretty smile, and brown eyes that were looking at something other than the camera lens. She was pretty but a little vulnerable.

"Lynette's ex-husband?"

The bartender carefully placed another glass of Jack Daniels in front of Ted. "Lynette had told us about this guy. They'd been married about nine years."

"You know why she got divorced? Were they swingers?"

Ted shook his head. "Ex-husband's an abusive alcoholic. She said that he used to beat the hell out of her."

"Good reason to leave him," I muttered.

He held his glass up to the light and studied the amber liquid. "In the end, Lynette made out okay, though. You said you saw George and Lynette's place out on the Landing?"

It was my turn to nod.

"George was some kind of millionaire. He mentioned that he worked for a bank or something. Lynette's first husband, Jim, owns an auto body shop. He does okay but he's no freakin' millionaire. You know what I mean?"

"I know you told me that you never talked much about last names," I probed, "but, by any chance, would you know Lynette's ex-husband's name?"

He winked. "Jim Brenner. I know because I recognized him when he showed up Wednesday night. Jim replaced a door panel on my Explorer last year. I knew him, but he didn't recognize me," Ted explained, then added, "I hope."

I took a hit of my vodka. Then I glanced at my notebook. "So this Jim Brenner showed up at the club last Wednesday night? Why, is he a swinger?"

"Oh, hell no. Lynette's ex is a jealous jerk. Lynette told us that when she was married to him, if she even looked at another guy, he'd beat the crap out of her. But after the divorce I guess he got religion. Swinging is all about recreational sex, no strings or commitments except to your own partner. Jim's not the kind of guy who could watch his wife, or ex-wife, have sex with another man or woman. Not without wanting to kick the bejeezus out of whoever was touching her."

"Is it widely known that there's a swingers' club in Sheffield?"

Ted shook his head. "You didn't know and you work for a newspaper."

"Then how did Lynette's ex-husband know where to find her?"

"I'm not sure, but let me tell you what happened and then I'll tell you how I think he got there."

"Okay."

"It was about eleven that night and that's when everyone starts to pair up. George and Lynette were quietly inviting people, including Sylvia and me, to come over to their place."

I didn't write down the name of Ted's wife because I was afraid I'd spook him. But I made a mental note...*Sylvia.*

"At that point, we'd been drinking and dancing and everyone was feeling pretty good. I don't know how Jim Brenner got in because there's someone at the door who checks in members and if you're a guy, you have to be paired up with a lady to get in. No single men allowed."

"But unescorted ladies can come in?"

"You can never have too many ladies in a swingers' club. Anyway, somehow this guy got in and was sitting off to one side of the bar by himself.

"I was leaning against the bar with one arm around Sylvia and the other arm around Lynette. The bunch of us, George, Kit and Kathy, Johnny and Martha, we were just finishing up our drinks, laughing and kidding around about driving over to Connor's Landing. That's when this guy walks up to us. It took me a minute because he was out of context, but I recognized him as the guy who'd fixed my SUV."

"What does he look like?"

Before he answered, he turned his head and scanned the interior of the restaurant.

I followed his line of sight but all I saw were about a dozen customers eating pizza and drinking beer. Beyond that, I saw traffic moving, taillights reflecting off the wet street. "What are you looking for?"

He shrugged and turned his attention back to me. "Brenner's in his mid-thirties, maybe, brownish hair, clean shaven, taller than me but built like a linebacker. When he came up to us, you could tell that he's pissed off about something."

"How?"

"He's scary lookin'. He's by himself so he shouldn't even be there. His eyes are wide and his face is red, but he's not saying anything. He comes up close and stands right in front of us."

Ted took another sip of his bourbon. "I felt Lynette tense up. She looks at this guy, takes my arm from around her waist and says, 'Jim, what are you doing here?' Then before he answers, she says, 'Everyone, this is my ex-husband, Jim.' None of us knew what to say. We all waited and held our breath to see what was gonna happen."

"What happened?"

"He starts shouting that Lynette's a filthy whore. He was slurring his words, like he's been drinking. Then he calls her a slut and points at me and says I'm an adulterer, a fornicator. Then he looks at George and calls him a pimp. That's when George steps in between Lynette and her ex-husband. And then Jim gets right in George's face and shouts, 'You let these other men lay down with Lynette? You let them touch her like she's a whore?'

"Lynette's ex-husband shoves George real hard so he falls back into where Lynette, Sylvia, and I are all standing. Thank God, the guy who runs the club shows up with two other big guys and the three of them tell Jim that he's got to leave. Jim stares at George and Lynette and he says, 'You're going straight to hell—straight to hell, and when you do I'll be laughing at you while the multitudes of demons peel the burning flesh from your bones.' That's when the three guys grab Brenner's arms and escort him out the door. Thank God, he leaves without a fight.

"After he was gone, George hugged Lynette and we all wondered how Jim had found the club. Lynette told us that she thought he might have been following her. She'd thought she'd seen him in his Mustang that afternoon while she was at the hairstylist and then again when she was at the grocery store."

I tapped my pen against the top of the bar. "'That must have been a buzz kill."

"Yeah, we all had another couple of drinks, talked about what had happened and tried to calm down, you know, get back into the mood. It's funny how much a couple of good, stiff drinks can mellow you out. Make things seem normal even when they're not."

Boy, if anyone knows that, it's me.

"It was pretty close to midnight and George and Lynette were working hard to convince the group to follow them out to Connor's Landing. There's a security guard at the bridge and that's the only one way on or off the island. They had a brand new porno they wanted everyone to see."

"But you and your wife didn't go."

Ted took a deep swallow of his drink and closed his eyes. "No, the mood was gone. It all felt wrong."

I was close to finishing my vodka. "So, are you telling me that you think Lynette's ex-husband, Jim Brenner, might have killed everyone that night?"

He glanced behind him again. Ted was clearly spooked. "I'm sure of it."

"You have to talk to the cops." I couldn't say anything to Mike because I protect my sources. But if Ted volunteered the information, I'd have this story locked up tight. Any other reporters out there chasing this down could kiss my ass.

He shook his head. "No, if I go to the cops, Brenner will know it was me. He'll come after me and my wife."

Abruptly, he grabbed his jacket off the back of his barstool and started for the door.

I couldn't let him leave without finding out his last name. I didn't have any way to get back in touch with him.

"Wait," I shouted.

He kept going, pushing open the door of the restaurant and rushing out into the rainy night.

I grabbed my bag and my windbreaker and started after him.

"Wait a minute, who's paying for the drinks?"

I looked behind me and saw the boy behind the bar, with angry, wide eyes and his arms outstretched.

Hands trembling, I fished around in my bag until I found two twenties and threw them on the bar. I hung my bag on my shoulder and ran out after Ted.

Once outside, I looked up and down the wet sidewalk. I didn't see him.

Damn it, where is he?

Brake lights flashed halfway up the block in front a parked cargo van. A red Ford Explorer pulled into traffic.

Damn it. I'm not close enough to read his license plate

Keeping to the wet sidewalk, I ran after him, hoping I could catch him before he got to the corner.

Ted accelerated.

I ran harder, cold pellets of rain stinging my face.

The stoplight at the corner was red.

He'll have to stop before he turns. I'll catch a break. Thank God, I'm wearing flats.

But before Ted even slowed down, the light turned green.

Shit.

I sprinted, bag digging into my shoulder, jacket clutched in my fist.

Ted turned the corner.

My lungs were on fire, I was sweating, my hair was wet and hanging in my face and my shoes were soaked.

And I was pissed. I'd missed him.

I didn't get the license.

What do I do now?

Chapter Eleven

Still smarting from losing my source, I hopped in my Sebring and drove by Brenner's Body Shop. It was tucked away in the dark corner of an industrial park not far from the harbor. The white cinderblock building was windowless except for tiny glass panes in a door to the office and in the three large roll-up doors to the repair bays. Wild clumps of grass and weeds stubbornly sprouted out of the cracks in the pavement in front of the garage. A small parking lot adjacent to the building was fenced in and topped with razor wire, protecting a dozen cars in varying degrees of repair, disrepair, or demolition.

I'm not sure what I expected to see. It was after ten and the place was dark and silent as a tomb.

The only way I knew for sure that I was at the right address was a faded red hand-painted sign over the office doorway proclaiming that this was indeed "Brenner's Body Shop."

I glanced down at my notebook. Officer Phil Gilmartin had given me Jim Brenner's home address.

Yes, it's the same Phil Gilmartin I'd struck in the eye during my squabble with Frank's wife at the Z Bar. He was also the one who had quietly urged the judge to show me leniency during my sentencing.

He has a crush on me. He's had it since high school, even though now he's married to a very nice woman who stays busy raising his two teenage boys. Maybe Phil has a secret attraction to "bad" girls.

Jim Brenner lived over on Wolfpit Avenue, coincidently about four blocks from Kevin's house. It was similar to the other homes in the neighborhood, a cookie-cutter Cape Cod with a small but well-kept yard and a thirteen-foot fishing boat on a trailer sitting in the driveway alongside an SUV.

The only illumination inside the house was the flickering light of a TV, flashing silver ghosts behind dark, heavy curtains. Was this the home of the man who stabbed and cut apart six people in a murderous alcoholic rage? Was the killer sitting back in his recliner, relaxing, drinking a beer, smoking a cigarette, and watching *Walking Dead?*

I briefly considered pulling into the driveway, knocking on the door, and asking Lynette Chadwick's ex-husband a few questions.

But I thought better of it. I might have more balls than brains, but I'm not entirely stupid.

Instead, I headed toward Kevin's place.

While negotiating my way to Random Road, I pulled the cell phone out of my bag and dialed Mike Dillon's number at the police station. I waited for an answer, glancing at my watch. It was about ten-thirty.

I got his voicemail, no surprise.

I didn't leave a message. I immediately dialed Kevin's number. My adrenaline was amped up pretty high from my meeting with Ted and I was looking for a little company. A couple of tumblers of vodka neat would go down real easy.

"Hello?" Kevin answered.

"Hey. It's me. I told you I'd call. Still up for that drink?"

The phone was quiet for a millisecond, then he answered, "Can I take a rain check?

I replied in a tone that I hoped didn't betray my disappoint-ment. "Of course, baby. Everything okay?"

"I was working on the kitchen cabinets and I think I pulled a muscle or something."

"Oh no, you okay?"

"Yeah, it's nothing a couple of Advil, another glass of scotch, and a good night's sleep won't fix."

I smiled to myself. "You sure it wasn't the sex? Was I too rough? I could give you a nice backrub and make it all better."

I don't usually tell guys this, but once during sex, I cracked one of my first husband's ribs. Guys are so stupid that if you tell them that, they're disappointed if you don't do the same thing to them. They think they're missing out on something really spectacular.

"You're sweet, but I've got to take a rain check."

"Hey, did Aunt Ruth say anything about me after I left?"

I could hear Kevin trying to formulate a diplomatic answer. "She thinks you're…really interesting."

"Yeah? You're full of crap. She's not there is she?" I was suddenly paranoid, picturing her in a black leather bustier, waiting with a whip for Kevin to come to bed.

"Who, Ruth? She left right after dinner. Can I buy you breakfast tomorrow? There's a place in Westport that serves the world's best pancakes."

"Are you going to feel better by then?

"Oh yeah," he said.

I smiled. "Then it's a date."

"I'll pick you up at your place."

"In your truck?"

"Yeah, my restricted license says that I can drive as long as it's daylight."

"What time?" I hoped it wouldn't be too early. Tomorrow was Sunday.

I could hear him thinking. "Ten too late?"

Personally, it was way too early.

"Perfect," I lied.

We said our good-byes and I drove home. I took Tucker for a quick walk along the waterfront, checked my e-mail, opened a couple of bills that had come snail mail and listened to my voice messages. There wasn't anything of interest and I was still really wired.

So I walked down to the Z Bar. I was still in the mood for a vodka rocks.

It was Saturday night and the place was throbbing with chest-hammering techno-industrial dance music, the floor was packed with sweaty couples writhing and grinding their bodies together, and the air was heavy with anticipatory sexual promise. The bar was a beehive of movement and noise as patrons vied for the attention of the attractive young bartenders.

I wedged my way up to the bar, leaned across the polished oak counter and literally grabbed one of the bartenders by the elbow. "Grey Goose and ice," I shouted, hoping the young Adonis could hear me above the music. He nodded and disappeared to get my drink.

I turned to look out over the dance floor and found myself staring right into Frank Mancini's smile. "Hi." I couldn't hear him but I could read his lips.

"Hi."

"How ya' doing?" he shouted, barely audible over the music.

I heard someone from behind me shout, "Hey!" I turned to see the bartender reaching out with my glass. I took it gratefully.

Then I turned back to Frank. He was standing there in a light gray suit, cobalt blue shirt, and dark charcoal tie, his teeth perfect, his hair perfect, and his dark brown eyes peering directly into my own.

He looked fabulous.

Leaning down, Frank put his lips close enough to my ear that I could feel his breath as he spoke. "You look great." He buried his face in my hair.

I reached up and touched his cheek.

"Let's go somewhere and talk." His words tickled the inside of my ear.

I took him by the hand and led him around the bar and down a set of stairs to the owner's office and the bathrooms. Most of the time, it was deserted and just far enough away from the music that you could actually have a conversation.

Once we found a place in the shadows, he pulled me close and kissed me hard.

I'm ashamed to say it, but I kissed him hard right back.

When our tongues finally unwrapped, he leaned back and smiled. "I missed you."

"We saw each other yesterday at lunch." I was still slightly out of breath. Frank's kisses can do that to me.

"I wanted to be with you last night."

"Too bad your wife was around."

"I would have rather been at that reception with you." Frank's hand massaged my wrist.

I smiled and squinted, "You know, the last time you and I were here at the Z Bar together, Evelyn showed up and I got arrested."

He nodded. "Evelyn's out of town tonight. She and one of her friends drove down to spend a few days in the Hamptons."

"So while the cat's away, Frankie can play?"

"Something like that. Want to go to your place?"

I didn't answer as quickly as I should have; the booze was probably slowing me down. But eventually I answered, "No."

"Do you want to go to my place?"

I shook my head.

"A nice hotel?"

I thought of Kevin. The way we'd snuggled last night, the way he smelled, the way he felt. And I remembered our shower together this morning.

Frank continued his attempt at my seduction, "I really want to be with you tonight."

I tried to change the subject. "Why are you out so late?"

"Why are *you* out so late?"

"I asked first."

He sighed. "I took a client out to dinner."

"And then you brought him here?"

He cleared his throat. "Her."

Unbelievable, he was with another woman and he was coming on to me.

"So why are you hitting on me? I don't do threesomes."

He put his forehead on mine. "I want to be with you, not her, not Evelyn. I want to be with *you.*

Chapter Twelve

Kevin rang my doorbell at five minutes after ten the next morning.

No, Frank Mancini wasn't lying naked in my bed, he wasn't hiding in my closet, and he wasn't drinking coffee while sitting at my kitchen table.

No, he wasn't there at all.

He'd left my apartment sometime around two a.m.

I'm not proud of the fact that I slept with Frank. Especially since I'd made love with Kevin in the same bed less then twenty-four hours earlier.

I don't know why I did it. I'd like to say that maybe it was to get even with Evelyn. Revenge for getting me arrested a few months ago, revenge for calling me a whore at the fundraiser on Friday night.

I'd like to say that maybe I had sex with Frank because I love him and he loves me. And in a quirky sort of way, I guess we do. I'd like to say that maybe it was because he's really good in the sack, which he is. Not better than Kevin, but good nonetheless.

No, the real reason that I slept with Frank was because I was stupid-ass drunk.

Let's count 'em. A white wine at Kevin's house along with two glasses of vodka. Another tumbler at Bricks while talking with Ted, the source. One more at my house after I walked Tucker. Then, well, then I lost count while I was at the Z Bar with Frank.

It's not a good excuse, but it's the only one I've got. It's one I've been using most of my adult life.

I greeted Kevin at my doorway with a barking dog, a pained smile, a nest of hangover rattlesnakes buzzing in my head, and a genuine sense of shame. Even though Kevin and I weren't in any kind of relationship, we were friends.

Passionate friends.

When I opened my front door and he pulled me close and kissed me, I felt like I'd betrayed him.

We were friends who'd become lovers. Frank Mancini and I were lovers, but we'd never ever really been friends, and probably never would be.

I mulled all of that around in the unrelenting sunshine and the godawful heat while we stood on line in Westport waiting to get into Kevin's pancake restaurant. Flap Jack's was so popular that we waited in the parking lot with about thirty other people, outside the front door, for nearly a half an hour before we got in and ordered.

Kevin seemed pretty chipper through it all, but I found it difficult to hold up my end of the conversation. "Beautiful day, huh?" He pointed his face into the direction of the sun while we stood on line.

"So how are you feeling?" I grunted, thinking that if he hadn't pulled a muscle, I wouldn't have slept with Frank last night. In a convoluted way, I could blame the whole thing on Kevin.

Without looking at me he said, "Just getting old, I guess."

I put my hand on his arm. "Don't ever let me hear you talk like that, okay? You and I are the same age. If you're getting old, I'm getting old. And that ain't happening."

He gave me his familiar smile and nodded toward the line behind us. "Look at all the people who brought newspapers with them."

He was right. Of the twenty or so people behind us, nearly half of them were reading a Sunday newspaper. Some of them were the *New York Times* of course, but most of them were holding *The Sheffield Post*. "Yeah, you wouldn't know that the industry's dying."

"Don't you get a kick out of knowing they're reading what you wrote?"

From where we stood, not far from the doorway of the restaurant, I could easily see that many people were reading about yesterday's arrest in the Stop-n-Shop parking lot, and they were talking about it.

"I'm not sure I'll ever know what that's like," Kevin said.

"What?"

"What it's like to have an impact on so many people."

I touched his arm again and then held onto his hand. "And I'll never know what it's like to raise a daughter. When everything's all said and done, this time tomorrow? No one will remember a single word I wrote. But for the rest of Caroline's life, and the lives of *her* children, what you've taught your daughter will shape other lives for generations to come. So who makes the bigger impact?"

What I said made him smile and blush at the same time. My words were off the top of my head, meant to be a simple gratuity for his compliment. But it was true and it made him feel like a million bucks.

For the first time that morning, I didn't feel like a complete shit.

• • ● • •

Kevin was right. Flap Jack's is an amazing place. The smells are incredible, hazelnut coffee, bacon, ham, biscuits, hash browns, frying eggs. But the best are the pancakes. Griddled with anything you can think of: fruit, chocolate, caramel, pecans, almonds and served up in stacks, steaming hot on plates soaked in maple or blueberry syrup.

I could literally feel buttery chunks of cholesterol clogging my arteries like a fleet of sixteen-wheelers jack-knifing on I-95. But the more I ate, the more my hangover dissolved.

I actually became chatty. "So tell me about Ruth. Caroline tells me that she's over at your house a lot."

"I told you about Ruth." He was perplexed, his eyebrows knitting together. "What else do you want to know?"

I finished chewing a mouthful of sausage and then pointed at him with my fork. "Well, have you and she, um, ever…?"

"What?"

"You know." I cleared my throat. "Knocked boots?"

Kevin's eyebrows shot up. Then he blinked and stared down at his plate.

I reached over and put my hand on his. "It's okay if you did."

He smiled and slowly shook his head, "No, we've never slept together."

Damn it. On the one hand, if he'd slept with Ruth, I wouldn't feel quite so guilty about my evening with Frank, but then again, I was relieved that he wasn't doing his sister-in-law. I was rummaging around in a mixed sack of wretched emotions like some morally bankrupt bag lady.

I sighed. "That's good. What's Caroline think about her?"

He took a moment to formulate his answer. "It's been good to have a woman around the house, you know, after Joanna passed away. But now I'm thinking that Ruth might be crowding her a little. Ruth can be a little in-your-face."

I shrugged. "Caroline's thirteen. She needs space."

"Yeah, now more than ever, though, I think she could use her mom."

"Losing a parent is pretty traumatic." I sipped my coffee.

Kevin's eyes focused on something in the distance, remembering. "All the while her mom was sick, Caroline was crying a lot. Maybe she was crying all the time. It was all so intense and I was so wrapped up in how I was dealing with it, I can't say for sure how bad it was for her. It must have been hell to see her mother in so much pain, dying an inch at a time. And then when it was over, Caroline went into a state of shock. She stopped crying. I don't think I've seen her cry since. At the funeral, people came up to me saying how well Caroline was taking it all. She was numb."

"Maybe she was grateful that it was over."

"Maybe."

"How's she doing now? She seems happy enough."

"I think she is. Most of the time. She can be moody."

"She's a teenager."

He rolled his eyes. "You know, one minute she can be a regular cheerful kid and the next she can shut herself up in her room like a hermit. I can't get her out of there with a stick of dynamite."

"Has she ever talked to a counselor or a therapist?"

"Yeah, it was Ruth's idea."

"Did it help?"

"It might have. What's normal when something like that happens?" he mused and shrugged his shoulders.

I could relate to the pain Caroline felt. My dad died back when I was in junior high. When that happened, I was devastated. I was certain it was my fault. When my mom passed away, two years ago, I was older and could handle it more maturely. Mom and I hadn't been close since dad died.

"The afternoon we scattered Joanna's ashes over Long Island Sound, she asked me why I thought her mom had to die," Kevin quietly said.

"What did you tell her?"

He put his fork down on his plate. "I told her that I didn't know. That God does things we can't understand."

"Is that what you think?"

He shook his head. "I don't believe in God. If there's a God, he wouldn't have made Joanna go through that kind of hell."

What could I say after that? We sat there and drank our coffee, lost in our own thoughts for what seemed like an eternity, but was really only a few minutes.

Finally, he tapped the table with his finger. "So, what are you doing this afternoon?"

I shrugged. "I think I'll go for a run."

Run to tone up my legs and ass, to burn off a couple of pounds of pancakes and to sweat out some guilt.

Kevin said, "I need to stop by my house to print up an invoice and then I'm driving out to the Elroys' place out on Connor's Landing. They're giving me a deposit check this afternoon. Want to come along and see their house? It's really something. Afterward, we can take a walk out on Shaker's Pier, catch some sun, maybe watch the sailboats, grab a margarita, and sit out on the deck over at the Sunset Inn?"

His face seemed so damned hopeful. How could I say no?

"I'd like that. I need to get my car and leave it at your place. Okay?"

In case I feel like dropping by Jim Brenner's place in the daylight.

• • ● • •

When I pulled into his driveway, Kevin was getting out of his truck.

Something about the yard looked different from the last time I'd seen it.

I got out of my car. "Did you cut the grass?"

"Yup."

"When did you do that?"

"I got up this morning about five a.m., took a look out the front window and thought it was looking a little raggedy. So I got out the lawnmower and got her done."

Guess he *was* feeling better.

"You cut the lawn at five this morning?"

"Yup."

"Five o'clock on a Sunday morning?"

"Yeah." He unlocked his front door.

"Your neighbors must really love you."

He thought a moment. "Probably." He puffed out his cheeks and then added, "Not."

"What are you doing getting up so early on a Sunday morning?"

He shrugged his shoulders. "Couldn't sleep. I was thinking about you."

After he said that, he ducked inside and started up the stairs to the second floor, taking two steps at a time. Once he got to the top, he asked, "Coming?"

I couldn't decide what Kevin reminded me the most of, that shy, self-effacing kid I knew in high school or a Labrador retriever.

I followed him up the steps, but by the time I got up to the second floor, he'd already disappeared. So I stuck my head in the first doorway I came to. It was Caroline's bedroom.

The room was very different from the rest of the house. The ceilings and walls were all intact. The room was complete. The walls were painted in a soft shade of coral and covered with posters of actors and pop stars. A comfortable, lime-green duvet was draped over her bed; overstuffed pillows were propped against the oaken headboard. Stuffed animals competed with cosmetics for space on her bureau. The mirror on her dresser was ringed with photos of her friends.

Caroline was sitting with her back to the door, facing a sunny window and a computer screen, her fingers flying across the keyboard with eye-blurring speed.

"Hi," I offered.

Her hands stopped jamming and she turned, smiling when she saw me. "Hi, Genie," she said cheerily.

"Writing a book?"

She chuckled. "Just talking with some friends. Did I hear Dad come home?" She glanced behind me.

I watched her computer monitor. Multiple conversations were scrolling down her screen, streaming in real time from who knows how many other homes? Messages firing up through the clouds, bouncing off a satellite locked in an undeviating position hundreds of miles above us, and then racing back down through the atmosphere and magically appearing here in Caroline's room.

If someone from the nineteenth century were standing in my place, they'd think it was witchcraft. I'm not a hundred percent sure that it's not.

"Yeah, your dad's home. I think he disappeared somewhere down the hall here."

"Well, the house isn't that big. Either he's in the john or in his bedroom." She reached around and picked up a handful of taco chips out of a bowl, dropped them on her desk, and put a couple into her mouth.

How the hell did that girl stay so thin? I've watched her put away the food and if I ate what Caroline ate, I'd be a blimp! I guess at her age, metabolism was everything.

"I'll tell him to stop in and see you," I said. "Okay?"

She gave me the thumbs-up and then went back to pounding away at her computer.

Turning away and heading up the hall, I momentarily wondered what Caroline thought of me. Did she think I was just her dad's old high school friend? Did she have the slightest inkling that we'd been intimate?

Did she give me a second thought at all?

When I found Kevin, he was much like his daughter, sitting in front of a computer screen. His fingers moved much more slowly across the keyboard, however. I stood and watched him as he struggled to punch up an invoice.

It gave me a chance to study his bedroom. Because of the darkness, it was difficult to get a good first impression. In spite of the bright sunny afternoon blazing away outside, Kevin's windows were completely covered by heavy drapes.

A tiny desk light perched next to the computer offered scant illumination and it took a second or two for my eyes to adjust. Eventually, I could make out that Kevin's bed was neatly made. Score one for him.

His closet doors were missing, much like the cupboard doors in the kitchen, so I could easily see that his clothes were pressed, hung up, and well organized. Score two.

A couple of paintings of flower gardens hung on the walls, along with a large photo of a woman's face that I surmised was Joanna's. That was nice. Score three.

And on the wall near where Kevin was sitting, there hung a *Sports Illustrated* swimsuit calendar. A skinny blonde was kneeling in the wet sand on a beach, wearing only a tiny bikini bottom, covering her naked chest with carefully folded arms.

All points lost. If we spent any time together, that would have to go.

I walked around his bed until I came up behind him.

Without looking back at me, he sensed that I was there. "I'm almost done."

I reached up and pulled open the curtains. The room was immediately flooded by sunshine.

Kevin looked up at me, blinking and squinting.

"Like you said at Flap Jacks, it's a beautiful day. Plus, how are you going to get a good look at Miss August over here if you don't get some light in this room?" I pointed my thumb at his calendar.

He faked a frown. "I forgot that damned thing was there."

"Right." I took the opportunity to take another look at his bedroom in the light. The bed was covered with a light blue, flowered comforter. The walls were painted in a similar, light pastel blue. There were two lamps on his dresser, topped by rose-colored shades.

It didn't take a genius to realize that Kevin's wife had decorated this room. No wonder he kept it dark. He was hoping her ghost was here.

When he slept, maybe she came to him in his dreams.

He punched a button on his keyboard and the printer on his computer table whirred to life. "This'll be out in a minute."

I'm not certain if her ghost came only to Kevin and only when he slept. I had a feeling that she might be here in this bedroom most of the time.

I made a silent promise to myself that I would never sleep in this room.

Kevin pulled a four-color document out of his printer. "Ready to drive out to Connor's Landing?"

And then he did the damnedest thing. He put his arms around my waist, lifted me up and placed me gently on his bed. Then, while lying on top of me, we kissed each other with unbridled passion.

And that was, of course, when I heard Caroline clear her throat.

Kevin and I both looked up at the same time, clearly embarrassed to see that his daughter was standing in the doorway.

"Um," she said, "Ruth called just before you got home. She wants to know if we want to come over to her house for dinner tonight."

Still on top of me, trying to be nonchalant, Kevin asked his daughter, "Do you want to go to Ruth's for dinner?"

She frowned. "We just saw her last night."

"That's what I was thinking. I'm going out to pick up a check this afternoon. Gonna' have money burning a hole in my pocket. How about the three of us go over to Poco Loco for Mexican?"

Since I was on the bottom and peering over my head at her, it was difficult to see her facial expression. "I could go for some chimichangas," Caroline said.

After she left, I mumbled, "Well, that was embarrassing."

"Could have been worse."

"Yeah, we could have been naked."

Kevin smiled. "I think she likes you."

"You're full of shit." Then I discovered just how ticklish he is.

Chapter Thirteen

The old man peered out at us from an open window in the tiny wooden gatehouse. Rheumy blue eyes stared over a pair of spectacles perched low on a nose made remarkable by its living roadmap of red and violet veins. White hair curled out around his forehead and ears from under a baseball cap emblazoned with a green and blue *Aztec Security* logo. Character was etched around the corners of his eyes and mouth by creases cut like dry riverbeds into his weathered face.

"Help you?" He put away a newspaper with a partially completed crossword puzzle.

Kevin smiled and pointed across the bridge. "We're going to the Elroy house, up on Smuggler's Road?"

"Yup," the old man nodded. Then he came slowly out of the gatehouse doorway, favoring his left leg, and handed Kevin a clipboard. The guard appeared to be somewhere in his early seventies and was dressed in tennis shoes, baggy beige pants, and a light blue polo shirt sporting the same logo as his hat. "Write your name here, please. Press down hard so it shows up on the copy underneath."

I leaned over onto Kevin's lap and looked up through the window. "Is there a guard on this bridge all the time?"

He bent down, put his arm on the door panel and gazed at me through the open driver's side window. "Twenty-four hours a day, seven days a week, even Christmas."

"Can you tell me who was working this past Wednesday night?"

He squinted at me and frowned. "Who wants to know?"

Playing a hunch that I might have hit pay dirt, I whispered to Kevin, "Give me a minute."

I deftly got out of Kevin's pickup and walked around the front bumper. Holding out my hand, I announced, "I'm Geneva Chase. I work for *The Sheffield Post.*"

He tapped his finger against the logo on his hat. "Yeah? I got orders that any questions from the press should go to the home office. We're not even letting any of those damned TV trucks across the bridge."

I cocked my head. "Yeah, I understand that. This is all off the record."

He shook his head, taking the clipboard back from Kevin. "Don't care. All questions go to the home office."

I sighed, stepped up a little closer, and gave him a smile. When I asked him my next question, I let my voice drop a little and put my lips near his ear. "I promise not to tell where I got the information. It'll never be in the newspaper and nobody will ever know. Can't you just tell me who was working that night?"

Older men like it when blondes flirt with them.

"I'm not supposed to." His voice got a little quieter.

I nodded and looked him straight in the eye. "Whoever was on duty, it must be really scary to know that a killer was out there on the island. It takes a very brave man to work out here alone at night. It's got to be spooky as heck."

He cocked his head and offered a tiny grin, letting me see his yellowed teeth. "Most times it's kind of nice, being out here all by myself late at night. I got a tiny light in the hut and I get a lot of reading done, mostly mystery books. It's real quiet. You can hear the waves lapping around the timbers of the bridge. Sometimes you hear a school of bluefish when they all come to the surface. In the winter you can even hear harbor seals when they swim ashore."

I was right. This was the guy who was watching the gate on Wednesday night!

"You work days *and* nights?"

"No, no." He held up a hand. "Right up until that night, I worked from eleven at night until seven in the morning, Monday through Friday. Nice and quiet. I love that shift. I always know it's time to go home when the sun creeps up over the water."

"No more?"

He could see Kevin was listening, so the old man took me gently by the arm and led me around to the other side of the gatehouse. From where we were standing, I could still see the short wooden bridge across the narrow waterway and the rest of the island beyond. Two waterside mansions were easily in sight, even though the owners had tried to hide their presence behind high stone fences partially covered by hydrangeas, roses, and ivy. Sheffield Harbor was off to our left, Long Island Sound to the right.

The humid air was still and the water was dead calm. I had no problem hearing the old man's words even though they were little more than a whisper. "My wife won't let me work nights no more. She says it just ain't safe."

"I don't blame her for thinking that. By the way, what's your name?"

He hesitated. "You ain't writin' any of this down, are ya'?"

I got up close to him again and put a finger on his chest. "This is between me and you. I call it color, background information. You'll never see it in the paper."

"I could lose my job. Social Security and my pension pay most of the bills, but I need to keep working so we can afford Loraine's prescription medicine. She had pneumonia last winter and still can't shake an infection got lodged in her chest."

"Nobody will ever know I was ever here, cross my heart."

He held out his hand, which I took with my own. He said, "Donnie Burke."

"Donnie Burke. Nice to meet you. You were working that night?"

"Yeah."

"Bet the cops spent some time talking to you, huh?"

Donnie rolled his eyes. "Hours. They took my clipboard from that night, kept asking me the same questions over and over again. Guess they thought that if they asked 'em enough times I'd give 'em a different answer."

"What did you tell them?"

"That Wednesday night, hardly anyone came through here 't all. Night was quieter than usual. Only folks comin' or goin' were residents…that and those people that came visitin' the Chadwick house at a little after midnight, God rest their poor souls. George Chadwick come through first, that night. Told me that two more couples were comin' up to his house for a visit."

"Oh?"

"Yeah, but you know something?"

"What?"

"I don't know what George was doing up at his place, but I don't think they were there for just a visit, know what I mean?"

I shrugged.

"He has a lot of parties up there."

"Parties?"

"Parties." Donnie winked.

"Yeah?"

"Oh, yeah." He used an appropriately conspiratorial whisper. "It's so quiet out here that I can hear 'em some nights. Drinkin', laughin', carrying on."

"Carrying on?" I thought about what Ted had told me last night about their swinging.

"Carrying on, doing things to each other. Most times they come off the island drunk as skunks. Sometimes, they don't come out 'til they've slept it off."

"What happened last Wednesday night?"

"I told the cops that after the last car went through, it got real quiet. And then I heard what I thought might be screaming."

"Screaming?"

Donnie whispered, holding up his hands. "Most times when I hear screaming its 'cause somebody's drunk and they're just having a good time."

"How about this time, Donnie? Did it sound like they were having a good time?"

He took a minute and looked at the ground. Then he looked up into my eyes. "This time it gave me the willies. But it was only for a minute or two and then it stopped. I wasn't sure what I heard and I couldn't say for sure where it had come from. Could have come from a boat out on the water, for all I knew."

"About what time was that?"

"Sometime after midnight, twelve-thirty, maybe."

That was the estimated time of the murders. And then the bodies weren't found for another seventeen hours. Nobody even knew they were dead, not until someone called the cops. Who, the killer? Did he have an attack of conscience? Who else would have called?

"You tell the cops this?"

He nodded to the affirmative.

"Did the cops ask you why you didn't call them when you heard the screaming?"

"Told them that I wasn't sure what I heard. And it only lasted just a real short time."

I looked back at the bridge again. It was low tide and the space between the mainland and the small island was little more than a tidal mud flat. Pointing, I asked, "Could somebody walk across that? Maybe cross over without you seeing them?"

"During low tide? It's possible, but you'd sink into the mud and silt right up to your waist. I've seen clammers out there in their hip boots. They come out of there a right old mess."

"But it's possible?"

"Yeah, it's possible," he shrugged. "But Wednesday night? When the police say those folks were killed? It was high tide. And the only way onto Connor's Landing at high tide is over this bridge or by boat."

By boat? I don't know why, but it hadn't occurred to me that the killer might have come in on a boat.

"Did you hear any boats that night?"

"Tell you the same thing I told the cops," he said slowly, his eyes looking a little sad. "I just can't recall. This here's an island.

You hear boats all the damned time. It's like living near an airport.
You kind of tune out the jets when they take off and land. With
me, it's the same with the boats. I don't hear 'em anymore. "

I sighed with disappointment.

"Anyways, if somebody's rowing in, *nobody's* gonna hear 'em."

I was pretty much out of questions so I thanked him, said my
good-byes, shook his hand, and walked back around the guard's
station. As I crawled back into the passenger's seat of the pickup,
Kevin turned to me. "So did you find out anything?"

"Not really. Mind if we drive by the Chadwick place?"

Connor's Landing has maybe thirty homes on it. Smuggler's
Road ran around the perimeter of the island with the most
expensive houses being on the waterfront. Out close to the
point, probably the most beautiful spot on the island, where
the harbor met the Sound, was where the Chadwicks had lived.

I recalled the house from a few nights ago when I'd stood
outside waiting for a quote from Mike Dillon. Even in the
dark, it was magnificent. But now, in the golden warmth of the
summer sunlight, it was breathtaking.

I'd done homework on its history for a sidebar to the murder
piece. Built in 1898, it originally belonged to Jonathan Hoyt,
owner of Sheffield Shipping and Receiving, a cargo company
that moved goods from New York and Boston to London.

In 1903, at nearly seventy years old, Hoyt died at sea during
a hurricane off the coast of Cuba.

I chalked it up to wanting to make one more trip to a sunny
location and being in the wrong place at the wrong time.

It was also the beginning of long string of bad luck for the
owners of that house.

Bartholomew Gault, a New York banker, bought the home
in 1910 when Hoyt's family went bankrupt. After installing
plumbing and electricity, he and his family lived comfortably on
Connor's Landing until the Great Depression wiped out Gault's
fortune. He drowned while fishing about six months after the
stock market crash. Rumors hinted at suicide.

Penniless, Gault's family left town, the bank took the over the estate and the house remained empty for nearly ten years, a home to raccoons, rats, and hobos.

In 1939 Carl Holden, the Broadway producer, bought the house and spent over a million dollars restoring it to its original grandeur.

Holden, best known for the musical *Paris Romance*, split his time between Manhattan and Connor's Landing until he died of a stroke in 1970. His grandson then lived in the house until George Chadwick purchased it ten years ago.

Holden's grandson was cursed with a lack of talent but was obsessed with Broadway. Many of the rooms were decorated with the actual props from famous plays and musicals: *42nd Street, Oklahoma, Who's Afraid of Virginia Wolf?, Streetcar Named Desire,* and of course *Paris Romance.* After he sold the house, it's said the grandson gave away all of his money to the Actor's Retirement Home and, ironically, died homeless during a particularly harsh winter a few years later.

And then George Chadwick bought it. Shortly after that, Chadwick's first wife, Brenda got fed up with George's unusual sexual predilections and filed for divorce and set up residence in the Virgin Islands. Okay, honestly, all I know for sure is the date of the divorce and where Brenda ended up.

The reason for the divorce, however, I'm guessing at. Not everyone likes the kinky life.

Two years after his divorce, George married Lynette. From a source that I can no longer locate, I was told that a few times a month, they're swingers.

The rest of the time, George Chadwick was a vice president of marketing and business development for Connecticut Sun Bank, the largest financial institution in the state. Even with that kind of position, George couldn't have afforded a house like this on Connor's Landing. His ten-million-dollar inheritance turned the trick.

Such a beautiful home. You have to wonder if George knew the house was cursed when he bought it, that he'd be one among a pile of bodies in a place that the cops called a slaughterhouse.

• • ● • •

As we drove by, I saw the house looming majestically behind the weathered stone wall that protected it from the rest of the world. Like last Thursday night, the wrought iron gate was open and I could see the perimeter of yellow police tape around the house, hanging limp in the heavy air. Two cop cars and an unmarked state police cruiser were easily visible in the driveway.

I'd heard from Phil Gilmartin that the forensic investigation wouldn't be completed until sometime on Monday. They were even draining the pool, looking for clues.

Kevin peered out of the driver's side window of his truck as we drove by. "Kind of creepy."

"Multiple murders are hell on property values."

He drove on. The address we wanted was only a couple of houses down the road.

While the Chadwick home was rich in history, the Elroy place was just the opposite. Hidden behind a ten-foot tall, wooden fence the two-story combination of contemporary and traditional was a stylish amalgamation of angles, redwood beams, and glass. A recent construction, it opened indoor and outdoor spaces to a southern exposure and the sweeping vista of the horizon, the water, and of small boats cruising over Long Island Sound.

Not much history here but there *was* new money.

Becky Elroy answered the door. She was dressed in what I call shabby chic—a light green, extra-large tee shirt that hung rakishly off one shoulder and a pair of denim shorts. Her dark hair was pulled back into a ponytail. She welcomed Kevin with enthusiasm and led us into the kitchen that, to my amazement, was nearly the size of my entire apartment. Sub-Zero, stainless steel appliances that were large enough to serve a good-sized restaurant, dominated the room. A young Hispanic woman in black shorts and white shirt ignored us, intent on chopping vegetables and mixing a sauce for barbeque chicken.

Mrs. Elroy and Kevin left me on my own and the two of them slowly strolled off to review his written estimate and timeline for the project. Knocking out a wall for a breakfast nook over here, hanging track lighting up there, installing eco-friendly recycled-glass countertops right over here, laying down Italian marble for the floors right there, and don't forget the custom backsplash, complete with genuine fossil imprints from the Jurassic era behind the sinks.

While they talked, I soaked in the view through the sliding glass door. The backyard embraced a half-acre of green shrubs and an eye-popping array of flowers, along with a koi pond, natural rock waterfall, and swimming pool. Beyond that, tethered to a long wooden dock, was a forty-two-foot powerboat floating lazily on the smooth, sparkling surface of Long Island Sound.

A half- dozen young men in swimming trunks and an equal number of anorexic young ladies in tiny bikinis played in the pool, tossing a soccer ball around, splashing and laughing. A dozen beer cans lined the edge of the pool. On the tables, under wide beach umbrellas, there was a wide selection of bottles and half-filled glasses.

I glanced at my watch. It was about three in the afternoon. Not quite happy hour, but obviously close enough for this crowd.

"Hi," said a voice behind me.

I turned to meet a man in his early fifties, with luminescent green eyes and light brown hair starting to turn gray around his temples. He was dressed in a red polo shirt and gray shorts. He was smiling at me and holding a plate of steaks. "I'm Pete," he announced quietly.

"Genie Chase, I'm with the contractor over there." I jerked my thumb in the direction of Kevin and Mrs. Elroy.

He'd noticed that I was watching the party outside. "Makes you want to be young and carefree again, doesn't it?"

"I'd settle for young and wearing one of those bikinis. Who are they?" I tipped my head in the direction of the pool.

"My boys and their friends. The one getting out of the pool over there? That's my oldest, Lance. He's a sophomore at Yale this year."

"Good looking kid." I wasn't kidding. He was about nineteen, a spitting image of dad, and didn't look to have a single ounce of fat on a body that was lean, tight, and solid muscle.

"And that young man playing video games under the cabana, that's Drew. He's a senior at the Handley Academy."

"I'm not sure I'm familiar with that." I picked the boy out of the crowd. Drew was as tall as his brother but larger, more muscular. He was broad-shouldered and from the looks of his chest and biceps, spent some time working out in the gym. His hair was cut short and he wasn't as handsome as his brother. Drew's face was a little too flat and his eyes too far apart. But that didn't seem to matter. Even though women in tiny thongs were cavorting mere feet from where he sat, his concentration was exclusively on the laptop on the table in front of him.

"Handley's a private school over in Greenwich," Pete Elroy announced proudly. "Graduating from Handley is guaranteed to make your kid an Ivy League candidate. Lance graduated from Handley two years ago. He was accepted by Harvard and Princeton before finally deciding on pre-law at Yale."

"Looks like quite a party."

"The boys have earned it. They both have summer jobs working as deck hands on the Sheffield Harbor Association ferry boat. Doesn't pay a lot, but it's honest work and that's the important thing, isn't it? It's a learning experience."

I looked around this spread. The beauty, the opulence, the excess, the carefree atmosphere—it was like something out of *The Great Gatsby*.

And just up the street? The Chadwick mansion stood as a testament that death can bring it all down in a sickening heartbeat.

Pete moved past me and slid open the glass door out to the deck. I could feel the hot, humid air from outside sneaking in around the air conditioning.

"Were you home Wednesday night?" I asked, too abruptly perhaps, but I didn't want to lose the opportunity.

He stopped dead and avoided looking at me, staring out at the pool instead. "Why do you ask?"

"Just nosy." I wasn't going to tell him that I'm a reporter. It's not good ethics, but what the hell. "It's a scary thing. Six people murdered in a house just down the street. Did you know the owners?"

He looked at me curiously. "We didn't know them at all. I wouldn't recognize either one of them if I saw them on the street. They never came to any of the Home Owners' Association meetings and, frankly, this isn't the kind of neighborhood where you stop by for a cup of coffee and trade gossip over the fence."

"Kind of spooky that nobody saw or heard anything."

He smiled now, filled with condescension, like he was explaining something to an idiot. "Lance and Drew were at a party that night, a friend's house in Greenwich. Becky and I stayed up until they got home around eleven. We had a late night snack and we were all in bed by midnight. We didn't hear a thing."

I nodded as if I understood.

"That's why we live out here on Connor's Landing. We mind our own business," he stated with finality, then walked outside and slid the glass door closed behind him.

It was Pete Elroy's way of telling me to do the same thing.

Chapter Fourteen

After Becky Elroy gave Kevin the deposit check, she politely offered us a cocktail before we left. The implication, of course, was that we'd have one drink and then be on our way. Don't stay for dinner, don't stay for a second helping of booze, and for God's sake, don't stay and talk to the guests. After all, now that she'd given Kevin money, we were paid help.

She told us, in addition to rewarding the Elroy brothers for getting summer jobs, they were preparing for a small party in honor of one of the partners in Pete's law firm. The partner had been appointed by the White House to be a legal advisor to the Environmental Protection Agency. They needed another high-powered, overpaid legal eagle to help them suck oil and drag the last of the trees out of our national wildlife refuges. You can't have too many lawyers or too few environmentalists for that sort of thing.

Indeed, as Kevin and I poured ourselves drinks in the back-yard bar, three couples about our age came out of the house and onto to the back lawn. Dressed in khakis, polo shirts, designer shorts, expensive jeans and deck shoes, they were all trying hard to appear casually chic as well as "barbeque-comfortable." Pete Elroy greeted them warmly, inviting them to take a look at his brand new, stainless steel gas grill, a shiny monster large enough to charbroil filet mignon for most of the Third World, should Pete decide to do so.

Seeing that their space was being invaded, Lance, Drew, and their nearly naked coterie of young friends quickly quieted down and clustered around several tables in the far corner of the pool area. They broke out a couple of decks of cards and started playing a little Texas Hold 'Em.

I'm guessing that all they wanted to do was stay out of the way of mom and dad's friends, get quietly drunk, smoke a little grass, and then leave to have mind-blowing sex someplace where the old folks weren't drinking martinis.

Kevin and I silently agreed that we should have our drinks and stay inconspicuous. We wandered out to the dock to look over the forty-two-foot powerboat and enjoy the unobstructed view of Long Island Sound.

"So how much did you get?" I crassly wondered about the size of his deposit check.

"Twenty thousand." With a big smile, he patted the pocket of his ubiquitous work shirt.

My eyebrows shot up in appreciation. "How much is the whole job costing them?"

"About eight times that." Then before I had a chance to say anything, he stepped up close, swept me up into his strong arms, and kissed me.

It might have been the sound of the water licking at the edges of the dock, it might have been the salty, pungent scent of the sea air, or it might have been the sweet, slow reggae song that Pete had just put on the CD player. It might have been the warm sunlight sparkling like diamonds on the surface of the Sound. Or it might have been that phenomenal kiss. All I know is that I melted into his body like a pat of warm butter left out in the summer sunshine. My hand reached behind his head to hold him closer, my breasts pressed hard against his chest, my hips tight against his. Right at that moment, I wanted to be so close to him that we'd never come apart.

When we finally broke for air, I heard him take a slow breath, clear his throat and say, "You know...I might be falling in love with you."

You know…I might be falling in love with you.

I kept repeating the words over and over in my head.

I'm not a kid anymore. This shouldn't happen to me, but my heart was beating so hard against my ribcage that I thought *he'd* feel it. All I could say was, "What?"

Oh, I'd heard him all right. I wanted him to say it again.

And he did. "Look, I know we've only been together a couple of days but I've known you all of my life, ever since we were kids. I've always loved you. I just didn't know it for sure until now."

Every woman wants to find her "soul mate." Every woman wants to find her hero. After three failed marriages and a long string of miserable relationships, I'm not completely stupid. I know what love really means. It means convenience, compatibility, an element of trust, good conversation, fun, and sex, if you can get it.

Not necessarily in that order or all at the same time with the same person.

I learned a long time ago that love doesn't mean a knight on a white charger, a lifetime with Prince Charming, or fairy tale magic. Sometimes the best love comes from a close friend. It comes from someone you truly like.

And I liked Kevin a lot.

I looked into his eyes. They were smiling at me.

I put my hand on his cheek and quietly replied, "I love you too."

Then we celebrated by kissing once more, this time with unbridled passion.

When we broke apart again I felt myself breathing hard. He placed his forehead against mine. "So what do we do now?" he whispered.

"Is it too early to go to bed?"

"That wasn't what I was thinking about."

I blinked and shook my head. "I know, I was just kidding," I lied. I wanted him so bad I could already taste him. I wanted to hold his body close to mine and never let him go.

"Look, I know I asked you to have a drink over at the boat club, but I also promised to take you and Caroline out for

Mexican. Margaritas are sounding real good to me. How about we go our separate ways for a few hours and then we hook back up at my place around seven?"

I couldn't stop looking into his beautiful blue eyes. "Okay."

"And after we eat, maybe we can drop Caroline off at her aunt's and then have a nightcap at your place?"

"Okay." I was on an incredible emotional high, supplemented of course by a vodka buzz. We walked back up the dock, across the perfectly manicured yard, past the waterfall, and onto the blue-green tiles that defined the perimeter of the pool.

"I'd better say good-bye to the Elroys," Kevin said.

I let him wander off to look for our hosts, after which we would drive away in Kevin's beat-up truck. It wasn't a white charger, but it was plenty good enough for me.

"Genie," purred a familiar voice behind me. "What a nice surprise."

My heart nearly stopped cold in my chest.

I turned. It wasn't a nice surprise at all. For the second time in less than twenty-four hours, I was looking right into Frank Mancini's chocolate brown eyes. "Jesus." I felt slightly off-balance. He was literally the last person I expected, or wanted, to run into. "I don't see you for over a month and then every time I turn around, you're right there. You're like a skin rash I can't get rid of."

Frank stepped up close to me with a smirk. "I guess it's fate." He was dressed in khaki shorts and a black polo shirt with the name of his boat emblazoned in red on the pocket, *Renegade*. "How do you know the Elroys?"

I don't know why I was surprised to see Frank there. He's a lawyer; Pete Elroy's a lawyer. Piranhas swim in schools.

"I'm here with a friend." I looked around, oddly relieved that Kevin wasn't standing next to me. After all, I'd slept with Frank last night and, only minutes ago, told Kevin that I love him. I don't hide guilt well.

Frank squinted out over the Sound, trying to recall what Kevin looked like. "Is it the guy you were with the other night at the Shorefront Club?"

"Yeah."

"Is he an attorney?" Frank asked.

"No, he has a real job."

Frank blinked and smiled. He takes a verbal punch pretty well.

"Are you here with Evelyn?"

"She's still in the Hamptons."

"Here alone?"

He shook his head. "Remember that client from last night? The one I dumped to spend time with you?"

"Sure, the bimbo with long blond hair and the boob job."

"Jill," he said. "Her name is Jill. I'm working on a probate case for her."

"I'll bet you are. You like women and probate cases." I looked across the patio until I spotted Kevin. He was talking to Pete Elroy, who was still obviously bragging about his grill. In the meantime, I was getting ready to call an end to this particular conversation. "So where is Jill?"

"Inside," he answered. "Bathroom."

I grabbed a crabcake off a tray as a young man in a white shirt came by with hors d'oeuvres. "Wish I could stay and chat, but I've got a life."

Frank frowned and grabbed me by the hand. "Stay for a minute. Have another drink."

I swallowed the crabcake and washed it down with the final swallows of my vodka. "The last thing I need to do is have another drink with *you*, Frank," I snarled as quietly as I could.

I noticed that the crowd on the patio was growing. There must have been thirty people now, not counting the Elroy boys and their friends. I tried to locate Kevin again, but couldn't find him. Had he gone inside to say good-bye to Becky?

"Why do you say that?" Frank asked.

"Frank, I really don't want to get into it here with you, but I think it's time we break it off."

If I'd expected to see a shocked expression on his face, I was sorely disappointed. He sipped his glass of wine and continued to gaze at me, as if he was studying a witness in a courtroom. "Have I done something to upset you?"

"Look, I've found something in Kevin that I really need, something that I've been looking for my entire life."

"Something I can't give you?" he remarked, dryly.

"Frank, you were a pleasurable distraction. A genuine ride on the Tilt-a-Whirl. But I'm done. I'd like to get my life back on track and it ain't gonna be with you."

"So we're done?"

I sighed. "Yeah, we're done."

"Then what was last night, a good-bye fuck?"

When he said it, I could hear the proverbial pin drop. The song on the CD player had just ended, conversation had hit an unnatural lull, and you couldn't hear any boats out on the Sound.

I was sure that the entire crowd on the patio heard what Frank said.

And from the profoundly hurt expression on his face, when I turned and saw him, I was certain that Kevin had.

He'd been standing right behind me.

Frank knew that. He'd watched as Kevin had walked up behind me.

A waiter came by with a silver tray of crystal flutes filled with champagne. I picked one up and threw the contents into Frank's face. Then I picked up a second one, put it to my lips and drank it one long gulp.

Before I was done, Kevin was already headed for his truck.

I looked back at Frank, who'd found a napkin to wipe his face. I hissed, "Asshole."

"You'll be back."

● ● ● ● ●

When I got there, Kevin was already sitting in his truck, staring absently at the steering wheel.

I stopped when I was about ten feet away to study him. The way he sat in the truck by himself thinking about what he'd just heard broke my heart.

I felt a malignant lump of sorrow swell in my throat. This might to be the shortest long-term relationship of my life. Kevin was hurt. And damn it, damn it all to fucking hell, I'd caused it.

Running into Frank last night, then seeing him again a few minutes ago, what was that? Random action that happens on its own? A bizarre coincidence? Or is it like Frank said? Fate? A perverse, twisted act of fate?

Why was God doing this to me? Was this some kind of karmic joke?

Or worse, had I done it to myself?

I walked around to the passenger's side and slid into the truck. Kevin started the engine without saying anything.

We rode in painful, awkward silence past the guard, his head down as he read one of his mystery novels in his tiny outpost, and across the bridge to the mainland. We never said a word as we took the back roads into Kevin's neighborhood, turned onto Random Road, and then into his driveway.

It wasn't until Kevin turned off the engine that I said, "I was drunk and stupid. I'm sorry."

How many times in my life have I said that?

Still sitting in the silent Ford, he shook his head. "It's not like we're married."

"I know. I'm still sorry."

He sighed, opened the door, and slid out of the truck.

I did the same and started walking slowly toward my Sebring, resigned that our relationship was dead before it had even really started.

Then Kevin said something that I couldn't quite make out.

I turned. I wasn't sure I wanted to hear what he'd just said, but I asked anyway, "What?"

His words were clearer, stronger, but it was obvious he was working to find a normal voice, "Still want to have dinner?"

I stopped in my tracks and took a step closer. "Dinner?"

"Yeah, do you want to come by and pick us up for dinner around seven?" He held up a hand to shade his eyes from the sun. He was struggling hard to make things okay.

I can't tell you what that tidal wave of relief felt like. I couldn't believe it. "Still feeling like margaritas?" My voice cracked with emotion, feeling tears of happiness welling up in my eyes and overflowing onto my cheeks.

He nodded and smiled gamely. "Yeah, hey?"

"What?" I was wiping tears away from my cheeks.

"Did you mean what you said back there?"

"Which part?"

"That you love me?"

I nodded and felt a fist sized lump in my throat. "Yeah, I love you." I managed to whisper, afraid that I was going to cry some more.

He offered a wan smile. "Don't sleep with Frank anymore, okay?"

I nodded again. "Okay."

He turned and I watched as he walked up his steps and into his house. I saw, but barely noticed, how he'd been sweating. His forehead had been slick with perspiration.

I hadn't taken serious note of any of it. I was too busy congratulating myself on my luck. I was too busy thinking that this was the guy I wanted to spend the rest of my life with.

Besotted, I was blissfully unaware of the nightmare that still lay ahead. For the first time in a long while, it felt like I was on course and Kevin was the reason why. I had no way of knowing that the two of us were headed into the dark winds of a lethal hurricane.

Chapter Fifteen

Driving away, I was a limp rag, twisted tight until every drop of energy was wrung out of me. It had been one hell of a Sunday and it was still only four o'clock in the afternoon.

Naturally, I wanted a drink.

The nail-biting tension and wild windstorm of emotion that had blown through the last forty-five minutes of my life had all but scoured away my pleasant vodka buzz from the Elroys' barbeque from hell. I considered driving down to the Sea View Tavern for an icy Absolute, but noticed that I was nearing Wolf-pit Avenue, Jim Brenner's street.

Less than twenty-four hours earlier, I'd been sitting in a bar listening to Ted, my source who drove away in the night, accuse Brenner of killing six people. I had another attack of guilt. Last night I should have gone to Mike Dillon and told him what I knew. Every minute that the cops didn't investigate this guy was another minute he had an opportunity to destroy evidence.

And every minute I didn't interview him was another minute lost on writing a great story.

That little bit of guilt about not talking to the cops quickly vanished. I wasn't supposed to do their job. I was supposed to do mine.

Pulling up to the front of his house, I noticed that the same Chevy Tahoe parked in the driveway last night was still there. It was gleaming black, newly washed and detailed. Shining in the afternoon sunlight, *Brenner's Auto Body* was emblazoned on the doors.

Next to the SUV sat a candy-apple red Mustang. Ted had told me that Lynette thought that she'd been stalked by her ex-husband in a Mustang.

Behind the Mustang, a pale blue Taurus station wagon was parked. From the mud spatters and obvious neglect, the vehicle appeared well-used but ill-maintained. The back bumper sported a bumper sticker—"God is Watching You."

A twenty-foot fishing boat covered with a tarp sat on a trailer next to the garage. Since I'd talked to the guard out on Connor's Landing, the boat had taken on a new significance. Had it been in the water on Wednesday night?

How would I find out?

I parked at the curb and studied the house. With its trimmed lawn and tidy sidewalk and shrubs, it all seemed normal enough. Not the sort of place where a vicious killer might lay his head.

Taking a deep breath, I did my best to forget the unpleas-antness with Frank Mancini on Connor's Landing. I had to get my head back on straight. Other media outlets were out there circling like hungry jackals. I needed to keep my ownership of this story.

I grabbed my bag, checked inside for my recorder and can of mace. Then I walked boldly up to the front door and pressed the bell.

Out of the corner of my eye, I noticed that the curtain to the living room window twitched, as if someone was checking me out surreptitiously through the window. Then a moment later, the door swung open.

"Can I help you?" a man asked. He was about five-ten, his shaved skull shining dully in the sunshine. He wore a closely cropped salt-and-pepper beard, and he studied me with blue eyes so light in color that they reminded me of polar ice.

Where had I seen him before?

"I'm Geneva Chase. I work for *The Sheffield Post*. Are you Jim Brenner?"

He didn't react like I'd anticipated. I'd expected suspicion, reticence or downright hostility. Instead he blinked. "For a minute I thought you might be a detective."

"Why?"

"I'm expecting their return."

"The police have been here?"

He squinted at me, cocking his head, not quite sure if I was putting him on. "Of course they have. In a homicide, the first person the police suspect is the husband."

"Or in this case, the ex-husband," I extrapolated. "Are you Jim Brenner?"

He shook his head. "I'm his brother, Aaron. And just for the record, I'm *Reverend* Aaron Brenner. Would you like to come in?"

I debated the wisdom of walking into Jim Brenner's house without letting anyone from my office know where I was. I had that tiny can of mace in my bag, and I also was sure that if anything happened, it would be pretty damned useless in keeping me alive. I don't pride myself on reckless courage and I don't normally put myself in a dangerous situation, but I needed this story. I didn't want to be working the cop beat in Sheffield for the rest of my life.

Walking into the house past Reverend Aaron Brenner, I noticed that he didn't look like most other men of God. He was lean, muscular, and dressed in khaki shorts and a faded gray tee shirt with the sleeves cut off. It didn't take a genius to surmise that the primitively etched tattoos on his shoulders were probably from a stint in prison. One of the tats proclaimed, "Vengeance is Mine, sayeth the Lord." The other tattoo right under it was a blue and scarlet stone cross, painted against a patch of dark purple clouds laced with lightning bolts. From the impressive size of his shoulders and biceps, I deduced that he'd spent a lot of his time working out in the prison gym.

"What church are you affiliated with, Mr. Brenner?"

"Reverend Brenner," he reminded me. "But you can call me Aaron. The United Christ's Church of Freewill."

I searched my memory. "I don't think I've ever heard of it."

He didn't bother to respond to my remark, but motioned me to follow him.

In the dark living room I could see a cloth couch, a leather recliner and a large flat screen television mounted on the wall. The walls were devoid of art and all the end tables had stacks of magazines and newspapers piled on top. This was a place that sorely needed some TLC.

I saw the indistinct figure of Jim Brenner across the room, outlined against bright sunlight, standing in the wide sliding-glass doorway leading to a back deck. He was like a shadow, gazing out into the backyard, his arms crossed in front of him.

From what little I could see, he was standing in what might be the only source of light in the whole house.

The curtains were drawn tight across the rest of the windows in the living room. The furthest corners lay in darkness. There was a faint odor of mildew. From my vantage point, I could see into the kitchen. The blinds in there were closed as well and I could barely make out the refrigerator and stove sitting heavily against the far wall in the shadows; green, red, and blue lights from the appliances glowed like lonely stars in an empty universe. I felt like I was in a tunnel and the proverbial light at the end of it was where Jim Brenner stood facing away from me.

I struggled with a brief bout of *déjà vu*. Earlier in the day I'd been in a place very much like this, Kevin's bedroom. It struck me that Kevin and Jim Brenner could be very similar—both hiding, both living in darkness. They had both lost their wives. Cancer had claimed Kevin's. A more grisly death had claimed Jim Brenner's.

"Jim, this is Geneva Chase," Aaron announced. "She's a reporter with *The Sheffield Post*."

Jim turned and looked at me.

That's when I recognized him. He was the speaker at the AA meeting on Thursday night, the same night I got the call about the murders on Connor's Landing.

What was it he'd said? That he wanted to hurt his wife and he wanted to hurt the man she married?

Then the paranoia set in.

Do I smell bourbon?

Jim had been staring out into the backyard. He took a moment to let his eyes adjust to the diminished light of his house. Then he stepped forward with an outstretched arm.

As I reached out and shook his hand, I could feel the strength in his grip and see the broadness of his shoulders. He wasn't much taller than me, but he occupied almost twice as much space.

How had Ted described him? Like a linebacker?

My heart skipped a beat when I saw he had a glass in his other hand.

"How can I help you?" he asked in a low, husky voice.

Unlike his brother, Jim Brenner had a full head of dark hair. His face was clean-shaven but from what I could make out in the shadows, he had the ruddy color of a man who'd spent a good deal of his life as a drinker. Jim's eyes were blue like his brother's but less like ice and more like sky. And they were marred with the glassy red rawness of someone who was crying.

Or drinking.

He attempted a disingenuous smile marred by a chipped front tooth that glinted in the scant light.

"First of all, I'd like to say how sorry I am for your loss," I said.

"Thank you."

"Would it be okay if I asked you some questions?"

"Sure," he said. "Would you like something to drink?" He held up his own glass.

"No, thank you."

Aaron was still standing by my side as he shrugged his shoulders and said, "I'm going fix myself something. If you change your mind, let me know."

Jim watched his brother disappear into the kitchen. "Would you like to sit down?" He gestured toward the sofa behind me.

Is he slurring his words or am I imagining it?

I hesitated before I sat down. "Does your brother live with you?"

Jim placed his glass on an end table and sat down in a recliner, leaning slightly forward, his hands resting on the tops of his legs. "No, Aaron lives in Maine in a place called Darwin. It's a tiny little town. He's got a church there."

"Been there a long time?" How was I going to get around to asking about his time in prison?

"Couple of years."

Aaron stepped back into the doorway. He'd apparently been listening to us and surmised where I was heading. "Before moving to Maine, I spent a few years at Garner for insurance fraud. I was stupid. But out of adversity comes opportunity. When I was in prison, I found the glory of Christ. And if I hadn't found the Lord, I'm not sure how we would have gotten through all of this."

"Our faith is what's keeping us going, Miss Chase." Jim sounded tired.

"Aaron said the police have already been here?"

"They talked to me and Aaron for a couple of hours. The first person suspected in a murder is usually the husband." He pointed to himself with his thumb.

"Aaron said he was expecting the police to come back. If the police were already here, why would they come back?"

Jim shrugged but didn't answer.

"How did you first meet Lynette?"

He looked up at the ceiling for a moment, finding the scene in his head. "She was raising money for the Women's Crisis Center. She came to my garage to see if I'd be a sponsor for some event they were having."

He smiled. "I told her that I would if she'd let me buy her a cup of coffee. The coffee cost me less than a buck. That sponsorship cost me five hundred dollars. But it was worth it. We started dating and we were married a year later."

"No children?"

He shook his head. "Docs said she couldn't have kids."

"Were you disappointed?"

He shrugged. "I always thought I'd make a pretty good dad."

I held my digital recorder in my lap. "How would you describe your marriage?"

His head dropped a bit. "I thought it was good. But Lynette was complicated. She had two sides. Her good side, she was always out there raising money for somebody—the United Way, March of Dimes, you name it, she was out there."

I glanced over at Aaron who was standing in the doorway, nodding in agreement. "Deep down, she had a really good heart."

I noticed that Aaron was now holding a glass.

What was *he* drinking?

Jim continued, "But she had another side. I think maybe it was why we got along so well, at least at first. I liked to party and so did she. We worked hard and we played hard. Both of us put away a lot of booze. Trouble is, I do stupid things when I drink."

That's what he'd said at AA.

"Did you ever hit her?"

He sighed. "Not at first."

"Not at first?"

He doubled up his hands into fists and then opened them again, letting them rest on his knees. "After the first time, I told her I'd never do it again."

"But you did, didn't you?"

He nodded.

Aaron took a seat next to me on the couch and turned to me. "Are you sure I can't get you something, Miss Chase?" He held up his own glass as an example.

I could feel sweat start to trail down my ribcage and my heart pump harder in my chest.

Was coming here a mistake?

I nodded toward the glass in Jim's hand. "Is that bourbon?"

Jim held the glass up in a toast he took a healthy swallow.

I looked Aaron in the eye. "Jim's in AA. Is that a good idea?"

He smiled and took a swallow from his own glass. "We're home. I'm here to watch out for him. You should be able to relax in your own home, don't you think?"

I don't like the way this is going.

I focused back on Jim. "When did Lynette leave you?"

"When she knew that I'd never stop drinking."

"You go to AA. Hasn't that helped?"

"Hasn't seemed to." He squinted. "I remember you, now. You were at the meeting. Your cell phone went off."

"Always nice to make an impression."

Aaron spoke up. "How long have you been sober, Ms. Chase?"

"About a month," I lied.

"Most times, someone from AA can tell you the exact date when they stopped drinking. Do you remember the date when you stopped?"

I needed to get back on point and then get the hell out of there. "Any idea who might have killed Lynette?"

Jim shook his head. "Did you know that she was having sex with multiple partners?"

"That's a dangerous way to live," Aaron added.

"So she was having sex with people other than George Chadwick, her husband? How do you know?"

"It's a small town." Jim swirled the bourbon and ice around in his glass.

I had to get this done and get out. "Tell me about last Wednesday."

Jim stared at me with angry, red eyes. "Wednesday should've been our tenth anniversary. I didn't go into work that day. Instead I got up and watched our wedding video." He shook his head. "That was stupid."

"Then he called me," Aaron said. "I could hear by his voice that he was in trouble so I hopped in my car and drove down so that I could be with him. I was planning on coming down anyway. I always try to be here on their anniversary."

"So you were here all day? You spent the entire day here in the house?"

Jim shook his head. "Sometime around ten in the morning, I drove down to the liquor store and picked up a bottle of Jack. I sat right there in the parking lot and took a couple of good sized hits. And that's when I saw her drive by."

"Who?"

"Lynette, behind the wheel of her fancy new Lincoln Navigator."

"What did you do?"

I watched him bite at his lip. "I followed her."

"Were you driving your Mustang?"

He nodded.

"How long did you follow her for?"

"A couple of hours, she got her hair done, did some window shopping in Westport, went to the Stop-n-Shop. And then she went home."

"What did you do next?"

"Then I came home and I waited for Aaron."

Aaron spoke up, "I got here about six-thirty that night and at that point, Jim was already passed out on the couch. He woke up around ten so I made him some dinner and then we prayed together."

"So you were here the entire evening?"

"Yes, ma'am," Jim said quietly.

"You were here all night? You didn't see Lynette at all?"

"We were here." Jim's eyes narrowed and his voice dropped to almost a low, malicious whisper. "Why, did you hear something different?"

What the hell was I thinking? I was in a dark house with two men, one or both of whom might be killers and they were sitting there getting hammered right in front of me. My heart thumped away at my ribcage in a swift drumbeat of escalating fear.

"No." I didn't sound convincing. "No, I just want to be accurate."

"We were here, Miss Chase," Aaron confirmed.

"Is that what you told the police?"

"Why would we tell them anything different?" His voice was almost a snarl. He picked up his glass, took a big swallow, then tapped the bottom of it against the top of the end table with irritation.

This was stupid. Go.

"Of course, you wouldn't." I put my recorder back in my bag and stood up. "Gentlemen, once again, let me tell you how sorry I am. You've been very helpful."

They both stood up. "Thanks," Jim mumbled. "Stop by anytime."

Aaron smiled at me, "I'm sure we'll be seeing each other again."

Holy Jesus, not if I can help it.

• • ● • •

The air outside Jim Brenner's home was oppressive, the epitome of hot, hazy, and humid. But I was thrilled to be in the sunshine and away from that house.

Were the Brenners lying to me?

Was my source lying?

Somebody wasn't telling the truth. I expected it was the Brenners. They were anticipating a return visit from the cops. They knew that sooner or later, the police would find out about the confrontation at the sex club.

I looked down at the shirt I was wearing. It was soaked with sweat, sticking to me like a second skin. I was thankful that I'd decided to put on a bra this morning.

If I hadn't wanted a drink before, I wanted one now.

Once inside my car, I reached into my bag for my cell phone. I intended to call Mike Dillon and tell him what I knew. As I drove away, I noticed again how pristine and shiny the Tahoe looked. It had been recently cleaned and I'm betting that it was *thoroughly* cleaned.

And then I wondered about the boat. Had that been washed and detailed as well?

What in hell would Mike Dillon find now that the Brenners have had a chance to get rid of evidence? But the cops had already been there and were apparently satisfied with their alibi.

Pulling up to a red light, I saw that there was a message on my phone. Hitting the code, I held the receiver up to my ear and listened.

As hot as the afternoon was, the message chilled me to the bone.

I heard Kevin's daughter, Caroline, as she said in a voice that was cracking with emotion and clearly afraid. *"Hi, Genie. I thought you should know that right after you left, Dad got really sick. I called 911 and they took him to the hospital!"*

Chapter Sixteen

The first time I'd ever been in an emergency room was when I was fourteen years old, waiting with my mom while three doctors and four nurses did the best they could to sew my father back into one piece. It's what happens when a man slides under an eighteen-wheeler going sixty miles an hour on his motorcycle.

It'd happened near the Westport exit on I-95 when a Saab abruptly changed lanes forcing a truck to slam on its brakes. The truck jackknifed. My father was right behind as the eighteen-wheeler twisted and careened out of control, metal against metal screaming in overheated agony, tires and axles disintegrating under cataclysmic, kinetic stress. Dad tried to avoid disaster but his synapses had fired way too late. The bike ditched and he skidded along the highway on his side, sliding in a cloud of sparks under the moving, buckling truck trailer until he was on the other side, and lying in a bloody heap in the breakdown lane.

But for fate, the truck should have crushed my old man. The cops said it was a miracle that he was still alive when they'd found him.

The spectacle might have been visually impressive, but it left my father with two broken legs, a punctured lung, a ruptured spleen, a mangled arm and shoulder, a fractured skull, a sliced aorta, and only faint heartbeats away from death.

My mother and I stayed in the ER for seven hours straight, waiting to see if my old man would live or die. I'm not sure, but I think it's the last time in my life that I ever prayed for anything.

I bargained with God with everything I had. If God would just let my dad live, I'd give every dime I ever earned to the church, I'd read the Bible from cover to cover, I'd build schools in Africa, I'd become a freaking nun.

At some point, after a hellish night, just before dawn, I looked up from where I was sitting, uncomfortably dozing in a hard plastic chair, and saw young Kevin Bell standing in front of me. He'd hiked five miles from his house to the hospital. His hair was matted, water dripped off his face, and his windbreaker and jeans were soaked through to his skin. He'd walked all that way in a driving thunderstorm.

He'd walked all that way just for me.

We hugged each really tight. I remember that I started to cry and couldn't stop. We sat next to each other in those hard plastic chairs for hours, Kevin holding my hand the whole time. I don't know why, but feeling his warm skin on mine helped take my fear away. He was my best friend.

My dad died on the operating table.

Since then, I've been in and out of a lot of emergency rooms. It's usually part of some story I'm working on. I try to stay detached, but I've never been able to shake the feeling that Death was sitting there in one of those waiting room seats. You couldn't see him, but he was always there.

Life was in the ER, too, but she was in where the action was, working with the doctors and nurses.

I suspect that when Death decides it's time to take someone, he walks into one of the cubicles where the doctors are struggling to keep someone's heart beating. Then, even though Life has put up a good fight, Death slides her off to one side. He smiles his skeletal grin, inexorably embraces the patient with his long cold arms, and bestows a final, icy kiss.

I don't like emergency rooms because, in the end, you can't negotiate, bribe, or trick Death into leaving you or a loved one alone. When it's your time, it's your time.

• • ● • •

The emergency room waiting area had changed a lot since I was fourteen. It had become more "friendly." The chairs were certainly more comfortable than I recalled. There was a flat-screen TV on one of the walls. There were toys for small children in a brightly colored plastic box on the floor.

But the magazines were still out of date, which made me really nervous.

When I got there, a half dozen people in twos and threes were sitting quietly around the room.

Caroline was seated alone in a corner. She was staring out a window that overlooked a courtyard.

"Hey, honey," I said. "How's your dad?"

She turned and looked up at me. I could see the red rims around her eyes. Her face seemed even thinner and paler than before. Caroline looked absolutely haunted. "I don't know." Her voice turned high and squeaky. Then her lips quivered, her face reddened, and she hid her tears behind a crushed-up ball of over-used tissue.

I leaned down and put my arms around her shoulders. She stood up and we hugged each other, much like what her father had done for me so many years before.

Just this morning, Kevin had told me that Caroline hadn't cried since her mom died. He'd thought that maybe his daughter had been squeezed dry, that Joanna's death had left the girl in a permanent state of shock.

But here she was, sobbing uncontrollably in my arms.

I knew what she was afraid of. She'd already lived through the tragedy of losing her mother. Being in an emergency room again for her dad was plain horrifying. Death wasn't a stranger to this little girl.

I dried her eyes with another ball of used tissue, but this one I found at the bottom of my bag. "What happened, honey?"

She swallowed. "Right after you left this afternoon, Dad came into the house and fixed himself a drink. He and I talked a little bit about how you guys had gone out to Connor's Landing to pick up a deposit check. He showed it to me, he was really proud.

He said to keep an eye on the time because we were going to Poco Loco for dinner in a couple of hours. But all the while he was talking to me, I could see sweat was dripping off his forehead.

"I asked him if he wanted me to turn up the air conditioner. But he shook his head, wiped his face with a paper towel and then took his drink into the living room. I'd stayed in the kitchen to get some ice water from the refrigerator when I heard him fall."

I felt fear clutch at the hairs on the back of my neck. "He fell?"

She slowly nodded. "I ran in and saw him struggling to get up off the floor. He couldn't get to his feet. His face was really red and all scrunched up like he was in a lot of pain. He had one hand over his stomach like it was hurting really bad, so I took his other hand and tried to help him, but he couldn't straighten up. He let go of me and just lay on the floor, groaning. I dialed 911. He kept trying to tell me not to call an ambulance, that he was okay. He just needed a few minutes and the pain in his stomach would go away."

"But it didn't."

"It always has in the past, but not this time," Caroline whispered.

"This has happened before? Has he seen a doctor?"

That was when I realized that Aunt Ruth was standing behind me. "Kevin hasn't been to a doctor in years," she stated flatly.

I spun to see her staring at me with an expression of both disdain and fear.

"Hi," I offered, not knowing what else to say.

"To answer your question," Ruth said, "yes, this has happened before. But it's never been this severe."

Caroline explained, "He gets the sweats and really bad pains in his stomach, sometimes so bad that he goes to bed and stays there for hours until it goes away."

"But he hasn't seen a doctor?"

Ruth told me what I should have known anyway. "He has health insurance but it's at some insane deductible."

I felt ashamed at the simplicity of her answer. "But there are free clinics," I argued. "He could have come into the emergency room. By law they have to treat him."

Ruth gave me a tight-lipped smile. "He knows that. And I offered to pay his way to see *my* doctor. But Kevin's stupid pride won't let him accept charity."

Yeah, that was Kevin. Independent to the point of being self-destructive.

"How long has this been going on?"

Caroline answered, "I don't know. Maybe three months? It's not like he's going to tell anyone."

"The last few weeks, Caroline's called me twice when Kevin was in a lot of pain," Ruth said. "I came over and suggested that we take him to the hospital…*strongly* suggested. He was adamant, even when it was obvious he was suffering. He'd shake his head and tell me that was okay. Just give him a minute and he'd walk it off."

For a moment, what Ruth said had taken me back to the first day I'd ever met Kevin. That day in the schoolyard when Danny Allan had used Kevin's face for a punching bag. Just as Mr. Wordin was leading the two boys back to the office, I walked along side Kevin for a couple of steps.

Neither of us knew the other's name, but I asked him if he was all right.

Even though his lips were swollen, one eye was almost closed shut and there was blood dripping from his nose, he managed to say, "I'm okay."

"You should have your mom take you to a doctor," I'd told him.

He tried to smile at me. Then he said, "Nah, I'll just walk it off."

When they finally let us in to see him, Kevin was in a tiny cubicle defined by white curtains hanging from roll-away aluminum supports. He was lying in a twin-sized bed, wearing one of those humiliating hospital gowns and covered by a single sheet. No wires were hooked up to his chest or miniature hoses running into his nose or arms.

I thought that was a good sign.

They must have given him some strong meds because his eyes were at half-mast and he had a difficult time focusing. "Genie," he said a little drunkenly. "You came to see me."

I kissed his forehead. "You okay?"

He frowned, "I shouldn't be here."

Caroline got up close and hugged him. "You okay, Daddy?"

He hugged her back and kissed her on her cheek. "I'm fine, honey."

"I'm sorry I called 911." Her voice was a little shaky. "I didn't know what else to do.

He waved his hand in the air. "Shows you love me. Awful scary for you, huh?"

"I don't want you to be sick, Daddy." She sounded like she might start crying again.

"I hear that this has been going on for a long time," I accused. "How the hell come you haven't gotten it checked out? And if you tell me that real men walk it off, I'm going to kill you."

He shrugged.

Ruth stepped up. "What did the doctor say? And bear in mind that I'm going out to check everything you tell me with the nurses."

Kevin shrugged a second time. "They want me to stay overnight and do some tests."

"What kind of tests?"

"The usual...blood work, MRI..."

"Does the doctor have any idea what's causing this?" I asked.

"If he does, he isn't sharing it with me. Personally, I think it's an ulcer."

Ruth grunted with impatience. "I'm finding the doctor," she snapped and turned on her heels, walking out of the cubicle.

After she swept out, we suffered through an embarrassing silence. Finally, Kevin broke it. "I think she'd be much mellower if the nurses gave her a couple of the same pills that they gave me."

I reached down and took his hand. "No pain?"

He shook his head.

"You're feeling pretty good?" I asked.

He nodded.

"Screw Aunt Ruth," I said. "See if you can score some for me."

• • ● • •

I stayed with Kevin for a little while longer, wishing that we could be alone for a few minutes. I wanted to apologize again for what had happened with Frank.

I couldn't shake the nagging suspicion that somehow I'd caused this.

Was his condition, whatever it was, exacerbated by the discovery of my adulterous disloyalty? All I wanted to do was drape myself over his chest and say that I was so very, very sorry.

Guilt sucks.

Caroline and I were quickly revisited by Ruth, who was now thoroughly annoyed. She'd been dismissed angrily by Kevin's doctor. Apparently, when she'd charged into a cubicle to grill him about Kevin's condition, he was sewing up a head laceration. The ER physician, on the tail end of a thirteen-hour shift, was in no mood for Ruth.

I'm not the only one she pisses off.

She did manage to talk to a nurse who confirmed what Kevin had told us.

They didn't know what was wrong with him and they were keeping him for observation and a round of tests.

I made certain that Caroline wouldn't be alone that night. She said that she was going to stay with Aunt Ruth. If I'd been Caroline, the last place I'd want to be is with Ruth, but I couldn't offer her an alternative without starting an argument.

So I kissed Kevin on the lips, jokingly told him to study hard for his tests, and said goodnight to everyone.

I went home and walked Tucker. After nuking some Lean Cuisine, I poured myself a vodka and ice and sat out on the porch. While heat lightning played hide and seek in the clouds on the horizon, I listened to the crickets and thought about the events of the day.

How Kevin and I had eaten a wonderful breakfast at Flap Jack's, seeing Kevin's bedroom, talking to the guard out on Connor's Landing, meeting the Elroys, and then running into that rat-bastard Frank near their pool.

Interviewing the Brenner brothers in that dark house and being thoroughly terrified.

Seeing Kevin in the hospital.

That was *the* scariest part of the day.

I looked at my watch. It was only nine-thirty, but I was exhausted.

When I finished my drink, I went back into my apartment, and remembering my visit with the Brenners, made certain the door was locked. I picked up a book I've been wading through for six months about war journalists. Then I grabbed the bottle of vodka out of the cupboard, took it and my book into the bedroom and drank myself to sleep.

Chapter Seventeen

I woke up with Tucker licking my face and a fierce hangover pushing hard against the back of my retinas. Painfully crawling out of bed and stumbling into the bathroom, I discovered a woman with witchy, bed-head hair and frighteningly red eyes staring back at me from the mirror. Sadly, she looked much older and more tired than the day before. Like I do every morning, I swore off drinking, fully intending to fulfill that promise yet knowing that I wouldn't.

I managed my way into a pair of shorts, a tee, and my Red Sox cap and then took Tucker down to the docks for his walk. After two aspirin, a hot shower, a half pot of Folgers, and part of a day-old muffin, I was feeling a little more human. I called the hospital.

A nurse told me that they'd already taken Kevin in for the first of his tests. I sighed and replaced the phone in its cradle and looked at the front page of Monday's newspaper. It's one of the only editions that I see objectively because I'm off the day before and none of the stories are mine.

Objectively I can say that it was dull as Minnesota dirt.

I shoved another stale clump of blueberry muffin into my mouth and silently wondered if I should ask Casper for a raise.

My phone rang.

"Yeah?" I was talking into the receiver with crumbs dropping from my lips.

"It's Mike Dillon. I didn't wake you, did I?"

It was nice of him to ask, since it was well after ten. The deputy chief of police knows that my shift doesn't officially start until two in the afternoon and there's no real reason for me to be up this early.

"I'm up," I answered succinctly. It suddenly occurred to me that I hadn't called Mike to tell him about what I knew about the Brenners. I'd gotten sidetracked when I'd heard that Kevin had been rushed to the hospital.

"Got time for coffee?" He was still being nice.

"What's the occasion?"

"Got some information about the Home Alone gang. We're holding a press briefing later this afternoon. You might want to get a jump on everyone else."

Now this wasn't a huge help to me because my deadline was the same as the other newspapers, and the TV guys were going to have it for their six o'clock broadcasts. But it *would* give me some exclusive face time with Mike and I had questions I wanted to ask without other news crews listening in.

I suggested, "East Side Diner in about a half hour?"

● ● ● ● ●

It wasn't quite lunchtime yet so the place was nearly empty. When I arrived, Mike was already sitting in a booth with a glass of iced tea and a copy of *The Sheffield Post* in front of him.

"Hey, Mike." I leaned down and kissed him on the cheek.

"Hey, Genie." He smiled at me as I sat down. "How ya' feeling? You took a hell of a jolt when that clown slammed his Hummer into the side of my Jeep." He gestured toward the bandage on my forehead.

It was my turn smile. "Should I sue him or the city for that?"

He held his hands up in mock defense. "Oh, Genie, don't even kid about that. I shouldn't have had you in my car in the first place."

"Yeah, I hope the newspapers don't get wind of that." I replied sarcastically. I motioned for the waitress. After I ordered a cup of coffee, I asked Mike, "So what's going on at the press briefing this afternoon?"

He pulled a tiny notebook out of his shirt pocket, flipped it open, and eyed his notes. "Early this morning, Lawrence Rhett, age thirty-seven, admitted to being the leader of the Home Alone gang and confessed to planning and executing thirteen home burglaries in Fairfield and Westchester Counties."

"Lawrence Rhett, he was the guy we arrested?"

Mike nodded.

"Thirteen robberies?"

He nodded again

"We reported that there were fifteen."

Mike sipped his tea and watched the waitress place a cup of coffee on the table. "There *were* fifteen. It appears that we're still looking for the perpetrators of two of them."

"Copycat burglars."

He nodded again.

By this time, I had my own notebook out and was scribbling away. "Any thoughts on who they might be?"

"Not at this time, but we're vigorously pursuing every possible lead," Mike stated in his official voice. He knew that this was all on the record and he's a pro.

"Any chance that this Lawrence Rhett is being less than honest and his gang did all fifteen?"

"No reason not to admit to all fifteen. The deal was to plead guilty and to give us the names of his gang. The end game is the same if there were thirteen, fifteen, or a hundred and fifteen."

"Plea bargain? Is he going to do any time?"

He gently scratched at his eyebrow. "You'll have to wait until the judge hands down the sentence. But, yeah, he'll do time."

"Just not as much time as he should."

Mike shrugged.

"So you got the names of the rest of the gang."

"Yeah, I'll make sure that you get a list of who they are. There're four of them out there and we've issued warrants for their arrest."

I tapped my pen against the tabletop. "Warrants but no actual arrests?"

"They're professionals. Once we picked up Rhett, they blew town."

"Where were they staying?"

"They were renting a house, 115 Canal Street."

I picked up my coffee cup. "That's right around the corner from me. I've walked my dog past there."

He took a swallow of his iced tea. "It's a nice quiet area. It's safe. Not a lot of crime."

I thought of my next set of questions. "So now you're sure there are copycat burglars out there."

"Looks that way."

"Any chance that *they* committed the Connor's Landing murders?"

He considered how he would frame his answer. "We're not discounting anything."

"So it's possible."

Mike's eyebrows shot up and he shrugged. "I doubt it. Look, what happened out there was a crime of rage, rage to the point of insanity. And we're pretty sure there were at least two killers."

"Pretty sure?"

"You can't have that much blood without *some* physical evidence."

"Fingerprints?"

"A lot of smears, nothing we can use," he said. "But what we *do* have are bloody footprints, two sets. We know there were at least two people out there that night. We know that they were most likely male, we know their shoe size and we know their approximate weight and their probable height."

Two people, two killers.

That was when the guilt struck home hard. I had to talk to Mike about Jim and Aaron Brenner. "You still interviewing family and friends of the victims?"

He flipped back a few pages in his notebook. "Yeah, and we've already searched the victims' homes."

"Find anything interesting?"

Mike studied my face carefully. "I know when you're tap dancing. Why don't you just tell me what you know, Genie."

I sighed and decided to ask another question. "Have you discovered how the victims all knew each other?"

He turned his head and looked out the window onto the busy street, deciding how much information he wanted to offer in trade for what I might have.

Rubbing his chin, he looked back at me. "We've only just started looking at the hard drives on their home computers, but it appears that the single common thread is that all three couples were extraordinarily interested in pornography."

I rolled my eyes. "That means they have something in common with almost every man in the world that has access to the Internet."

He pointed his finger in my direction. "And a very large population of women as well, Miss Chase."

"Pretty weak," I said. "There must be something else that ties them all together."

He smiled crookedly. "Well, in addition to an appreciation of erotica, all three couples apparently had an interest in swinging."

I leaned back against the backrest in the booth. It was my turn to carefully consider my words.

"Now tell me what you know, Genie."

"Have you talked with Lynette Chadwick's ex-husband, Jim Brenner?"

His eyes studied mine. "Two of my detectives interviewed him yesterday. Why?"

"Is he a suspect?"

"Right now, everyone's a suspect. But Jim Brenner claims to have been home with his brother on the night of the murders. His brother confirms his alibi, for what that's worth."

"A brother who happens to be an ordained minister. Theoretically adding credibility to his alibi?"

He massaged his eyebrow again, clearly annoyed. "Are you going to tell me what you know or am I going to have to take you down to the station and sweat it out of you? I swear, Genie, I love you, but sometimes you just drive me nuts."

"A couple more questions, Mike. Is that what those victims were doing out on Connor's Landing. Having sex? Swinging?"

He eyed me carefully. "Possibly."

"I'd say most likely. Is it possible they were killed in a jealous rage?"

"Talk to me, Genie."

I glanced around the diner. "I talked with a source two nights ago who said he saw Lynette Chadwick's ex-husband, Jim Brenner, go bat-shit crazy on her and her husband."

Mike's expression turned serious. "You waited two days to tell me this? Who's your source?"

"I can't, ethically, and I can't even if I wanted to…because I don't know who he is."

"You don't know who he is?" He sounded doubtful.

"When I suggested he talk to you, he ran out into the night like I tried to set him on fire. He never told me his name." At least not his last name.

Mike was writing in his notebook. "Where did he say Brenner accosted the Chadwicks?"

"Sex club…swingers club." *I wasn't sure what to call it.*

"Where?"

"He wouldn't tell me. Just that it was in town."

That wasn't honest. I'd found it on the web. If you wanted the address, you had to call a number listed on the site. The club was called Temptation House and it was located in the Matthews Hill section of town. There was a photo on their website. It was an old Victorian home tucked away and surrounded by trees and lush landscaping. It looked more like the house where a spinster aunt might live."

"Was your source there when it happened?"

"He said he was. He said that all the victims were there."

"Did he describe the scene?"

"He said that Jim Brenner snuck into the club, he looked drunk, and he started name-calling and he physically accosted

George Chadwick. A couple of guys at the club escorted him out. After that, the Chadwicks invited the Singewalds and the Websters back to their place."

"Is your source a swinger?"

I drank my coffee and ignored his question.

"Genie, if you're withholding evidence, I swear I'm going to come down on you like a ton of bricks," he growled.

"Mike, I just gave you a big freaking clue here, so don't be giving me an attitude," I argued back.

He stewed silently for a moment and looked out through the window at the cars going by on the street. Finally he nodded and looked back at me, the anger apparently behind him. "Okay, look, you just did me a favor, I'm going to do you a favor." He still had a light edge clinging to his voice. "Want a human interest story?"

"Sure."

"Check the police reports from last night. There's one in there for an attempted robbery over on Briar Street at around nine. The perpetrator broke into a ground floor condo without realizing that someone was home at the time. The resident confronted the burglar and chased him away."

I blinked and shrugged. "Okay, a story with a happy ending. Not like this doesn't happen with some regularity."

Mike smiled. "The reason that the erstwhile robber thought it was safe to break and enter was that the condo was dark and he thought the owner was away."

"Was the owner asleep?" I wondered aloud, thinking that nine was pretty early to be hitting the hay. The story was still pedestrian.

Mike took his time. "What makes this story worth your while, darling, is that the woman who chased the robber away is blind."

It hit me. "The reason the condo was dark."

Mike raised his eyebrows. "She chased the punk out of there with a chisel. Want her phone number?"

What are you kidding? Mike was right. A blind woman chasing a burglar out of her home? Hell, yeah.

"Sure."

"Going to tell me who your source is?" He handed me a slip of paper with the phone number on it.

"Honest to God, Mike, even if I wanted to, I can't. I lost him. Ran off in the night.

"Okay." He sounded satisfied with that.

"I'll pick up the tab for your iced tea, though, how's that?"

He smiled again. "I'll tell you what, how about you buy me a drink some night?"

I frowned at him. He's always flirted with me, but it never went much further than being playful. "I stopped drinking. You know that."

He stood up and tossed some money down on the table. As he started to walk away, he used a hint of sarcasm. "If you ever start again, let me know."

Chapter Eighteen

I got to the hospital just before noon. Before I got out of my car I studied the big brick building. Staring back at me were countless windows and the dark, double glass doors of the lobby.

How many people have gotten bad news in that building? How many people have died?

I shook my head. I couldn't be thinking that way. Focus on how many people have been cured, gotten better, and made whole again.

Glass half-full or half-empty...doesn't matter as long as it's vodka.

Deep down, I wanted to believe that whatever was wrong with Kevin was minor. Worst-case scenario, they put him on some medication and we'd still grab a late dinner and a drink tonight once I was done with my shift. Continue with our lives, never miss a beat.

I shook off whatever sense of dread lingered and got out of the Sebring.

Walking into his hospital room on the third floor, I was pleasantly surprised to find Kevin lying in bed, covered up to his chest by a sheet, his hands clasped behind his head and his eyes studying the television. I noticed that there were flowers in a vase off to one side of the small room on a counter and a "Get Well Soon" balloon tied to the aluminum side of the hospital bed. The flowers weren't fragrant enough to ward off the pervasive scent of ethyl alcohol and ammonia that permeates a hospital room.

Ruth was nowhere to be seen.

"Hi," I said brightly. "I'm going to be your nurse this morning. Are you ready for your sponge bath?"

He winked and put a finger to his lips. "Shhhh," he warned, pointing his thumb toward a curtain hanging next to his bed. "I have a roommate."

I peeked around the curtain and, sure enough, there was another man lying in a bed on the other side of it. Like Kevin, he was covered by a thin sheet, but he looked to be in his late eighties and fast asleep. He had an IV dripping into his arm and his eyes were closed. But for his regular breathing, he could have been dead.

"Does that mean the sponge bath is out?" I whispered.

He grinned. "Not only do I have a roommate," he said in a conspiratorial voice, "but Caroline and Ruth will be back in a few minutes. They just went down to the cafeteria to get me coffee and something to eat. I'm starving."

"Coffee, huh? You must be feeling better. Why don't we stop on the way home? There's a Starbucks on the way. I can take you home, you know. Ruth doesn't have to do it."

I bent over and kissed him on the forehead.

He reached up and gently pulled my head down, my lips finding his. We kissed long and hard.

When we were done, I stayed close to him and looked into his eyes. "Wow, you seem pretty healthy to me. You can leave, right? They didn't find anything seriously wrong, did they?"

He took my hand and squeezed it. "They're not done yet."

I looked at him and frowned. "More tests?"

He cocked his head to one side. "Yeah, more tests."

Cold, butterfly wings of fear were starting to flutter in my chest. "What are they looking for?"

He took a breath. "They want to see how much of my liver is still functioning."

My arms and legs went numb. "How much of your liver is functioning?"

He shrugged. "I never took real good care of it."

"How serious is this?"

He waved his hand. "It's nothing."

"What have you told Caroline?"

"At this point there's nothing to tell. Ruth knows, but I didn't see any point in spooking Caroline."

I wanted to say something else, ask more questions, but I heard Ruth and Caroline coming through the doorway. Aunt Ruth was holding a steaming Styrofoam cup in each hand when she spotted me. She stopped for a moment, searching into my eyes, trying to discern how much I knew.

It only took her a second to realize that Kevin had already told me everything.

"Stupid cafeteria didn't have any lids for the cups. I must have scalded my hands a dozen times coming up in the elevator."

"Genie!" Caroline exclaimed happily, rushing up to give me a hug.

Feeling her arms around my shoulders was a pleasant surprise. I hugged her back.

Ruth gave one of the cups to Kevin who sipped at it gratefully.

"Should you be having coffee, Daddy?" Caroline held out a paper bag.

I wondered the same thing.

He gave her a "who-gives-a-crap" look and waved it off. "Coffee's the best thing for me. I read it in the latest *Journal of American Medicine*. What's in the bag?"

"Cherry Danish." She waved the bag at him.

Kevin took the bag from his daughter's hand and slowly opened it. Then he smiled and tore off the corner of his pastry and put it into his mouth.

I noticed that, in spite of claiming to be hungry, he was chewing with a lot more deliberation than when he'd eaten his breakfast yesterday at Flap Jacks.

"So," I asked, "when are they going to let you outa here?"

"Not sure, but they said they'd do the last test sometime this afternoon. They said it's simple enough. I can go home when they're done."

"Hey, look, how about if I call in sick?" I suggested. "That way I can drive you home when it's over."

Ruth jumped in, "I'll drive him home." Her voice was definitely definitive.

Kevin reached out and took my hand. "Tell you what. Let Ruth drive me home and then, if you get off a little early, maybe you and I can grab a bite to eat?"

"I'd like that." I leaned down and kissed him again on the lips. "Call me if you hear anything, okay?"

"Cross my heart."

I hugged Caroline again and nodded at Ruth who, to my surprise, followed me out the door and into the hallway.

When we were out of earshot, Ruth asked, "Kevin told you?"

I nodded.

"I think it's best if we don't tell Caroline," Ruth continued. "There's no point in alarming her until we know for sure."

"Until we know what for sure?"

"That it's catastrophic liver failure." Her voice cracked, her eyes reddened.

"Who said anything about catastrophic liver failure?" I shot back.

"Well, I pray that it's not," Ruth whispered. "It wouldn't be fair. Not to Kevin and not to Caroline. She's still not recovered from Joanna's death."

"So Kevin's told me."

She shook her head very quickly. "Even Kevin doesn't know how bad it is. Caroline helps him shop. She helps him cook. She helps him keep house. She's trying to fill the void that Joanna left after she died. Caroline wants to be perfect, more than perfect for her father, more perfect than any daughter can ever be. She's taken it to the extreme. On top of which, Caroline has an eating disorder. Did you know she's bulimic?"

Was that why she never gains an ounce even though she's constantly eating?

I could feel the anger rising as I looked at Ruth. "Kevin doesn't know?" I asked incredulously.

"I've been taking Caroline secretly to a doctor, a specialist that I'm paying for. She says that Caroline is making progress. I'm concerned that if anything *is* seriously wrong with Kevin, then Caroline is just going to completely spiral out of control."

"You haven't told Kevin that you're taking his daughter to a doctor?"

"I don't want him to worry. And he doesn't have the money. He's proud and he can be pig-headed."

Yeah, but not telling Kevin isn't right.

"What makes you think Caroline is bulimic?"

Her cheeks colored crimson as she answered, "Because, I'd suspected for months that there might be something wrong with her. Then one night, back in May when I was having dinner at Kevin's house, he went into the kitchen to get us all some ice cream. Caroline excused herself to use the bathroom. I followed her and listened at the door."

Nosy bitch.

"I could hear her in there, throwing up. Purging, that's what they call it," Ruth continued in a quiet voice. "I confronted her when she came out of the bathroom. She lied and told me her stomach was upset."

"What makes you think she was lying?"

Ruth stared at me. "I can always tell when someone is lying to me. I told her that I had to tell her father. She begged me not to. Caroline doesn't want to disappoint Kevin. She told me that if I said anything to him she'd kill herself."

"And you believed her?"

"Yes, I could see the defiance in her face. I've seen the same expression on Kevin. I told Caroline that if she saw a doctor, a therapist, I wouldn't say anything to her dad."

"How's it going?"

"She's been making good progress. She's starting to gain back a little weight and she's looking healthy again." Ruth stopped and slowly shook her head. "But I'm worried."

"You think she might relapse?"

She stared at me with wide eyes. "I think she's already relapsed. I think she's purging again."

"What makes you think that?"

"I'm not stupid, Miss Chase," she stated. "Neither are you. Look at her. There's no color in her face and her weight's dropping."

"Is this recent?"

"Very recent." Ruth's lips were drawn tight. "It started again when Kevin brought *you* into his house."

Chapter Nineteen

Now, I'm acquainted with guilt.

The afternoon that my dad slid his Harley-Davidson under the trailer of a jackknifing truck, the afternoon he died, he was on his way to my high school. Mrs. Bowler, my math teacher, had caught me and Mary Sue Wilcox smoking a joint in the girl's room and the principal wanted to see both of our parents or else we'd be expelled.

Danny Allen was the one who ratted us out, the same boy who'd beaten Kevin so badly on my first day at the school, years ago. He told me he did it to get even for me taking Kevin's side that day. *Who would have thought he'd hold a silly grudge for so long?*

If it hadn't been for that, my dad wouldn't have been where he was when that Saab cut off the truck and it went out of control. If it hadn't been for me pissing off Danny Allen or smoking a joint in the girl's room, my dad might be alive today. If…if…if.

More than once, in the throes of the medication her doctors prescribed for her depression, my mother told me that. *"If it hadn't been for you…if it hadn't been for you."*

I drove away from the hospital in a haze, considering what I'd just seen and heard. Kevin was getting tested to see how much of his liver was functioning. The question was—how much of it was already dead?

And what about Ruth's accusation that Caroline was bulimic and it was my fault? What was that based on—one of Ruth's Truths? It was obvious she hated me. She'd lie to me.

But, despite my best efforts, both of those monstrously nasty prospects kept sneaking into my thoughts like snakes crawling under an old barn wall.

Knowing that Kevin was lying in that bed waiting to hear if he was about to face the fight of his life, and the possibility that Caroline was facing a psychological struggle that I might have triggered, yeah, I felt guilty as hell.

Yes, I'm acquainted with guilt.

I needed a drink. The digital clock in my dashboard told me that it was only a little after noon and it was too early, even for me, to be sitting in a dark bar somewhere hunched over a vodka rocks.

Better that I drink alone at home.

So I drove back to my apartment and poured myself an Absolut on ice. While Tucker sat at my feet and enjoyed my quiet company, I leaned against the counter in the kitchen and sipped my drink. The more I sipped, the better I felt.

Halfway through the vodka, I recalled what my third husband, Sal, had once said. "When you drink, you're trying to run away from something. But you know what? You're always carrying that baggage around. Your responsibilities are still waiting for you in the morning, the bad guys are still running the country, and the monster's still hiding under the bed."

Of all of my husbands, Sal probably knew me the best.

I wanted that drink in my hand. Right at that moment it was my best friend. I was really worried about Kevin. I was really worried about Caroline. Hell, I was worried about me.

The monster was, indeed, still hiding under the bed.

●　●　●　●　●

While I sipped my second Absolut, I called the number that Mike Dillon had given me. The blind woman who'd chased a robber out of her home answered the phone. I told her who I was and asked if I could stop by to interview her. She hesitated for only a moment before she said yes, but only if I could stop by right away. Her daughter was coming to pick her up in an hour to take her to Cape Cod.

I didn't mind. I needed to stay busy. If I stayed home I would get hammered.

On my way over to Briar Avenue, I was envisioning a woman in her sixties, slightly overweight but sturdy, liked to knit, and loved listening to Lake Woebegone. But still spunky enough to chase off a burglar.

The woman who answered the door was nothing like that at all.

She was tall, lean, and in her early fifties. Her shoulder-length black hair was flecked with random strands of gray. She wore no makeup but didn't need any. She was attractive in an exotic way. Her facial features mixed Mediterranean and Middle Eastern with high cheekbones, distinct eyebrows, a patrician nose, and full lips. I guessed that most men would find this woman irresistible.

There was only one flaw in her appearance. Her eyes were covered with a milky-white membrane.

When the door to her condo swung open, I said, "Hi, I'm Geneva Chase, from *The Sheffield Post.*"

It was a bit disconcerting to watch her cock her head to listen, not looking at me but in the vague direction of my words. "I'm Isadora Orleans." Her voice low and smoky. "Would you like to come in out of the heat?"

She had a slight accent that I couldn't identify, Greek or perhaps Turkish.

"I'm sorry I made you come over so quickly." She waved me into the living room. "But my daughter is arriving in a few minutes. She's taking me to my brother's house in Chatham. It's lovely there. I can hear the ocean, smell the sea breeze, and I love the crabcakes and chowder."

She had a beautiful smile.

"I love Cape Cod," I said.

Isadora nodded and closed the door. "Can I get you a drink?"

Her nostrils flared as she sniffed the air. I've heard that, because of the lack of sight, a blind person can develop the other senses to incredible heights. I wondered if this woman knew that I'd already had a couple of drinks. I was hoping that I'd covered my breath with a handful of breath mints.

"It's a little early for me."

She frowned. "I'm going to have one. I have some Stolichnaya in the freezer. I'll pour you some."

Oh, okay.

This would make my third drink and it wasn't even one o'clock. I'd have to make sure that I stopped off to get something to eat before I went into the office.

"It would be rude if I refused."

She smiled again. "Yes, rude."

While Isadora disappeared into the kitchen, I scanned the apartment. I was pleased to see that the curtains were wide open and the place was flooded with sunlight. I wasn't surprised to see that the room was spartan—an overstuffed chair and a leather couch, and an entertainment center holding a television and a stereo. No bookcases, no coffee tables, nothing with hard, sharp corners that a blind woman might trip over if she lost her concentration.

What was startling, however, was the large easel that dominated the center of the room. And the dozens of dark paintings that sat on the hardwood floor, leaning against the walls.

I stepped up to the easel to see a work in progress. It was three-dimensional. Upon closer inspection, I saw that it wasn't a canvas but a panel of wood, several inches thick, with abstract, flowing designs carved into its surface.

I walked over to the wall closest to me and squatted down to look at what I'd thought were paintings. None of them were actually canvases. Intricate designs had been carved into panels of oak, cherry, and walnut and then exquisitely stained. They were mesmerizing. Like peering into a dark, dreamlike waterscape, the wood grain random, yet somehow familiar, depicting an image that was just beyond my grasp, just on the far edge of my imagination.

I stared at the carving closest to me, my eyes studying hard at the odd design. It was like there was something in the carved grooves and grain that I was supposed to see.

It slowly came to me. I saw an eye, then two eyes, shadows under the cheekbones, lips, a receding hairline. It was a man's face.

Suddenly I stood up, my hand clasped over my mouth.

It was Kevin's face.

I was certain. Kevin's face was carved into that wood, the wood grain and odd coloring fleshing out his features. It was as if I was looking at him through a film of viscous liquid, but Kevin nonetheless.

Who was this woman?

"Are you looking at my work?"

Hearing her words, I turned with a slight gasp. I cleared my throat. "Yes. It's very striking."

Isadora smiled. "Thank you." She held out my glass.

I took it and she sipped at hers. "They're how I support myself. I'm always surprised at how well they sell."

"I'd like to talk to you about them." I was still a little unnerved.

She cocked her head. "If we have time," she replied. "You came over to talk to me about the burglar?"

I glanced back at the carving that had spooked me so much. Now that I was standing away from it, I couldn't see Kevin's face at all.

Had I imagined it?

"Um, the police say a man broke into your apartment last night."

"Idiot," she snapped. "The curtains were wide open and there were no lights on so the moron must have thought was no one home. Since I'm on the first floor, he thought this would be easy."

"Were you in bed?"

"It was only around nine. I was working. Obviously I don't need any light, so the place was dark. I heard something in my kitchen, a scratching at the window. At first I thought it was my cat."

I scribbled in my notebook.

"So I stayed very still. Sometimes I have on the radio to keep me company. But last night I was enjoying the silence. It was easy to hear how clumsy the robber was."

I walked over to the doorway and peered into the kitchen. The usual appliances were on the counters, a microwave, a toaster, and a blender. All neat and tidy. Not like my kitchen where there were dishes in the sink, a coffeepot still half full, or a loaf of bread left out to go moldy.

The only window was right over the sink. "Is that where he came in?" I pointed.

Then I felt like an idiot. She couldn't see me.

She sipped at her vodka and smiled at me. "The window in the kitchen, yes. The window was open but he had to come in past the screen. The police tell me that he used a knife to pry it open."

"So he actually got into in your apartment?"

Isadora nodded. "I could hear him climbing in. Once the screen was off, he was very fast. I could hear his feet on the tile in there."

"You must have been terrified."

"Terrified, yes," she answered. "I sat very still, not wanting to make a sound. But I knew that when he came into the living room, he'd see me."

"And did he?"

She shrugged. "I guess it was very dark. Must be some light coming in through the windows, even at night, but he didn't know I was here. I heard him come in and bump into the cabinet over there." She gestured in the direction of an entertainment unit that held the stereo system.

"I was so scared that he would hurt me, maybe kill or rape me. I just reacted, at first in fear and then in anger. How dare this man break into my home? I grabbed one of my chisels and screamed like a crazy person."

Even though I was grinning at her story, I could feel my heart beating a little faster as she told it. I know what that kind of fear is like. It's like being an animal trapped in a corner.

"What happened?"

She took a quick drink. "I must have scared the shit out him. I heard him try to run, but I think he tripped over his own feet because I heard a big thump when his ass hit the floor."

"No." I laughed.

"I kept screaming and slashing the air with my chisel. I heard that bastard crawl like a baby across the kitchen floor going fifty miles an hour until he got to the sink. Then I heard him shout, 'crazy bitch.' And then he was gone."

"You're very brave."

She shook her head. "He was right, I'm a crazy bitch."

"Any precautions so it doesn't happen again?"

"My daughter wants to install bars on the windows. I think it will ruin my view."

She had quick sense of humor. Quotable.

"That answers most of my questions about the burglar. I'm very taken with your art. How long have you been doing it?"

She walked deliberately over to the easel in the center of the room. Running her fingers gently over the face of the wood, she responded, "Since I was a small child. My grandmother taught me. I grew up near Mount Athos in Greece. You know it?"

Shaking my head, I answered, "No."

"There are many monasteries there. Inside these monasteries are special rooms where icons from the Byzantine period are kept. These icons are paintings or carvings on wooden panels of holy figures, the Virgin Mary, Christ, the apostles, saints. Some of these icons were said to have been created by St. Luke and have miraculous healing powers."

She sipped at her drink for a moment while I waited for her to continue.

"I was born without sight. I've never seen sunlight. I've never seen a tree. I never saw the face of my mother or grandmother or my own daughter. When I was very, very small, my grandmother took me to one of these rooms and the monks let me touch one of the icons. They told me that I was touching the face of Christ and if it was His will, He would let me see."

I stayed silent.

She smiled. "As you already know, I'm still blind, but that doesn't mean I can't see."

She lovingly ran her fingers over the wooden panel on the easel. "My grandmother taught me to carve flowing designs onto wood. And she taught me that the wood would tell its own story, unique to each person who sees it."

Isadora stopped speaking and her long, callused fingers lightly stroked the carving, slowly, as one would touch a lover. Her face was relaxed, her eyes half closed, in a self-induced state of bliss.

I walked slowly over to the panel that I'd seen earlier. I squatted down and took another look. There were ripples and currents where Isadora had carved them into the face of the wood. A finish, thickly applied, added to the impression that you were peering at a scene locked in amber.

But through it, I could see a conscious design.

And once again, I saw Kevin's face.

"What do you see?" Isadora asked.

"I see a friend."

"Your friend is very important to you?"

"Yes. I don't understand how you do this. His name is Kevin Bell. Do you know him?"

With another smile, she shook her head. "Everyone sees something in my work. The carving in the face of the panels I do by touch. The designs that the wood grain makes with the stain, well, I'm afraid that's completely random."

I looked back at the icon. It was Kevin. I was certain.

"I understand that people see things when they look at clouds."

I stood up, still looking at the wooden carving at my feet. "Yes."

"Same thing here. People see what they want to see. Their senses demand it. They need to see the design. A monk once told me that people need order. No one can live thinking that there isn't a plan for all of us."

"So do you believe in fate? That there's a grand design?"

She shrugged. "What I create, there's no plan. It's all chance."

I thanked her for her time and started for the door. Then I turned. "Orleans. That doesn't sound Greek."

"It's not. It was my husband's name, Michael Orleans. He died seven years ago. He was a jazz pianist. One night after a gig in the city, he was driving back through Westchester County at around two in the morning and was hit head-on by a drunk driver."

To punctuate her statement, she held up her drink and then took a healthy sip.

I took a deep breath and looked at my own glass. There was still vodka in it. "I'm so sorry, um… I'm going to put my glass in the kitchen."

I poured the rest of my vodka into the sink, rinsed it out with water from the tap and closed my eyes for a moment.

"Miss Chase?"

I opened my eyes and found myself looking directly at the woman standing in the doorway. "Yes?"

"Don't feel bad. It was a long time ago and it happens to all of us sooner or later, doesn't it?"

"It does," I replied.

"Then enjoy each day as it comes, yes?"

She made me smile. "Enjoy your crabcakes and chowder, Isadora Orleans."

Chapter Twenty

The time I'd spent with Isadora Orleans will make an interesting piece, but it had been a very unsettling experience. Did her art reflect life? Was there really no grand design, only what we want to see? That fate doesn't exist, that it's something that our minds conjure up when we need it? That when something bad happens we struggle to find a reason for it? That we can't stand the thought that we're alone in the universe and that our lives are dictated by random events?

Or was I reading way too much into it? Knowing that Kevin could be seriously ill, I wanted desperately for the universe to have meaning, that there was a plan, that there was a happy ending.

I still had time to kill before I started my shift so I drove over to Mathews Hill. It's a neighborhood in the northern part of Sheffield that's a New England cliché. All residential, it's a collection of historic homes tucked away on a secluded, wooded two-lane road with easy access to the Merritt Parkway.

While driving, I called a number I'd gotten off a website devoted to swingers. A man answered and I told him that my boyfriend and I were interested in joining his club and I wondered if I might stop by to take a look. Since these types of establishments are notoriously publicity shy, I skipped the part about being a reporter.

The man on the phone sounded friendly enough and asked when I'd like to come by. I told him that I was already in the neighborhood, could I stop in now?

He gave me the address and directions.

The house was a white Victorian with black shutters, set discretely behind a lush wall of landscaping, complete with a widow's walk on the roof and graced with a large front porch. It wasn't at all what I would have expected a sex club to look like.

I drove up the driveway and around back of the house, as instructed, to a gravel parking lot large enough to hold about forty cars. Even before I'd gotten out of my car, a man dressed in faded denim shorts, work boots, and a sweat-stained UConn shirt was standing on the landing waiting for me. He was in his late fifties, sported a salt-and-pepper goatee, and had a healthy head of jet-black hair. I strongly suspected the hair color was the result of chemicals rather than his DNA.

As I walked up the steps, he said with a smile, "Welcome to Temptation House." He held out his hand and announced, "I'm Walt."

I shook his hand. "I'm Genie."

I was wearing a pair of black shorts and a sleeveless top. I could feel Walt's eyes giving my body the once over.

"What's your boyfriend's name?"

"Kevin," I answered without hesitation.

"Have you been together a long time?"

I nodded knowingly, "About three years."

"How long have you been in the lifestyle?"

"Only recently."

He nodded back. "Not a problem. Newbies are always welcome. C'mon in."

An attractive woman waited for us at the end of the hallway. In her early forties, she was wearing designer jeans, sneakers, and a short-sleeved shirt similar to Walt's, without the perspiration stains. Her long blond hair peeked out from under a New York Giants cap and she was appraising me with mirthful green eyes. Her broad smile exposed perfect teeth that were professionally whitened.

She held out her hand the way Walt had. "I'm Sue, Walt's better half."

"Genie." I shook her hand.

She quickly looked me up and down the same way her husband had.

"Well, Genie, forgive the way we look. Since we're closed for a couple of weeks, we're getting some work done around here that needed some attention."

"You're closed for a couple of weeks?"

Walt took the opportunity to answer. "We had some of our members pass away unexpectedly in a tragic accident," he said with proper sobriety. "We're honoring their memory by staying closed for a little while. Genie, I've got to get back to work but it's very nice to meet you. I hope you and your boyfriend join our group. You'd fit right in here. I'd very much like to see more of you," he said with a lascivious grin on his face.

He left us standing in the doorway of a large room, quite possibly what used to be the ballroom or dining area of the original house. All of the windows were covered by thick, velvet curtains and the lighting was supplied by a dozen or so faux-Tiffany lamps hanging on golden chains suspended from the twelve-foot high ceiling. Cocktail tables and chairs gave the room a nightclub vibe complete with a dance floor and a small, raised stage with a DJ's sound equipment and speakers.

In the center of the room was a horseshoe-shaped bar made of polished walnut and surrounded by leather padded bar stools. Hanging above it were shelves of crystal glasses and bottles, dozens of them, filled with various types of alcohol.

That's when I realized that, tragically, my buzz was wearing off.

"That's our bar. Those bottles are brought in by our members and tagged. It's BYOB, so when we serve alcohol, there's no money that changes hands. That way we steer clear of any pesky Connecticut liquor laws."

Sue walked out into the middle of the room and spread her arms. "This is where we start the evening." She pointed toward the small table we'd walked past. "That's where members check in. We have a bouncer there watching the door the entire evening. We're very strict about who comes in. No single men and you must be a member."

"How much is a membership?"

She smiled, "It's a thousand dollars a year, and fifty dollars a couple per visit, payable at the door."

I whistled. "It seems a little steep."

"I inherited this house from my grandmother so Walt and I own it outright, but there are considerable expenses in keeping it up. Plus, we have a very classy clientele here. The membership dues help keep out the riffraff."

I thought about the intrusion by Jim Brenner last Wednesday night. The "clientele" must have been absolutely apoplectic.

"At the beginning of the evening, we have food set out—it might be designer pizza or it might be heavy hors d'oeuvres. Most nights we have a DJ and this is the place we all chill out, dance a little, have a few drinks, and meet and greet. Then at eleven-thirty we open the rooms."

"The rooms?"

"Playrooms. Come on, I'll show you." She took me by the arm and led me to a staircase. At the top was a landing and along its walls were sets of polished, wooden clothes lockers. "This is where everyone gets naked. We also have another locker room and a couple of playrooms downstairs."

She then pulled me toward a doorway and we peeked inside. She flipped on a light switch and soft pink illumination came from tiny lights around the perimeter of the ceiling. It was supplemented by a small, mirrored disco ball throwing shards of light around the room. The room seemed almost infinitely large by virtue of the ceiling-to-floor mirrors covering the walls.

The only furnishing in the room was a king-sized bed.

I felt myself blushing when I murmured, "Party."

We took a look at two more rooms that were similar except one also had a leather-and-rope swing apparatus hanging from the ceiling. Another had something that looked a little like a workout machine, complete with a movable seat, stirrups, and hand grips. It reminded me of my last visit to the gynecologist. I pointed to it and asked, "What's that for?"

She smiled enigmatically. "For just about anything you can imagine," she purred. "I hope you get a chance to try it out, Genie. I'd love to show you how it works."

Then she led me to one last room. It was twice the size of the other rooms, filled with a wall-to-wall mattress. She leaned in close so that her shoulder touched mine and whispered, "This is the orgy room."

"Wow," I said, barely under my breath. "How many people will this accommodate?"

She shrugged. "I've seen as many as fifty people in here. Of course, it was pretty tight, but then again, isn't that what it's all about?"

She was staring at me and smiling.

I tried to visualize what fifty naked bodies in one room might look like.

As if reading my mind, Sue said in a husky voice, "Seeing all that flesh is delicious, but even better are the sounds, the pure animal moans and groans of pleasure, the low grunting from the physical exertion, the yelps and cries of release." She turned to me. "Yum."

As we walked back down the stairs, Walt was standing on a step ladder at an emergency exit, struggling with some wires.

"So are you and your boyfriend going to join our club?" Sue asked.

"I'm going to try to talk Kevin into it," I lied. "I think he'll want to take a look himself. I hope you don't mind?"

Sue smiled again. "I don't mind at all. I love checking out potential new members, if you know what I mean."

Reaching the ground floor, I asked, "What's Walt working on?"

"Oh, we're installing alarms on the two emergency exits," she answered. "Some of our members like to go outside to smoke and they've been sneaking out those doors. Once in a while when they come back in they'll accidentally leave the door unlocked. We had someone who wasn't a member sneak through one of those doors and crash our party the other night. It caused a bit of a scene."

"Oh no." I feigned surprise. "Did he threaten anyone?"

Sue held up a hand and, for the first time, looked at me with the hint of suspicion. "It wasn't a problem. We always have a couple of security guys here on party nights."

I thought I should lighten the mood. "Your security guys, are they good looking?"

Sue glanced over at her husband and whispered in my ear, "Darlin', they are smokin' hot. Every once in a while, we let em join in on the fun. You would have a ball."

As I was saying my good-byes, I visualized what Walt and Sue looked like naked. Maybe being in a house that specializes in group sex was leaving a lusty impression on me.

I still had more than an hour before I officially started my shift, so I parked my car on the street in front of my apartment and walked to Bricks. The last time I'd been there, it had been late at night, it was raining, and I was sharing bar space with a man named Ted, who may have been one of the last swingers on Earth to see six people alive before they were brutally butchered.

Now it was warm and sunny outside, but I had a dark, disquieting, overriding anxiety that I couldn't shake. Sitting at the bar, the first thing I did was order a spinach salad and an Absolut over ice with a twist.

Thankfully, the drink came first. As I took my first cool sip, my cell phone twittered. I looked at the caller's number on the tiny screen with disbelief.

It was Frank Mancini.

"What the hell do you want?" My voice was as nasty as I could make it without bothering the other diners.

"I want to apologize. I was completely out of line."

"You're an asshole." I wanted to take my conversation outside. I discounted that idea because it would take me too damned far away my drink.

"Look." His tone as low and as genuine as only years of practice in law can offer. "I need to explain my behavior, but I need to do it in person."

"What are you, stupid?"

"I understand your anger. If I were you I'd be furious. What I did was childish and, you're right, it was stupid."

I took a deep hit of my vodka while I watched the bartender drop off my salad. I took a fork and speared a tomato, wishing it was one of Frank's testicles. "Well, we're both in agreement. You have my attention."

"I need to see you in person."

I sighed. "This is totally tiresome. Now, right now is your only chance, Frank."

There was a moment of silence as Frank seemed to gather his thoughts. Finally he said, "I did it because I was jealous. I didn't like seeing you there with that guy. I don't want to lose you."

It took me by surprise. His words sounded heartfelt. I always thought that I could tell when Frank was lying and when he was telling the truth.

But I also know that Frank is a first-class bastard, capable of weaving together a colorful but believable tapestry of lies that you hoped like hell was the truth. The man sways juries. When Frank is talking to me, I want to believe him.

"Genie?"

"Yes?"

He was silent again, as if agonizing about what he was going to say.

Then Frank said, "I love you."

For a brief moment, I remembered the good times I'd had with Frank. Excellent lunches and dinners in some of the best restaurants in Connecticut and Manhattan, spirited conversations ranging from the historic implications of religious violence to the political implications of horror movies. Weekend trips all up and down the East Coast, including Cape Cod, the Outer Banks, and Key West and the hot, sweaty afternoons and evenings in anonymous hotels, backseats, and even the occasional elevator.

I don't regret my time spent with Frank.

But I remembered the man who was in the hospital. Kevin Bell was honest, hard-working and when he said something he meant it. You didn't have to think about his words and try to wade through the rising tide of implications and half-truths.

Kevin Bell was a decent man, a man who should be treated with the respect that he effortlessly offers.

I was in love with Kevin Bell, not Frank Mancini.

"Frank?"

"Yes?"

"Good-bye." I pressed the End Call button.

Just as I finished my conversation, I noticed that the bartender was watching me. He smiled. "Sounded serious."

"It was. Once."

• • ● • •

I ate my salad, finished my drink and then went back to my apartment. I intended to walk Tucker and then drive to the newspaper office.

Tucker got a quick turn around the backyard. But seeing there was time left before I needed to leave for work, I poured myself another cocktail, a very generous cocktail.

I don't even recall going into my bedroom to lie down. Nearly two hours later, I was awakened by the phone.

"Yes?" I said sleepily into the receiver.

"Geneva? It's Casper."

Recognizing the voice on the telephone jolted me back to complete, heart-pounding awareness. I looked at the digital clock on my headboard. I was way late for work!

"Casper."

"Are you okay?"

I hesitated, then I said, "Yes, why?"

"You missed the assignment meeting."

Taking a breath I tried to think of an excuse. "I got a tip for a story from Mike Dillon."

"Oh?"

"Man broke into a woman's apartment last night and she chased him out with a chisel."

"Oh?" He was clearly unimpressed.

"Woman's blind, Casper."

"Oh!"

"The only time I could interview her was this afternoon," I was stretching the truth.

"Uh huh," he mumbled. "Well, next time, call and tell us what you're doing. We were worried about you. For all we knew, you were in a car accident or something."

Or drunk and in a ditch. That's what he really wanted to say.

"I'm on my way in now to write it up. Sorry if I worried you."

I could hear him clearing his throat. "I tried calling your cell and didn't get an answer, so I called your home phone number. If you were interviewing this blind woman, what are you doing back at your apartment?"

Good question. Casper had been a really sharp reporter in his day.

"Had to walk my dog, Chief." Not a lie. I just neglected to include salient bits of the truth.

"Right. So you're on your way in?"

I sighed and rubbed my forehead. It was only slightly after four in the afternoon and I had a skull-splitting headache. "I'll be there in a few minutes."

A midday hangover is the worst. The best part of the day is already behind you.

Unless you go back to the trough.

Which I wouldn't do. I needed to get to the office and write stories.

After I got to the *Post* building and settled into my chair, I noticed that Laura, the day editor, was still in her office. She was standing in the doorway glaring at me.

While I hammered out the Isadora Orleans story, Casper stepped into Laura's doorway and I watched as they quietly conferred about something. By the way they surreptitiously stole glances in my direction I surmised that they were talking about me.

Shrugging it off, I called Mike Dillon's office to see what the latest was on the Connor's Landing homicides. To my surprise, he was in.

"Hello?"

"Mike. It's Genie."

"Are you calling to ask me out for that drink?"

I felt my temple throb and contemplated how nice a little hair of the dog might be. "Sorry, pal. I'm on the clock."

"Too bad, I'm off my shift in another hour. What's up?"

"That's my question. What's the latest on Connor's Landing?"

There was a poignant moment of silence and I could feel the tension coming through the phone line. "What are you, psychic?"

I wasn't sure what my next line should be. "Mike, this is just a routine follow-up call. What's going on?"

"We arrested Jim and Aaron Brenner a few minutes ago."

I shook my head, not quite believing what I was hearing. "What?"

"We just took them into custody."

"Who else knows this?"

He chuckled. "You're the only one, darling. We *were* going to issue a release to the press in the morning, but if you get down here in the next few minutes, you've got yourself an exclusive."

"I'm on my way." As I hung up, I grabbed my oversized bag and started for the door.

But before I got three steps, Casper called out to me. "Genie!"

I stopped dead in my tracks. Looking over at him, I saw that he was standing next to Laura and neither of them looked happy. "What?"

"We need to talk to you."

There were half a dozen other reporters in the newsroom and every one of them stopped typing for a split second. Then, being the news people that they are, they pretended to start working again but listened to what was surely going to be something interesting.

"Look." I walked toward them. "I just heard from Mike Dillon...."

"We need to talk to you!" Laura interrupted.

Looking around the newsroom, everyone's heads were down but I could feel them all scoping me out from the corners of their eyes. "I really have to…"

"Now!" Laura shut me off a second time. "In my office."

Weird. As I walked quickly over to where they were both standing, I suddenly realized that someone had fixed the air conditioning. I don't know why I hadn't noticed it before, but it felt cold enough to hang meat in there. It reminded me of the last time I interviewed the coroner while in the morgue. It had that same feeling of cold and dread.

They closed the door behind me as I sat down. "I really have to get going." I tried to explain.

Laura wasn't having any of it. "Genie, you have a drinking problem."

I was so shocked at her bluntness that I sat straight back in my chair.

"I don't know how many times you've come in here with alcohol on your breath. Once you were so drunk, I actually had to send you home and take your shift."

The night I thought she had been doing me a favor. Now I know that she hadn't been covering for me at all. She was keeping me from doing something stupid in the office.

"According to company policy, we should have fired you after you were arrested for public intoxication and assaulting a police officer."

Casper jumped in, "But you're a good writer, Geneva. When the court dictated that you had to stop drinking, we thought we'd give you one more chance."

Even though the AC was cranked up, Casper was wiping away sweat from his bushy eyebrows.

Were they going to fire me?

"Look." I kept my voice level, taking what might be my last shot at keeping this job, careful that I wasn't slurring my words. "I interviewed Mike Dillon this morning. I just called him to follow up and he told me they've arrested two men on the Connor's Landing homicides. We're getting an exclusive on this and the only reason we are is that *I'm* on the story. But…" I paused for effect and then continued, "I've got to get over there in the next few minutes."

They both stared at me in silence. Then Laura asked, "Were you drinking before you came into the office? Is that why you're late?"

Jesus, she wasn't going to let up.

"No." I looked her straight in the eye.

She stared at me expectantly, waiting for me to confess.

"No," I repeated emphatically.

"You're very good at what you do," she finally said. "As a matter of fact, you're overqualified for this job and for this newspaper. But when it comes right down to it, I think we both know that nobody else out there will hire you."

Ouch.

"You've got a reputation as a juicer and, frankly, I haven't seen anything to show me differently. I truly think that you're going to drink yourself right out of a career. Maybe drink yourself to death."

I wanted to argue the point. Debate her. Show her how wrong she was.

I couldn't. She was dead right.

"Casper and I have talked to Ben and we all agree we're going to give you one last chance. One…last…chance."

Ben was Ben Sumner, the owner, publisher, and managing editor. I liked Ben because I'd partied with him at social functions disguised as business events and he can put it away like a thirsty sailor. The fact that he was giving me one last chance trended past the hypocritical.

Or maybe he understood the situation better than I was giving him credit.

"If you show up drunk," Laura said, "or if we even think that we smell booze on your breath, we'll terminate you." She held up a single sheet of paper. "This is your final written warning. We need you to sign it."

I felt a thick knot of humiliation in my throat as I took the warning and pretended to look at it. Honestly, my eyes were so hazy with tears that I couldn't read it at all. I took a pen off Laura's desk and scribbled my name.

I took a deep breath and gathered up what dignity I still had. "I need to go see Mike Dillon. Are we done?"

Casper and Laura nodded in unison.

I walked out, hoping that the rest of the newsroom couldn't see the tears in my eyes.

Laura was right. I was overqualified for the *Post* but she was also dead on when she said that I couldn't find a job with anyone else. If I lost my position here, it would be the final humiliation. I was already at the end of the road. There was nowhere else to go.

And the funny thing? I wanted another drink.

I fought off the urge to go back to my apartment and pour myself a tall, cold one. Instead, I drove to the police department and did my job.

But before I got out of my car, I took my cell phone out of my bag and dialed the hospital. I immediately got the receptionist who after a few of my questions sent me to information who after a few more questions sent me to the floor nurse in Kevin's wing. After an interminable period on hold, I talked to the nurse who summarily told me that Kevin had been discharged.

I tried Kevin's home number.

No answer. But I left a message on his voicemail. "Hey, Kevin, I got a phone call from the hospital. They said you left without settling up your bill. I told them I'd sell my car. That ought to be enough for a deposit. Hey, give me a call when you get a chance, okay? I want to know how you're doing."

After a lengthy pause I did something I hadn't expected.

I said, "I love you."

Oh, my God! What if Caroline listens in while Kevin checks his phone calls? Or what if Ruth hears it? Well, that's okay, for sure.

I shook my head and put the cell phone back into my bag. Then, even though I was parked in the police station parking lot, I locked the doors.

Mike met me at the front desk with a kiss on the cheek and escorted me down the dingy hallway to his office. The harsh, fluorescent lights were much too bright.

Hangovers will do that to ya'.

"So after you and I talked, I found the sex club online. You know, they've got their own website and everything," Mike said as we walked. "I'm sure you know that it's a house over on Matthews Hill."

I smiled. "Did you go over and interview Walt and Sue?"

"Walt and Sue, so you met them?" He wasn't smiling at me when he said it.

"Part of my job."

"You could have damaged this investigation."

"But I didn't."

He opened the door to his office and ushered me in. It's not much bigger than a closet and has no windows. I'm mildly claustrophobic so I've never liked spending time in Mike's office.

I settled into a scuffed-up plastic chair while he sat down at his desk. Photos of his kids hung on the walls next to framed commendations and awards. There were places on the wall where photos had once hung. Now were only vacant spaces marked by empty nail holes. I stored the information away in my head in a file marked 'useless.'

Mike opened. "The owner of the club, Walter Holland, told me the same story you did. Last Wednesday night, around eleven or so, a white male made a scene and threatened to assault a few of the guests. Two paid staff working as security escorted the guy out. We showed Mr. and Mrs. Holland some old arrest photos and they identified that guy as Jim Brenner."

"And?" I was scribbling notes like crazy.

"We immediately got a warrant to search Brenner's house," he explained. "We found enough evidence to lead to the arrests of Jim and Aaron Brenner."

"What evidence?"

"Evidence of blood on their clothing and in their boat and on knives we found on their boat."

Their boat. I knew it.

"Have you gotten a DNA match on the blood found on Jim Brenner's property with any of the victims?"

Mike frowned. "What do you think? I can put samples into a magic DNA machine and out pops the answer? It's going to take a couple of days."

I glared at him. "Don't get surly. I'm just doing my job here."

"We arrested the Brenners, read them their rights, and brought them in for questioning. They want to lawyer up so we have to wait until their attorney gets here."

"Can I talk to them?" I already knew the answer.

"Before we talk to them?" Mike shot back, laughing. "Go write your story, Genie. Be comforted in the knowledge that you helped us get two vicious killers off the street."

And indeed, I should have been elated.

I don't know if it was because I had just been given a formal warning from my bosses at the newspaper and was a hairsbreadth from getting fired. I don't know if it was the time I spent with Isabella Orleans or my confrontation with Frank Mancini.

I don't know if it was because Kevin was out of the hospital and I didn't know what the prognosis was.

I've owned the Connor's Landing story right from the very beginning. I was there the night the bodies were found and I was instrumental in helping the police catch the killers. It was my byline, and my newspaper was the only media outlet that would carry the story come tomorrow morning.

But, instead of being happy, I felt as if I was standing on a beach and in the far distance, I could see the dark shadow of a tsunami rising up on the horizon. It was a hunch that something bad was coming and I couldn't stop it.

Chapter Twenty-one

On my way back to the office, I tried to call Kevin again. The machine picked up and I looked at my watch. It was after six.

Where the hell is he? He left the hospital hours ago. Why isn't he home?

I tried his cell phone and it went straight to his voicemail.

Maybe he's gotten good news. And to celebrate, they're all at Coldstone Creamery for ice cream. That had to be it!

I didn't leave a message and I fought back the urge to drive by his house.

Instead, I went straight back to the office. The last thing I needed was to add fuel to the fire of anxiety and doubt already burning in Laura's and Casper's suspicious minds.

As I sat down at my desk, I saw that Laura had left for the night and Casper was glued to his computer screen. There were only a few reporters left in the newsroom but I felt their eyes sneaking glances at me like those lasers on a cop's rifle that light up where the target is.

I ignored them all and went to work.

I needed as much background information as I could get on both Jim and Aaron Brenner. When I was a young reporter, I would have painstakingly gone through the newspaper's voluminous library of press clippings to find any relevant stories that might shed some light on their lives. Then I would have spent time on the phone, interviewing neighbors and friends to get an idea of how these men were perceived in the community.

I still like to do that.

But now that we're in the twenty-first century, I Googled them.

Jim and Aaron moved to Sheffield with their family when they were both in their teens. Their father was an auto mechanic right up until he died of a heart attack at the age of fifty-three.

Their mother worked as a clerk at McCurdie's, a small department store and died a year after her husband passed away.

I found a piece on Jim and Lynette's wedding that had taken place ten years ago, coincidentally in the same church that Kevin's Uncle Jack had belonged to. The same one where Uncle Jack had been struck by lightning.

There was a news report on Jim Brenner's arrest for assaulting his wife in a bar. He'd pled guilty and was sentenced to a five-hundred-dollar fine and probation.

I found out when Jim started his body shop, bought his house, and when he and Lynette got divorced.

I even managed to punch up the announcement about Lynette's engagement to George Chadwick. There was no mention of Jim Brenner in that story.

I'm very good at finding things on the Internet.

I finished with Jim and turned my attention to Aaron. That's when I found something that I hadn't expected.

According to a news story, Aaron borrowed nearly a half million dollars from Connecticut Sun Bank to buy an apartment building in Bridgeport. He immediately took out an insurance policy worth a million and a half dollars on the building. Two months after the purchase, the building burned down. Miraculously, no one was killed but ten residents, including three children, were treated for smoke inhalation and minor burns.

Aaron filed his claim.

If it hadn't been for the tenacity of a suspicious young executive at the insurance agency who pressed for further investigation, Aaron would have gotten the money, paid off the bank, and walked away with a million dollars. As it turned out, the police eventually were able to ascertain that the fire had been deliberately set "with flagrant disregard for human life."

Aaron received three years in prison.

The young executive who had relentlessly pressured the police into further investigation? John Singewald, who eventually rose to the level of CEO.

The same John Singewald who'd been hacked to pieces along with his wife and four other people out on Connor's Landing last Wednesday night.

On a whim, I called Mike Dillon's cell phone.

When he answered, I immediately asked, "So how long have you known about the connection between Aaron Brenner and John Singewald?"

I heard Mike Dillon chuckle. "After you told me about Jim Brenner showing up at the sex club, we punched up both Jim and Aaron's records. It made it much easier to go to the judge for a search warrant."

"Why didn't you tell me?" I was peevish that he'd made me waste so much time researching Aaron's past.

"Consider it payback for not telling me who gave you the tip about the incident at the club."

I countered, "I can't tell you who my source is. You know that. But let's not forget that I'm the one who told you about the incident in the first place."

Nothing but aggravated silence on the other end of the phone.

"Who gave you the information that helped you make this arrest?" I asked testily.

Finally, he answered, "You did."

"Who's going to get dinner out of this?"

"You are." I could almost hear him smiling over the phone.

"Okay, then. Is there anything else you're holding back on me?"

"Nope, that's pretty much it. I'm going home."

"Say hello to Beth for me." I'd never met his wife, but heard from some of the other cops that she could be a real ball-buster. Rumors said that she disliked the long, crazy hours Mike had to put in and she was making his life miserable.

Another silence hung for a moment before he said quietly, "Genie, one more thing I haven't told you. Beth left me five months ago."

Those empty spots on his office wall? Where his wife's photos had once hung?

I tried to think of something comforting or glib to say. When I couldn't come up with anything, I settled for honest.

"Her loss, Mike."

Chapter Twenty-two

I hung up the phone feeling vaguely depressed. Whether or not Mike's wife was a bitch was irrelevant. He loved her and she left him. She'd hurt him and that made me sad.

I did my best to shake it off and wrote the story about the police arresting Jim and Aaron Brenner. I finished my shift, grateful that I didn't have to interact with Casper again. The clock on my computer screen showed it was a little after ten. Any other time, I would have headed home for a cocktail and some cuddle time with Tucker.

But I wanted to see why the hell I hadn't heard from Kevin.

Less than twenty minutes after I'd left the office, I was parked in Kevin's driveway.

His pickup truck was sitting in its usual spot. Lights were on in his house and even from my car I could hear the high-pitched shriek of a power saw.

Was that why he hadn't heard my phone calls?

I walked up to the door and rang the bell.

My only answer was the shrill screech of a circular metal blade tearing through wood.

I knocked as firmly as I could on the door but the noise continued to drown me out. Finally I tried the doorknob. It was unlocked, so I let myself in.

The air was filled with wooden particulates and the sweet smell of sawdust. "Hey," I shouted.

The earsplitting, metallic scream continued unabated so I walked toward it, into the kitchen where Kevin was carefully slicing a thin line off the top of a panel of wood stretching across two sawhorses.

For a moment I thought of Isadora Orleans and her slow, steady workmanship with oak and pine. She created almost supernatural pieces of art.

Watching him work, total concentration etched across his face, I knew that what he was doing was equally magical.

I am so in love with him.

Kevin must have seen me out of the corner of his eye, because he looked up, switched off the saw and pulled his plastic goggles up onto his head. He was covered in wood dust. He smiled. "Genie."

I waved back at him. "Hi. I tried to call you a couple of times. I was worried."

I want…need to know what the doctors say.

He put the saw down on the kitchen counter next to the sink. "I'm sorry, I didn't check my voicemail."

I had a vague feeling that he was lying to me. I pushed ahead anyway. "So…what did the tests show?"

"Genie." Caroline came up behind me.

I turned to greet her and was gratified when she hugged me.

I wrapped my arms around her shoulders, feeling the soft cotton of her tee shirt against the palms of my hands. I squeezed her back, "Hi, honey. Shouldn't you be in bed?"

She nodded toward her father's work area. "Yeah. Have you ever tried sleeping at a construction site?"

I took a look around and appreciated how much he'd accomplished since the last time I'd been in the kitchen. The ceiling was complete, the recessed lighting was installed and the walls had been repaired. They weren't painted or wallpapered but at least no insulation or wires were showing.

It looked like the counters were all where they were supposed to be and half the cabinet doors had been hung. It was a huge improvement.

I patted the girl. "I see what you mean."

Caroline still had her arms around my waist.

She sure doesn't act like I'm traumatizing her into an eating disorder. Aunt Ruth is a walking, talking bag of crap.

"When did you guys get home?"

"The hospital released Dad around five-thirty but then Ruth dragged us out to Giordano's for dinner," the girl explained.

I looked over at Kevin. I noticed for the first time the sheen of sweat covering his face. Smudges of sawdust streaked across his face that only confirmed to me that this guy was hard, rugged, and rough around the edges.

My carpenter warrior.

"You stopped for dinner? And then come home to work your ass off? I would have figured that all those tests would have worn you out. So what's the verdict?"

He shrugged. "It's all good."

Relief washed over me like a tide of holy water. I wanted Kevin to be good…to be better than good. I wanted him to be great.

"It's good? So you're okay?"

"It's good. I'm like a horse."

I hugged him and held him close. "I think you're more like a horse's behind."

Kevin squeezed me back and then broke away, making a small show out of unplugging his saw. "I'm done for the night." He came over and gently kissed Caroline on the forehead. "Go to bed. We'll start again in the morning."

She hugged her dad. "Okay, see you in the morning. I'm glad you're okay."

He put his forehead against hers. "Me too, baby. Tuck yourself in. I'm going ask Genie to take a short walk with me. I need to get some air, okay?"

Caroline's smile faltered a moment. Then she reached out and squeezed my hand.

Does she know, or suspect, something that I don't?

Caroline left and Kevin touched my arm. "Give me a minute to wipe off my face. I'll be right back."

When I was alone, I studied the work he'd done. It was first class, but there were telltale signs that he was hurrying, a rough edge on one of the counters, ceiling trim that didn't fit snug in the corner, a cupboard door that hung a fraction of an inch too low.

I opened up one of the cabinets and moved things around until I found what I was looking for. A bottle of Dewar's poorly hidden among containers of cooking oil, spices, and condiments.

I pulled out the scotch and found two small glasses.

Hesitating, I thought about what Kevin had said in the hospital. That they wanted to see how much of his liver was functional. *No scotch for Kevin.*

Before I could put the bottle back, Kevin came back into the kitchen. His face looked scrubbed and he was wearing a clean shirt.

In one practiced movement, he took the bottle and poured two glasses. He picked up his and downed it in one gulp, closing his eyes with content. He opened them again, still holding the bottle. "Let's go sit in the backyard."

"This first." I stepped up to kiss him. I could smell the soap he'd used to wash his face and the deodorant he'd put on in a vain attempt to cover the scent of his sweat.

I couldn't help myself. I wrapped my arms around his waist and hugged him tight, my face pressed hard against his chest.

"You shouldn't, I'm a mess," he mumbled, hugging me back, still holding the half empty bottle, kissing my neck.

"That's why I love you."

"C'mon," Kevin led me out the kitchen door.

The temperature was easily twenty degrees steamier outside and a hundred percent more humid. Immediately, I felt beads of perspiration under my arms.

A slice of new moon hung like a neon hook in the sky, barely illuminating the stacks of lumber and piles of scrap that were the professional rubble of Kevin's backyard. Invisible crickets chirped a soothing symphony in the tall grass along the fence.

We sat side by side at the picnic table and Kevin poured himself another drink. I hadn't yet sipped at mine.

"So what's the deal at the hospital? What was that business about liver function?"

He looked up at the sky. "You ever really look at the stars?"

I didn't look up at the sky. I already knew what was there. Instead, I concentrated on sipping at my scotch and nervously watched his face.

"I read someplace that we're looking at light that's been traveling through space for millions of years. We're looking into the past, seeing stars that may have already flamed out. They're already dead. But we can still see their light; still see what they looked like when they were burning, when they were still alive."

I don't like the way this is sounding.

"What did the doctors say, Kevin?"

"So it's like we're looking at ghosts. We can see them, but some of those stars are already dead."

"What did the doctors say, Kevin?"

His eyes left the sky and looked into my own. He sighed. "Liver failure."

I glanced down at the bottle of scotch sitting on the table. "Should you be drinking that?"

"Damage is done."

"How bad?"

"Close to total."

I blinked my eyes. "What's that mean?"

"It means I have maybe three months."

As those words left his mouth, in my mind, the crickets stopped their symphony, the cars on the highway ceased their incessant hiss, the crescent moon dimmed and the stars flickered. At those words, it felt as if my heart stopped beating.

"What?" I asked, stupidly.

He reached out and put his hand over mine. "It's terminal."

"No, it's not!"

He slowly nodded and his grip tightened on my hand.

"I'm serious. I don't care what they say. We'll do what we have to do to beat this. What about a transplant? They do it all the time."

"They were very honest. I'm an alcoholic. I brought this on myself. I'm not a candidate."

"Bullshit. We'll fix this."

Simple as that. You can do anything if you set your mind to it. You have a plan and be ready to do what's necessary to get the job done. Right?

"We'll get a second opinion. I know one of the top gastro guys at Yale. I'll make an appointment for you tomorrow morning."

Kevin gazed into my eyes, silent.

Don't answer me. Let me take care of you. Let me make you better.

He nodded. "Sure."

I cannot cry. No crying.

"I haven't said anything to Caroline, yet." His words were simple, stunning in their meaning.

I took a hard sip on my scotch and felt the amber liquid light a fire all the way down my throat into my stomach. "Yeah, I think it's too soon. Let's find out for sure how bad this really is." I sounded braver than I actually was. "No point getting her worried over something we can get fixed."

Denial is such a wonderful thing.

We stopped talking for a few minutes and listened to the sounds of the night and looked up at Kevin's stars. They truly were beautiful. The ambient illumination of the city streetlamps wiped away the more nuanced and subtle of the tiniest stars, but the bold ones poked their way through the night like the hot, brave souls that they were.

"I ever tell you that when I was a kid," Kevin said, "I wanted to be an astronaut?"

"I thought you wanted to be James Bond."

"That too. I thought I could be both."

We both sat quietly for a moment. I was surprised to see silent flashes of heat lightning in the distance. That's a phenomenon that always amazed me. These strange flashes of light with no attendant rumbles of thunder—a meteorological magic trick.

I could use a magic trick right about now, a really good one.

"I didn't get to be James Bond and I didn't get to be an astronaut. In the end, I really didn't do anything meaningful at all."

I surprised both of us when I reached out and cuffed him hard along the back of his head.

"Oowwww," he complained. "That hurt. Why'd you do that?"

I'm angry, angry at the doctors, angry at God…angry at him.

I pointed my finger at him and felt tears burning in my eyes. "Just because you're sick, don't think you're going drag me down a fucking black, rat hole of depression. I'm not going to let you take me there and, goddamn it, I'm *not* going to let *you* go there either."

He blinked and rubbed his head, not really knowing what to say.

I felt the wet heat of tears in my eyes when I growled, "You're a wonderful father, a great friend, and a terrific lover. You're a good goddamned human being. Don't trivialize that… or the next time I'm breaking your freakin' nose and don't think I can't do it."

He blinked again at my harsh words. Then he leaned forward and kissed me, long and hard.

Oh no, horrible. He's kissing me and I'm crying.

Kevin withdrew his lips only slightly from my own and whispered, "I love you."

I leaned forward and locked my lips onto his for a second time, sobbing uncontrollably.

Then I slowly pulled away, wiped the trails of tears off my face and gruffly whispered in a voice I barely recognized as my own, "I love you too. Are you going to let me help you?"

"Yeah."

I touched his face with my fingers, wiping the moistness from my tears off the stubble on his cheeks.

"Are you going to pull through this so that we can live together and drive each other crazy?" I was having a hard time keeping from falling into another crying jag.

"You already drive me crazy."

"You want to come home with me and have sex? I hear it's therapeutic as hell." I tried to laugh.

"You know what I really want?"

"What?"

"For you to take me up to my bedroom and hold me until I go to sleep."

I did that.

We snuck up the stairs and past Caroline's bedroom. As I crept by her door, I stopped and peeked in. She was motionless under a sheet except for the rise and fall of her breathing. After the tension of the last two days, she must have been exhausted.

Her hug tonight—so sweet.

When we got to Kevin's room, he practically fell onto the bed.

I crawled in next to him. I laid my head on his shoulder and my hand on his chest. We were both completely clothed, but somehow it was as intimate as I've ever been with anyone in my entire life.

"It's going to be okay," I said softly.

"I know."

We lay there holding each other for a long time. No one said anything because there weren't any words that could possibly be adequate or appropriate for what Kevin was facing.

For what all of us were facing.

I know what I wanted to say. I wanted to offer a long litany of encouraging platitudes and advice, some of which I'd already said while we'd been sitting in the backyard. I wanted to rail against God. How could a just and loving deity do something so horrible to such a wonderful human being?

How could God do this to Kevin's daughter? She'd already suffered through the awful death of her mother.

Was she going to have to face it all one more time?

I wanted to cry again.

I knew the moment Kevin had blessedly fallen asleep when I felt his breathing slow down and it became deep and regular. I think I dozed off myself because the next time I checked my watch, it was nearly three in the morning.

I carefully crawled out of bed and covered Kevin up with a blanket. I took a clean sheet of paper out of his printer and wrote him a note that said that I love him and I'll call him in the morning.

I went home and walked Tucker.

Then I drank two more glasses of wine while I curled up on my couch and I cried until I didn't have any tears left. When I finally fell into my own bed, I swore to all that was holy that I would find a way to keep Kevin alive.

By God, I'm not going to let him die.

Chapter Twenty-three

I was making coffee when my cell phone went off. "Yes?"

"Genie?"

It was Laura Ostrowski. For the briefest of terrifying seconds, I irrationally wondered if I was late to work again. Then I recalled that I wasn't due in the office until three that afternoon.

"Yeah," I repeated, watching Tucker eye me anxiously. I hadn't taken him for his morning walk yet.

"Did I wake you?"

"Nope. I've been up for a whole five minutes."

"Good." She didn't sound convincing. "I just got a phone call from Paula Ramos, the attorney who's representing Jim and Aaron Brenner."

"Oh yeah?"

"Yeah. Aaron Brenner wants to do a jailhouse interview, against his attorney's advice."

"He does?"

I heard Laura sigh with irritation. "He specifically asked for you."

"When?"

"Eleven this morning."

"Police station?"

"That's where he's being held." She sounded clearly annoyed. And why wouldn't she, after all, last night she'd threatened to fire me.

And now she had to tell me that Aaron Brenner specifically wanted to talk to me.

That had to piss her off.

"I'll be there." I expected that would be the end of our conversation.

"One more assignment," Laura added. "For this evening."

I wanted to remind her that, if I was interviewing Aaron Brenner at eleven, I was starting my shift early. And because the company hated to pay overtime, I should clock out early. But knowing how close I was to being terminated, I stayed quiet and listened.

"A group of paranormal investigators are going out on the Sheffield Seaport Association ferry boat."

I rolled my eyes. "Why?"

"Apparently, on this night sometime during the Great Depression, a rich guy by the name of Bartholomew Gault jumped off his fishing boat and drowned himself in the harbor."

That name sounds vaguely familiar.

"Ring any bells?" Laura asked.

"Yeah, but I can't say why."

"You wrote about him just a couple of days ago."

Now the bells were ringing.

"The Chadwick house out on Connor's Landing," I said quietly. "Bartholomew Gault bought it in 1910."

"And died on this very night in 1930."

I paused before I asked my next question. I didn't want to sound like a wise ass. "Okay, what's that got to do with me?"

"Ghost hunter by the name of Stella Barry says that a strange light has been seen out on the harbor every year on this night not far from the lighthouse on Fisher's Island. She's going out on the ferry tonight to take some pictures and invited one of our reporters to come along."

I closed my eyes and counted, one, two, three, four...

Around the time I got to ten, Laura added, "Stella Barry requested you by name. It seems she read your story on the Chadwick House and its inherent bad fortune."

Asked for by name by the Brenners' lawyer and by a ghost-buster named Stella. Notoriety has its plusses and minuses.

Any other time I would have wheedled and complained and found a way to get out of a paranormal investigator's obvious attempt at free publicity, but I was on thin ice here. So I simply said, "What time and where does the ferry leave from?"

I could almost hear the sound of quiet satisfaction in the short silence on the phone. She knew I hated doing features like this. "Be at the city dock at nine-thirty. I'd bring some bug spray."

Without saying good-bye, she hung up.

Bitch.

I had time before I needed to be at the police station to talk with Aaron Brenner. There was a shower to be taken, makeup to be applied, coffee to be consumed, and a dog to be walked, but first I wanted to spend a few minutes in front of my computer.

There was something in the world that was more important than my job with *The Sheffield Post,* an interview with a killer, or even a walk with Tucker.

Kevin Bell was sick…really sick.

I had to find a way to save him.

Hitting the familiar keys to work the magic of my favorite search engines, I looked for information on catastrophic liver failure. It wasn't good news. Causes could be any one or a combination of factors—hepatitis, cancer, diabetes, overuse of acetaminophen, abuse of drugs, alcoholism.

Bingo.

Prognosis was bad. Really bad. He was looking at becoming jaundiced, suffering from a painful buildup of fluid in the abdomen, fatigue, depression, and reduced brain function.

Oh, and death. Let's not forget that.

I reached for my cell phone and found the number for Dr. Paul Durham, a gastroenterologist at Yale. I'd done a piece on him a few years ago when I was freelancing in New York. Durham was articulate, good looking, and arrogant.

He was also one of the best in his field.

I reached his answering service and left a message, reminding him who I was and requested a return phone call. I was sure he'd remember me. He'd aggressively hit on me all during the interview. It's not professional to be seduced by your story subject, not to mention, I was married to a very jealous New York City cop at the time. So I'd gently rebuffed him with the vague promise that we might get together sometime in the future.

Yes, I was reasonably confident that he'd remember me.

And I knew that if anyone could increase Kevin's chances of survival, it would be Durham.

• • ● • •

"I've warned Aaron against doing this interview with you," Paula Ramos stated. The attorney was in her mid-thirties, about five-three, slightly overweight, and exhibited the warmth of an ice cube. Her hair was brown and unremarkable. She wore black-rimmed no-nonsense glasses through which she stared at me without blinking.

"I'm not particularly comfortable with this either," Mike Dillon added.

The three of us stood in front of a closed doorway. Mike had his arms folded. He said, "Depending on the way the story is presented, it could improperly influence a jury seated at the Brenners' trial."

The attorney nodded slightly. "It could just as easily influence them to be biased against the Brenners."

I had my heavy bag slung over my shoulder and the strap was digging into my shoulder. "So what do we do?"

Mike shrugged. "I guess we do the interview."

I knew that if Mike really wanted to keep the interview from happening, he could.

The same with Paula Ramos.

They each had an agenda. Mike would be sitting behind one-way glass listening to my questions, hoping that he'd learn something more than he already knew.

The attorney was hoping that I'd write a piece that would plant the seeds of doubt in the populace of Sheffield, so that when the jury was chosen, part of her job will have already been done by me.

I wanted a good story.

I recognized Aaron Brenner immediately from his shaved head, broad shoulders, trimmed beard, and piercing ice-blue eyes. He was seated behind a heavy, wooden table and wore an orange jumpsuit.

"Miss Chase," he announced with a nod of his head, "thank you for coming. Pardon me for not standing." He jangled the handcuffs that attached his wrists to a chain locked around his waist. "I'm afraid that all of this is attached to an eyebolt in the floor."

Ramos turned to Mike. "This is unnecessary." Then she looked at me and ordered, "You will not put the fact that Aaron is chained up like some kind of animal in your story."

By way of explanation, Mike stated flatly, "He's been charged with six counts of murder."

I noticed that a uniformed cop had followed Mike into the room.

"He's not going to be in here during the interview," Ramos said, pointing angrily at the beefy officer.

Mike smiled. "He most certainly is or this isn't going to happen. I'm not letting two women sit in here alone with a killer."

"Alleged," the attorney reminded.

"Right," Mike said dryly. "Half an hour, Genie."

"Thanks, Mike."

After the door closed behind the deputy chief, both Ramos and I sat down across the table from Aaron. The big cop behind us remained standing, clasped his hands behind his back, and stared silently at an invisible spot on the opposite wall.

I took my recorder out of my bag and placed it on the table. Switching it on, I asked, "So Mr. Brenner. I'm afraid this is a little different than the last time we talked. Are you doing okay?"

"Reverend," he reminded me.

"Of course, I'm sorry…how are you doing, Reverend?"

He glanced at the tiny voice recorder and then looked back up at me, nodding. "My faith in the Lord sustains me. That, and Jim and I are innocent."

I leaned forward, putting my notebook on the table and holding my pen in my hand. "Where *is* Jim? How come he's not here?"

Aaron glanced at Ramos. Then he looked back at me. "As you probably know, I'm doing this against the advice of our attorney. Perhaps Jim is a better listener than I am. He's waiting in his cell hoping that I don't say something stupid."

"If your attorney advised you against this interview, why are you doing it?"

"I want the truth to see the light of day, Miss Chase, because sometimes the truth is trivialized, marginalized, or never makes it into the courtroom."

Like the unfair outcome of the Jimmy Fitzgerald manslaughter case last week, I had to agree with Aaron Brenner. The truth certainly didn't have much to do with that verdict.

I checked my recorder to make certain it was running. I locked eyes with Aaron. "The last time I saw you, I asked you where you and your brother were last Wednesday night. You told me that you and Jim were home the entire evening. We both know that's not true."

Paula Ramos grunted painfully and then groaned, "I hope this isn't the tone you're going to take all the way through this interview."

Aaron shook his head and held his hand up as far as the chains would allow. "It's okay, Paula." Then he directed his attention back to me, "Ever since Jim and Lynette split up, I've been driving down from Maine to comfort my brother on the day of his wedding anniversary."

I glanced over at the attorney who appeared to be studying her reflection in the large mirror on the wall. In reality, I knew she was wondering who was behind the one-way glass.

Aaron continued, "I'm always afraid Jim might do something stupid."

"Like start drinking again?"

"Like start drinking again," he repeated. "This would have been their tenth anniversary. Over the weeks leading up to it, Jim and I'd been talking on the phone a lot. This particular anniversary was going to be hard for him. He was still hopelessly in love with Lynette."

"So you drove down on Wednesday?"

"I got to Jim's place at around five," he stated. "He wasn't around, but I've got a key to his house and let myself in. I waited around for about an hour and then called him on his cell phone."

"Where was he?"

Aaron hesitated and glanced over at his attorney who only shrugged. "Jim was sitting in the parking lot at the Stop-n-Shop."

"What was he doing there?"

He waited again before he answered. "He was following Lynette."

"Why?"

For the first time, Aaron appeared agitated. "It was his anniversary. He wanted to see his wife."

"Ex-wife."

He nodded.

I took a deep breath and measured my next words carefully. "Did he confront Lynette?"

"No," Aaron answered. "I told him that it would be a good idea for him to come home."

"Did he come home?"

"Yes, then I saw he'd been drinking."

"How bad was he?"

"Hammered," Aaron replied.

"What happened next?"

"I told him to go sleep it off."

"And did he?" I asked.

Aaron nodded. "He slept a few hours…until about nine-thirty."

"At what point did your brother drive to the club in Matthews Hill?"

Aaron sat for a moment, thinking about what he was going to say. "When he got up, I could tell Jim was still buzzed. I tried to get some coffee into him and he told me how this wasn't the first time he'd followed Lynette. He'd apparently done it a number of times over the last few weeks. Three of those times, three consecutive Wednesday nights, he'd followed her and her husband from Connor's Landing to a house in Matthews Hill, a place he was convinced was a sex club, a place where the wicked perform sinful, perverted acts of adultery."

"So, last Wednesday, Jim figured that Lynette and George Chadwick were probably going to be at that house?"

Aaron sneered with disgust. "On the night of their anniversary, Lynette was going to violate herself with other men."

"And this upset Jim."

"Miss Chase, have you ever been in a similar situation? When someone you love was fornicating for the amusement of others? Do you know that kind of humiliation and shame?"

In my own way, I did. I still recall what it felt like when I caught my first husband naked in bed with another woman. It was like he'd torn my heart right out of my chest.

And then I realized that must have been what Kevin felt when he heard that I'd slept with Frank. For a brief, illuminating moment I wanted walk out of the interview, go out into the hallway, and cry the guilt out of my soul.

I did my best to shake it off. "Yeah, I've been there."

"Me too," Aaron remarked. "I was married when I went to prison. Barb was really better than I deserved. She's bright, pretty, and deserved better than me. After I'd been in prison for about two months I heard that my wife was sleeping with another man. After only two months, with our next door neighbor. At first I was so angry I wanted to kill them both. Then for a while I wanted to kill myself. But in the end, it was the tipping point in my life that made me find God. God gave me the strength to go on. Now multiply that kind of pain by the number of men that Lynette would lie down with that night."

"So when did Jim decide to drive to Matthews Hill?" I asked again.

Aaron shook his head. "I don't know. After we talked and we prayed and we argued and prayed some more, Jim said he was going to that house to talk to Lynette, and he was going to do it whether I liked it or not. Miss Chase, I couldn't let my brother go alone. I was genuinely concerned about what he might do."

"He's a violent man, isn't he?"

The attorney interrupted, "Don't answer that!"

Aaron responded with a pained, awkward silence.

"What time did you get to the club?"

"I'm not sure, sometime around eleven?"

Just before they open the "rooms."

"So what happened?" I prodded.

"I drove Jim to that…place. We found Lynette's SUV in the parking lot around back. I was supposed to wait in the car while Jim found a way in to talk to her."

I decided to momentarily switch gears. "Aaron, did either one of you have anything to drink after Jim woke up?"

Aaron looked down at his feet and was silent for a long moment. When he looked back up at me, his face reflected a profound expression of personal sadness. "Both of us. When I'd tried to make him drink the coffee, he opened another bottle of Jack. We argued. Then in a fit of my own stupidity and rage I told him that if he was going to ruin his life again, I would too." He remembered that night. "He just dared me. He thought I was bluffing."

"So you had something to drink too."

"Yes."

"How much did you have?"

"Any alcohol for either of us is too much."

I thought about this for a moment. I know just how stupid you can be when you drink. And once you start, you can't stop. "What was he hoping to accomplish, confronting Lynette at that house?"

Aaron shrugged. "I don't know. Maybe she'd see how much he still loved her. Maybe he could talk her out of debasing herself with those other men. Maybe he needed to see her. Whatever the reason, I watched as he went through a side entrance. I waited in the car and it felt like an eternity but, really, I think I was only out there for about ten or fifteen minutes. I got worried and I went in to look for him."

"What did you see?" I asked.

"The doorway I went through opened up into a kitchen. No one was there but I heard music, Motown, and walked through another door. It was a big room with high ceilings. It was kind of dark. The only light was from some colorful lamps hanging from the ceiling. There were couples dancing, there was a DJ. It all seemed normal. I was very relieved to see that everyone still had their clothes on."

If they'd gone in a half hour later, all bets on that would be off.

"Then I saw the bar in the middle of the room and spotted Jim. He was sitting on a barstool, hunched over the counter," Aaron sighed, shaking his head. "Jim was watching a small group of people standing maybe about fifteen feet from him. Lynette was one of them."

Aaron continued, "I stood there keeping my eye on Jim and then I saw a guy come up behind Lynette and put his arms around her. That's when Jim got up."

I held my hand up to stop Aaron for a moment. I asked him, "The guy who put his arms around Lynette. Was it John Singewald?"

Aaron Brenner shifted in his chair and bent his head from side to side, as if trying to relieve a stiff neck. Finally, he said, "No, Miss Chase. It wasn't John Singewald. But I recognized Singewald right away, even in that dark room, standing with those folks, right next to Lynette. I'd spent a lot of time thinking about him while I was in prison. Imagine my surprise when I saw that he was there that night, a member of that immoral party. Another reason he'll spend everlasting eternity in hell."

"Let me just be absolutely clear here," I said. "This is the same John Singewald who helped put you in prison?"

He took a breath. "Yes, Miss Chase."

I took a moment before I asked my next question. "So, Jim sees a man put his arm around Lynette. What happened next?"

I already knew who had put his arm around Lynette. It was Ted, the source who'd called me and blew the whistle on Jim Brenner.

"Jim gets up in this guy's face and starts saying something that I can't hear, but I know that Jim's been drinking and I know that this isn't going to end well. Anyway, I see this guy step back and Lynette's husband, George, puts himself between Jim and Lynette. I start to walk over now and I can hear Jim saying words like 'whore' and 'adulterer' and then I see Jim push George really hard so that he falls against Lynette and the guy who had his arm around her."

"Then what happened?"

"By the time I got there, a couple of other guys, I don't know, bouncers maybe, were right beside me. We all grabbed Jim by the arms and escorted him out of the house."

Now we reach the most important part of the interview.

I leaned forward. "What happened after that?"

Aaron sat in his chair in silence.

"Aaron?"

He remained silent, staring into his lap.

"Aaron?" I insisted. "Did you go out to Connor's Landing?"

His piercing blue eyes looked up into my own and he shook his head. "No." His voice barely a whisper. "We went down to Riley's. It's a bar just up the street from Jim's house."

I shook my head. "You and Jim went to a bar?"

He nodded, almost imperceptibly. "We were there until closing time and got blind, stinking drunk. The bartender will remember us. I know there's a video camera behind the bar. And I paid by credit card. Check with them, the credit card receipt will show we couldn't have been out on Connor's Landing."

At almost the second that Aaron Brenner was finishing his story, the door to the interrogation room flew open. Mike Dillon stood in the doorway and from the dark expression on his face, he was really pissed.

"Why didn't you tell us about Riley's?" Mike demanded.

Aaron looked up at the cop with incredible sadness in his expression. "It's not something that Jim and I are proud of. There's nothing about last Wednesday night that we're proud of."

Mike couldn't believe what he was hearing. "You'd rather we arrest you for murder?"

Aaron looked down into his lap, silent.

Mike continued his tirade, "You mean to tell me that you had nothing to do with what happened on Connor's Landing?

Brenner slowly shook his head.

"You're telling me that Jim's ex-wife and the same guy who sent you to prison both died out on Connor's Landing and it's all a big coincidence?" Mike shouted.

Aaron looked up at Mike. "Yes."

The cop had one more question. "In Jim's closet, we found shoes with traces of blood on them. We also found blood on a knife in his boat. Whose blood is it?"

The prisoner stared at me when he answered. "Nobody's blood."

"What do you mean?" I asked. "Nobody's blood."

"It's not human. Jim likes to fish. He hooked into a school of blues last week and never cleaned up the mess."

I heard Mike behind me say, "Jesus H. Christ."

As Mike walked out and Paula Ramos followed him, she insisted, "I want my clients released immediately."

Mike responded, "Don't hold your breath."

The guard remained silent behind me. Aaron sat without a word across the table. I wondered what my next question should be.

Finally, I asked, "Aaron?"

"Yes?"

"What's the real reason you didn't tell the police you had an alibi?"

He smiled slightly. "Off the record?"

"Sure, why not." I turned off my recorder.

"I wanted to see this in the paper." His voice low. "I wanted the world to know the sins taking place at that house."

"Did you want to embarrass the cops too?"

He grinned. "Yeah, maybe a little."

"Well, you did that. Do you think that those people out on Connor's Landing died for a reason?"

He leaned slowly back in his chair before he answered. "Everything happens for a reason."

"Do you think they died because they were sinners?"

"In Romans 6:23, the Bible says that the wages of sin is death."

"So you're saying that God wanted those people dead?"

His brow furrowed. "I can't pretend to know what God is thinking, Miss Chase. But I hear Albert Einstein said something that I'll always remember."

"What's that Aaron?"

"God doesn't play dice with the universe."

Could be true. All I knew was that if the Brenners are innocent, my days of being out front on this story had just ended.

Chapter Twenty-four

It took me about an hour to knock out the story about the arrest and release, pending confirmation of their alibi, of the Brenner brothers. Unfortunately, this meant publicly outing Temptation House since it was now an integral part of the story. This was the first time the "swingers" aspect of the murder would appear in print. It would most likely put the club out of business.

I felt a twinge of regret about that. The owners seemed like really nice people and the people who visited the club weren't hurting anyone.

Laura Ostrowski paced up and down the newsroom while I pounded away at my keyboard. When I finished, I hit the button sending the story to her computer. I nodded to her, signaling that it was done.

She nearly broke into a sprint to get back to her office. Laura smelled the hot, mouth-watering scent of the salacious, six-column, front page lead on tomorrow morning's paper.

At that point, what I really wanted to do was to walk in with the warning letter that she and Casper had forced me sign last night and tell her to bend over so that I could stick it up her dowdy posterior.

But instead I punched up Kevin's number on my office phone while watching Laura devour my story with her eyes about the Brenner boys and the sex club.

"Hello?" Caroline answered.

"Hey, sweetie." I spoke as brightly as I could. I still didn't know for sure how much she knew about Kevin. "I was thinking about taking your dad out to lunch. Is he around?"

"Aunt Ruth drove him to Mount Sinai Hospital in New York. He's not supposed to be back until around two-thirty."

Suddenly I was very, very jealous of Aunt Ruth. If anyone was going to save Kevin's life, I wanted it to be me.

How petty can I be? What's more important? Curing Kevin or beating Ruth?

Well, the answer was both. Kevin came first, of course.

But beating Ruth was a really close second.

As I talked with Caroline, I pulled the cell phone out of my bag and looked for messages. Sure enough, Dr. Durham had returned my call.

Damn it. It was probably while I was interviewing Aaron Brenner. I'd had my phone turned off.

"Genie?" Caroline snapped my attention back to the landline.

"Yeah, hon?"

"I'd really like it if we could talk. Just you and me."

I glanced at my watch. It was nearly a quarter to one. "Tell you what. I am starving. How about if I buy you lunch?" It would give me a chance to talk with Caroline and check her out myself to see if she was, actually, suffering from some sort of eating disorder.

"Cool," she bubbled.

"I'll pick you up in about fifteen minutes."

As I walked by Laura Ostrowski's office, I could almost see her forming the words with her lips as she read my story.

Damn, I'm good.

On the drive over to Random Road, I called Dr. Durham.

It was his private line and he answered on the second ring. "Durham," he announced, brusquely, the important physician.

"Paul, its Geneva Chase."

"Genie." His voice took on an audible smile. "What a nice

surprise it was to get your message. Are you taking me up on my offer for dinner?"

"No, I'm sorry. I wish I was calling you under different circumstances. I have a very dear friend who was just diagnosed with liver disease…they're telling him that it's terminal."

I felt the words catch in my throat. Saying it out loud makes it more real.

He held a brief silence before he said, "That doesn't sound good."

"But there're ways to treat it?"

"Well, I'd have to have a look at him."

"We can beat this thing."

"Has he consulted anyone about a transplant?"

"He's not a candidate. What are our options?"

I heard him sigh. "Well, there are certainly protocols."

Protocols? What the hell did that mean?

He continued, "Look, Genie, why don't you bring your friend in here so that we can assess his situation. We're working on some cutting edge treatments that have exhibited some very promising results. It's very possible he could be a good candidate for one of them."

My brain heard Paul's words and translated them. He was saying that Kevin didn't have a snowball's chance in hell so let's make him a guinea pig and try out something really experimental. Hell, why not? He's got nothing to lose.

But my heart heard something completely different. That they were working with something brand new. Hopeful treatments that might actually keep Kevin alive. Bring him in. He's got everything to gain.

I wanted to believe my heart. "How soon can you see him?"

"You can bring him in Friday afternoon, say about three. This friend of yours? He's special to you?"

"He's special, Paul. You don't know how special."

I picked up Caroline and drove us both to a small place on the water called Sound Bites. It's a hamburger shack with little to offer in the way of a menu, but once you ordered your food, you can eat outside on a deck that overlooks a marina right on the shoreline of Long Island Sound. The food's little more than commercial grill and grease pit but the view is fabulous.

We sat on either side of a weatherbeaten, wooden picnic table. The hard pine, stained with years of condiments, displayed a litany of names that had been cut into its surface. A plastic garbage can near the corner of the building, almost filled to the brim with dirty paper plates, napkins, and soda cups, attracted about a dozen bees.

With the sun playing hide and seek behind a growing bank of clouds, the air was temperate and the breeze from the sound was exhilarating. The boats in the marina floated and bobbed on the water with a regal insouciance.

All in all, it was a pleasant afternoon to be outside. Too bad Sound Bites didn't have a liquor license.

Before I took a big bite out of a greasy cheeseburger, I asked, "So how're you doin'?"

Caroline swatted away a bee and looked out over the water. "I'm okay," but then quickly cut to the chase. "I need for you to tell me the truth."

I chewed slowly. This really wasn't a conversation I wanted to have. With my mouth still half-filled with food, I asked, "What do you want to know?"

She looked me right in the eye. "Is Daddy dying?"

Her bluntness nearly took my breath away. "What's your dad told you?"

"Just that he might be sick."

"Well," I answered inconclusively and shrugged.

"Is he?" She pushed for an answer.

I thought, this is a discussion Kevin should be having with his daughter.

Before I had a chance to answer, Caroline told me, "Aunt Ruth says that Dad's extremely ill, that he might not live."

What?

That bitch! That heartless, cold-hearted, stone-faced bitch.

Trying hard to hold my temper, I gritted my teeth. "What else did Aunt Ruth say?"

Caroline's hands formed tight fists resting in front of her on the rough, wooden surface of the picnic table. "She said that she was taking him to see doctors in New York. If they can't help him, nobody can."

I reached over and put my hands over hers. "Let's see what those guys at Mount Sinai say, honey. But just so you know, I talked with a doctor from Yale this morning who wants to see us on Friday. He's the absolute best in the business. If I have anything to say about it, your dad's going to be okay."

She looked down at her lap. "Aunt Ruth said that if anything happens to Daddy, she wants me live with her."

Let me see if I've got this straight. Ruth wants to hook up with her dead sister's husband? And then when it looks like he might die, she goes after the daughter? What is she, a vampire that feeds on grief?

Caroline continued to look down. "If something happens, I don't want to live with Aunt Ruth."

"Nothing's going to happen."

"Can I live with you?" She started biting her lower lip.

That took me by surprise. I tried to wrap my mind around what I'd just heard from her.

It's not like I never wanted kids. I think that if you catch them on a good day, they can be kind of cute, like puppies. But I can barely take care of myself, how could I even think about taking care of someone else?

I must have waited a little too long to answer because Caroline cast her gaze out over the water again and quietly mumbled, "I was just kidding."

I was still holding her hands when she tried to pull away.

I held tight. "Caroline, you hardly know me."

She continued to look away from me, staring out over the water. "I know that my dad loves you. And that you love my dad. And my dad says he's known you his whole life."

I squeezed her hands even tighter until she turned back to

face me. Caroline had tears in her eyes. "Dad says you're a good person. He says you have a good heart."

I shrugged. "When we were kids, I once saw your dad eat a bug to win a bet. So what's he know?"

She smiled nervously for a second and then we stared at each other for an uncomfortably long time until Caroline asked, "So, can I?"

I sighed. "Nothing's going to happen to your dad, honey. I won't let it."

She kept looking at me with eyes so much like Kevin's that I could have cried. Finally, I said, "But in case anything happens, and it's not going to, you can come live with me."

That's when the tears really started, both hers and mine.

She stood up and came around the picnic table. I stood up at the same time and we just hugged each other. We hugged each other so tight I didn't think we'd ever let go.

We had nothing in common and we had everything in common

We both loved Kevin.

So we both loved each other.

Chapter Twenty-five

When we finished crying, we talked and laughed, finished our cheeseburgers, fries and learned about each other. I gave her the sanitized version of my life, leaving out the ugliness of three failed marriages and a drinking problem. I figured that if she ever did become my roommate, she'd learn about all of that in its own sweet time.

I discovered that, for the most part, Caroline likes school. She aces English and History but struggles with Math. Her best friend is Jessica Oberon who lives with her two moms on Evans Road just three blocks from Caroline's house. She told me about Rob Wempen who's in her English class and is kind of dorky and cute all at the same time but she finds him interesting because he reads poetry and wants to write novels.

That was the segue to her mom. She told me how much her mother had enjoyed books, all kinds of books—mysteries, romance, travel, adventure, poetry, even the classics. And Caroline talked about how they all like watching movies together in their family room. Their favorites were *National Lampoon's Christmas Vacation* and all the *Toy Story* and *Shrek* movies but their absolute favorite was *Princess Bride*.

She talked about how strong her mom had been when her dad was sick for an extended time and they were, as her mom put it, "a little strapped for cash." But her mom never complained and her dad eventually went away for a little while.

That's particularly curious. It sounds suspiciously like a stint in rehab.

She went on to tell me how her mom got sick right after that, and then it was her father's turn to be strong.

I knew this part of the story wasn't going to have a happy ending so I feigned looking at my watch and suggested we'd better head back to her house just in case her dad got home before us and started to worry.

As we drove back, I wanted to ask her a tough question. She was looking out the passenger's side window of my Sebring, staring at her neighbors' houses as I drove past them on Providence Avenue. "Caroline?" I raised my voice to be heard over a Taylor Swift song on the radio.

She turned toward me, cheerfully. "Yeah?"

"Don't get pissed off at me if I ask you something, okay?"

She shrugged. "Okay."

"It's serious."

"Okay."

"Do you have an eating disorder?"

I cringed inside even as I asked it. I'd watched her as she ate her lunch, a big, fat double grease burger, a bucket of fries, and a large Pepsi. She hadn't wolfed it down, but she'd finished most of it.

She rolled her eyes and groaned. "Who told you that? Aunt Ruth?"

I'm a fanatic about protecting my sources, but I really don't like Ruth. "Yeah."

Caroline turned off the radio so that she wouldn't have to shout. "Sometime last May, Aunt Ruth was over at our house for dinner. I had a stomach bug. Dad grilled some scallops. I hate scallops. After we ate, I ran off to the bathroom and barfed. When I came out, Aunt Ruth was standing there waiting for me. She asked the same question you did. She asked me if I had an eating disorder. I told her no, but she wasn't hearing any of it. She told me that she wanted me to see her stupid therapist, Dr. Tina Beaufort. She said that if I had a disorder or I didn't, it would be a good idea to talk to the doctor because I'd been through a lot, what with Mom dying and all."

I swung my eyes away from the road for a moment and studied her face. She was gazing out the windshield, looking in the distance at something that wasn't there. "Well, honey, you *did* go through a lot. Did this Dr. Tina help you?"

She cocked her head to one side when she answered. "I had a couple of sessions with her and then she gave me a prescription for antidepressants."

"This doctor gave you pills? Do you think you're depressed?"

"I dunno, maybe I was. It was pretty bad when Mom got sick."

Even worse when she died. And now this kid is facing the same thing with her father.

"Are you still taking the pills?"

"I took 'em for a couple of weeks," Caroline said. "Then I stopped. I know that Aunt Ruth is on some kind of meds. I don't want to be like her. I don't want to spend the rest of my life looking at the world through a pill bottle."

We didn't say anything more for a while which gave me time to consider it all. I wasn't altogether sure that Caroline still didn't suffer from a mild form of depression. A couple of weeks in therapy isn't much. But who wouldn't be depressed? She'd watched her mother die a little at a time, inch by agonizing inch, right in front of her eyes.

There's nothing about death that's fun. And for someone as young as Caroline, it's particularly hard. When you're that age, you don't think that anyone should die.

Period.

But Caroline didn't have bulimia. She was thirteen and had the metabolism of caffeinated ferret. Anything she ate, her body burned off. I'd been the same way right up until I got to college and everything I ingested took up permanent residence on my hips.

"So Ruth told you I had bulimia?" Caroline asked.

I sighed. "Yup."

"Why?"

"Don't know."

But secretly, I did know. I'd left out the part about Ruth blaming me. Aunt Ruth was hoping I'd catch a bad case of the guilts and disappear, leaving her the queen bee of the Bell hive again.

That Ruth was one twisted woman. Maybe Dr. Tina should ramp up the dosage on *her* meds.

• • ● • •

As we got to the corner of Random Road, Ruth was just driving her powder blue Mercedes into Kevin's driveway, parking behind his truck. I pulled my dusty Sebring in right next to her.

Before I'd switched the motor off, Caroline was out of the car and dashing up to her father. I watched them hug each other as I got out.

"How'd it go?" I lifted my hand up to shield my eyes from the sun.

Before Kevin could respond, Ruth answered brightly, "The doctors at Mount Sinai think Kevin is an excellent candidate for a promising, new procedure they're trying."

I reached out, put my arms around Kevin, and then gave him a long, lingering kiss. I wanted to make certain that Ruth got an eyeful.

His lips are the best. He's a wonderful kisser, soulful, passionate, and willing.

When we finished, I took a breath. "New procedure?"

He attempted a smile. "Promising new procedure."

I nodded. "Well, that sounds great!"

I was surprised to see that Ruth had gotten close enough to touch my elbow. She said in a low voice, "They said that this is Kevin's best chance."

Hearing her words, Kevin's face twitched like he'd just been zapped with a snapping jolt of static electricity.

I said, "Well, I called a friend of mine. He's a gastro specialist at Yale. He has some new protocols he wants to talk to us about. We have an appointment Friday afternoon. I'll drive us up to New Haven." I reached up and massaged his arm. "Maybe we'll grab some pizza while we're there."

"Protocols?" Ruth arched her eyebrows.

"Specific to this type of illness," I said in whisper, aware that Caroline was listening.

"We already have a plan of action, "she said.

"Only a fool wouldn't look at all the options."

"Time is of the essence," she argued. "Every second wasted reduces Kevin's chances at survival."

Before I could say anything, Kevin reached out and put his hand on each of our shoulders. "Time out."

I couldn't help but notice that tiny diamonds of perspiration were slowly trickling down from his hairline, etching crooked lines next to his eyes. It was hot, but not that hot. His face was flushed and his eyes were glassy.

"We'll look at all of it, okay? Right now, I need to go in and take a handful of those pain pills."

Ruth and I stood by the rear bumper of her sports car. We watched Kevin walk deliberately up the sidewalk with Caroline at his elbow, open the door, and disappear into the house.

Concerned about his sudden pain, I was ready to follow him when Ruth grabbed my wrist and put her nose only inches from my own. "You have no idea what we're facing here."

I stared right back at her. "Gee, Ruth, I think I do."

"Really?" Her voice low and guttural. "He has a zero chance of surviving this. Zero! Unless we do something radical."

I leaned in close. "That's why I've got an appointment with the best liver guy at Yale."

Her eyes were angry slits. Ruth hissed, "You know he brought this on himself."

"What?"

Ruth nearly growled when she announced, "He's an alcoholic. They won't even consider him for a transplant."

"He's been trying to get his life back together."

Ruth stepped back. "Did he tell you what he put his family through?"

I crossed my arms, staring at her, waiting.

She balled up her fists. "Up until Joanna got sick, Kevin was a worthless drunk. He pissed everything away."

Don't believe her.

"For years he made my little sister's life a living hell. She's from a good family and he treated her like trash. Kevin ruined his life and he ruined hers too."

As she talked, I shook my head in denial.

She's lying. Kevin would never do that.

Ruth continued spinning her venomous web, "Kevin lost everything. When he and Joanna were married, he had a good reputation and a thriving business. They had money in the bank, they bought this house, had a beautiful daughter and a real future. Kevin threw it all away. By the time he was done their universe was a cesspool. He inflicted indescribable pain on this family. He was a bad husband and a horrible father. As far as Joanna and Caroline were concerned, during that time, the best thing he could have done for them was die quietly in some gutter."

"What?"

"The only thing that got him straight was when Joanna got sick." She set her jaw in defiance. "Her sickness saved his life. He got himself clean, at least until she died."

I stepped back away from her. I was so angry at her my hands were shaking. "If he was so bad to your sister," I asked with difficulty, trying hard to force my voice through a throat that was tight with fear and rage, "why are you trying to take care of him?"

She straightened her back and walked around to the driver's side of her car. "Because, on her deathbed, Joanna asked me to," Ruth said. "She begged me to take care of Kevin and Caroline. And, by God, that's what I'll do."

With that, she got into her car, backed it out of the driveway and roared away.

I lost track of how long I stood in the merciless heat and humidity, staring out at the empty street.

Don't believe her.

My Kevin? The man I love?

It's Ruth. Don't believe her.

I held him to a higher standard that any man that I'd ever known. Did Kevin put his family through a booze-induced hell?

Ruth lied to you about Caroline. Why is she telling you the truth now?

The answer was simple. Ask Kevin. He'd tell me.

He'd tell me the truth.

Would he?

When I walked into his house, I was shocked to see Kevin up on a ladder in the corner of the living room, nailing a last bit of crown molding to the wall.

"What the hell are you doing up there?"

He looked down at me with a serious expression. "Finishing up."

"I thought you were in pain."

He hammered in the last of the nail and started down the ladder. "I was. Listening to Ruth was killing me." Suddenly he bobbed his head from side to side to peek around behind me. "Is she still here?"

I shook my head. "She drove off in a cloud of fire and brimstone. So what are you doing?"

He glanced around the room. "I'm tying up loose ends. I think most of it will be done by the end of today."

Scanning the room, I had to agree. It looked pretty nice. "The whole house?" I asked.

He nodded. "It'll need a little spackle and paint, but the heavy lifting is almost done."

How early had he gotten up this morning? I was amazed at his progress. Was this sudden urgency an unexpected byproduct of his illness?

I changed subjects, "So your meeting at Mount Sinai went well?"

He turned around to put his hammer into his toolbox. "About like I expected."

I'd hoped to hear a little more optimism in his voice. "And what were you expecting?"

Wiping his hands off on a rag, he turned back to look at me. "That whatever they suggested was going to be long odds, really long odds."

Not sounding good.

I reached out and took his hand. "But did they sound hopeful?"

"Do you want me to tell you what you want to hear? Or do you want me to tell you the truth?"

Please. Tell me what I want to hear.

I answered, "I want you to be honest with me."

"Ruth and I spent the morning learning about all the experimental drugs and therapies that they want to try. Then after Ruth left the room, I asked the doctor what my chances really are?"

I don't really want to know.

I asked the question anyway. "What did he say?

"I have a one percent chance of lasting more than a year. The actual odds? I've got maybe a few months…tops."

Christ Almighty.

Not going to accept that. I moved in close to him, put my arms around his waist, and my face against his chest. "Look, let's see what my guy at Yale says."

He held me tight but ignored my offer. "So what are your plans for tonight?"

"At nine, I'm covering a boat cruise full of ghost hunters. But I'm free for dinner before that."

"Ghost hunters?"

"My job's full of surprises."

"Dinner sounds like a plan. What are you doing after your cruise?"

"I should be done around midnight," I answered. "Want to grab a drink?"

The man has liver failure, stupid.

"That was beyond thoughtless," I mumbled.

He laughed. "Told you, the damage is done. I want to grab a drink and then grab you. I'll pick you up for dinner around six-thirty?"

"You're driving? You get your license back?"

He frowned and shook his head. "What are they going to do to me?"

He had a point. I guess they could give him a ticket. They might take his license away completely. But Kevin didn't care. He had bigger fish to fry.

Before I kissed him good-bye, I considered asking him if Ruth was telling me the truth about what he'd put his family through. I've been with him…I've been drinking with him. I didn't see it.

This wasn't the time or the place to ask him. It was a subject that could wait.

Chapter Twenty-six

I started driving home so I could walk Tucker. Three blocks from Kevin's house, I burst out crying and couldn't stop. I cried so hard that I had to pull off the road and park in the CVS parking lot.

Years ago, I saw a therapist who, after only a few sessions, told me that I was clinically depressed.

Big surprise. Almost everyone I know has the blues.

But he also told me that I was highly functional and would be fine if I continued to see him at a hundred bucks an hour and take a regimen of antidepressants.

Much like Caroline, I hated the idea of living from the inside of a pill bottle. The allure of a liquor decanter was much more appealing. Taking Kevin's advice from childhood, I figured I could walk it off, as long as I self-medicated.

On that summer afternoon, it all caught up with me.

I don't know how long I sat in my parked car, but I know I cried until my throat burned and my eyes ached. And when the storm was finally over, I put my soggy, torn wad of Kleenex back into my bag, switched on the key, and drove home, determined that I was going to somehow make things right.

Tucker always makes me feel better. His slobbering, unbridled enthusiasm when I walk through the front door is like a fresh breath of puppy air. Walking him is one of my great joys in life. Consequently, I always feel guilty when I have to leave him alone in my apartment again.

Yet I had to earn a living to pay for dog food and needed to get back to my office, so after a quick walk around the backyard, I checked my mailbox, stuffed a handful of bills into my bag, and started for the car.

The cell phone ringing in my bag stopped me in my tracks.

I recognized the digital number on the screen immediately. "Mike Dillon? I was just thinking about you." Yes, I was lying but often that's what a good reporter does.

He replied, "Yeah? Why?"

"I have follow up questions from the interview with Aaron Brenner."

"What a coincidence, I have a few things I need to talk to you about as well. I just clocked out early. How about I buy you a drink?"

"I stopped drinking, you know that."

"Bullshit. Do you want a drink?"

Being cognizant of the scrutiny that I was likely to face at the newspaper due to my past cocktailing indiscretions, I'd honestly planned on tee-totaling the rest of the day. However, meeting Mike for a quick drink certainly wouldn't do any harm?

Could it?

"Where?" I asked.

"Bricks."

"Bricks it is."

• • ● • •

As I pulled up in front of the restaurant, daylight was slowly waning, it was overcast and there was an oven-warm breeze drifting in from the Sound. There was a tropical storm moving in from the south and we were looking at several days of heavy rain.

It was still a few hours from sunset and hot enough that, by the time I walked to the front door from the curb, I was perspiring. Inside the restaurant the air conditioned, recycled air felt like a cold compress on my face.

Mike was at the bar with a glass of red wine sitting in front of him. I wasn't certain what time he'd clocked out, but he was already out of his uniform and into khakis and a golf shirt. Ever the gentleman, he stood up and greeted me with a kiss on the cheek. "Hey, Genie. I can't believe that I'm finally buying you that drink."

"And I appreciate it." I caught the bartender's eye and ordered vodka on the rocks.

As we took sips from our respective glasses, Mike began, "So you said you had follow-up questions to the Aaron Brenner interview?"

The vodka made a warm, familiar fire in my stomach. "How come the Brenners didn't tell you about their alibi up front? It would have kept them out of jail for the night and saved everyone a lot of time and trouble."

Mike took another sip of his Cabernet. "Well, you know Aaron has had some seriously unpleasant confrontations with the law. What better way to embarrass us than to do it in the newspaper?"

"He's a man of the cloth," I countered. "A minister or something."

"My ass. Once a con, always a con. I bet he tries to sue the department."

"Have you released them yet?"

He grinned. "Well, we haven't been able to talk to anyone at Riley's bar. So far, we haven't been able to establish the validity of their alibi."

"And you're not in any hurry."

Mike slowly shook his head.

"They're still in custody."

"Much to the dismay of that butch attorney."

I looked at him and scowled. "I don't think she's a lesbian."

He shrugged. "Who would know for sure?"

"What's the matter? She's not interested in you?"

He leaned forward. "She's not. Are you?"

I don't know why, but he took me by surprise.

Buying time, I responded, "I have another question."

He leaned back again, massaging his cheek. "Shoot."

"You got an anonymous call nearly twenty-four hours after the murders telling you where you could find six bodies. Any idea who's the caller?"

He took another sip of his wine before he answered. "Someone with a restricted number called city hall and left a message with Mary Carlyle, the town clerk. Whoever it is was smart enough not to call 911. He told her that there were dead people at 104 Smuggler's Road out on Connor's Landing. That's all he said. So no, we don't know who the caller is."

That tells me absolutely nothing.

"Anything else?" he asked.

"Yeah, you guys have never said anything about a murder weapon."

He looked down at the top of the bar for a moment and then back up at me. "You know that we always hold back some information."

"Come on," I wheedled.

He ran his finger around the rim of his glass as he spoke. "Multiple weapons used by at least two killers. Remember I said we found two sets of footprints, which by the way, are the same size as the Brenners."

"So you're not convinced they're innocent."

"Nope."

"Weapons?" I tried to get back on track.

"George Chadwick collected antiques. He had an eye for it. He had a special passion for antique military weapons. There's a whole room filled with them. I saw some of them, beautiful pieces from all over the world, eighteenth-century Navy cutlasses, Middle Eastern scimitars, dueling pistols from the Revolutionary War. It's a truly remarkable display."

I took long sip of my vodka and waited for him to continue.

"Some of them appear to be missing. We think the killers may have used them to cut up the victims."

"Oh my God."

"Genie, it was as bad in there as I've ever seen. There was

blood everywhere, on the walls, on the ceiling. I've investigated my share of murder scenes. This was the worst."

"You haven't found the weapons yet?

He shook his head. "The murders took place on an island. Long Island Sound is a pretty good place to hide things. Any other questions?"

I shook my head and raised my eyebrows as I took another long drink. "Nope."

"Well," he said, "then it's my turn."

"Go."

"The stories you've written so far? You've been uncharacteristically restrained in the, um, sexual overtones of the victims' relationships."

"You mean the fact that they were swingers?"

He nodded. "Yeah, you haven't mentioned a word of it in any of your stories."

"What's your point?"

"Is it going to continue along that line?"

I looked at him with curiosity, wondering where the hell this was headed. "Once the Brenners were arrested, the sexual overtones of the murders became an integral part the story, didn't they? Why is this of interest to you?"

He tapped his fingers against the polished wood grain of the bar. "I got a phone call from an old friend of mine this afternoon, Larry Abernathy, the headmaster of the Handley Academy."

The Handley Academy is the preeminent prep school in this part of Connecticut. It's where the *really* rich parents sent their kids.

"He was asking if I had any pull with the local press."

"Do you?" I batted my eyes.

"Larry knows that he might not be able to keep the school's name out of the newspaper. But he was hoping to have it mentioned a minimal number of times."

I didn't want to sound stupid, but I didn't know how else to ask the question. "Why would I mention it at all?"

Mike cocked his head to one side. "Two of the Connor's Landing victims, Kit and Kathy Webster. They were both teachers at the Handley Academy."

Oh?

"Larry Abernathy is worried how it will look if it gets out that two of their teachers were sexual deviates."

I took a deep gulp of my drink. "They were swingers. I'm not sure if what they were doing qualifies the two of them as deviates. But I understand why your friend is concerned. How does this affect you?"

"I'm trying to get my thirteen year-old son, David, into Handley."

Now how in hell does Mike think he can afford to send his son to Handley?

"Is this a conflict of interest, Mike?"

"No," he stated flatly.

I didn't agree but I decided not to disagree either. "I'll see what I can do."

He finished his glass of wine and pushed it forward on the bar. Then Mike caught the bartender's eye and motioned that he'd like a refill. "Look, I'm not asking you to do this without something in return." He turned his attention back to me. "Remember the blind woman who chased away the burglar a couple of nights ago?"

"Isadora Orleans," I answered. "What about her?"

"We've been interviewing some of the neighbors to see if anyone remembered anything unusual about that night. One of them recalls seeing a sports car driving away from the scene at a high rate of speed. A convertible."

I smiled condescendingly. "That's not a lot, Mike. That's all the neighbor said? It was some kind of generic sports car with a rag top? Did the neighbor at least get a partial plate?"

"Neighbor thinks that maybe there was dark plastic taped over the plate…oh, and the car looked expensive."

"Well, that's a whole lot of nothing."

He put his hand on mine. "I've got something else."

"Wow me."

"An old friend of yours got busted this afternoon. A police report hasn't been issued yet."

"Who?" I was suddenly interested.

"Jimmy Fitzgerald."

The rich kid from Greenwich whose old man bought his way out of a manslaughter rap after he ran over the mother of three kids with his Porsche. Yeah, that got my attention.

Hearing the name, I got a little tingle. "What was the young Mr. Fitzgerald busted for?" I was already amused.

"Selling methamphetamines to an undercover agent." Mike drained the last of his wine.

"That scamp."

Mike said, "Jimmy's been marketing the stuff on the Internet and selling it off his daddy's fifty-two foot Hatteras yacht out at Indian Cove Marina."

Before the bartender brought Mike another Cabernet, I finished my vodka and asked for a refill.

Then I mused, "I don't get it. Here's a kid who has everything and I mean everything. Why the hell does he feel the need to deal drugs?"

As the young man behind the bar dropped off our drinks, Mike answered, "I don't know. I think rich kids get bored. They already feel detached from the rest of the world, better than everyone else. They don't know where the boundaries are or they don't care. Maybe for them, the rules don't apply."

"So is Jimmy's dad going to buy his way out of this one?"

Mike pulled a folded sheet of paper out of his sport coat pocket and handed it to me. "A copy of Jimmy's arrest report."

Ah, a scoop.

"And in return, I show restraint using the Handley Academy name?"

"I'm not asking that you don't print it. Just don't beat it to death."

Hell, up until a few minutes ago, I didn't care where Kit and Kathy Webster had worked. What is Mike getting out of this? A break on tuition, a scholarship? Maybe he thinks if he can get the kid into Handley, he can buy himself another chance with his estranged wife?

I took the copy of the arrest report from Mike's hand. "I'll see what I can do." I tucked it into my bag, and I looked up at him. "So you don't have to answer me or nothing, but you doing okay?"

He knew what I was asking about and he nodded. "Yeah. Beth and I were married for over fourteen years. Everything has a life cycle. Nothing lasts forever."

I looked at him and knew him well enough to see that he was lying. "It's none of my business, but whose idea was it to call it quits?"

Rude of me to ask. I knew that. It's the reporter in me.

"She moved in with the guy who does our taxes, for Christ's sake," he answered. "But I really don't blame her. Being married to a cop is the worst. I work all hours, she never knows where I am. Hell, there were some nights she was afraid that the next time she saw me would be in a body bag. It's stressful as hell and on top of that I can be a real pain in the ass."

I smiled. "And the bean counter is an exact opposite."

"So, I find myself back on the market." He reached out and took my hand.

I gently took my hand back and then placed it on his cheek. I looked right into his eyes. "I'm sorry, Mike, but I'm in love with Kevin Bell. I don't want to screw that up. Plus you're on the rebound."

He took my hand off his cheek and kissed my fingers. "I know," he whispered.

"But you're a hell of catch, Mike Dillon."

He smiled. "You change your mind, let me know, okay?"

I gently kissed him on the cheek. "It's a deal."

● ● ● ● ●

Back in my office, I managed to keep away from both Laura Ostrowski and Casper Staples. My breath was covered by the handful of Altoids I was chewing on, but I was a little concerned about the lush flush on my cheeks.

I took enormous delight in writing up the story about Jimmy Fitzgerald. I even tried to call his father for a statement. Whoever answered the phone claimed that the elder Mr. Fitzgerald was in a meeting, but a press release would be issued sometime in the morning.

It must be nice to have your own PR firm at your disposal.

Then I went back into our computer records and dug out pictures of the Connor's Landing victims. I was particularly interested in Kit and Kathy Webster, the teachers from the Handley Academy.

The photos I was looking at were school publicity shots. But it was easy to see, even though they were both in their early forties, Kit and Kathy made an attractive couple. They were both blond, had big eyes, and bright smiles. He wore his hair cropped close to his scalp and wore a pair of dashing wireframe glasses. She wore her curly hair long in a way that made her look younger than her age. The expression on her face looked both worldly and mischievous all at the same time.

They were a good looking couple, much too pretty to die in such a horrible way.

I saved the photos in my Connor's Landing file.

And then I rushed out to meet Kevin for what would turn out to be the unique dinner of my life.

Chapter Twenty-seven

Kevin was full of surprises.

At a little after six-thirty he came to my place to pick me up for dinner. He'd told me that he'd drive even though it was illegal, so that was expected.

What was totally unexpected was the car he came in.

Instead of his beat-to-crap work truck, Kevin pulled up to the curb in a gunmetal blue, BMW Z4 convertible.

I was sitting in a wicker chair on the front porch of my apartment house waiting for him with a glass of Pinot Grigio in my hand. Seeing him roar up in that expensive sports car was surprise enough, but it was replaced with complete shock and awe when he opened the door and got out wearing a tuxedo.

I stood and watched him stride up the sidewalk. The words *wickedly handsome* came to my mind. "Hey, Kevin Bell," I called out. "You look just like James freakin' Bond."

He sauntered up the steps of the porch and swept me into his arms. When his lips touched mine, I absolutely swooned.

Gazing into my eyes he said quietly, "Good, that's the look I was going for."

Still in his arms, I smiled up into his face and whispered, "You always wanted to be James Bond."

He smiled back. "Bell, Kevin Bell."

James Bond. Kevin Bell. Right then, to me, they were one and the same.

I kissed him again.

When we broke apart, I stepped back to get a better look at him. "I can't believe it. Man, you look so cool. And what's with the car? You rob a bank?"

He cocked his head and gave me a dashing smile. "You only live once."

I held up two fingers. "Wrong. The Bond film was *You Only Live Twice*. Seriously, where'd you get the car?"

"Place in New Canaan rents them for special occasions."

"The tux?"

"Different place rents those as well," he explained innocently.

"Where the hell are you taking me for dinner?" I asked. I pointed to what I was wearing. Khaki shorts, a sleeveless top, and sneakers. "I'm not exactly dressed for the Ritz."

"It's a surprise," he said. "And you're dressed perfectly."

I'll be damned. For a moment there, he sounded like Daniel Craig.

• • ● • •

I swear there's nothing better than being in the passenger's seat of a hot fast convertible on a summer's evening with the wind blowing through your hair and the man that you love at the wheel.

"Where'd you say we were going?"

"I didn't."

Hmmm, out of questions, my brilliant journalistic interviewing skills were getting me nowhere. Best just to relax and enjoy the ride.

Unfortunately, the ride only lasted ten minutes. A few miles from my house, we pulled into a neighborhood of homes clustered together on the shore. The houses were small and packed in close, but they overlooked Sheffield Harbor and, because of the exclusive location, the property there was ridiculously expensive.

Kevin parked the BMW in the driveway of a two-story white Cape Cod. There was a low picket fence that encircled the Lilliputian front lawn, green shutters accenting the windows, and brilliant splashes of flowers planted around the low shrubbery that ran along the front of the house. While gulls wheeled and squealed overhead, I could smell the pungent sea breeze.

"Here we are."

"Where we are?"

Saying no more, he got out of the car and opened the trunk. By the time I got out, he was carrying a green and white plastic cooler by the handles and balancing a large rectangular, wicker basket on top of it.

Cognizant of how sick he was, I joined him with my arms out. "Here, let me give you a hand."

He shook his head. "I've got it." Then he started for the back yard. "Can you can open the gate for me?"

I unlatched the wooden gate and then followed Kevin as he walked behind the house and climbed the steps to the deck. Once there, he carefully placed the cooler and the wicker basket on the railing. Then he took his coat off and hung it on the back of one of the deck chairs.

I could see that his face was flushed and there were beads of perspiration on his forehead. "Jesus, honey, are you okay?"

"Yeah, just hotter'n hell."

I felt like the temperature had dropped a little since we'd arrived on the waterfront. He turned away and looked out over the harbor. Sailboats bobbed lazily in the swells. The sky was overcast but the sun still stubbornly stabbed its way through the clouds with pink-gray beams of color.

"This is nice," I grinned at the view.

"Really nice." Then he turned to start the fire on the gas grill. Once he was satisfied with the flame, he pulled a plastic container out of the cooler, opened it up, picked out half a dozen pieces of chicken, and placed them on the grill. "I've been marinating these all afternoon."

I enjoyed the water view and felt the sudden cool breeze of a weather front seductively sliding in over the water. I sighed with satisfaction. "Kevin?"

"Yes?"

"Whose house is this?"

"Drink?"

"Sure," I answered. "You wouldn't happen to have some vodka and ice in that magic cooler of yours, would you?"

The boy was just full of surprises. He lifted out a chilled bottle of Absolut. "Ta da!" he sang. Then he dropped a couple of ice cubes into two crystal glasses, poured vodka in mine, and Dewar's in his and we both took a drink.

"This is really swell, Kevin. But, seriously, whose house is this?"

He rubbed his chin. "Harry and Nancy Brill."

I nodded and looked around. "Nice place they have, the Brills. Harry and Nancy are home?"

He continued to rub his chin. "They're vacationing on the Outer Banks."

"Ah."

He went back into the wicker basket, pulled out a linen cloth, and draped it over the wrought-iron deck table. Once more, he reached into the basket and brought out two candles in glass holders which he lit with a flourish.

I watched him go back to the grill to check the sizzling chicken. "So the Brills, do they know that we're having dinner on their back deck?"

He turned the chicken and the fire flared for a moment. "Well, last April, I built this deck. They said I should come over for dinner sometime."

I held up my glass. "And here we are. Using the Brill's grill."

"Can you get the place settings out of the basket and put them on the table?" He was laying down some aluminum foil and carefully placing sliced vegetables over the fire.

I opened the wicker container for the plates, the silverware. and the napkins. As I took it all out, I saw a photograph lying at the bottom of the basket. I picked it up to see it in the diminishing light.

I recognized the moment right away. A faded Polaroid photo showed two sixteen-year-olds in an awkward embrace, slow dancing with each other. The boy looked embarrassed and was wearing a brown suit that was slightly too big for him. The girl had hair that was over-teased, used too much eye makeup, and wore a dress that was too tight for her ripening body.

It was us.

High school, the Junior Prom. Kevin and I hadn't gone as dates. I went with Tony Pollack, linebacker for the varsity football team. He was a big guy, sweet, but not too bright. After he graduated from high school he was planning to be a cartoonist. Last I heard he was selling life insurance.

Kevin was on the dance committee and had been working the front table, taking tickets. He was there stag.

I don't recall the exact circumstances, but I think that when Tony discovered I wasn't going to show him my boobs in the backseat of his Camaro, he disappeared with his buddies to go buy beer.

During one of the last songs of the night—I'm pretty sure it was *Unchained Melody*—and I was standing along the wall feeling pissed off at my date, embarrassed, and trying hard to fade into the crepe paper decorations. Kevin walked up to me, smiled, and asked me if I'd like to dance.

It was so natural. I remember wondering why *we* hadn't come to the dance together. And then we were out on the dance floor holding each other and swaying to the music.

Our Biology teacher, Mrs. Van Skiver, took the photo.

"I fell in love with you that night," Kevin whispered, looking over my shoulder at the Polaroid, taking my hand.

I turned back to see his eyes. "How come we wasted so much time with so many other people when it's so obvious we're supposed to be together?"

He beamed. "Because it made us into what we are now. I don't think you would have liked me much when I was younger."

I frowned. "I knew you when you were younger. I liked you just fine."

He squeezed my hand and then walked over to the grill to turn the chicken. "I need to ask you for a favor."

I waited.

He turned, serious. "It's a big one."

"So ask."

"Actually, I think Caroline might have already talked to you about it. When the time comes…"

I put my fingers on his lips and stopped him in mid-sentence. I finished it for him, "And that's not going to be for a long time. But if it does, I've already agreed that Caroline can live with me."

He nodded and held up his glass in a toast. "Thanks. That's a load off."

"Still not sure why you wouldn't rather have Caroline live with Ruth."

He struggled to find the best answer. "Ruth's a loon."

"Granted, but Ruth has a lot of money."

"Money isn't everything. But just so you know, I met with an attorney this afternoon and wrote a will."

A knot started to swell in my throat and I wished he'd just stop talking.

But he kept going. "I'm leaving everything to you."

I put my hand on his chest. "Don't say any more."

"We have to talk about this. I'm leaving everything to you. There isn't a lot, some money in a savings account. Some equity in the house and the house has nearly doubled in value since I bought it."

"I don't want to talk about it," I mumbled, head down.

"Some insurance money."

"Kevin, please let's talk about something else."

"And I've left instructions that you're to be Caroline's guardian."

I lifted my head forward until my lips found his. Kissing him was the only way I knew to shut him up.

His lips felt hot, not sexed-up hot, feverish hot.

I stepped back. "You okay?" Wondering if I was going to cry.

He gave me a sheepish grin even though it was obvious he was sweating through some pain. "No, honey. That's kind of what I've been trying to tell you. I'm not okay."

I got up close again and hugged him.

"I've got to check the food." He gently disengaged.

I watched him go back to the grill and tend the chicken and vegetables.

I wanted to talk about something else, anything else. "So what's Ruth's problem, anyway? Do you know she tried to convince me that Caroline has an eating disorder? And that it was my fault?"

He drained his glass and headed to the cooler for a refill. Holding up the bottle of vodka he asked me, "Ready for another?"

I finished the last drabs from my own tumbler and held it out.

He dropped fresh ice cubes into our glasses. "I think you've already discovered that Ruth is a relentless drama queen." Pouring a second helping of our respective vices, he continued, "Caroline doesn't have an eating disorder."

"I know. This afternoon I watched your daughter eat a double chili cheeseburger and fries from Sound Bites and she didn't puke."

He handed me my drink. "Damned near a miracle for anyone."

"But you know, Ruth told me something else that was even more disturbing."

I watched him stiffen. He already knew what I was about to say and turned back to the grill. "What was that?"

"That you used to be an out-of-control drunk, a really bad one. That you hurt your family. Not what you are now."

"You believe it?" He speared the pieces of chicken with a long fork and dropped them on a serving plate.

"I'll believe whatever you tell me."

He put the serving plate on the table, pulled out my chair, and I sat down.

He brought out a bowl filled with salad and settled into his chair. Without looking at me, in a deliberate voice, he slowly said, "She's right. There was a time when I was out of control. I hurt Joanna. I hurt Caroline. I hurt all of my friends and family. I can never make up for the pain I inflicted. I went to rehab and got straight…for a while. I had to because Joanna was sick and I had to take care of her and Caroline. I accept that I can't change the past but I can affect what happens now."

So it was true.

I didn't say a word. I waited to see if he added anything else.

"Joanna forgave me. Caroline forgave me. Even Ruth, in her own strange way, forgave me. And for everything I put them through, they had every reason not to. And for that, I'll always love them."

I stared at the glass in his hand.

He swirled his scotch around. "Too late, way too late, I can control it. But in the end, it's what'll kill me."

I reached out and squeezed his hand.

He stared down at his lap for a long time. Then he looked up into my eyes. "Anything else you want to know?"

"No. There's something that I want *you* to know."

"What?"

"I love you."

He allowed a short sigh and tried to smile. There were tears in his eyes when he answered me. "I love you so much."

We sat in silence for what seemed to be a long time, letting our dinners go cold. I listened to the water gently lapping at the shore. I spoke first. "Look, I'm so confident that things are going to turn out okay and you're going to beat this thing. I'm going to ask you something and this is serious."

I had his attention. "What?"

It took every bit of confidence I had to say it. "Marry me."

He blinked, not believing what he was hearing. "Forgive me for saying, but you have a spotty record on this marriage thing."

I waved at the air. "Bygones. What do you say?"

The silence in the air hung like an evil omen.

Oh, my God, he's going to say no.

"Okay. I'm in." The look of confusion on his face gave way to a big grin.

We fell into each other's arms and held each other tight, not wanting to let go. We were quiet again.

"So," I broke the silence, wondering, "all kidding aside. Do Harry and Nancy Brill know we're here?"

He glanced around at the empty decks of the houses on either side of us. "I'm thinking we should probably eat before the neighbors start to wonder."

Chapter Twenty-eight

To call the Sheffield Harbor Association's vessel a "ferry boat" is a tad misleading. It's not one of those husky ships that take hundreds of people and cars across challenging bodies of water. Nor is it one of the many lithe, dependable vessels that ferry commuters in and around Manhattan seven days a week in all sorts of weather.

No, the *Harbor Express* is a pontoon boat that runs a few months in the summer and maxes out at twenty tourists per trip.

It's a refitted party barge.

When I got to the dock at a little after nine, streetlights reflected like lazy, slithering, illuminated eels on the black surface of the harbor. Small clouds of mosquitoes silently hovered and hunted in the reeds on the edge of the shore. We were only a couple of blocks from the bars and the nightclubs and, every once in a while, I could hear the shrill, screaming laughter of someone who already had too much to drink rise above the low, ambient rumble of traffic.

The man standing next to me on the dock touched my elbow to get my attention.

"The Harbor Association is a non-profit environmental organization dedicated to the preservation of Long Island Sound. We're able to fund a lot of our programs with this ferry boat," explained Daryl Zelfin, the president of the association's board of trustees. "Over the summer, we take hundreds of people for harbor tours and out to visit Fisher's Lighthouse."

He was in his mid-fifties, wore tiny wire-frame glasses, had a full mustache and, when he smiled, displayed a set of unusually big teeth. Daryl was an uncanny cross between a leprechaun and Teddy Roosevelt. He wore a dark blue Harbor Association polo shirt and khaki slacks.

We were standing on the dock, out of everyone's way, while a dozen men and women loaded equipment onto the boat.

"But tonight," I stated, holding my digital recorder between us, "we're not taking a harbor tour."

He leaned forward so that he could speak directly into the machine. I'd heard that Daryl was an unabashed publicity hound. "No, Geneva. Tonight we're carrying thirteen paranormal investigators."

"Thirteen?" I asked. "Isn't that unlucky?"

He chuckled, "It's only unlucky if we run into a storm."

Which isn't entirely out of the question.

On the way over, I'd seen lightning flashing in the distance. Once I was parked, I checked the weather app on my phone and saw a bright red and orange blob, a nasty thunderstorm, south of us moving from west to east. The vanguard of the tropical depression bearing down on us.

While the ghost hunters got their gear onboard, silent spears of electricity flashed and played tag along the horizon. Granted, it was so far away I couldn't hear accompanying thunder, but it was out there nonetheless.

A slightly zaftig woman in her early forties, wearing jeans, a short-sleeved top, and a silver and black feathered hairstyle that was popular around the time that the original *Charlie's Angels* was broadcasting, walked up between Daryl and me and introduced herself. "I'm Stella Barry. Are you the reporter?" She was smiling, slightly breathless, and her green eyes were wide with excitement.

"Yeah," I put out my hand. "Geneva Chase."

She ignored it. "When's the photographer getting here?"

This lady obviously thought that the newspaper was working for *her*. I tried to smile. "I'll be taking the pictures tonight."

She studied me dubiously. "You want some background info?"

"Okay."

"You already know my name is Stella Barry. I've been a para-normal investigator for over twenty-five years." She gestured to the people who were nearly finished loading the *Harbor Express*. "These folks are the New England Paranormal Investigations Team. Some of them have been with me for over ten years and some of them are newbies-in-training. I've personally done a hundred and fifteen investigations. Seven of them have been documented and broadcast on the Discovery and the Travel channels."

No need to ask questions. This was the Stella Barry Show.

"Have you ever heard of Newford Hospital?" she asked.

Before I could answer, she continued, "Mental institution, built in 1898, it once housed as many as a thousand patients. It closed in 1977 and it's been deserted ever since. There's a cemetery onsite with nearly five hundred unmarked graves. We did an investigation two months ago and found over forty active spirits there. Got eleven of them on film, got another seven on audio. *The Hartford Courant* covered it. Maybe you read the story?"

This woman was exhausting.

I shook my head no.

"Too bad," she said. "Tonight, we're going to investigate reports of an unexplained light seen out on the harbor every year on this night, the anniversary of the mysterious disappearance of Bartholomew Gault."

Without saying another word, she whirled and dramatically boarded the boat.

Daryl watched her. "She's a force of nature, huh?"

"Yup."

A good-looking, muscular young man with short black hair, dressed in a dark blue Harbor Association polo shirt and khaki shorts walked up to us. "The captain is asking everyone to please board now."

Kid was a real heartbreaker. He looks familiar.

A second young man stood at the open entrance to the boat and helped us aboard. He was dressed exactly the same as the other boy, except this one was taller, broad in the shoulders with closely cropped hair.

That's when I recognized them. They were the young men I'd seen by the pool when Kevin and I had been at the Elroys' place out on Connor's Landing. It took me a moment, but by the time I found a place to sit down, I'd even recalled their names.

The older, good-looking boy was Lance Elroy, a sophomore at Yale. The younger boy, who looked like he spent too much time in the gym, was named Drew.

I also recalled, from my short discussion with their father, how proud Pete Elroy was that they were gainfully employed working on this ferry, and that Drew was a senior at the Handley Academy, the prep school that was every rich boy's best chance to get into an Ivy League college.

The same exclusive prep school where, until their untimely deaths, Kit and Kathy Webster had been teachers.

Suddenly, this boat trip became very interesting.

• • ● • •

Once the two boys finished casting us off, the captain powered the boat slowly away from the dock. I took a bottle of insect repellent out of my bag and started to slather it on my face, neck, and legs.

"Once we get out of the harbor, the breeze will pick up and it'll help keep the bugs off us," Daryl said cheerily.

"Have you ever seen this mysterious light?"

"You mean the ghost?" He held up his hands and wriggled his fingers in a mocking, pseudo-scary way.

"Yeah." I wasn't feeling particularly amused.

Realizing that I wasn't in a playful mood, the association president's face became serious. "No, but I understand a lot of people have seen it, or claim to have seen it."

I nodded absently. "Why did you agree to this?"

"Hosting this investigation?"

"Yeah."

"Off the record?"

"Okay."

He leaned forward and whispered, "Ferry ticket sales are off so far this summer. A little publicity about a ghost out on the harbor might be good for business, you know what I mean?"

I looked straight at him. "On the record, do you believe we're going to see a ghost out here tonight?"

He swallowed and sat back, thinking. Finally, he answered, "I'm keeping an open mind. No, wait, what I meant to say was, if there's a ghost out here, we're going to find it."

I smiled. "You sure you want to go with that?"

He frowned. "Can I get back to you?"

We were both sitting on a padded bench and before I could say anything more to Daryl, Stella Barry slid in next to me. "So you want to get the lowdown on what we're going to be doing tonight?"

"You bet." Now, admittedly, I was still a little buzzed from having cocktails with Mike Dillon and dinner with Kevin. But I'm a pro, I know when too much is too much. And right after I said "you bet" to the ghost hunter queen, I realized that I was going to have to rein in my sarcasm.

Luckily, Stella Barry hadn't picked up on my tone. She went ahead and got started. "Bartholomew Gault was the oldest of seven children, born into a wealthy family on Long Island. He attended Princeton University and got a job right out of school with a bank in New York. He worked hard, and by 1909, he was the bank's general manager. That same year, he married a woman named Elizabeth who bore him two children. Elizabeth Gault insisted that they leave the grit and the grime of the city and that they move to the country, so Bartholomew bought the Hoyt mansion out on Connor's Landing."

"Yeah, yeah, I wrote about that," I said. "Jonathon Hoyt was the guy who built that house. He died in a shipwreck off the coast of Cuba."

Stella nodded somberly. "The house is plagued with bad luck," she intoned mysteriously.

Six people were recently hacked to death there. I'm not psychic, but hell yes, I'll say that house was bad luck.

Standing up, Stella shook out her hair and ran both hands through it. As we sliced through the black water, she gazed out at the darkness. "Soon after he bought it, Gault spent a small fortune upgrading and modernizing his new residence. He added electricity and indoor plumbing that was still very rare for that time. He moved his family into it in 1912. They were all very happy on Connor's Landing."

As we got to the mouth of the harbor and entered Long Island Sound, I could feel air start to move around me. Gliding out over the open water, the tiny breeze quickly strengthened into a sustained wind.

Stella brushed renegade strands of hair away from her eyes. She had to practically shout to be heard over the boat's engines and the wind. "In 1917, Bartholomew Gault became president of Manufacturers' Bank and Trust. He spent more and more time on the train to New York. As the economy grew, so did Gault's tireless pursuit of wealth.

Stella lifted her face, flaring her nostrils as she sniffed the air. "Life was good, until history and the Great Depression caught up with him. Like everyone else in America, he was heavily invested in the stock market. October of 1929 wiped out his fortune in an instant. By the following March, his bank had failed. By August, he was penniless. Bill collectors and solicitors started to knock on the front door of his grand house on Connor's Landing. Suddenly, the man who had everything couldn't buy food for his family."

I could feel Daryl Zelfin sitting by my side on the bench, waiting for the rest of the story. Except for the man's breathing, he was absolutely motionless.

I followed Stella's line of sight. Only darkness lay ahead of us. The stars and the moon were obliterated by the storm clouds. The wind rose and fell like the breath of a mythical beast. The boat's engines hummed like electricity through an exposed wire.

"On August fifteenth, 1930, Bartholomew Gault inexplicably told his wife that he was going to go fishing. It was the last time anyone ever saw him. The next afternoon, an oyster trawler found his boat run aground on Fisher's Island. There was no sign of Gault.

"The police investigated and concluded that Gault had probably slipped off his boat by accident and drowned in the cold, unforgiving waters of the Sound. The locals say that the water was calm as glass that night, no wind, no chop." She paused for a dramatic moment and took a breath.

I glanced at Daryl. He was staring up at Stella's face, waiting breathlessly.

She looked down at him and smiled, pleased with the effect of her tale. "They say Gault couldn't stand being poor. Better to be dead than a pauper standing in a breadline, so he tied something heavy around his waist and quietly slid over the side of his fishing boat."

Stella finished with the simple sentence, "They never found his body and coincidently, they never found the boat's anchor."

She stopped talking and gazed pensively out over the water, hands clasped.

This is all properly spooky.

I stood up. "Nicely told. I think I'm going to go forward and get a better view. Let's connect again when we get closer to the, um, point of contact."

What I really wanted to do was put some distance between me and the creepy lady. That and I was hoping to get some alone time with the Elroy brothers.

The captain, a short, potbellied man in his early sixties, was dressed in a baseball cap and the requisite Harbor Association polo shirt and khaki pants. He stood at the wheel in the bow, steering the boat and peering seriously into the darkness ahead. We were moving toward the islands beyond Sheffield Harbor. It's an area known for hidden rocks and shifting sandbars. He squinted into the darkness with steely concentration.

I sincerely hoped he knew what he was doing.

The Elroy boys were seated on a bench not far from the captain. "Hey." I spoke with as much enthusiasm as I could muster. "Aren't you Pete and Becky's kids?"

I was standing right behind them when they both turned toward me. From the blank looks on their faces, they had absolutely no clue who I was.

"I was over at your house the other day for the party," I explained, implying that I had been one of the invited guests. "You boys were by the pool with some very attractive young ladies."

That made them both smile. Lance stood up politely and Drew, seeing his brother on his feet, followed suit.

"My name's Geneva Chase. And if memory serves me right, you're Lance and you're Drew." I poured warm honey into my voice.

Before we could say another word, the captain shouted in a voice that sounded like a hundred miles of hard gravel road, "Lance, go aft and check the steering cable on the port engine."

The tall boy gave me an engaging grin and shrugged. "It's nice to meet you, Miss Chase. I'll tell my parents that I ran into you. I've got to go to work." He walked quickly up the center aisle to the back of the boat.

"So, Drew," I said, "do you mind if I sit down here next to you?"

"No, ma'am." We both sat down on the padded bench.

"You're dad's pretty proud of you guys," I started.

"He is?"

"He thinks it's great you both are working this summer."

Drew nodded slightly with a hesitant smile. "He says it builds character."

"Well, he's right," I responded. "You guys are doing a great job tonight. Hey, this is kind of spooky, isn't it? Going out at night to try to find a ghost?"

He offered a shy grin. "I don't really believe in ghosts."

"Speaking of spooky, when I was out at your house, your dad was telling me about the night of the murders."

Drew's eyebrows knitted together with puzzlement. "He did?"

I pushed on. "That's all pretty gruesome stuff. He tells me you and Lance were both at a party that night."

"Yeah, we were at a friend's place in Greenwich."

"You weren't at Greg and Missy Henderson's house, were you? Their son's about your age. I think it was his birthday last week."

Okay, it was a complete fabrication. I didn't know any Greg and Missy Henderson.

"No." Drew shook his head. "What's the son's name?"

I took a minute like I was trying to recall it, when in reality, I was making it up. Finally, I said, "Bobby," snapping my fingers. "Yeah, Bobby. You know him?"

It was Drew's turn to see if he could place the name. "Nope, don't know any Bobby Henderson. We were on Jimmy Fitzgerald's boat. It's tied off at Indian Cove Marina. Well, it's his dad's boat. You know the Fitzgeralds? His dad's got more money than God."

Jimmy Fitzgerald? Oh man, yeah, Drew. I know the freaking Fitzgeralds.

Obviously, this kid had no clue that his buddy had been busted that very afternoon for selling meth to an undercover cop.

I suddenly noticed that we were cruising by Connor's Landing. "Hey," I stood up again and looked out over the railing. "Can you see your house from here?"

Drew stood up beside me. "Yeah," he pointed. "It's over there, see those lights?"

"A couple of houses over, isn't that the Chadwick place where those people were killed?"

He didn't say anything at first. Then he bobbed his head and answered in a voice I could barely hear over the boat's twin motors. "Yeah."

"So tragic. I heard there were a couple of teachers killed in there. I think they were from the Handley Academy."

Drew stared out over the water, transfixed by the sight of the Chadwick house as we steamed past it, dark and cemetery silent, a black monolith in the night. Once a home, now a massive tombstone.

"So sad."

"One of them was my biology teacher. Mrs. Webster." His voice was barely audible. "She didn't deserve to die like that. She was a beautiful lady, beautiful in the way she looked. But beautiful in her soul, too. You know what I mean?"

"Beautiful in her soul?"

"She wouldn't just teach us about science," he explained. "She didn't talk to us like a teacher talks to students. She talked to us like we were adults. She talked to us about real stuff. Life lessons, she called it."

I was about to ask another question, when the captain shouted. "Drew, see what the hell is holding up your brother, will ya? I'll bet he's chattin' up some good-lookin' chippie back there."

Drew looked at me and blinked, like he was awakening from a dream. "I've got to go. Nice meeting you."

And then he was gone.

By the time I wandered aft, Stella Barry was helping one of her team attach an odd-looking camera to a tripod.

"You hoping to actually get a photo?"

She stared at me. "You never know. Sometimes we get lucky."

"What's a ghost look like on film?"

The woman smiled. "Not always the same. Sometimes a spirit will look like a wisp of smoke. Sometimes, it will look like a person. Mostly we get orbs of light."

"Orbs of light."

"Well," she finished with the camera, "that only makes sense now doesn't it?"

It does?

Stella Barry watched her crew get their equipment ready. "I never studied physics. But I understand that energy is never lost. It changes form, but it's never lost. I believe that when you die, your energy still exists. Your soul goes on."

"That's what those orbs of light are? Souls? Energy?"

The ghost hunter nodded. "Yeah, in a philosophical nutshell."

"Are you a religious person, Stella?"

She smiled. "Of course I am."

"Aren't souls supposed go somewhere? Like heaven?"

"Most do. Some don't. Some don't know they're dead. Others feel that they have unfinished business to take care of. But for most spirits who linger here, it wasn't the right time for them to die."

Like Kevin.

"So you think all us of have a specific time we're supposed to die?"

The paranormal investigator shrugged. "Everyone dies. And I think that God has a plan mapped out for us. Sometimes it doesn't all go according to plan, or at least according to our plan."

At any other time, I would have avoided like the plague getting sucked into a religious discussion. But with Kevin being so sick, it was simply something I needed to talk about. "When we die, is it for a reason?"

As she looked into my eyes, I saw sadness in her face. Like she understood where my question was coming from. Stella surprised me when she took my hand. He voice was soft. "I believe everything happens for a reason, honey. We don't always know what it is. And sometimes, that's why a spirit may linger. They're simply trying to understand."

Almost at the same time that she said that, the wind picked up and in the distance I could hear the low reverberation of thunder.

The captain hollered, "Daryl, can I see you please?"

The Harbor Association president stood and walked briskly up the aisle. The captain and Daryl Zelfin put their heads close together to talk.

As they did, an attractive young woman in her early twenties, with long hair tucked under a baseball cap, lifted up her arms to the night. Like some kind of signal, the other investigators stopped their conversations, remained absolutely motionless and watched her.

Stella leaned in close and whispered in my ear, "That's Marie. She's an intuitive."

"You mean like a psychic?"

"We have several. Marie is the most sensitive."

The young woman then held her palms out straight, as if warding off an unseen danger, before she announced, "I can feel movement. He's here."

"This must be where Bartholomew Gault went overboard," Stella said. Then she shouted, "Mr. Zelfin? Can we cut the engines?"

Daryl looked at us with wide eyes and conferred with the captain again. Nodding, he walked toward us and the engines went silent. The association's president came close. "We can't stay long. The captain is concerned about the storm. He radioed the Coast Guard. They told him that the wind has shifted and it's moving faster than we thought."

Not wasting another moment, Stella shouted, "Let's get set up! We've got a storm moving in."

Suddenly the boat was a beehive of activity.

Stella Barry had brought a dozen people along on this investigation. I'd expected a crew full of geeks and freaks. In actuality, they were painfully normal. After talking with some of them, I discovered they were plumbers, architects, waiters, insurance adjusters, landscapers, and housewives.

Nothing marked them as being particularly different or special, except that right at that moment, they were all hustling to get cameras, audio recorders, electromagnetic sensors, motion detectors, and divining rods in place so they could find the ghost of Bartholomew Gault.

In minutes, everything was in place and, except for the rising wind, the night was silent. The boat rocked with sea swells that were growing in size, but I could still feel, more than hear, the cameras shooting and the recorders humming.

Someone behind me whispered, "Energy spike."

Another quietly added, "Ten degree temperature drop."

I peered out into the dark that surrounded us. Indeed, I could feel the change in temperature.

Of course. A storm front's barreling down on us!

We stayed as still as we could for another few minutes, holding tight to anything available to steady us on the rolling deck, straining to hear or to see something magical.

"Another energy spike, ten points," the voice whispered behind me.

I thought I'd jump right out of my skin when a jagged spear of lightning split the sky and thunder clapped like God's hammer of justice.

"That's it," the captain shouted. "We've got to go."

"Five more minutes, please!" Stella pleaded.

The wind swirled up around us like a hungry snake. The water suddenly started to roil.

Without a word, the captain turned on the engines.

Stella sighed. "Pack it up."

As quickly as they had broken it all out, they put it all away. No one said a word. It was easy to see how disappointed they were.

Hell, I was disappointed.

As we cruised away from the spot that the intuitive, Marie, announced was the place where Bartholomew Gault had drowned, I heard something that, to this day, gives me a chill when I recall it.

"There he is!"

I don't know who said it. Suddenly, there was a rush to one side of the boat and I could feel the boat leaning dangerously to port.

"Don't crowd up like that," yelled the captain.

Okay, I couldn't help myself. I was part of that crowd.

We were all looking over the side.

And deep under the water? Where it should have been totally black?

We could see light.

It was vague, faint, and a light shade of green.

But it was light.

About the size and shape of an antique lantern at a depth of about six feet, right under our boat. It was moving. It disappeared as it went under the boat.

We rushed to the other side.

"I said don't crowd over like that," the captain shouted.

The boat listed to other side as we gazed into the water.

The light appeared again, brighter now. Growing stronger as it rose closer to the surface.

It didn't look like an antique lantern at all.

It was a man's face. Mouth, chin, mustache, open eyes staring at us.

Then gone.

It vanished when the wave broke over the side of the boat, washing over our shoes and the deck.

"Save the equipment," Stella screamed.

A ferocious wind hurled a gray curtain of stinging rain sideways into the boat. People shrieked in surprise.

The captain accelerated at the same time another brutal gust of wind twisted the boat around. I lost my footing and fell back onto a bench.

The captain shouted, "Lance, Drew, pass out the life jackets."

The two boys pulled the seats of unoccupied benches up and hauled out bright orange safety vests, staggering about the deck, handing them to the ghost hunters.

"Save the equipment," Stella screeched, putting on her vest, kneeling down on the deck, awash with brackish water, securing a motion detector.

Others were trying to do the same.

The captain shouted one more time, "Sit your asses down on a bench until we're safe."

The ferry bounced over peaks of the waves and dove headfirst into the moving valleys they left behind. Sprays of foam and water splashed back from the bow, adding to the discomfort of the driving rain.

It was long, wet ride home.

• ● ● ● •

The rain had let up by the time we tied to dock. While the ghost hunters inspected what was left of their equipment, I had a chance to talk to the captain.

"So what the hell was that?" I was referring to the mysterious light.

We both watched the Elroy boys finish securing the boat while flashes of lightning danced high above our heads.

His voice that was low and dirt rough. "Plankton, most likely. If you disturb it, it shines phosphorescent. Got a real spooky glow to it. It's not that unusual, Miss Chase."

It sounded like a reasonable response.

Picking up my bag, I slung it onto my shoulder and started down the dock. Then I turned around. "You really think that's what it was?"

He grinned, showing me teeth yellowed by years of cigarette smoke. "Don't know," he shrugged. "Could've even been a jellyfish. Some of them are bioluminescent, you know, like fireflies."

I thanked him and started to carry my bag down the dock when I heard the captain holler and chuckle, "But since you asked, I'm inclined to think was the ghoulie of Bartholomew Gault."

• • ● • •

I got to my car and checked my watch. A little before eleven, an hour ahead of schedule. I was in the process of digging the cell phone out of my bag to see if Kevin wanted to join me for a drink at my place and then maybe a little hanky panky, when I dropped my keys.

Fatigue? More like exhaustion.

I was so bone tired that when I leaned over to pick them up I thought for a second I might tip over and crumple in a heap onto the parking lot. But I kept my balance and as I scooped up my key ring, I noticed the license plate of the car parked next to me.

It was a Nissan 370Z, steel gray, convertible.

The car suddenly chirped as the doors were remotely unlocked and Lance and Drew walked up behind me.

"It was nice to meet you, Miss Chase." Lance got into the driver's seat, sporting a thousand-watt smile. "Sorry we didn't get to see more of the ghost. That would have really been cool."

Drew didn't say anything, but nodded morosely and slid into the passenger's side.

I watched as they carefully backed the sports car out of their spot and slowly growled out of the parking lot and onto the street.

What had drawn my attention to their car?

While I was picking up my keys, I saw ragged pieces of duct tape and tiny, torn shreds of black plastic attached to the edge of their license plate. Coincidence? On a night with lightning flashing and ghosts about, who knows?

Chapter Twenty-nine

The universe put on a spectacular light show for Kevin and me as we sat on the porch. With each flash of lightning, a burst of white and pink neon illuminated the inside of the clouds, accompanied by a low, rumbling tremor, like the warning growl of a rabid Rottweiler.

A second band of storms was moving in. The first drops of rain had yet to fall but the air was filled with anticipatory ozone. It was only a matter of time before electricity would split the air and spear the Earth with a bone-rattling, nerve-racking crackle of thunder joined by the generous applause of pouring rain.

Kevin and I waited for the deluge. We each had our choice of poison—vodka for me, Dewar's for him. As we tasted our respective cocktails, I looked out over the freshly trimmed grass and manicured hedges freshly painted silver and gray by the streetlight. It amused me to see the rented BMW sports car, top up, sitting quietly in the apartment house's parking area off the driveway. I hoped all my nosy neighbors were both curious and jealous.

"So you don't know if you saw a ghost." Kevin sipped his drink. "Or a just a school of radioactive, single-celled shrimp."

I frowned. "Duh, of course it was a ghost. Before we got off the ferry boat, Stella Barry announced it was the spirit of Bartholomew Gault. She was quite adamant that I quote her correctly."

"No kidding." He feigned a serious demeanor.

"She said that Gault is out there looking for his family."

"Really? Who told her that?

"Marie, only the best intuitive on the boat," I stated in a lofty manner, as if he should have already known.

"Ah." He stared at his tumbler of scotch. "I'm thinking the only spirits that I really know about are swirling around in our glasses tonight."

We sat in wicker chairs, our feet resting on the table in front of us, our bare toes touching and occasionally playing tag with each other. I held his hand. "Do you believe in heaven?"

He took another sip of his drink before he answered with another question. "You mean do I believe in an afterlife?"

"Okay."

"I want to. I didn't, up until Joanna died." His voice became low and serious. "I'd always thought that before you were born you were nothing. And when you died, you went back to being nothing."

"Ashes to ashes."

"But then someone you really love passes away. I just never wanted to believe that she was completely gone. I guess that I hope, believe, pray that she's gone someplace and that she's happy." When he said all of that, Kevin's eyes looked so sad.

I had a question I needed to ask, but hated to because it was just so damned trite. "Do you think you'll ever see her again?"

Am I really asking, so are you going to hook up with your dead wife when you get to heaven?

I squeezed my hand while he mulled over his answer. "I loved her for a lot of years. I still love her. I put her through hell and she stuck with me. But you have to know that I love *you*. Are you really asking if you and I will be together after we both die?"

Well, yeah, that was what I was asking. But then I realized how unfair the question was.

Dropping my feet off the table and leaning forward, I put both my hands on his face and then kissed him. When I took my lips off his, I looked into his eyes and said, "Let's not worry about that. How about we just enjoy each other now? We're getting married, you know?"

He reached up and touched my face. "I'll always love you. Don't ever doubt that."

Thunder rumbled in the heavens above us while we stared into each other's eyes.

He whispered, "Do *you* believe in heaven?"

"I believe that there's something after we die. I'm not sure it's green fields and angels, but I think Stella had it right when she said that energy is never lost. It may change forms, but it goes on forever."

"How about reincarnation?" he asked.

"I love reincarnation," I answered. "How about we go with that?"

He nodded and appeared thoughtful. "If we come back in another life, how will we know each other? After all, we won't look like we do now, will we?"

"How about if we have a word, a word almost nobody uses. Like a password."

"I've got one." He leaned in close. "Sidereal."

"Sidereal," I said, feeling the word in my mouth. I didn't know the definition but I like how it almost rhymed with ethereal. "I'm not a hundred percent sure I know what it means."

"If I remember right, it's got something to do with stars, constellations, and time."

"Sidereal. I like it. There's something eternal about it.

● ● ● ● ●

When the storm started for real, the wind swirled up hard and a gray spray of rain drove onto the porch, stinging us like an angry cloud of wet bees. We quickly drained our glasses and headed for the dry safety of my apartment.

I was only mildly surprised to see that, because lightning had knocked out a transformer along the power grid, my electricity was gone. Except for the stuttering lightning strikes outside, the place was dark and unnaturally silent.

I lit a candle and looked into Kevin's eyes.

He was so beautiful.

Without a word, we carried the candle into my bedroom, took off each other's wet clothes, pulled back the sheets and made love.

It started with slow, warm caresses but became breathlessly passionate and furious. We were as driven as the storm that beat relentlessly against my window.

It wasn't just sex, it was our love and bodies chasing away the furies.

When we were finished, we lay for a long time listening to the rain and the sound of our own breathing. I had my face on his chest and with each rise and fall, I could hear his heart beating.

I don't know how long we stayed that way, it might have been minutes.

It might have been days.

Kevin broke the spell when he whispered, "Genie?"

"Yeah?"

He didn't answer.

I lifted my head from his chest and asked, "What?"

"I'm scared," he whispered.

I didn't know what to say. Kevin was my hero. He wasn't supposed to be afraid.

"It's okay," I said quietly.

"What if there isn't anything after we die?"

"There is."

He sighed and I could tell from the tension in his body that he didn't believe me. "Promise me you'll take care of Caroline."

"You know I will," I answered. "But nothing's going to happen."

We were silent again for a few heartbeats before Kevin whispered, "It is, you know. Something *is* going to happen. We both have to face that."

My throat tightened up again. I didn't want to cry. "Let's not talk about this."

He sighed. 'Whatever happens, whatever treatment, protocol, experiment, I can't afford it. By the time it's over there won't be anything left to leave Caroline, no money, no house."

"You have insurance."

"You know how far that'll go," he growled.

"Please let's not talk about this. We'll do what we have to do."

He didn't say anything more and for a few minutes I thought he might have drifted off to sleep. But then he whispered, "Do you think that people die for a reason?"

Please, oh please, I don't want to talk about this now.

"I don't know."

"It's like when lightning struck my Uncle Jack. I wondered about that for years," he whispered. "But then I stopped wondering, until Joanna passed away."

I just lay there and listened to him while the storm raged outside.

He gently stroked my shoulder. "I wondered how God could let someone so young die, and in so much pain."

"I don't know," I repeated.

"I do. If she hadn't gotten sick, I'd still be a hopeless drunk. It's what made me get straight."

Neither one of us said anything for a minute.

"It's just so damned stupid. My business was good. I had a dozen people working for me. I had a beautiful wife and daughter. Everything was going my way. I thought I could do anything. I was invulnerable. The rules didn't apply. It was all just one long party."

We both stayed silent again.

He's thinking he's being punished for putting his wife through hell.

"And what's worse," he said, "is the pain I'll be putting Caroline through again. She watched her mother die. Toward the end, it didn't matter how many painkillers Joanna took, she suffered horribly. And Caroline saw it all. She's such a good kid. I can't stand the thought of her going through that again."

When he sighed it was a sigh of the damned.

It reminded me of the first time I'd seen him in the schoolyard, beaten and bloody. He'd sighed that same way. Back in the schoolyard, even after the beating, Kevin had a look of defiance on his face. He'd been beaten but not knocked down.

He stood up to it.
He hadn't won.
But he hadn't lost.
Now, right now, I wish I could see that defiance again.

Chapter Thirty

I woke up before Kevin. A light rain tapped against the roof as the rust-colored morning light stole through the gaps in the curtains. My bedroom was filled with long, brown shadows.

Illuminated blue zeros on my digital alarm clock blinked annoyingly on and off. The electricity had returned sometime during the night and now all the electronic timepieces needed to be reset. I looked at my watch and saw that it was nine-twenty. I lay there and listened to the steady rain and to Kevin's heavy breathing. Feeling his warm body next to mine made me feel comfortable and safe and I wanted to stay there for the rest of my life.

But I sighed and slowly, quietly, swung my legs over the side of the bed and sat up. I had it in my head that I was going to make us breakfast. Honestly, I'm not much of a cook. I don't enjoy it. But I can scramble eggs and make toast and that was the plan.

I showered, made myself presentable, threw on a pair of shorts and a sleeveless top, and carrying my umbrella, took Tucker out for a short walk. Then I got out the frying pan, plates, and whole wheat bread so that it all would be ready when Kevin crawled out of bed.

I disconnected my cell phone from the charger and noticed that I'd gotten a text from Mike Dillon. Time-stamped at seven-thirty-seven this morning, it simply said, "Call me."

Recognizing my number, he answered on the second ring, "Morning, Genie."

"Hey, Mike, what's up?" keeping my voice artificially low so I wouldn't wake Kevin in the next room.

"First off, let me say I'm sorry about yesterday afternoon. I shouldn't have come on to you like that. That was way out of line."

I smiled to myself. "It's not your fault I'm so damned irresistible."

"Yeah, well, I don't want to screw up our friendship," he said. "That's what we are, right…friends?"

I closed my eyes. Men and women that are on the bad end of a break-up have the pitiful need to feel wanted. That's human nature. It always makes me sad, especially since I've been there. "Of course we are."

"I'm going to make it up to you."

"No need," I answered, although I eagerly listened for what he had to offer.

"Late last night, we got a warrant to go out to Greenwich and search the home of Henry Morris Fitzgerald."

"Jimmy's dad. Bet the old man and his lawyers loved that."

Then Mike said, "We were looking for drug evidence but found something else. In the old man's library, newly mounted on the wall over the stone fireplace, we found an antique samurai sword."

If there is still any sleep fogging this old mind, that simple statement completely blows it away.

"Is it from Connor's Landing?"

"We don't know yet. We've compared it to a manifest that George Chadwick kept and it looks like it matches but we're waiting for the FBI to check it for any traces of residual blood or tissue."

It was far too early in the morning for my heart to be pumping this hard. Was it really possible that Jimmy Fitzgerald was there at Connor's Landing the night those people were killed?

"How soon are you going to know?"

"It could be sometime this afternoon. We asked the old man where he got the weapon and he told us that it was a gift from his son. He said it was a show of gratitude for everything he's done for the boy."

I got a genuine chill that ran up my spine.

Mike continued, "We asked Jimmy how he came by the blade."

"What did he say?"

"He says he found it out near Fisher's Island this past weekend while he was out casting for blues. He claims that while he was cruising by at low tide, he saw something underwater reflecting the sunlight. When he anchored and took a look, low and behold, it was an antique Japanese fighting sword."

"I guess it's possible," I said doubtfully. "One of the killers throws it into the water and it washes up near the island."

"Sure, it's like winning the lottery, happens all the time. Even so, we're going to sweat Jimmy a little. One thing the kid has going for him is his shoe size doesn't fit any of the footprints. But who knows? We could get lucky and Jimmy turns on some of his friends."

"You wouldn't cut a deal with that piece of crap, would you, Mike? He's already beaten one rap for killing somebody."

"Hell, Genie. We'll get the names and, trust me on this, Jimmy *will* do time."

"But not the time he deserves."

"Don't be a pessimist. Let's see what forensics has to say about the blade. Would you like to be the only reporter here when we get the answer?"

"You're the best, Mike Dillon. Give me a call when you know," I kept my voice down, trying hard not to wake Kevin.

I glanced around the kitchen. Everything was where it should be when Kevin arose. This would be the first time I'd ever cooked anything for him.

But it would have to wait.

That wealthy little weasel Jimmy Fitzgerald was going to turn on his friends and take a deal, I just knew it. There was no way I was going to let that son of a bitch catch a ride on this.

I walked into my bedroom and sat down on the bed next to where Kevin was still sleeping. I leaned down and kissed his cheek.

He slowly opened his eyes and smiled at me.

"Morning, sleepy head."

"Morning," he answered in a hoarse growl. "What time is it?"

The tiny light on my alarm was still blinking so I quickly consulted my watch. "Around ten."

He groaned and sat up. "I never sleep this late."

"You must have been comfortable."

He smiled. "Very."

"Hey, I was going to make us breakfast, but I've got to go out and cover something. I won't be long, how about you just laze about here and I'll scramble some eggs when I get back?"

He gently put his hand on my waist. "Nice idea." His voice was still heavy with sleep. "But I want to give Caroline a big hug and then I've got to get the Bond-mobile back to the rental company."

There was something in his voice when he talked about hugging his daughter that struck me as odd. He'd told me that she was spending the night at Aunt Ruth's so I knew she was safe.

I shrugged it off. "Can we connect later this afternoon?"

His fingers pushed tighter into my waist, and he gave a slight bob of the head. "Sure."

I frowned and slid off the bed. "Okay then. I'm going to run."

"Genie?"

"Yeah?"

His eyes locked onto mine. "I love you…don't you forget."

I smiled. "Love you too."

As I walked out of the house, into the rain, I was struck by a vague uneasiness. Something wasn't right and I couldn't quite get my hands on it. But hopping into my car, I quickly chalked it up to the depressing weather.

It took me twenty minutes to get to the wooden bridge leading to Connor's Landing. The door to the guard's shack swung open and a figure came out dressed in a blue slicker and a baseball cap with the Aztec Security logo on the front. I was a little disappointed to see that it wasn't Donnie Burke, the elderly gentleman who'd been working the night of the murders.

I rolled down the window and the guard asked, "Who are you here to see?" He was of medium height and young, maybe in his late twenties. There was blond stubble on his face and his eyes were bloodshot like he'd been up all night. He had in his hand the ubiquitous clipboard.

"Becky Elroy."

"Is she expecting you?"

"Yeah," I lied. "Hey, where's Donnie Burke?"

He looked up from the clipboard and into my eyes. "You know Donnie?"

"Yeah, he's a great guy." I was hoping to distract him from calling the Elroy residence to see if they were expecting a guest.

He took a long breath and exhaled. "Apparently, he had some chest pains last night and they rushed him to the hospital."

"Oh my God, is he okay?"

"I don't know. I haven't heard anything. This is Donnie's shift. I've been here since eleven last night 'cause the company hasn't found someone who can fill in."

"Oh man, I'm sorry." I dredged up as much sympathy as I could muster. "Hey, am I good to go?"

He waved his hand. "Oh yeah, yeah, you're a friend a' Donnie's, you're cool."

I drove through Checkpoint Aztec.

I hadn't planned to stop at the Chadwick house but as I drove slowly past it I could see that the yellow tape and the police cruisers were gone. Instead, two white vans marked with the Gold Coast Biohazard Specialists logo were parked in the driveway.

Once the police finish a murder investigation, one of the most wrenching tasks facing the survivors and family is cleaning the crime scene. What's left is often blood and tissue. Not only is it emotionally draining and traumatizing beyond the actual crime itself, but it's literally considered a biohazard to be handled by professionals. I stopped my car and backed up. Then I pulled into the driveway and parked behind one of the vans. The unceasing precipitation made the dash from my Sebring to the front door uncomfortable and I wished that I'd brought an umbrella.

Any other time I would have rung the doorbell, but instead, I tried the door and discovered it was unlocked. Letting myself in, the first thing I noticed was the pungent, throat-searing smell of chlorine and hospital-grade disinfectant that immediately made my eyes water.

I closed the door quietly behind me and cupped my hand around my mouth and nose in a vain attempt to keep out the chemicals I was certain were burning my lungs. I walked gingerly through an entryway and into the living room bathed in the glow of intense floodlights where I found four figures in yellow haz-mat suits, filtration masks, and goggles ripping up the carpeting.

One of them noticed me out of the corner of his eye. Pulling the mask away from his face, he asked, "Who are you?

It took two full heartbeats before I answered, "Realtor."

He studied me carefully for a moment. "We're not ready for you yet."

I figured I was on a roll. "The attorney for the estate asked if I'd come by and take a look. He'd like my opinion on an asking price."

"We've still got a lot of work ahead of us. This place ain't near ready to show. This room is going to have to be completely repainted. There was blood everywhere."

I nodded. "That's what I hear. Look, I just need to take a real quick look around. I promise to stay out of your way. Please?"

The cleaner mulled that over for a couple of seconds, then slid the mask off and placed the goggles on the top of his head. He glanced around at the other three men and said, "Okay, let's take fifteen. Give the lady a chance to look around." The men on their knees stood up and they all slowly trudged out the front door and trotted out into the gray weather to their vans, leaving me in the living room alone with the project foreman. He held up hands to show me the rubber gloves he had on. "I'm Carl. I'd shake your hand, but right now it wouldn't be such a good idea."

"Gotcha', I'm Geneva Chase." I glanced around the room remembering my source's description. The room was huge, nearly the size of my entire apartment. The couches and plush pillows had been removed, as had the rest of the furniture. The fireplace was where he said it was, but there was a spot above it, a large, pale rectangle with wiring in the center, where a large-screen television must have been. The curtains had been taken down and a slate gray light pushed oppressively against the glass. Much of the carpeting had already been torn up, leaving exposed hardwood.

The room felt completely devoid of life, sterile.

"It was bad?" I asked.

Carl frowned. "Bad as I've ever seen. Coroner got all the body parts up but there was still plenty of tissue in the carpeting and on the walls."

I sighed. "Any of the other rooms have any damage?"

"The armory," Carl answered. "No blood, just some broken glass."

"The armory."

"It's where Mr. Chadwick kept his weapons collection."

"Can I see?"

He nodded and led me to an adjoining door. Indeed, over the top of the doorjamb was a wooden coat of arms with a single word on it, Armory, in an Old English font.

The walls were lush, dark wooden panels, like something you see in a castle. The windows were stained glass. Thick carpeting muted any sounds. Tall cabinets with glass doors displayed a dazzling array of antique pistols, rifles, muskets, knives, and swords. It was like walking into a museum.

Carl pointed to a cabinet across the room. "That glass was busted out and all over the floor. Cops cleaned that up. They think that maybe two of the swords in that exhibit right there were taken the night of the murders."

I stepped closer and studied the cabinet. It appeared that there was room for two long fighting blades that might have once been on display but now were conspicuously missing. One of which, hopefully, had been discovered in the home of Henry Morris Fitzgerald.

"So do you want to take a look at the rest of the house?" Carl offered.

I didn't, not really. I'd seen what I came to see, but for Carl to believe I was who I said I was, I said, "Yes, look, I'm only going to be five minutes. Why don't you take a break with your guys and I'll be out of here before you know it."

Carl smiled. "I do hear the coffee in my thermos calling me. You sure you'll be okay?"

I smiled back and made a show of pulling my notebook out of my bag. "Hey, I'm a professional."

Then I spent the next ten minutes poking around the Chadwick place. It was two stories and beautiful. The ceilings were easily twelve feet high, multiple bathrooms and fireplaces, five bedrooms, a library, and a spacious kitchen. Whether the furnishings were antiques or contemporary, everything in the house was first class and expensive.

It was difficult to believe that only two people lived in the massive, marvelous old home.

But I know the long, sad history of this house. I know the stories of the people who owned it and how they died. There are ghosts in this house. Maybe not the spirits that Stella Barry looks for in the dead of night in lonely cemeteries and old asylums, but ghosts nonetheless. They're a history that haunts the quiet rooms and lurks in the shadows of the long hallways. They're victims of chance and ill fortune. I was quite happy to bid good-bye to the house and relieved as I waved to the guys sitting in the vans drinking their coffee while the mist and drizzle enveloped us in a wet, gray blanket.

Stopping at the Chadwick house had only made me more apprehensive of my next and final visit on Connor's Landing.

Chapter Thirty-one

I pulled into the paved circle in front of the Elroy home and parked behind Lance's gray Nissan 370Z. Getting out of my car, I walked over and took another look at the rear license plate. The same tiny shreds of black plastic and duct tape that I'd seen last night were still there.

I trotted along the wet flagstone sidewalk that was lined with well cared-for rose bushes and climbed the brick steps to the front doorway. As I fingered the doorbell, I expected Mrs. Elroy to open the door dressed in her suburban fashionista designer shorts and top. Instead, when the door swung open, I recognized the pleasant face of the young Hispanic woman who'd helped prepare for the party in the Elroy kitchen a few days ago. Today she was wearing a pair of denim shorts and a navy blue sport shirt.

"Can I help you?" she asked with a smile.

"I'm Geneva Chase. I work for *The Sheffield Post*," I said. "Are Lance and Drew home? I see Lance's car is parked over there."

Hearing that I worked for a newspaper, the smile disappeared and she eyed me with suspicion. "Are they expecting you?"

"Yes," I lied. "I'm doing a story on local students who took on summer jobs working for the Harbor Association."

She studied me briefly and then decided that it all sounded eminently plausible. She told me, "Lance is in the shower and Drew is having breakfast out by the pool."

Is she giving me a choice of where I want to go?

"Come with me." She led me through the house and into the kitchen that smelled deliciously like bacon. Sliding open the glass door, she motioned with an open hand that I should find my own way to the pool.

I mumbled a thank you as she slid the door closed again. I negotiated my way through the falling rain and the shallow puddles until I got to the pool. The chlorine scent emanating from the water reminded me vaguely of my visit to the Chadwick house. Drew was hunched over a wrought iron table under a canvas awning attached to the pool house. He was wearing a swimming suit and an unbuttoned short-sleeved shirt. A steaming plate loaded with bacon, eggs, and toast lay off to one side of the table. He was staring intently at his open laptop, his thumbs working maniacally at a small, black plastic control panel.

Focused completely on the computer screen and wearing earbuds, he was oblivious to my approach when I walked up next to him. I stepped back so I could watch as he played.

I've never been a believer that watching violent movies or playing abhorrent video games makes someone a serial killer. After all, I grew up watching Roadrunner cartoons and I don't go around dropping anvils on people's heads.

But I think that being overly exposed to violent material can desensitize you. And what I was seeing on Drew's computer screen chilled me right to the bone.

It was all happening from the point of view of Drew's avatar, a futuristic warrior with the musculature of a steroid addict. He was running through a dark, massive stone hallway and from almost every hiding place, shadow enemies, both human and alien, leaped out in attack. At first Drew's avatar simply blew them away one at a time with a shotgun but when he ran out of ammunition, he pulled an AK-47 out of a leather sling he carried on his back. Firing at a ridiculous rate of speed, the body count added up quickly. When he emptied the clip, he pulled a fighting blade from a scabbard at his waist and began the carnage with eager bloodlust.

The avatar sliced through throats and hacked off limbs, one after another. Simulated blood fairly exploded from his victims' dying bodies. Even though Drew was wearing earbuds, I could hear the shrill screams of agony and despair.

Finally, deciding that I'd seen enough, I tapped the young man on the shoulder. He twisted around until he could look up from his chair to see me. His eyes stared at me dully, blinking, until the spark of recognition hit. He smiled, put the game on hold and took the tiny speakers out of his ears. "Hi." He made an effort to stand up.

I put a gentle hand on his shoulder and pushed him back down into his seat. "Don't get up. You're fine."

"You're the lady from the ferry last night."

"Aren't you sweet to remember."

As he blushed, I sat down at the table across from him. I noticed a full-length mirror was hung on the wall of the pool house behind where Drew was sitting. Knowing the narcissism of the Elroy family, I wasn't surprised. From my viewpoint, in the mirror I could see the back of Drew's head, part of his computer screen and my own reflection, at least from the eyes up. The rest of my face was hidden by the open laptop.

On the glass surface of the table in front of me was an empty plate, bowl, coffee cup, and cutlery. "Is Lance joining you for breakfast?"

"If he ever gets out of the shower."

Dying for a cup of coffee, I reached over to a ceramic carafe and poured some steaming brew into the mug I'm sure was meant for Drew's brother. Then I took a grateful sip and asked, "What's the game you're playing?"

He smiled again. "*Final Apocalypse III.*"

How many final apocalypses can you have?

Swallowing another delicious sip of caffeine, I said, "Look Drew, my name's Geneva Chase and I work for *The Sheffield Post*. I've got some questions I need to ask you. Is that okay?"

He frowned. "I guess."

"Whose car did you guys take off in last night? What is it? A Nissan convertible?"

Drew nodded. "370Z...it's Lance's. Mine's just like it only black. It's in the garage."

"Did your dad get that for you?"

The young man nodded. "Yeah, I got it for acing my grades this year."

"At the Handley Academy?"

"Yeah, I'm going to be a senior when school starts back up in August."

"That's a good school." I sat back in my chair. "Why do you suppose there are bits of duct tape and black plastic on Lance's rear license plate?"

He jerked. Shaking his head, he said quietly, "I don't know."

"Sometimes thieves obscure their license plates with plastic and tape. That way if someone spots their car, a witness can't catch the number. And once they've gotten away, it's real easy to tear off."

He didn't answer.

"Drew, did the two of you break into a woman's apartment over on Briar Street a couple of nights ago?"

Silence.

"One of the neighbors identified Lance's car," I said. It was only a tiny lie. The neighbor described it as an expensive sports car with a rag top and a license plate that was blacked out.

Drew chewed his lower lip, thinking while he stared at the screen of his laptop.

"Nobody got hurt, Drew. No harm, no foul. Tell me what happened that night."

The only sounds in that backyard came from the fountain and raindrops as they fell onto the surface of the pool and dripped off the edge of the awning. Somewhere in the distance, the faint music of a wind chime floated on the air as metal struck slowly against metal in the delicate breeze.

I decided to take a different tack. "Jimmy Fitzgerald was arrested last night. Did you know that?"

Drew looked up at me, across the top of his computer screen. He frowned, his wide-set eyes focused on me with extreme interest. "What for?"

"Weren't you and Lance out partying on Jimmy's boat last Wednesday night?"

His eyes narrowed as he studied me. "What was he arrested for?"

"Jimmy was busted for selling methamphetamines to an undercover cop. Were you doing meth the night you were partying on Jimmy's boat?"

Drew nodded slowly.

"Isn't meth a little ghetto for you boys? I expected you'd be doing something a little more high-rent, like coke."

Drew didn't say anything and I saw his eyes drop briefly to his computer screen. He tapped out a couple of short sentences on his keyboard and then looked back up at me. "It's a good high."

"Anyway, the meth isn't the most interesting part. No, what's really interesting is when they searched Jimmy's place they found an antique samurai sword."

His eyes widened for a brief moment and he sucked in a deep breath. Almost at the same time, he tapped out another short sentence on his laptop.

"Who're you talking to, Drew?"

He was quiet for a minute as he looked across the top of his computer screen at me. Finally, he replied, "Guy I was playing the game with. He's wondering why I stopped playing. Did Jimmy lawyer up?"

"I don't know. But what I do know is that Jimmy likes making deals." I leaned down and took the recorder out of my bag. I hit the on button and set it in front of me. "Let's start with something easy. Whose idea was it to copy the Home Alone gang?"

"I don't know what you're talking about."

I sighed. "How old are you, Drew?"

"I'll be seventeen next month."

Interviewing a minor without parental consent is a journalistic fuzzy area, especially when talking about drugs.

But I'm not letting that get in my way.

"You're a minor. Nothing's going to happen to you," I said.

His shifted his eyes to the computer screen again. I could see he was reading something. It only took him a moment and then he slowly reached up and closed the laptop. "Okay, it was Jimmy's idea."

That's it, Drew. Throw Jimmy under the bus.

"Jimmy," I repeated.

"He said it would be a real adrenaline rush. He'd read all about that gang in the newspaper. He figured if they could do it then we could do it. Jimmy knows a guy who works IT for Aztec Security. For a couple hundred dollars he'd switch off the alarm when and where Jimmy told him to. The first house we did was in Westport. It was kind of scary and cool all at the same time, like we were doing a heist. It was like something out of a movie."

"Pretty smart. Everyone thought it was the pros. You guys play the game, somebody else gets the blame. What all did you get?"

He thought for a moment. "I don't know…some cash, a bunch of jewelry, an antique coin collection, some other stuff."

"How did you unload it?"

"Jimmy knows a guy in the city." Jimmy Fitzgerald is his own one-man crime syndicate, I thought.

"Some of it we sold on E-bay."

"How many houses did you guys hit?" I was assuming it was at least two.

Drew didn't answer. Instead he turned his head and gazed out over the dark, moving surface of Long Island Sound.

"Drew," I interrupted, "help me out here. I know you broke into at least two houses, nicely done, professional. But what was the deal with breaking into the blind woman's apartment? That wasn't like the others, now was it? This was, well, sloppy."

I could see his jaw working as he ground his teeth. He looked back at me and replied, "Jimmy got pissed off at us."

"You and Lance."

"Yeah, he didn't want to have anything to do with us anymore."

"Why?"

Drew shrugged and continued, "After he got pissed off at us, Lance wanted to show Jimmy that we didn't need his sorry ass. So we were over on Briar Street a couple of nights ago smoking a little weed and talking, just killin' some time until we had to come home. We noticed that as it got darker, nobody was turning any lights on in one of the ground-floor apartments. We figured the place must be empty."

They figured wrong.

"Who broke in that night? Was it you?"

He slowly shook his head. "It was Lance. When he came back to the car, he was freakin' out. He said he'd been attacked by some crazy bitch with a butcher knife. Did you say she's blind?"

Big tough guy, chased away by a blind woman wielding a chisel.

"How come Jimmy didn't want to have anything to do with you and Lance anymore?"

He just stared down at his closed laptop.

I decided to go for broke. "Last Wednesday night, did you guys break into the Chadwick house?"

He stared at the table, refusing to answer.

"Was there really a party on Jimmy's boat last Wednesday night?"

"Yes."

"But it was just the three of you."

"Yes."

"Were you doing drugs?"

"Yes."

"Meth?"

"Tequila first," he answered softly. "Then some grass. a little coke, then some meth."

"Okay, so you guys got toasty. What happened then?"

"Me and Lance left the marina and drove back home. Jimmy followed in his dad's Hatteras a little later and tied up to our dock." He motioned toward the water with his jaw.

"Why'd you pick the Chadwick house?"

He pursed his lips while he thought about his answer. "A few years ago. Lance and I shoveled snow out of Mr. Chadwick's driveway. When we went inside his house to get our money, he showed us his room full of antique weapons. He called it his armory. He was real proud of it."

"And you told Jimmy about the armory."

"He said that some collectors will pay serious cash for those old guns and swords."

"Drew, wouldn't it be easier just to ask your dad to bump up your allowance?"

I was startled to see him look up at me in anger, shaking his head. "You don't know, you don't know what it's like. My father, he's self-made, he came from nothin'. He put himself through college, he earned every dime. I hear that *every* day... *every fucking day*. That's why he wants us to work on that stupid ferry boat. He wants us to earn our own way like he did. But that ferry boat gig? It doesn't pay shit."

"Not like earning a thirty-thousand-dollar sports car by getting good grades?"

He stayed silent and stared at me through angry slits.

"Why did you boys pick last Wednesday to hit the Chadwick place?

He still glared at me. "We've heard mom and dad talking about the Chadwicks, about how they were perverts and how they went to sex parties. So Lance and I started watching their house."

"You watched their house? Why?"

He shrugged. "We've never seen a sex party. We were hoping to sneak a look through one of their windows."

"And?"

Drew frowned again. "We watched their house for a whole month and we never saw them throw any kind of party. But every Wednesday night, they went out and didn't come home until real late, sometimes around five or six in the morning."

Five or six in the morning? Was George Chadwick so far up the corporate food chain that he didn't have to work office hours like a normal person? Was he so rich and important that he could party like a porn star and then take all the next day to recover?

"So it was a safe bet that no one would be around if you hit their house. Did you walk over there?"

"Yes."

"How did you guys get in?"

"Basement window."

"What time?"

"I don't know, eleven-thirty, maybe closer to midnight."

"And once you were in," I said, "the Chadwicks came home."

He tapped his hand on the top of the closed laptop while he stared past me, thinking about that night.

"What happened?"

He stayed silent, thinking. The only sounds were from the raindrops and the distant wind chime and the lapping of the water on the sides of the dock and against the hull of the powerboat.

"Drew, the Chadwicks came home while you, Lance, and Jimmy were in the house. What happened?"

He licked his lips. When he began talking, it was little more than a whisper. "Lance and I were in the armory. Jimmy went upstairs to look for cash and jewelry. We'd just busted out the locks on two of the display cases. And then we heard them come home.

"Lance and I just stood there, looking at each other. He was high and I remember that he was having a hard time not laughing. He thought it was all hilarious. Me, I was freaking out. We turned off our flashlights and stood there in the dark. I couldn't breathe, I was so afraid they'd hear us. While I was standing there in total darkness, I was thinking to myself that we were standing in a room full of antique weapons. The question ran through my head, how many guns, real guns firing real bullets, did Mr. Chadwick have in the house? There in the dark, in my head, I could see him coming into the armory, putting a gun barrel up to my face and pulling the trigger."

"But that's not what happened," I suggested. "Is it?"

He slowly shook his head. "At first, all we could hear were the Chadwicks. She said something about getting the wine open and he said something about getting the movie started. Then Mrs.

Chadwick said something about a guy named Jim and how he's a crazy bastard. But I couldn't hear her real good.

"And then there were other voices. I couldn't tell how many. Lance and I listened to them talking and laughing. Mr. Chadwick said something about how the movie was made in some club in New York and how he and Mrs. Chadwick had been there a couple of times. They talked a little more and then I guess they started watching the movie because it got pretty quiet."

"By that time, how long had you been hiding in the armory?"

He shrugged again. "I don't know, maybe fifteen minutes."

"What happened next?"

He turned his face away from me again and looked out over the black waters of the sound.

"Drew?"

No answer.

"Tell me about Mrs. Webster, Drew."

He continued to stay silent.

"Was she a good teacher?"

Drew stared out at the water.

"I know how a good teacher can change your life, Drew," I said. "For me it was Mr. Sibelius, my English Lit teacher in high school. He taught me the beauty of language. He showed me the poetry of life. He was someone I related to…he made me feel like an adult. Even now, I think about him with great affection. Was Kathy Webster that kind of teacher, Drew?"

He turned slowly back to me. "Yes, she was that kind of teacher. She taught me not to be ashamed of myself."

"Drew, why would you be ashamed of yourself?"

I could see tears welling up in his eyes. "Just look at me and then look at Lance. He's older and better-looking, smarter. Girls are always all over him. I've heard the way my father talks about Lance. How proud he is of him."

I frowned. "You're father is proud of both of you. He told me that the afternoon I was here."

"Dad thinks I'm a stupid freak."

That sat me back in my chair. I wasn't sure what my next question would be.

"But I'm not," Drew said. "Mrs. Webster saw something special in me. And she fell in love with me."

"Were you in love with Mrs. Webster?"

"And she was in love with me."

"Did she say that?"

"Yes. She said I was an old soul, a lost soul. She said I was a boy yearning to be a man. She was interested in what I had to say, my thoughts, my opinions. She talked with me and she listened to me, I mean really listened."

I stayed quiet for a moment. "Was this strictly an emotional love, Drew? Did it go beyond that?"

He nodded slightly. "Yes, it started with kisses on my forehead and my cheek, and long hugs."

"Where did the two of you get together?"

"In her classroom, after school, eventually at her house. She lived here in Sheffield."

"Was Mr. Webster ever home when you were there?"

"Sometimes," he answered. "He mostly stayed in his office upstairs."

"Did you ever do more than kiss?"

He bobbed his head. "She could tell I'd never done it before. She said she'd helped other boys become men. She said she wanted to help me too."

"So the two of you had sex?"

His whole body took on an air of belligerence. "We made love."

"Sorry, was Mr. Webster in the house?"

Suddenly his face flushed crimson. "Yes," he whispered. "He never knew. We were very quiet."

I bet Kit Webster not only knew but recorded it on video.

"How many times did you and Mrs. Webster make love?"

"Three times," he answered. "The first time I was kind of clumsy and it was all over really fast. But the last time it was slow and beautiful. I know she came at least twice. She told me. She said I was the best she'd ever been with." He puffed out his chest.

"When was the last time?"

"It was only two weeks ago." I watched as a deep sadness replaced the pride that had so briefly dominated his demeanor.

I leaned forward. "Drew," I said in a voice that could barely be heard. "When you and Lance were in the armory and it got really quiet in the living room, what was happening?"

That's when I saw Lance's reflection in the mirror and my blood turned to ice water. He was standing directly behind me, holding a butcher knife in his right hand.

"Jesus, Drew, when I told you to keep talking and keep her here, I didn't expect you were going to give her a complete confession." Lance leaned over my left shoulder and reached out. He picked up my recorder off the table and hit the off button. Then I watched his reflection as he placed the tiny machine in the pocket of his blue jeans.

It had been Lance that Drew was talking to on his computer, not some guy he was playing a video game with.

I started to stand up and Lance put both of his hands on my shoulders, pushing me roughly back into my chair. The knife was clenched tightly in his right fist, the blade aimed at my throat. My heart was hammering so hard I could feel the pressure in my ears.

"What happened next, Miss Chase?" Lance growled in a voice much too close to my ear for comfort. "When it got real quiet in the living room I decided I wanted to see what was going on. So I opened the door just a crack and took a look. A skin flick was on the big screen on the wall over the fireplace. But the real show was on the floor. They'd laid blankets down and all six of them were as naked as the day they were born. And they were having themselves a good old time, playing with each other, sucking... fucking. Soft moans and groans, it was hard to tell what was coming from the movie and what was coming from the floor."

I glanced at Drew. He wore a pained expression. He already knew what the next part of the story was.

Lance was leaning close to my ear. I watched him in the mirror as he slowly straightened himself back up. He was also looking into the mirror, straight into my eyes.

"I thought it was hilarious, but hell, I was pretty fucked up, wasn't I, Drew?"

The young man nodded again.

"So I told Drew that he had to take a look. But Drew didn't think it was quite as funny as I did."

I didn't know just how afraid I was until I tried to find my voice. I had to clear my throat twice before I could coax my vocal chords to ask, "Did you recognize Mrs. Webster, Drew?"

The young man stared straight ahead. His eyes were focused on what was happening in his head. "She was naked, on her back. Men were using her, using her like a whore."

He sounds exactly like Jim Brenner.

Lance spoke up. "Old Drew just snapped, didn't ya, Drew?"

He sat across the table from me without making a sound, still visualizing that night.

Lance spoke again. "Drew was holding a three-hundred-year-old samurai sword. I looked it up and the correct name for it is a 'katana.' The blade is made of several layers of forged steel sharpened and balanced to the point where it'll cut through bone like butter. Isn't that right, Drew?"

The young man remained stone-still.

"Well, I'm standing next to Drew and the next thing I know, he's in the middle of all those naked bodies and I'm watching through the doorway. He's holding the katana with both hands and then he's bringing it up to his shoulder like he was getting ready to swing a baseball bat. Somebody on the floor must have seen him because there's this piercing scream and Drew brings the blade down on somebody's neck."

Drew muttered but it was so low that I couldn't understand him. Lance asked, "What's that, Drew?"

"Mr. Chadwick," he whispered in a low growl. "It was Mr. Chadwick. He was on top of her. He was on top of Kathy... Mrs. Webster."

"Oh, yeah," Lance acknowledged, "took his head completely off."

Drew huddled over his laptop in misery.

"And then all of the sudden, everyone was screaming," Lance said. "They were starting to get up off the floor. Some guy actually had his hand on Drew's arm. The next thing I knew, I was there swinging my own katana. I took that guy's arm off at the shoulder."

I studied Lance's reflection in the mirror. His face was flushed and his eyes were glassy. I was guessing he was high. "Lance," I managed to croak, glancing down at the knife blade he held inches from my neck. "How stoned were you that night?"

He laughed out loud. "Oh, I was fucked up bad."

I need a way out, any way out.

"Those are mitigating circumstances." I hoped I sounded like I knew what I was talking about. "Involuntary manslaughter. There's a good chance you can get out of this with probation."

I watched Lance smile and shake his head. "I'm fucked up now, Miss Chase. When I kill you, will I get off on probation?"

Definitely taken the wrong road. Find a different direction.

"Why did Jimmy get so pissed off at you guys?"

Drew started whispering again. "He saw us. He stood at the top of the steps and watched us. Once we started, we couldn't stop. I just kept swinging the blade, over and over. Until the screaming ended."

"What about Mrs. Webster?"

Neither Lance nor Drew answered.

Finally Drew took in a deep breath and sighed. "She was still alive, everyone else was already dead. One of us, I don't know which one, had sliced her from here to here." He moved a finger down his collarbone to the top of his swim trunks to show me. "She was bleeding, bad. She had her hands down there, trying to keep her guts in. She was on her knees, she begged me to help her. All I could see was those men using her over and over."

The rain fell on the backyard and the pool. No one spoke.

Lance leaned down close to my ear again. "Drew finished her, one stroke and it was done. You know what the weirdest part was?"

It could honestly get weirder?

"When it was all over, Drew and I were standing there in the middle of those dead people…blood was splashed everywhere, our shoes, our clothes, the walls, the ceiling, the TV screen…and the skin flick was still playing. Those people on the big screen were still having sex, just like nothing had happened.

"What about Jimmy Fitzgerald?"

This time Lance sighed. For him, this might have been the saddest part of the story. He recalled, "I heard Jimmy say, 'Holy Christ, holy Jesus Christ, what the fuck did you guys do?' And then he said, 'We got to get the hell out of here.' Then he told us to gather up everyone's clothes. We'd take their wallets and purses and get some cash out of this if nothing else. He said to bring the swords too, don't leave evidence.

"When we got back to our dock, where Jimmy's boat was tied up, he made us strip down and hand over our clothes. They were soaked in blood. He was going to put everything, clothes, swords, in a canvas bag he had on the boat and tie an anchor to it. Drop it into the sound. Nobody would ever find it. Not ever."

"Two killers, two sets of bloody footprints," I said in a low voice. "But three people were there. Jimmy didn't do the killing and he steered clear of the bloodstains. Smart boy, that Jimmy Fitzgerald. Except he didn't throw everything into the water like he told you he was going to. He kept at least one sword and gave it to his dad. I don't think Drew had the chance to tell you, but the cops arrested Jimmy last night and found the sword. I think right about now, he's ratting you boys out."

Lance jerked up quickly. I could see his face in the mirror, covered in a crimson cloud of rage. "That miserable son of a bitch kept one of the swords? That night on the dock, *our* dock, he told us he didn't want to have anything to do with either one of us. He said we were meth-heads, that our brains were fried. He kicked us to the curb like we were garbage. He said we, *we*, were incompetent and stupid. And we were like brothers, Jimmy and me, like fucking brothers."

I looked over at Drew again. His misery was absolute. He'd heard it. Jimmy and Lance were like brothers. Not Lance and Drew.

"Drew?" I quietly asked.

When he looked at me, there were tears trailing down his cheeks.

"Was it you who called the police and told them about the bodies in the Chadwick house?"

"I couldn't stand knowing that they were all dead, that she was dead, and lying on the floor, just up the road from here."

Lance's left hand strengthened its grip on my shoulder and his right hand pressed the knife blade against my neck. "Now the only question that's left, Miss Chase, is what are we going to do with you? You're kind of a loose end."

I could feel the cold steel of the knife against my carotid artery. These guys butchered six people. One more certainly wasn't going to make any difference.

I worked hard to find a voice through my escalating terror. "If the police are talking to Jimmy, you know it won't take long for him to give you up. The cops are probably on their way here now."

"Maybe," Lance mused, "but once they get here, it's not going to help us if you're here telling them our story."

I was willing to try anything. "Take off now. Get a head start. Take my cell phone, disable my car. When the cops get here, I won't say anything. They'll already have Jimmy's testimony. They won't need mine."

Lance was grinning in the mirror, looking at himself, admiring his own reflection. "Yeah, the reporter won't say anything," he repeated sarcastically. "I can make sure of that. We're going to take a boat ride, Miss Chase."

I involuntarily glanced at the dock where the powerboat was tied.

"Drew, come here, get around back, get her by the neck."

The boy got up and moved fast, behind me. The steel blade of the knife vanished, replaced by the crook of Drew's thick, muscular arm, pressed hard against my windpipe.

Lance stood in front of me, looking me up and down. "You're pretty, Miss Chase. I think we'll have some fun with you before you go for a swim."

No. Gotta be a way out.

Lance turned and led the way, still holding the butcher knife.

Rain falling, we followed. I tried to walk but my legs didn't work right. Drew half-carried me by the neck across the yard to the dock.

Weapon, I need a weapon.

I tried kicking my feet against the ground.

Not working.

I pulled at his arm.

Too strong.

We moved up the dock, got to where the boat was tied off. Lance hopped across onto the deck and turned. "Can you get her across okay, Drew?"

"I got her."

He put his other arm around my waist and carried me onto the boat.

I tried kicking him. All I got was air.

Lance ordered. "Get her below and into the master stateroom. Use one of the lines and tie her up if you have to. I'll cast off." Then he stared right at me and held up the knife. "It won't take long to get those wet clothes off."

Drew dragged, walked, carried me down the steps down to the lounge. The engines growled to life.

I glanced around. Teak walls, padded benches, TV on the counter, small stove, refrigerator.

Weapon, I need a goddamned weapon.

Drew carried me through the galley. The table was littered with paper plates, a pizza box, empty beer bottles, a pack of cards

The doorway ahead of us led to the bed inside the stateroom. Too big for the tiny room.

Desperate, I flailed out.

My hand found the neck of a beer bottle, smashed it down on the counter, rammed the jagged edge hard into Drew's forearm. Hit bone.

Blood splattered my face.

Drew shouted, "Fuck!"

His grip tightened. I couldn't breathe.

I stabbed the ragged glass into his arm, over and over. Every time, feeling it, hearing it hit bone.

He roared and let go.

I turned. Drew was between me and the steps up to the deck. The vessel's twin engines growled and we started to move.

Gotta get past Drew.

His head was down, inspecting blood draining out of his torn arm, dripping onto the deck.

Gotta get past Drew.

Panic-stricken, I leaped forward, screaming, slashing at his face. He held up his hands and I ripped the broken bottle into the palms of his hands.

He grunted, twisted and fell against the table, dropping onto a bench.

Run.

I dashed up the steps onto the deck and, without looking, hurled myself over the transom of the boat, throwing myself into the air, falling into the cold, bubbling wake of the twin engines.

Underwater, swimming.

When I surfaced, I saw we hadn't gotten far from shore. A hundred feet from the dock.

Behind me, the boat was still moving away from me, nearly invisible now behind the gray curtain of rain.

That's good.

I kicked off my shoes and swam for the dock.

The noise from the twin engines suddenly changed. I stole a look behind me again. Lance had throttled down. The boat was turning. Coming back for me.

I swam harder, adrenaline firing through my veins, swimming for my life.

Too slow.

The engines got louder, closer. Lance was accelerating.

I reached out for the ladder of the dock and hoisted myself up, my heart pumping like a hammer against my chest, my lungs on fire, straining for oxygen. Running in bare feet down the dock.

I saw the boat drawing up to the dock. Drew stood on deck with a towel around his arm. His chest and shirt were covered in blood. Lance was tying off the lines.

Legs pumping, feet splashing, I sprinted across the yard, past the pool, up to the steps to the house, slid open the glass door to the kitchen.

The maid stood at the counter, mixing something in a bowl with a spoon. She stared at me with wide eyes.

Where was my phone? Where were my keys? In my bag, next to the table by the pool.

I turned and looked through the glass door. Lance and Drew trotted across the yard.

"What's going on here?"

I whirled. Becky Elroy stood in the kitchen doorway.

"Call 911," I screamed.

"What are you doing here?" She shouted back, mystified at seeing me standing there, soaked and muddy.

"Call 911." My voice howled with desperation.

Suddenly the boys slid the glass door open, They were in the kitchen.

Becky, seeing the blood-soaked towel on her son's arm and blood dripping from the palms of his hands, shrieked, "What's happening?"

The boys glowered hard at me.

Where do I run?

"There's a break-in at 32 Smuggler's Road," shouted the maid into her cell phone. "On Connor's Landing. Yes, I'll stay on the phone."

Drew glared at me with unbridled hatred. Then he turned and mumbled at Lance. "Jesus Christ, what are we going to do?"

Lance narrowed his eyes, sizing me up. Then he glanced at his mother, at her horrified expression. "Let's go, Drew."

The two of them turned and marched out the open door, disappearing into the rain. Moments later, I heard the purr and then roar of a sports car start and then accelerate down the driveway.

Suddenly my legs had no strength in them. I needed to sit down. But first I had to get my cell phone.

I looked at the two women. The maid still had her phone pressed to her ear, holding a meat cleaver with the other hand, watching me cautiously. Becky Elroy's gaze moved from the blood spatters on her kitchen floor to my face.

"You're the contractor's wife," she hissed.

"Close enough."

Holding my hands out in front of me, I was amazed at how badly they were shaking. I found enough strength to walk to the doorway, still open, and down the steps and into the cold rain.

I staggered to the table under the awning by the pool house where Drew had left his laptop. Exhausted, I dropped into a metal chair. Water dripped from my hair and down my face.

What was I trying to do? Get a story? Get a confession so Mike Dillon wouldn't have to make a deal with Jimmy Fitzgerald? Show how smart I was?

I've done some incredibly stupid things in my life, but most of them were fueled by too much alcohol.

This morning I was stone cold sober.

What about those two boys? They had every advantage, money, privilege, a good family. What went wrong? Drugs? A feeling of invulnerability? Pressure from their father? Undue influence from a bad seed like Jimmy Fitzgerald? A seductive teacher?

There was no good reason for those six people to be dead. They were simply in the wrong place at the wrong time.

I needed to call Mike Dillon. I reached down into my bag for my cell phone.

My hands were shaking so badly that it took three tries before I could punch the number onto the screen.

When he answered, I made an effort to calm my voice down so I wouldn't sound hysterical. "Mike, it's Drew and Lance Elroy."

"Genie."

"It's Drew and Lance Elroy. They're the killers."

"We know, Jimmy Fitzgerald told us. We just got the warrants. We're on our way out there now to arrest them."

"They just took off." The words tumbled out much too quickly. "They're driving a gray Nissan 370Z convertible."

"Where are you?"

"I'm here, at the Elroy house."

"Are you okay? Are you in any danger? I just heard someone made a 911 call from that address."

"I'm good. Their maid called that in. She thinks I'm crazy."

"We've already got a car at the bridge," Mike said. "They won't even get off the island."

Thank Christ.

"Genie," he said somberly. "I have some bad news."

Nobody likes to hear a cop say he has bad news. The fear that gripped me in its icy fingers only moments ago doubled down with a vengeance.

"Genie, Kevin Bell was in a car accident about a half hour ago."

Oh, my dear God, no!

"Is he okay?"

Mike was silent for a heartbeat. Then…"Genie, I'm sorry. He's dead."

Chapter Thirty-two

Remembering the rest of that day is like trying to recall bits and pieces of a nightmare you can't wake up from.

One of Mike Dillon's cops, I don't remember which one, took my statement as we sat by the Elroy's pool. The rest of them, faceless to me, swarmed through the house, looking for evidence. At Mike's instruction, when we were done, the young officer offered to drive me home. I politely declined.

Even before I drove off Connor's Landing, I could see the blue-and-red stuttering lights of police cruisers. On the other side of the bridge, two of them were parked at the side of the road while a familiar gray Nissan convertible was being loaded onto a flatbed truck. I didn't see Lance or Drew. I'd been told they were already in custody.

I went straight to Ruth Spence's house in Darien. It was the first time I'd ever laid eyes on it. It was two stories, constructed of stone. Perfect for Aunt Ruth. Like most homes in this exclusive bedroom community, it's tucked behind a high fence and quietly cocooned by trees and landscaping.

Mike Dillon, bless his heart, parked his squad car behind my Sebring. He was there at my request.

I couldn't be the one to tell Caroline.

He wore his uniform but respectfully carried his hat in his hand. When Ruth opened the door and saw us both there, she already knew something was wrong. Caroline was standing right behind her, eyes wide, fear already spreading across her face.

I only vaguely recall what Mike said that day.

He told us how around eleven o'clock that morning, Kevin was on the Merritt Parkway heading to New Canaan to return the rented BMW. Because of the rain, the conditions were slippery. Kevin, apparently while traveling at a high rate of speed, overshot his exit, lost control of the vehicle, and hit the stone overpass. For whatever reason, the driver's airbag didn't deploy.

Mike assured us that Kevin died instantly. He told us how sorry he was and asked us if there was anything he could do.

We thanked him and said that we'd handle everything from here. From the way he hugged me in the doorway, I knew he was telling the truth about being sorry.

Then we all sat on the sofa in Ruth's living room and held each other while Caroline cried it out. Ruth and I cried as well, but I think we were determined to stay as strong as we could for Kevin's daughter. Now she was truly an orphan. First she'd lost her mother and now her father. She was utterly alone.

When I left late in the afternoon, I promised to return later that evening.

The depressing weather was lifting and pockets of sunshine struggled to find their way around the dark clouds. I drove home in a fog, numb and exhausted. When I got to my apartment, I picked up Tucker and held him so tight he must have thought I meant to crush him. He needed to be walked so I took him down to the waterfront where Kevin and I had been the first night we were together. That was so long ago and it felt so lonely.

I'd fully planned that when I got back to my apartment I'd pour myself a vodka rocks. But I bypassed my kitchen and went into my bedroom instead.

Kevin had made the bed.

I sat down on it and thought about how we had both been in that bed only hours ago. How comfortable I'd been snuggled up next to his warm body...how happy and content I was. How alive and vibrant he was.

I could smell him here...his scent.

Then I saw the folded slip of paper tucked underneath my pillow. I picked up the note, unfolded it, and read Kevin's handwriting.

> *I love you...I've always loved you.*
> *I'll love you for all eternity.*
> *Me.*

That's when I started to sob...truly sob.

No, I didn't have that vodka rocks. My eyes might have been red but it was from crying. I was sober when I went to the newspaper and wrote up the story about Drew and Lance Elroy, the copycat burglaries, Jimmy Fitzgerald's meth arrest, and Drew's confession to me about the brutal mess that happened on Connor's Landing. I can't tell you if what I wrote that night was cogent or coherent but I know that Casper was absolutely delirious with joy.

And then I wrote Kevin's obituary. I insisted.

I didn't have a drink that night and I haven't had a drink since. I've been sober for eleven months and twenty-six days. Yes, I attend AA meetings. You can't be a drunken role model.

Drew and Lance Elroy were tried and convicted of six counts of murder. Even though he was seventeen when he committed the crimes, Drew was tried as an adult. They were both sentenced to life.

Jimmy Fitzpatrick testified against the Elroys in order to receive leniency. He got off with fifteen years. He'll be out in ten.

I'm officially Caroline's guardian and I'm in the process of adopting her.

Two weeks after his funeral, I sublet my apartment and moved into Kevin's place. He had a four-hundred-thousand-dollar life insurance policy. He'd named me as beneficiary. That paid off the mortgage and gave us some breathing room.

Before he died, Kevin had restored the missing cabinet doors, the countertops, the light fixtures, and finished dozens of other repairs that he'd started. But it was all still rough around the edges so Caroline and I spent evenings and weekends spackling, sanding, and painting. I'd say the place is pretty much complete, and for a couple of amateurs, looks pretty damned good.

Yes, I know there are ghosts here.

But they're benevolent spirits. Sometimes I think I can feel Joanna, mostly in Caroline's room. And Kevin…I feel him all the time.

Sitting on my bed, reading his note that day, I was overcome with grief. Then the grieving turned to anger. Kevin had cheated me out of what little time we had left together by dying. We'd misspent our lives by not understanding we were supposed to be a couple and then when we'd finally found each other, he lost it.

Aunt Ruth surprised me by not fighting for Caroline's custody. She huffed and puffed but in her heart Ruth knew where Kevin's daughter wanted to be. The only concession I had to offer was that Caroline spend time with Dr. Tina Beaufort. I don't know why I was surprised that Dr. Tina was not only likable, but very competent. Maybe because she was Aunt Ruth's therapist as well…and hell, up until now, Ruth wasn't making much progress out of Uptight Heights.

Dr. Tina told me that, as horrible as it was, losing her father so suddenly may have been less traumatic than watching him die slowly…like her mom did. We were all surprised that she seemed to recover faster than we'd anticipated.

Dr. Tina had a theory for that as well. She thought that Caroline could see my pain and she needed to be strong for me. Caroline was taking on the responsibility of getting *me* through this.

I recall Kevin telling me that was what she did for him when Joanna died.

So Caroline and I worked on the house together and we learned to cook. I've never been much of a chef, but most nights now I make dinner. I've discovered that not only am I pretty good at it, I enjoy it.

Casper retired back in December and, because it pays more money, Laura took over as nighttime copy editor. She promoted me to her old spot as editor on days. It was a vote of confidence I needed, as well as little more in my paycheck and a schedule where I could be home in the evening for Caroline. I guess Laura's not such a bitch after all.

Aunt Ruth comes over for dinner once every two or three weeks. Maybe my sobriety has made me more tolerant of her presence…or maybe she's just not as crazy as I thought. There are some evenings I actually enjoy her company.

I heard through the grapevine that Frank Mancini's wife kicked him out of their Westport home and filed for divorce after she'd caught him, yet again, with another woman. A few months later, someone told me that she'd called off the divorce proceedings and agreed to let him move back into their house. Probably contingent on his testicles being kept in a locked box for which only she has the key. Shortly after Kevin died, Frank surprised me by calling my cell phone and leaving a message. He said, "Genie, I can't tell you how sorry I am. I know how much Kevin meant to you. It makes me realize how appallingly awful I was to you that day you both were out on Connor's Landing. I hope you can find it in your heart to forgive me."

I couldn't make myself call him so I texted him instead. "I forgive you."

I've had dinner a couple of times with Mike Dillon. Our relationship is strictly platonic and we're both content with that. After everything that happened, including the bad publicity, Mike decided that having his son attend the Hanley Academy wasn't such a good idea after all. He's a freshman at the same school that Caroline attends.

The nights are the hardest for me. When I'm alone in the dark in Kevin's bed, I feel cheated. There's so much more of Kevin that I wanted.

I'm not angry with him anymore. I know why I feel lost.

Did anything good come out of it? Of course…I'm clean and sober now. Kevin's death probably saved me from killing myself, either from alcoholism or dying in a drunk driving accident and possibly killing someone else. He gave me Caroline, a beautiful young lady to share my life with.

So is it chance or is there a plan?

Ultimately the plan is we all die, that's pretty obvious. None of us gets out of here alive. But beyond that, is there a meaning to our being here at all?

I've thought about it a lot. I guess while we're alive, it's up to us to enjoy and appreciate each and every moment to give our own purpose to our existence. And after we're gone, I suppose it's up to the people who know and love us to figure out what we've done and who we were that gives meaning to their own lives.

To see more Poisoned Pen Press titles:

Visit our website: poisonedpenpress.com/
Request a digital catalog: info@poisonedpenpress.com